SKANDAR
AND THE
CHAOS
TRIALS

A.F. STEADMAN

Simon & Schuster Books for Young Readers
New York   London   Toronto   Sydney   New Delhi

SIMON & SCHUSTER BOOKS FOR YOUNG READERS
An imprint of Simon & Schuster Children's Publishing Division
1230 Avenue of the Americas, New York, New York 10020

Simon & Schuster: Celebrating 100 Years of Publishing in 2024
For information about special discounts for bulk purchases, please contact Simon & Schuster Special Sales at 1-866-506-1949 or business@simonandschuster.com.
The Simon & Schuster Speakers Bureau can bring authors to your live event. For more information or to book an event, contact the Simon & Schuster Speakers Bureau at 1-866-248-3049 or visit our website at www.simonspeakers.com.
Interior design by Tom Daly
The text for this book was set in Adobe Caslon Pro.
Manufactured in the United States of America
0324 BVG
First Edition
10 9 8 7 6 5 4 3 2 1
CIP data for this book is available from the Library of Congress.
ISBN 9781665912792
ISBN 9781665912815 (ebook)

For my mum, Helen—who showed me how to dream

THE ISLAND

WILDERNESS

FIRE ZONE

THE LAVA
BOWL

THE
ARENA

THE DESERT
OASIS

THE
EYRIE

THE
TERRACED
VALLEYS

FOURPOINT

AIR ZONE

THE SKY
FOREST

CONTENTS

CONTENTS

Prologue

COMMODORE NINA KAZAMA HAS COME TO inspect the damage to the Hatchery.

She does not know.

Instructor Rex Manning rides with her, his silver unicorn glinting as the sun hits the clifftop.

He has no idea.

Five proud sentinels guard the gaping wound in the Hatchery's grassy side.

They have not realized.

The sentinels allow the two most important riders on the Island to approach.

Nobody has noticed.

Commodore Kazama peers through to the inner chamber. Rex Manning, the new head of the Silver Circle, joins her.

They will not believe their eyes.

Commodore Kazama blinks, her vision adjusting to the gloom.

"Why aren't the eggs for next solstice in their stands?" she demands.

But the sentinels have been guarding the monument from outward attack.

They still do not realize it has all been in vain.

The Commodore climbs through the hole, scattering loose earth in her haste.

Rex follows.

Every egg stand in the inner chamber is empty.

Every single one grasps thin air.

They are starting to suspect.

Rex is the first one to think it. Nina looks at him and fear snatches at her breath. Their footsteps ring out in the silent chamber as they sprint to the storage level below.

No unicorn eggs.

And the level below that.

No unicorn eggs.

And every level: down, down into the bowels of the ancient mound.

Empty.

And finally they understand.

No unicorns will be hatched here for thirteen years.

An entire generation of riders lost.

Now they stand on the clifftop as the waves crash against the Mirror Cliffs below.

"Nobody can know," Nina says. "Promise me!"

"We'll find the eggs," Rex agrees. "The two of us."

Yet the weight of the truth hangs heavy in the air between them.

The Hatchery is empty.

CHAPTER ONE

Sally's Sandwiches

SKANDAR SMITH WAS SEARCHING FOR Scoundrel's Luck. Again. Some might say it should be impossible to misplace a bloodthirsty unicorn. But those people had clearly never met one who was beginning third-year training at the Eyrie. Over the summer, the behavior of the Fledgling unicorns had become so bad, Skandar was pretty sure they were now *completely* beyond their riders' control. And that included Scoundrel's Luck.

It was the last day of the break before training restarted. Skandar had been searching for Scoundrel for most of the morning: Shekoni saddle balancing on one arm, bridle looped round the other. Now he sat on the Eyrie's hill, ripping up handfuls of grass in frustration. Scoundrel had been disappearing all summer—Skandar had no idea to where—but they were supposed to be riding into Fourpoint for lunch with the quartet.

On cue, Bobby Bruna came thundering down the hillside on Falcon's Wrath. She looked quite the ferocious air wielder: with the sleeves of her battered rider's jacket rolled up, the slate-gray feathers of her mutation visible all the way to her elbows.

Falcon was galloping straight for Skandar, and Bobby waited just a little *too* long to slow her. Bobby's mouth twitched as Skandar scrambled to his feet in alarm. Well, that confirmed it—she'd definitely done it on purpose.

"Have you found him yet, spirit boy?" Bobby demanded, ignoring Skandar's ashen face.

Skandar debated complaining about her dangerous riding, but it was nearly lunchtime, and a hungry Bobby was not a happy Bobby.

Instead, he sighed. "Nope. You go ahead without us."

"But we're meeting your sister afterward, remember? Outside the Stronghold." Bobby dropped her reins so Falcon could snap up a passing rabbit.

Skandar winced as bunny bones crunched.

Bobby ignored him. "We need to leave now if we're going to get lunch at the unbe*liev*able place I found. It gets busy!"

"I still don't get why you can't tell us its name."

"It's a surprise," she said evasively. "Er . . . since when is *he* the late one?"

Mitchell Henderson was riding toward them on Red Night's Delight. Red looked more demon than unicorn—her mane and tail were flaming brightly, along with her eyes and hooves. But Skandar barely noticed because his own unicorn, Scoundrel's Luck, was trotting happily beside his fiery best friend.

"There you are!" Skandar hugged Scoundrel's onyx neck—equal parts relieved and scolding. The unicorn tossed his head happily, the white spirit blaze under his horn flashing in the sunlight. The bond rippled with their combined joy at being reunited, though Skandar was less happy when he noticed that Scoundrel's black coat—which had been shiny yesterday—was covered in a thick layer of dust.

"Why's he so filthy?" Bobby asked, as Falcon skittered sideways—she detested dirt.

"I do hate to interrupt," Mitchell said sarcastically. "But isn't anyone going to ask if *I'm* okay?"

For some reason the entire zip was missing from Mitchell's green jacket, and it was hanging open to reveal the brown skin of his chest.

Bobby snorted.

"Do not laugh, Roberta. I'm warning you."

"What happened?" Skandar asked gently.

Mitchell sighed, the flaming hair of his mutation billowing. "Red happened. She's been setting fire to things all summer—and now she's widened her targets to include *me*."

Skandar frowned. "But she wouldn't hurt you, would

she?" Okay, the quartet unicorns had been getting more chaotic lately, but surely they wouldn't intentionally hurt their own riders?

"That's why I took my T-shirt off!" Mitchell said, exasperated. "Did you think I was just a bit hot?"

"I . . ." Skandar glanced at Bobby, who was biting her hand to stop herself from laughing. "I'm not following."

"Red scorched the fabric around the zip of my jacket, so I couldn't do it up," Mitchell raved. "Then she did the same to my T-shirt, and burned my spare before I could even get it over my head. I can feel through our bond that she finds the whole thing hilarious. She only stopped when I wasn't wearing anything on my top half at all!"

"I hope Red doesn't start on his trousers next," Bobby murmured to Skandar, who tried to hide his grin.

"What are you whispering about?" Mitchell demanded.

Bobby recovered quickly. "Come on, we're already late for lunch. Flo's meeting us in Fourpoint once she's dropped Kenna off. I invited the blacksmith bard, too."

Mitchell's eyes widened. "*Jamie's* going to be there? This is a disaster." He gestured to his destroyed jacket, fire pin catching the light as it flapped open in the breeze.

Skandar had an idea. "Why don't you tie Scoundrel's lead rope round you?" He passed it up to Mitchell. "Then at least the jacket will stay shut."

Mitchell eyed the blue rope suspiciously but appeared to realize that if he wanted to make it to lunch on time, there was no other choice. And Mitchell hated lateness.

"You might start a new trend," Bobby said mischievously.

"Oh, do shut up," Mitchell snapped, as he fastened the rope round his middle.

Skandar mounted Scoundrel and followed the others down the Eyrie's hill toward Fourpoint's main shopping street. Skandar was happy to see that many of its vibrant treehouses—in tones of red, blue, green, and yellow—had been repaired after the elemental destruction during Skandar's Nestling year. And, in the distance, the Spear of the Silver Stronghold pierced the sky once again.

But many other buildings across the Island were yet to be repaired, and Skandar too still felt a little broken by everything that'd happened in June. On the summer solstice, the Island had been minutes from tearing itself apart with its own unbalanced magic—the result of the Silver Circle killing wild unicorns. Skandar, Bobby, Flo, and Mitchell had managed to work out how to save the Island by winning the bone staff from the First Rider and his Wild Unicorn Queen. But then Skandar had been faced with a nightmare beyond anything he could have imagined. His sister, Kenna, had been bonded to a wild unicorn foal. The Weaver—their mother—had forged Kenna a bond just like her own.

Commodore Kazama, horrified yet fair, had allowed Kenna to remain with Skandar while a decision was made about her future with the wild unicorn. At first Skandar had tried to see the bright side. It had been wonderful writing to Dad, telling him that Kenna was at the Eyrie. But once the dust settled, Skandar had started worrying about the forged bond clasped round his sister's heart. He'd begun checking on Kenna's destined unicorn—the dapple-gray—in the Wilderness of his Mender dreams. And the longer Nina delayed in making her decision, the more he let himself wonder if there was a way to get that unicorn—that life—back for Kenna.

"You're thinking unusually hard about something," Bobby observed, slate-gray Falcon falling into step beside Scoundrel.

"How d'you know?"

"You get a dent in your forehead," she said. Bobby might be loud, but she paid quiet attention to people's feelings—especially Skandar's.

"My sister," he said simply. He wasn't ready to say anything about reuniting Kenna with her destined unicorn just yet. He needed more information.

"What *is* Nina playing at?" Bobby exploded. "This whole delaying thing is properly out of character for an air wielder. Just make a decision! What does she think these investigations are going to show? The Weaver hiding in Kenna's saddlebags?"

Bobby had been furious from the start about the tests on Kenna and her wild unicorn foal at the Silver Stronghold—the Silver Circle's base. She scoffed whenever Flo said that the new leader of the Silver Circle—Rex Manning—was much nicer than his father, Dorian Manning, had been.

"Well, that's not exactly hard, is it?" Bobby had snapped eventually. "Rex's dad almost destroyed the Island last year. Had *us* arrested for the unicorn murders *he* was committing."

Skandar didn't like Kenna being behind the Stronghold's shield wall either. An exclusive group for riders with silver unicorns, the Silver Circle was the most powerful organization on the Island. They had a rivalry with spirit wielders that went back centuries.

"The Stronghold is the safest place to do the tests, Skar," Flo had insisted. "For Kenna *and* the rest of the Island. Injuries from wild unicorn magic never heal, remember?"

Now, a month or so later, Skandar was happy to accept that Flo had been right. Kenna was regularly summoned to the Stronghold, and nothing bad ever seemed to happen. She'd be questioned about her time with the Weaver, interrogated about her forged bond, and then asked to attempt elemental magic. The sentinels wouldn't let Kenna ride; she was only permitted to place a palm on her wild unicorn's neck. So far she hadn't been able to summon even a spark.

"Do you ever wonder," Bobby asked Skandar, as they rode side by side, "what Kenna was doing with the Weaver all that time?" She sounded hesitant, less sure of herself than usual.

"Kenna told us that they hardly spoke; the Weaver was focused on preparing to forge her bond," Skandar said stiffly. "And I believe her."

"Obviously I believe her too, but . . . why would Erika Everhart forge a bond for her daughter and then abandon her to skip on up to the Eyrie? It doesn't feel very . . . Weavery."

"No," Skandar said grimly. "It doesn't. But I'm sure Kenna's told us everything she knows. She understands how evil the Weaver is now. She wants to be at the Eyrie training as a unicorn rider—just like we always dreamed."

Though a wild unicorn hadn't been what either of them had imagined, had it?

Bobby pointed. "This way!"

The three friends turned off the shopping street and entered a thicket of trees with a collection of restaurants in their branches. Relaxed chatter filled the air along with the clinking of cutlery. The smells were mouthwatering. Skandar's stomach rumbled as they passed Island Tacos, but he also spotted options for pizza, curry, tapas, falafel, ramen, jerk chicken, and even pancakes.

There was a sudden change in the chatter above: hushed awe in the voices.

"It's the Eyrie's silver!"

"Olu Shekoni's daughter."

"Look at that unicorn shine!"

Flo Shekoni had arrived. Silver Blade glimmered along

the narrow street to meet the rest of the quartet. Silver unicorns were rare and powerful on the Island, and Blade never failed to inspire wonder, however much Flo hated the attention.

Flo caught Skandar's eye first and smiled reassuringly. "Kenna's fine—more than fine. When I dropped her at the Stronghold, Rex said this was likely to be the final time she'd be called in for tests."

Skandar's heart soared with hope. Maybe the new head of the Silver Circle really was an improvement?

Flo looked at Mitchell, who was reknotting Scoundrel's lead rope round his jacket. She raised a questioning eyebrow at Skandar.

He chuckled. "I'll tell you later."

Blade followed behind Scoundrel, and Flo inhaled deeply. "It all smells so good! My mum always says the food got so much better on the Island after the Treaty."

Skandar leaned over Scoundrel's wing, reading some of the menus fixed to tree trunks. He felt a bit daunted. He'd never tried most of the options, and he knew that wasn't because he was a Mainlander. There hadn't been the money for eating out when he was growing up.

As Flo, Mitchell, and Bobby chatted about foods he'd barely heard of, Skandar threaded his fingers through Scoundrel's mane. The black unicorn rumbled softly, his stomach vibrating under Skandar's legs. And somehow, not knowing about different kinds of foods seemed to matter a lot less. Scoundrel didn't care about any of that stuff.

"Well, if it isn't the blacksmith bard!" Bobby's loud cry made Skandar look up.

"*Please* don't call me that," Jamie moaned, as he approached the four riders.

"You look really nice, Jamie," Flo said.

Gone was the blacksmith's leather apron with pockets of clanking tools; gone were the smears of ash from working at the forge. He was even wearing a collared green shirt.

"Oh yeah, d'you think? Thanks," Jamie said distractedly, running a hand through his golden-brown hair. His mismatched brown and green eyes found Mitchell, who'd frozen halfway through dismounting from Red's back.

"Need a hand there?" Jamie asked, the ghost of a smile on his lips.

Mitchell released the front of his Taiting saddle and thumped to the ground. "N-no, I'm good, I'm fine, I'm excellent," he stuttered, pushing his brown glasses back up his nose and desperately adjusting his jacket.

Jamie's gaze came to rest on the blue lead rope round Mitchell's middle.

Mitchell's flaming hair grew brighter. "Erm, yes, long story. It was Red; she—"

"TA-DAHHH!" Bobby shouted. They'd reached a place called Sally's Succulent Sandwiches. Bobby was jabbing a finger at the menu on its tree trunk, beaming. Flo and Skandar glanced at each other, confused.

Mitchell was outraged. "Are you telling me that your grand plan for this lunch—this lunch you made people attend *half-dressed*—is a sandwich shop?"

"It's not a sandwich shop, Mitchell. Sally's is a sandwich *delicatessen*. A sandwich *restaurant*—if you will." Bobby stared lovingly at the menu.

"Sally's is class," Jamie agreed. "I come here quite a lot, to be fair."

"Well, naturally, there's nothing *wrong* with sandwiches," Mitchell said quickly.

Skandar and Flo dismounted so they could read the menu.

September Menu: Sally's Succulent Sandwiches

Water zone tuna with anchovy mayo
Earth zone mixed-vegetable deluxe
Fire zone spicy chicken and bacon
Air zone wasabi with zingy prawn
Sandwich of the month:
The Emergency Sandwich
by Bobby Bruna

ALL SERVED ON FRESH BROWN OR WHITE AIR ZONE BREAD
WITH OR WITHOUT SUNFLOWER SEEDS.

"You are kidding me," Skandar said, already laughing.

"Bobby, how did you get Sally to agree to this?" Flo asked, clearly worried there'd been blackmail involved. For

Bobby's emergency sandwiches were well known to her quartet. Butter, cheese, raspberry jam, and Marmite.

Mitchell's mouth was hanging open. "But your sandwiches are a health hazard."

"Sally said they've been really popular," Bobby announced proudly. "Come on!" She looped Falcon's reins through one of the metal rings provided for rider customers and climbed the shop ladder three rungs at a time, leaving the others to follow.

Inside the treehouse, a woman stood behind the counter. "Well, if it isn't our sandwich of the month creator," she cooed as the quartet approached. She had curly black hair, a rainbow-colored apron, and a smiley—slightly pink—face.

"Hi, Sally!" Bobby was bouncing on her toes, her olive skin flushed with excitement. "Five Emergency Sandwiches, please."

"Umm, Bobby, I was actually hoping to get the one with mayo," Skandar said quickly.

"Fire zone chicken for me," Mitchell said.

"I'd like the zingy prawn," Flo added guiltily.

Sally tutted. "You're missing out. The Emergency is our top seller."

"But does anyone ever order it twice?" Mitchell muttered to Skandar.

In the end, Jamie agreed to try Bobby's sandwich if she promised to stop calling him the blacksmith bard. Jamie had never wanted to follow in his parents' footsteps and become a bard, despite having sung his truesong back in June.

The sandwich shop was clearly well liked. They squeezed past Falcon's blacksmith, Reece, on their way in, who grunted to Bobby in greeting. He was older, with a graying beard, and not particularly friendly. The story was similar with Red's blacksmith, who'd made armor for four different riders during her career. Unlike Jamie, they weren't interested in making friends with Fledglings.

There was only one table left on the platform outside. Jamie waved to a particularly raucous group, and a young woman came over, sandwich in hand. She had bright blond hair scraped into a ponytail.

"This is Clara." Jamie introduced her, respect in his voice. "She's blacksmith to the Commodore's unicorn."

But Clara was looking at Mitchell. "What happened to that?" She gestured to his singed jacket.

Jamie answered to save Mitchell the embarrassment. "He's a Fledgling at the Eyrie."

"Ohhh. Third year. You should have seen how rebellious Lightning's Mistake was at the beginning of Nina's Chaos Trials; I could hardly get her armor on."

"So this behavior is normal, then?" Mitchell asked sheepishly.

"Very," Clara reassured him.

"And a unicorn disappearing whenever he likes?" Skandar asked in a small voice.

"Rarer, but don't sweat it."

"Falcon hasn't changed at all," Bobby said. "She's still perfect."

"It's not nice to boast, Bobby," Flo chided.

"What's the latest with Nina?" Jamie sounded worried.

"The same." Clara sighed. "She's gone for hours every day, but I know she isn't training because she never wears armor. Lightning comes back exhausted. Nina comes back depressed."

"What's wrong with her?" Skandar asked—thinking of Kenna and the decision being made about her future.

"No idea." Clara shrugged, the tools in her apron pockets clinking. She turned in Flo's direction. "Your dad tried to talk to her, but she's avoiding him."

Flo's dad was Olu Shekoni—the best saddler on the Island. Like Skandar, Nina had a Shekoni saddle.

"If Nina carries on like this, she's never going to qualify for the Chaos Cup this year." Clara sounded frustrated. "We're supposed to be going for the hat trick. Nobody has ever done it!"

Skandar's stomach clenched. The only other Commodore who'd been close to winning three Chaos Cups had been his mum, Erika Everhart, and her unicorn Blood-Moon's Equinox. But then Blood-Moon had been killed mid-race on their third try, and Erika had embraced the darkness of her wild unicorn, becoming the Weaver.

"Are you all right, Skar?" Flo asked gently while the others were still talking to Clara. "Are you worried about training starting tomorrow? Mitchell's sure the instructors are going to tell us more about our Chaos Trials."

"A little," he said, not meaning it. All the other Fledglings had been trying to find out as much as they could about the challenges they'd be facing during their third year. Especially as—just like the Training Trial and Nestling Joust—they'd need to pass the Chaos Trials to remain in the Eyrie. According to Skandar's older friends at the Peregrine Society, the third-year challenges took place in the elemental zones. They changed every year to make them impossible to prepare for.

Of course, that hadn't stopped Mitchell from studying previous Chaos Trials all summer. But when he'd moved from book research to asking real-life Rookies and Preds to describe their experiences, many hadn't been keen to talk. Flo worried they were traumatized. Bobby said they were keeping secrets to reduce competition for future Chaos Cups. But Skandar hadn't really paid attention—he'd been researching something of his own.

"I'm just going to talk to Craig a second," Skandar said, noticing the bookseller across the platform.

Craig owned Chapters of Chaos. He was a friend to spirit wielders, collecting knowledge from older riders whose spirit unicorns had been executed when their element was declared illegal. And he was also the only other person who knew Skandar's secret hope of reuniting Kenna with her destined unicorn.

Just before he reached Craig, the memory of Kenna appearing in the self-destructing Eyrie resurfaced, and Skandar froze. Once again, Skandar heard Kenna confronting him with all the lies he'd told her: about his allied element, about their mother. He'd tried to explain that he was a Mender—a spirit wielder who could use dreams to find and bond riders to the unicorn they should have hatched. Tried to say how he'd dreamed of a wild dapple-gray unicorn that had been destined for *her*. But it had all been too late. Skandar's stomach turned over as he remembered that distant look on Kenna's face, the look that'd made him think he'd lost her forever.

But then Skandar had said how sorry he was. And Kenna had told him how she'd been so desperate for a unicorn that she'd left the Mainland with the then head of the Silver Circle, Dorian Manning, only to escape him and be taken in by their mother's promises. Then, with all their mistakes out in the open, the siblings had forgiven each other.

"What is *in* this?" Craig asked, when he spotted Skandar hovering by his table. He was inspecting the jam and Marmite oozing between his bread.

The question broke Skandar out of his memory. He chuckled. "You don't want to know."

"How's Kenna?" Craig asked kindly, waving Skandar into a chair.

"At the Stronghold again." Skandar took a deep breath. "Have you found anything?"

Craig shook his head, bun wobbling. "None of the spirit wielders I've spoken to so far knows anything about forged bonds, let alone whether they can be broken. They've never even tried to break a *destined* bond—killing a bonded unicorn has been a crime for centuries. And we know what havoc can come from killing a *wild* unicorn."

There was a retching sound.

Mitchell was crying with laughter. "I did warn you!"

Jamie had taken a bite from his Emergency Sandwich.

"I think I might save mine for later," Craig said tactfully, as he stood up to leave. "I'll keep searching for the answer, but you have to think about how far you're willing to go with this. Kenna loves that wild unicorn, doesn't she?" The bookseller's brown eyes searched Skandar's own.

"I know, but I—I haven't even decided whether I'll say anything," Skandar said, faltering. "It depends how things turn out for Kenna, you know? I have to keep her safe."

"Safe is not always the same as happy, Skandar," Craig warned. "Remember that."

The quartet waited to meet Kenna Smith at the end of a silver birch avenue. They'd only been there a few minutes when Scoundrel and Red teamed up to incinerate a branch above Falcon, making her screech with indignation. Then, as she shook ash out of her perfectly combed mane, the entry shield in the Silver Stronghold's wall lifted.

A lone rider appeared, leading a wild unicorn foal.

Skandar locked eyes with Goshawk's Fury. The staring contest only lasted a few moments before Skandar blinked, shivering despite the warm September afternoon. The wild unicorn's eyes were filled with endless shadows and immortal suffering. Goshawk's Fury was condemned to a life lived in death. And Skandar's bighearted, very much *alive* sister was bonded to her.

Just like Scoundrel as a Hatchling, the wild foal had grown to the size of a horse in the last couple of months. But that was where the similarities ended. Scoundrel's horn was black like his shining coat; Goshawk's was transparent and ghostly, her honey-colored coat already balding and dull. After two years of Eyrie training, Scoundrel's muscles rippled, his wings full-feathered and powerful. But Goshawk's bones were visible in places—a couple of knobbly vertebrae along her back, five thin ribs rising and falling as she walked, a hint of a femur as she lifted her front leg. Some of her wing feathers had already fallen out, creating leathery patches, as though they belonged to an oversized bat rather than a great bird of prey.

For Goshawk's Fury would always be wild. Her bond was forged, not destined. Goshawk had been meant for another rider who'd never made it to the Hatchery on the summer solstice of their thirteenth year. And Kenna had been destined for a different unicorn—the dapple-gray— still out in the Wilderness alone.

As Kenna smiled at Skandar, Agatha Everhart's warning about Kenna's wild unicorn bond came floating back to him: *Look at what the forged bond did to Erika. . . . Five allegiances pulling you different ways. . . . Five ways for the unicorn's power to take over.*

Skandar had always dreamed that Kenna would come to the Island, that they would become Chaos riders together. But what if the Island believed she was too dangerous to be one of them? What if the Eyrie excluded her? What would Skandar do then?

The thought scared him, and his mind turned again to his half-formed plans, the possibility of a different future for his sister. He resolved to sleep in Scoundrel's stable tonight and find his sister's dapple-gray through a Mender dream. To make sure Kenna's *destined* unicorn was safe.

Just in case.

CHAPTER TWO

Wild Mutation

LATER THAT EVENING, SKANDAR ENTERED
Scoundrel's stable. The unicorn opened one eye and it flashed
between red and black in warning, the bond vibrating with
irritation—Scoundrel was annoyed at being woken up.

"Can I join you, boy? Please?" Until recently Skandar
had never had to ask permission to sleep under Scoundrel's wing. But now it was necessary. On a few occasions
over the summer, he'd been on the receiving end of warning flames or icy winds when Scoundrel had wanted the
stable to himself. But tonight the black unicorn ruffled his
feathers, as if to say, *Oh, all right, then—if you must,* and
lifted one great black wing, allowing Skandar to snuggle
up beside him.

"What's going on with you, hey?" Skandar whispered, stroking Scoundrel's side.

Scoundrel rumbled low in his chest, but the emotions Skandar felt through the bond were confused. Skandar rested his head on Scoundrel's side, listening to the unicorn's breathing, and tried to reassure himself that the Commodore's blacksmith had said this was normal for Fledgling unicorns.

And in no time at all, rider and unicorn were asleep inside a Mender dream.

Skandar was getting better at this. His dream presence only collided with Kenna's for a second—a flash of a hand that wasn't his own—before he escaped to sit beside her. The siblings dangled their legs over the edge of a treehouse platform. They had to be somewhere in the Eyrie because when Skandar looked up, all he saw was green. And he'd learned that the dream location matched where the rider was in real life. He didn't stay long here—it wasn't Kenna he'd come to check on.

The bond tugged on Skandar's heart. He and Scoundrel had done this so many times over the past month that he barely glanced at their shining bond stretching out toward the Wilderness.

Skandar touched the white cord, and he rushed along it, then collided with—

Where is she?

As Skandar's dream presence joined with Kenna's destined unicorn, he sensed the same question coming from the dapple-gray as in every single one of the Mender dreams.

Where is she?

Skandar tried to channel soothing thoughts, tried to picture his sister's face, but—

Kill. Blood. Alone. Angry.

Skandar shuddered. The wild unicorn was particularly furious today, and he was struggling to leave its body, struggling to separate their feelings. He felt a terrible rage descend, dark shadows clouding his vision—and then the pain started. His chest was burning, his head thundering. He'd stayed too long. He always stayed too long. *He cried out.*

"Skar?"

Someone was shaking him awake, rescuing him from the unicorn's endless suffering.

Kenna stood in front of her brother: brown hair tangled, concern on her face. Instinctively Skandar reached out for her like he'd done since he was little, and she responded without hesitation. They hugged tight, and the pain in his chest and head ebbed away. She smelled like the salt of Margate and the pine of the Eyrie—like home.

"Was that a nightmare?"

Skandar nodded. It was a good excuse—he'd had nightmares growing up. And he didn't want to get into the detail of his Mender dreams with Kenna just yet. She knew that he'd dreamed of her destined unicorn last year, but she didn't know that he was still doing it—or that it hurt him.

"What are you doing down here?" Skandar asked, changing the subject.

"Just checking on Goshawk. Do you want to come?" There was something mischievous in Kenna's voice, but he followed her along the curve of stables, lanterns lighting up unicorn horns over the doors. He liked it when it was just the two of them—they didn't get much chance, especially because Kenna was currently required to sleep in the water instructor's treehouse.

Hisses and shrieks echoed behind them, as they approached Goshawk's stable. It was sandwiched between two of the strongest unicorns at the Eyrie: Celestial Seabird, who belonged to the water instructor, Persephone O'Sullivan; and Silver Sorceress, who belonged to Rex Manning. For Rex Manning wasn't only the new head of the Silver Circle. He had also recently been installed as the Eyrie's new air instructor.

According to Flo, Rex hadn't wanted to make a big deal of being the first head of the Silver Circle ever to hold an instructor position at the Eyrie. Skandar suspected it had something to do with Rex's disgraced father having hunted down wild unicorns last year. He'd tried to kill as many as possible, so that Skandar could never reunite them with their destined riders—the lost spirit wielders who'd been barred from the Hatchery door.

Kenna unbolted Goshawk's stable door and tried to coax her over with one of Scoundrel's Jelly Babies. Skandar's breath hitched with nerves. He didn't trust the wild unicorn with his sister. Not yet. Possibly not *ever*. The wild unicorn would outlive Kenna. The forged bond meant Goshawk had not given up her immortality the way Scoundrel had for Skandar. They would never be equals. He tried to comfort himself by thinking of the Mender dream he'd just had—Kenna's destined unicorn was still out there, still safe.

"Why won't Gos eat it?" Kenna gave up and stuffed the sweets Dad had sent them into her black trouser pocket. Kenna wore the official rider uniform: short black boots, black T-shirt, black trousers. But until her membership in the Eyrie was approved, she wasn't allowed to wear an elemental rider jacket.

Skandar shrugged. "Scoundrel ate one just after he hatched. He probably wouldn't even like them if I hadn't given him one as a baby."

"There wasn't much time for Jelly Babies when Gos hatched," Kenna said quietly, and Skandar stayed very still. She hardly ever brought up the time she'd spent with the Weaver, and whenever *he* did, she shut him down. Bobby's words from earlier echoed in his mind. *Do you ever wonder . . . ?*

"Kenn," Skandar prompted, "what d'you mean there wasn't time?"

"I wasn't supposed to be inside the Hatchery, was I? Mum was worried people would find us."

"Did you and the Weaver talk much?" Skandar asked carefully. "When you spent those weeks with her?"

Kenna sighed. "I don't know what to tell you, Skar. I

know everyone wants me to spill all the Weaver's secrets, but honestly? We hardly spoke. She was obviously planning to . . . to abandon me after she forged my bond," Kenna choked out. "She left me, remember? I just want to forget about it all."

"Yeah, I know. I'm sorry, I shouldn't have—"

But Kenna was looking over her shoulder at Goshawk, and then back toward Scoundrel's stable, her face shining with sudden determination.

She grabbed Skandar's arm. "Okay, so Instructor O'Sullivan *may* have mentioned that the instructors have a big meeting this evening about you Fledglings—something about trials? And I was wondering if *maybe*"—Kenna took a deep breath—"you'd help me ride Goshawk's Fury?"

The last phrase was a blur of nervous words, and Skandar realized Kenna had been working up to asking him. "Kenn, you know you're not allowed to ride yet, and—"

"I'm going to be so behind the other Hatchlings," Kenna interrupted. "I'm sure Commodore Kazama will approve my training any minute. I'm going to look ridiculous if I've never even *ridden* Gos before."

"You'll catch up in no time!" Skandar reassured her.

But Kenna was tucking the same strand of hair behind her ear over and over in frustration. "I feel so detached from her, and I *know* riding will help. *Please*, Skar!"

Skandar hesitated. He understood how Kenna was feeling. Only a couple of months ago, Scoundrel had been placed under guard after the Island's unbalanced magic had affected their bond and filled Skandar with a dangerous, bloodthirsty rage. For a few weeks, Skandar hadn't even been allowed to touch his own unicorn. "I don't—"

Kenna crossed her arms, eyes suddenly hard. "I'll ride Goshawk on my own if I have to. I'm asking for your help, not your permission." The fierce look on his sister's face was her *I'm older than you, do as I say* look. It was a look she'd learned growing up because Dad hadn't always been well enough to wear it.

Skandar had defeated the Weaver and saved New-Age Frost. He'd won the bone staff from the First Rider and the Wild Unicorn Queen. Despite wielding the illegal spirit element, he'd made it to his third year of training. He was on his way to becoming the Chaos rider he'd always dreamed of. So Skandar knew he should've been able to stand up to his older sister. But he couldn't bring himself to disappoint her.

Ten minutes later, Skandar and Scoundrel passed through the wall's east door, with Kenna and Goshawk following in the shadows of the tall trees. Scoundrel's unease churned in the bond. Skandar tried to send a bubble of positivity back, but it was half-hearted. He was already regretting this. Every burst of chatter from the treehouses above made his stomach lurch; every swaying branch made him jump. And Goshawk kept making creepy hissing noises that sounded like she was about to eat something. He just prayed she wouldn't set off any rancid blasts of wild unicorn magic—there was no way the Eyrie residents wouldn't smell *that*.

They reached the Nomad Tree. It was the first place that had popped into Skandar's head where riders were unlikely to be hanging out. The Nomad Tree glistened in the moonlight filtering through the leafy canopy. Shards of elemental pins studded the bark—pins that had belonged to riders declared nomads, who'd been required to leave the Eyrie. Nobody liked coming here. It reminded them of the friends they'd lost—and the possibility that if they didn't keep excelling, a smashed piece of their own pin might end up here too.

Kenna wasn't interested in the tree. She was already looking over at Skandar expectantly, and the excitement in her eyes was blazing so brightly it softened his heart a little.

Skandar made himself relax. There was no one around. The instructors were holed up in Instructor O'Sullivan's treehouse. Kenna was going to sit on Goshawk's back for a couple of minutes, and then they'd put the unicorns to bed and nobody would have to know a thing. Skandar might not even tell the rest of his quartet.

He could imagine their responses. Flo would be horrified that he'd let Kenna do something the instructors had forbidden. Mitchell would reel off the plan they should have had in place. Bobby would just be annoyed that Skandar hadn't brought her along for the ride.

No, he *definitely* wouldn't tell them.

"Watch me get on Scoundrel first, and then I'll talk you through it," Skandar said, pulling himself up onto Scoundrel's bare back. It felt odd to be teaching Kenna something. Growing up, she'd always been better than him at most things.

Kenna shrugged. "Looks easy." But there was a wobble in her voice.

"Okay?" Skandar checked. "I was pretty nervous the first time I rode Scoundrel."

"I'm fine."

"You don't have to do this right now, you know."

"I do," Kenna said fiercely.

Skandar gave in. "All right, then. Face Goshawk's side like I did."

Goshawk let out a snarl as Kenna approached, and his sister tried to hide her nervous jump. Scoundrel's wing joints twitched near Skandar's knees, as he rumbled a warning at the wild unicorn foal. Scoundrel could sense how important Kenna was to Skandar; they were both ready to summon magic into the bond at the first sign of trouble.

"And then you need to—"

But Kenna had already launched herself upward, balancing precariously over the wild unicorn's back on her stomach. Goshawk bellowed loudly, tossing her ghostly horn from side to side. Seemingly unfazed, Kenna swung her right leg over and sat up, clutching at Goshawk's honey-colored mane. "Oh yeah!" Kenna cried, all traces of fear gone.

"Keep your voice down!" Skandar warned, although he couldn't keep the grin off his face. His sister was riding a unicorn at last, and her position on Goshawk's back was perfect.

"Trust you to make riding a wild unicorn look easy," Skandar pretended to grumble, his heart bursting with pride.

Kenna's laugh was gleeful. "It's like that time we tried skateboarding. We thought it would help us when we became riders, because of the balance! *I* was fine, but you fell right on your—"

"Oi!" Skandar cried, but he started to laugh too. "It is *not* like that! I'm a member of—"

"The *Peregrine* Society," Kenna interrupted in a grand voice. "The Eyrie's elite flying squad blah-blah-blah. The Grins this, the Grins that—you talk about them ten times a day."

"I do not," Skandar mumbled, but he felt giddy. For so long, he and Kenna had had to be sensible. Looking after Dad, there'd been no time for adventures or rule breaking. But now they were on the Island; Dad was happy; they were unicorn riders; and everything was going to be all—

A green glow reflected off the nearest armored trunk. At first Skandar couldn't see where it was coming from because it was so bright. But once he blinked, he realized it was Kenna's Hatchery wound.

"What are you doing?" he half shouted, aware of the riders in the treehouses above.

Kenna's face was only visible in flashes of green light, then red, then yellow, then blue, then white. She didn't look worried. If anything, she looked triumphant.

"Stop it, Kenn!" Skandar suddenly felt unsure of her. She hadn't been able to summon any magic at the Stronghold, had she? "You're not ready; you haven't learned to control it. Someone will see!"

BOOM!

Soil, roots, and bark exploded upward. There was so much debris that Skandar couldn't see anything until Scoundrel blasted a gust of air to clear it.

Goshawk's Fury was rearing on her hind legs, swirling black smog rising from her back, the visible bones of her skeleton shining in the moonlight. Kenna's hand had stopped glowing, and she was now clinging for dear life to the unicorn's neck. Incredibly, this wasn't the most terrifying thing Skandar saw. It was the Nomad Tree. Kenna and Goshawk's magic had created an enormous crater round the famous tree. *Under* the famous tree. And the remaining roots looked rotten, like they'd caught a terrible disease. The tree creaked ominously. Time seemed to slow. Scoundrel looked up at the sparkling trunk, eyes flashing between black and red. Goshawk's front hooves thumped back down to the forest floor. The trunk of the Nomad Tree groaned, and then it began to tilt—

"WE HAVE TO GET OUT OF HERE!" Skandar yelled to Kenna—and, as though they understood the danger, both unicorns careered toward the Eyrie's wall.

Skandar looked over his shoulder: once, twice—they were still in the fall zone. The sound of splintering wood filled his ears; the tree's leaves whooshed like heavy rainfall as they caught on neighboring branches; the pins studding its trunk dislodged, landing in Skandar's hair like golden hailstones.

Kenna screamed as a falling branch brushed her shoulder. Panicking, Skandar swerved Scoundrel, forcing Goshawk to the left. Miraculously the unicorns burst through the arched door of the Eyrie wall, hooves clattering on the stone.

Skandar threw himself from Scoundrel, and then pulled a shaking Kenna off Goshawk's back. All he could think was: *They can't find out she did this.* Goshawk was spitting sparks as Skandar and Kenna pushed her back into her stable; a smoldering cinder landed on Skandar's left thumb and burned his skin.

CRASH!

The Nomad Tree had finally reached the ground. The stone floor of the stables vibrated with the force of its fall. Somebody was going to see them. They were running out of time.

Skandar ignored the searing pain in his thumb and grabbed Kenna's hand. Scoundrel cantered ahead of them, sensing their urgency. They hurtled along the line of stables, lanterns flickering wildly as they rushed by. Finally Scoundrel let out a shriek of greeting to Red, as Falcon and Blade peered over their stable doors at the sweaty arrivals.

Only after Skandar had bolted Scoundrel's door did he notice how pale his sister was. Her cheeks were ghostly white, and she was wincing in pain.

Skandar rushed to Kenna, who was hunched over. "Are you hurt?"

"Skar," she whispered, "something's happening to me. Look at my veins!"

Skandar caught her shaking hand as she reached out. Bile rose in his throat. The veins in Kenna's arm were the deep green of the earth element. Then before his eyes, they solidified into snaking vines that began to bulge out of her skin. He could feel one right on her wrist.

"Is it a mutation?" Kenna's voice was a mixture of terror and excitement.

Skandar was about to answer when Kenna cried out in pain. A thorn had burst through her skin.

Shouts echoed along the wall. The fallen Nomad Tree had been discovered.

"Argh!" Kenna cried. More thorns were coming through from vines that now snaked all round Kenna's right arm.

"Come on, Kenn," Skandar said, his voice unsteady. He supported her weight as they hobbled back out to the forest, ignoring the shouts coming from the direction of the fallen

Nomad Tree. Kenna yelped as she climbed the last ladder up to the treehouse, and the two of them practically fell through the metal door.

Skandar's quartet were settled on beanbags. Bobby was midway through a sandwich. Mitchell was reading a book. Flo was folding a letter. Three pairs of eyes stared back at Skandar for a heartbeat. Then—

"Help," he said in a small voice. He didn't know what he wanted them to do. All he knew was that he needed them.

Bobby and Flo immediately took Kenna's weight from Skandar and lowered her down onto the red beanbag. More thorns were bursting through her skin, but she'd stopped reacting. Her face was gray; she barely looked conscious. Mitchell was kneeling down, squinting at the vines encircling her right arm—all the way up and under the sleeve of her black T-shirt.

Skandar was still standing by the open door. This was all his fault. It took him a moment to realize Mitchell was asking a question.

"What happened, Skandar? It looks like a mutation. How could she mutate without using magic?"

Skandar took a deep breath. "She rode Goshawk."

Flo spoke first. "You found her like this?"

"No. I"—Skandar hesitated—"I helped her. She was sad. I didn't know what else to do." At the expressions on their faces, he started to panic. "She had to ride Goshawk sometime!"

Bobby eyed him curiously, though for once she kept whatever opinion she had to herself.

But Mitchell exploded, gesturing wildly. "Flaming fireballs! Have you lost your mind? Have you got any idea what the instructors are going to do if they find out that you, a spirit wielder—yes, the spirit element *is* still illegal on this Island, Skandar—helped your sister, who was bonded to a wild unicorn *by the Weaver* to—to—" He spluttered. "What exactly were you helping her to do?"

"How could you take the risk, Skar?" Flo asked gently, but there was something else in her voice. Anger? Hurt?

Kenna stirred on the beanbag. "It's not his fault." Color was returning to her cheeks. "I asked him to help me ride Gos."

Mitchell's hair flared ominously. "Skandar is not an amoeba. He has his very own brain, though he *clearly* wasn't using it."

Skandar ignored him, more concerned about Kenna. "Has it stopped hurting?"

She nodded, eyes wide. "It only itches a bit now. The pain was only while the mutation was actually happening." She suddenly looked brighter. "Can you believe I've mutated already? Is it normal for it to hurt?"

"No," Skandar, Flo, and Mitchell said together.

Bobby swallowed the last of her sandwich. "What's a bit of pain? There's no harm done. Look at her! She's fine! You lot are more dramatic than a snake in a snowstorm."

Kenna giggled, and then looked a bit sheepish. "I did sort of destroy a tree."

Now that she was safe, Skandar felt his anger at Kenna kick in. "It wasn't just any old tree, Kenn! It was the Nomad Tree."

"You destroyed the Nomad Tree?" Flo asked, stunned.

"Toppled it," Skandar said, failing to make it sound like less of a disaster. He turned back to Kenna. "What were you thinking, summoning magic into the bond?"

But Kenna was already fast asleep on the beanbag.

Skandar went to fetch a blanket. He was careful to avoid the mutation on Kenna's arm as he tucked it round her—thorns visible along the vines.

Bobby shrugged. "Well, nobody liked the Nomad Tree anyway."

"That's not really the point," Flo said quietly.

"It's an earth mutation," Mitchell murmured. "But she's not earth-allied. There'll be more of them, won't there?"

"Do you think the others will hurt her too?" Flo asked, sounding horrified.

Even Bobby looked a little worried. And Skandar knew that his three best friends were thinking exactly the same as him: Kenna was allied to all five elements. She had four mutations to go.

What if they got more painful each time? What if she was in more danger than Skandar had realized? His mind went to the dapple-gray unicorn in the Wilderness, to his half-formed plans.

Finding out if a forged bond could be broken suddenly felt a lot more urgent.

Later that evening, Skandar's hopes that nobody had noticed Kenna's tree-felling were shattered by the arrival of Instructor O'Sullivan.

The metal door of the treehouse crashed open—startling Kenna awake—and the water instructor stood silhouetted in the doorway, whirlpool eyes swirling dangerously between Skandar and his sister. She spoke only three furious words.

"With. Me. *Now.*"

The siblings didn't dare speak as they kept up with Instructor O'Sullivan's swift pace. They crossed swinging bridges and climbed multiple ladders, until eventually they reached the instructor treehouses. In different circumstances, Skandar might have appreciated the platform's flowered entrance arch and the large tree—with lanterns spiraling up its trunk—breaking through its center. But instead he focused on four grand colored treehouses, one nestled at each of the platform's corner trunks, painted to match each instructor's element. Agatha's treehouse was a whole bridge away—there were still *officially* only four elements after all.

The porch of the water treehouse curled over Skandar and Kenna in a breaking wave, as they followed Instructor O'Sullivan's billowing blue cloak inside.

Though Kenna had been living at the water instructor's house since she'd arrived at the Eyrie, Skandar had never been inside. He was struck immediately by the glow of glass tanks built into the walls, which were filled with fish of different sizes and colors.

Instructor O'Sullivan saw him staring. "In my spare time I re-home injured fish," she snapped. "Everybody needs a hobby. And my fish are the *least* of your worries right now."

Skandar and Instructor O'Sullivan had developed quite a close relationship during his first two years at the Eyrie, but she was often as spiky as her gray hairstyle. He found it impossible to imagine her gently nursing fish back to health.

She rounded on Kenna. "I have had multiple reports that you were—" She broke off, her blue eyes raking up Kenna's vine-covered arm. "You've mutated."

"Yes, but—" Kenna started.

"The thing is—" Skandar said at the same time.

"Enough!" Instructor O'Sullivan boomed. "There is no use trying to deny anything. The Nomad Tree may well be beyond repair, and I've had ten different riders in here saying they saw you two underneath it before it fell."

She fixed her swirling eyes on Skandar. "You *knew* Kenna wasn't allowed to ride Goshawk's Fury. Floundering floods, what possessed you to break the rules like this?"

"I didn't think anyone would s—" Skandar started, but he was immediately cut off.

"See? You didn't think anyone would *see* the only spirit wielder in training and the girl with the wild unicorn topple one of the biggest and most ancient of the Eyrie's trees?"

Instructor O'Sullivan turned to face a nearby fish tank and inhaled deeply. "If the pair of you had been a bit more *subtle*, it might have been possible to keep Kenna's magic between us. But Rex Manning was *in* my treehouse—all the instructors were—when riders came reporting the news. I'm afraid the Commodore will have to be informed. Why would you risk this, Kenna? The Stronghold investigations were almost over!"

Skandar started to panic. "But riders and unicorns destroy things by accident all the time. That's why some of the trees have armor!"

"Those riders are *not* bonded to wild unicorns. Their fate is *not* currently hanging in the balance."

Kenna looked like she was going to burst into tears. "Do you think Commodore Kazama will decide I can't train now?"

Instructor O'Sullivan sighed. "I don't think this will turn Nina against you, Kenna—even considering the strength of the magic you must have used."

"It was an accident!" Skandar insisted.

Instructor O'Sullivan ignored him. "Commodore Kazama has been on your side since the beginning. But it's convincing her Council and the Silver Circle to allow you to train that has always been the difficulty. No doubt they'll want to study your new mutation."

"Can't we keep my mutation a secret?" Kenna asked quietly. "For now?"

Instructor O'Sullivan gave her a stern look. "Absolutely not. It's hard enough for the Island to trust you as it is; it will be impossible if you cover up truths about yourself."

Kenna nodded mutely.

"From now on I suggest that you *both* be on your absolute best behavior."

"Yes, Instructor," Skandar and Kenna chimed.

Instructor O'Sullivan pierced Skandar with her swirling gaze. "I have fought very hard for Kenna and Goshawk's Fury even to be allowed to *sleep* inside the Eyrie. Please do not let me down like this again."

Guilt flooded Skandar. He hadn't realized how much Instructor O'Sullivan had been helping them.

The water instructor opened the door. "Get some sleep, Skandar. It's a big day for you Fledglings tomorrow."

Skandar glanced at Kenna. He couldn't tell if she looked paler, or whether it was just the eerie light of the fish tanks.

"Your sister will be fine," Instructor O'Sullivan said firmly.

"I'll see you tomorrow, Skar." Kenna waved feebly, the thorny vines of her brand-new mutation catching the lamplight.

CHAPTER THREE

Solstice Stones

"INSTRUCTOR O'SULLIVAN HAS A FISH HOS-
pital!" Bobby's voice was gleeful the next morning. "She has
an actual *ambulance aquarium* in her treehouse!"

Flo, Mitchell, and Bobby had waited up for Skandar the
night before, terrified about the consequences of the Nomad
Tree incident. He'd barely got through the door before Flo
had thrown her arms round him in relief. When Skandar
had finished explaining everything, Mitchell had said happily, "Of course, rationally I knew they wouldn't just cart you
both off to prison, but I still couldn't stop worrying!"

Bobby, on the other hand, had been much more interested in the water instructor's hobby.

"*FISH*, though?" Bobby repeated, descending into

gales of laughter for the fifth time that morning.

The quartet were astride their unicorns on the Fledgling plateau—the third level down from the Eyrie itself. The plateau encircled the grassy hillside, with the four elemental training grounds positioned at its compass points.

"Roberta, will you please stop?" Mitchell snapped. "This is the first training session of Fledgling year—probably the most important of our lives, and we went to bed ridiculously late, and I'm having a hard enough time stopping Red from spontaneously combusting without you going on about Instructor O'Sullivan!" Red was, at that very moment, attempting to set fire to her own reins.

"But she rescues fish, Mitchell. FISH!"

"Enough now, Bobby," Flo said firmly, and Bobby quieted.

Watching the other Fledglings on the plateau, they looked almost like Hatchlings again. Romily was clinging desperately to Midnight Star's mane as he reared on his back legs, lightning bolts erupting from his front hooves. Earth-allied Elias was yelling at Star to stop, as his own unicorn, Marauding Magnet, blasted columns of sand from his mouth. Toxic Thyme, Farooq's unicorn, was refusing to move forward, stamping his hooves on the ground so hard it cracked. Marissa's and Mabel's unicorns—Demonic Nymph and Seaborne Lament— were spraying water over each other and then freezing it with blasts of cold air, so their whole bodies ended up frosted.

Even Scoundrel was trying to gallop forward for takeoff.

"No, boy!" Skandar cried, turning him in a circle. "We're not flying right now!"

"What's got into them all?" Flo moaned, as the ground beneath Blade's feet quaked and smoke billowed around the silver unicorn's wings.

"*We're* fine," Bobby said, shrugging, as Falcon stepped calmly away from Red's igniting tail.

A white unicorn passed overhead, circled, and started to descend. The Fledgling unicorns all looked up, wary of the unfamiliar unicorn soaring toward them.

"Who's that?" asked Gabriel, who'd managed to line up Queen's Price on Scoundrel's left.

Sarika paused in braiding her long black hair under her helmet, looking up. "He's so beautiful. Does anyone know which unicorn that is?" Her own unicorn, Equator's Conundrum, snorted sparks jealously.

But Skandar was smiling. Because he'd met this white unicorn once before in a communal garden in Margate.

"That's Arctic Swansong," Skandar murmured.

And a fully grown spirit wielder landed on the Fledgling plateau for the first time in almost two decades.

"Sorry I'm late," Agatha Everhart said breezily. "I had to collect someone." A chuckle burst from her smiling mouth as she gestured down at Swan's snowy neck.

"Not sure I've ever seen Agatha smile before," Bobby observed. "It's unnerving."

"She's happier than . . . a woodworm in a wardrobe?" Flo said, and Bobby clapped.

Mitchell shook his head. "Oh, not you as well."

"I've been giving her lessons on Mainland sayings," Bobby said proudly.

Skandar was too distracted to point out that Bobby's sayings were certainly *not* from the Mainland. Instead, he was watching Rex Manning greet Agatha. As Swan settled beside Silver Sorceress, Skandar tried to squash his worries. Rex had *freed* Arctic Swansong, despite his own mother having died as a direct result of the Weaver—a spirit wielder—murdering her unicorn. He'd been kind to Kenna throughout her questioning at the Stronghold. Skandar had to trust that Rex was different from his prejudiced—and now incarcerated—father. As the Weaver's son, Skandar knew he of all people should understand that a child was not responsible for their parent's mistakes.

Instructor O'Sullivan blew her whistle, though it made absolutely no difference to the roaring, shrieking, and elemental magic coming from the Fledgling unicorns, who'd now recovered from the shock of Arctic Swansong's arrival.

"You may have noticed," Instructor O'Sullivan shouted, "that over the summer break, your unicorns have become less obedient than you have come to expect."

"That's an understatement," Mitchell muttered, as all four of Red's hooves burst into flame beneath him.

"When unicorns reach Fledgling age, it's common for

them to rebel. They know you well enough to understand how to test you. They are clever enough to know their own strength and power. To put it frankly, they are wise enough to have worked out that they don't have to do exactly as you tell them."

"But what about the bond?" Farooq called out. "Surely Toxic Thyme will have to do as I say eventually? We share feelings!" The earth wielder sounded panicked, as he fidgeted with the long sprigs of fragrant thyme that snaked through his ponytail.

Instructor O'Sullivan shook her head. "You cannot rely only on the bond between your hearts any longer. You must work on your non-magical relationship. You must build up the trust between you: show your unicorn *why* they should do as you say, *why* they should fight with you. Show them what your future together will look like. And this next step in your rider training is exactly why the Eyrie requires all Fledglings to undertake the Chaos Trials. Instructor Webb?"

This was the moment the Fledglings had been waiting for.

"My heartfelt congratulations to you all for reaching your third year of training at the Eyrie." Instructor Webb looked pleased to have the undivided attention of the crowd for once.

"Get on with it," Bobby muttered. Falcon flapped her gray wings in agreement.

Instructor Webb gave them a stony look from Moonlight

Dust's back. "Fledgling year is the most brutal of them all. For the first time, you will be tested during each elemental season, completing a trial in all four elemental zones. These challenges will force you to rely on your relationship with your unicorn by putting you in different—and often dangerous—situations."

"Dangerous?" Flo squeaked.

Four seasons. Four zones. Skandar felt a pang of disappointment. The Chaos Trials would still be operating on the basis that there were four elements, not five.

Instructor Webb continued, voice gravelly. "Throughout the trials you must draw on the elemental magic you have learned so far, quickly adapt to new environments, and rely on your instincts, courage, and skill. If you pass, your rider-unicorn bond—both magical and emotional—will be stronger, preparing you for the last two years at the Eyrie and the ultimate goal of qualifying for the Chaos Cup."

Celestial Seabird snorted, and Instructor O'Sullivan took over. "To advance from third-year Fledgling to fourth-year Rookie, a rider must collect four solstice stones throughout the trials—an earth, fire, water, and air stone."

At her words each instructor—except Agatha, who grimaced awkwardly—opened their left hand. There was a collective gasp from the Fledglings. On each palm shone a stone that matched the color of the instructor's allied element. They were like large gemstones: oblong in shape, with sharp edges and smooth facets that flashed in the morning sun. Mitchell had mentioned something about the trials involving stones, but Skandar had never thought they'd be so beautiful. When Instructor O'Sullivan moved forward, he saw that the glassy blue gem was etched all over with the droplet symbol of the water element.

"Three things to know about solstice stones." Instructor Manning spoke up for the first time, sounding nervous. "First, they are sacred objects—symbols of the elements as the source of the Island's power. Between each trial the stones you've collected will be locked away safely in the Silver Stronghold."

How come the Silver Circle gets to have them? Skandar thought.

"Secondly, you may be wondering why we're allowing your rebellious unicorns anywhere near these stones, given that they are precious artifacts." Electricity sparked playfully around Rex's mutated cheeks.

There was some whispering down the line. It was Marissa, Aisha, and Ivan, who'd been in a quartet with Albert—the fire wielder who'd been declared a nomad partway through Hatchling year.

Aisha sighed, stroking Dagger's Emerald. "Isn't Instructor Manning just the *nicest?*"

"I wonder if he's got a boyfriend," Ivan whispered, electricity sparking round his irises.

"Or girlfriend," Marissa said wistfully, adjusting her blue-framed glasses.

Niamh shushed them from Snow Swimmer. The water wielder had one ice spike through each ear, like very cool piercings—she wasn't someone to mess with.

The new air instructor was still speaking. "Luckily, solstice stones are indestructible. They've been here on the Island for as long as the unicorns; legend has it that the First Rider's great-granddaughter invented the Chaos Trials and first used the stones in third-year training. The Eyrie has continued her tradition. And lastly"—there was a loud clinking sound—"they're magnetic!" Rex had attached the yellow stone to his armored chest. "Once you've secured a stone, you must wear it visibly until that particular trial is over."

"Rex is making it sound like we'll be fighting over the stones," Flo said worriedly on Skandar's right. "Won't there be enough for everyone?"

"From what I've read, I highly doubt it." Mitchell looked a bit green, though Red *had* just burped—noisily—in the direction of his face.

Instructor Anderson summed up. "After the trials are over, those of you who have secured stones in all four elements will advance to Rookie year. For those without a complete set, you must wait at the Eyrie's entrance to see if one of your fellow riders—some of whom may have secured spare stones—will decide to save you, by handing over the ones you are missing. If your collection is complete, you can re-enter the Eyrie. Anything less, and you'll be declared a nomad."

"I'm going to get so many spares," Bobby murmured to herself. "Imagine the power!"

"If people can get spares, that means we *will* be fighting over stones," Flo said anxiously.

Mitchell looked slightly more confident. "I think it'll be mostly about tactics."

Skandar was horrified by the idea of reaching the Eyrie's entrance and not being allowed to re-enter. Especially when the future of the spirit element depended on him reaching his fifth year of training.

Then Instructor Webb made them all feel a lot worse. "Fledgling year sees the biggest cull of riders. It is during the Chaos Trials that true riders are born. Quartets will shatter, friendships will fracture, chivalry will give way to ambition. Many of you will fail. But for those who succeed, what will be the cost of collecting every elemental stone? And is a place at the Eyrie worth the price?"

Instructor O'Sullivan rolled her eyes. "Yes, thank you, Instructor Webb, for that encouraging description."

He inclined his mossy head graciously, oblivious to her sarcasm. "The Chaos Trials follow the elemental seasons. The final challenge will be the Air Trial, to which your families will be invited."

Skandar felt a warm glow of excitement. Maybe Dad and Kenna could watch him together?

Instructor O'Sullivan waited for the whispering to

subside. "Therefore, the first trial will be the Earth Trial in mid-September."

"That's only two weeks away!" Zac cried from Yesterday's Ghost.

Instructor O'Sullivan ignored him. "Until then, training will take place in quartets. You'll be practicing sky battles in groups. You'll need allies out in the zones, and these initial sessions will teach you how to cooperate. The instructors will mostly just observe today to assess your standard. Be wary—your unicorns may well rebel against your commands. And if you no longer have a full quartet, please come to see the instructors now."

By unhappy coincidence, Skandar's quartet was drawn against the Threat Quartet.

"Look at Alastair's face," Flo said when the battles were announced. "He looks like he wants to kill us."

"Half his face being rock doesn't exactly help him look friendly," Skandar agreed, as Red sidled up close to Scoundrel.

"Here's what we do," Bobby said breezily. "Skandar and Flo target Meiyi and Amber. Mitchell can attack Alastair and Kobi with me."

"It's a good plan," Mitchell conceded. "If we stick to that, we're using our best elements against their worst."

But as Skandar watched the first two quartets battling, he began to lose hope in their plan. Riders were attempting to engage each other in sky battles, but their unicorns were intent on doing their own thing. Instead of battling, Old Starlight and Queen's Price were shooting lightning bolts toward the air pavilion—determined to explode it—leaving Mariam and Gabriel powerless. Savage Salamander had swerved away from Sarika and Equator's Conundrum, not as a tactical move by his rider, Walker, but because Salamander had spotted a juicy-looking bird. The instructors called out occasional pieces of advice from the sidelines, but Skandar wasn't convinced the riders could hear them. Eventually they called time—without either quartet the clear winner.

Next, the whistle sounded for the Threat Quartet to face Skandar's. The eight Fledgling unicorns thundered forward and snapped out their wings to take off, heading right for each other. Their roars vibrated through the air, making Skandar's ribs rattle under his chain mail. And, as he'd predicted, the plan the riders had come up with went up in battle smoke.

Ice Prince, Rose-Briar's Darling, and Dusk Seeker headed straight for Silver Blade, preparing to neutralize the powerful silver unicorn first. Amber and Whirlwind Thief had already veered left toward Bobby and Falcon, and looked surprised that Kobi, Alastair, and Meiyi were targeting Flo. Clearly, Amber hadn't been in on the strategy.

Blade reared in the air, bellowing at his attackers. Flo had gone into full defensive mode, her silver armor flashing as she lifted her palm to create shield after shield: ice to block a volley of fire arrows from Meiyi, sand to cushion a barrage of rocks from Alastair, fire to melt Kobi's frozen scythe as he swung it toward her chest. She was holding them off well, but with three opponents, she was never going to get time to fight back and escape.

Skandar looked around for Mitchell and Bobby, but Bobby was already battling Amber over the air pavilion, and Mitchell, well . . . Red had clearly decided she'd rather still be in bed and was flying purposefully back up toward the Eyrie's forest. Scoundrel was luckily still responding to Skandar's commands, so they left the rest of the quartet behind and swooped closer to Blade, unnoticed.

Skandar summoned the spirit element into the bond, his palm turning white. Immediately the colorful cords between the hearts of the riders and unicorns below shone green, red, and blue. Only spirit wielders could see and manipulate bonds, and Skandar fully intended to use that to his advantage.

He let the magic build into a glowing mass between his hands, before letting three separate tendrils of spirit magic fly from his palm. The spiraling power snaked toward the hearts of the enemy riders and entered their bonds, extinguishing the elemental glow in their hands. Skandar had been training in the spirit element all summer, despite the other Fledglings taking a break. And when Agatha cheered from the ground, he knew it had paid off.

Flo looked up at Skandar, and time stood still for a

moment. He shrugged, she grinned, and then—with calm determination—she showed absolutely no mercy. She threw out a tornado so strong that it spiraled larger and larger as it loomed toward her attackers. Then she switched to firing sandy arrows into the spiral of air so it grew even bigger, picking up the elemental debris.

Snow-colored Ice Prince abandoned the attack on Blade and hurtled to the ground, refusing Kobi's attempts to fly him back toward the silver unicorn. Then Blade roared practically an entire waterfall from his mouth and knocked Rose-Briar's Darling back like a bowling pin. Had Flo lost control? Skandar caught sight of her terrified face before Meiyi and Briar were spiraling toward *him*.

Summoning the air element, Skandar quickly molded a trident with lightning sparking between its prongs. He prepared to throw it at Meiyi's armored chest. But Scoundrel had other ideas.

The black unicorn flew up over Briar's horned head, taking Skandar out of range, and then dive-bombed the ground instead.

"Scouuuundrelll!" Skandar cried. "What are you doing?!" But as the ground rushed up to meet them, Scoundrel arched his neck upward and they rocketed back into the sky. Skandar attempted to turn him back toward Briar, pouring his desire to finish the battle into the bond between them, but all he could feel from Scoundrel was a kind of nervous excitement. The black unicorn *liked* being a rebel right now.

Meanwhile, Bobby and Amber had forced each other to the ground, still battling near the yellow pavilion. They seemed extremely well matched—until Bobby drew back her arm to throw a flaming javelin and Falcon chose that exact moment to rear up on her hind legs. Bobby was catapulted out of her Henning-Dove saddle, javelin extinguishing as she hit the ground with a thud of armor. A hush went over the training ground. Falcon had *never* thrown Bobby off before.

Scoundrel finally allowed Skandar to return to the central battle. Only Alastair and Dusk Seeker remained fighting Flo and Blade, but the boy was clearly panicking—teeth set in a grimace of concentration as he threw his trusty diamond axe at Flo's chest. Mitchell—having convinced Red to turn back from the Eyrie—pointed toward Seeker and then—

KABOOM!

Glittering diamond pieces rained past Skandar.

Flo had exploded the axe in midair.

A whistle sounded for the end of the battle.

"Well, wasn't that fun?" Mitchell said sarcastically, as Red landed by Scoundrel. "They weren't joking about the unicorns rebelling."

"I feel like a Hatchling again," Skandar grumbled. How was he supposed to get through the Chaos Trials if Scoundrel wouldn't even *fly* in the right direction?

"I'm not sure Hatchling Flo could have exploded that

axe," Mitchell observed. "Diamond is the hardest substance in the world. How did she *do* that?"

"She's a silver," Skandar murmured, worrying what this rebellious year would look like for Flo. There were so many horror stories about silvers accidentally killing their own riders in battle—it was the reason so few had ever qualified for the Chaos Cup.

"Is everyone okay?" Flo asked, joining them. Blade's eyes were still smoking.

Bobby trudged dejectedly behind. Falcon looked sheepish, and Skandar couldn't help feeling a *little* pleased that Bobby's perfect unicorn wasn't immune to the Fledgling rebellion.

"Bobby?" Flo prompted. "Are *you* okay?"

"Don't want to talk about it," Bobby grunted, her hair frazzled by Amber's electrical attacks.

"Suddenly feels a little unsafe being a unicorn rider, doesn't it?" Mitchell said.

Flo actually laughed. "What do you mean *suddenly* feels unsafe? And why are you all looking so gloomy? We won the quartet battle, didn't we? I thought you all loved winning?"

"Technically we did win, yes," Mitchell conceded.

"Our unicorns were definitely rebelling *less* than the Threat Quartet's," Bobby said.

Skandar listened to his quartet finding the positives, seeing their way through the chaos ahead, and felt a burst of hope. They had worked together against terrible odds ever since they'd arrived. And their unicorns had been through it all with them. Their bonds were strong, even if the unicorns were testing them now. In the year to come, surely those foundations were going to matter more than anything else?

"You know?" Skandar said, grinning. "I think we've got a chance in these Chaos Trials."

"Why are you lot in such a rush?" Kenna asked half an hour later as Skandar, Bobby, Flo, and Mitchell hurtled into the treehouse.

Instructor Anderson had mentioned very casually at the end of training that instructions for the Earth Trial had just been pinned to their treehouse noticeboards.

"We'll explain in a second!" Skandar called. And, sure enough, among the feed schedules, training timetables, and a note about extra jam, there was a green-dyed piece of paper that read:

> Earth is a generous, productive element with fairness at its core. Therefore, in this first trial, the key is cooperation. Each Fledgling will have an earth stone and must finish the trial with it attached visibly to their armor. Quartets will succeed or fail together; if one member loses their stone, all four will fail.

There is nothing to be gained by attacking others—the earth provides enough for everyone. And in its generosity, it will reward those who work together and conquer their highest fears— a reward that may make all the difference in smoothing the path ahead.

"Nothing to be gained by attacking," Flo said, relieved. "That doesn't sound too bad."

"Speak for yourself," Bobby moaned. "Cooperation isn't exactly my strong point."

"But it doesn't say what we have to do," Skandar complained, as Kenna peered at the instructions too.

"Well, it was never going to explain exactly. It's the Eyrie, Skandar. They wouldn't want to make anything *easy*," Mitchell scoffed.

"We all start with an earth stone, though. That's good." Flo was still trying to be positive.

"And to keep it, everyone in our quartet has to pass the trial," Mitchell said, reading again. "The only bit I don't understand is *highest fears*."

"Is this the Fledgling challenge you've all been worried about?" Kenna asked.

"That's right," Mitchell said, heading for the bookshelf.

Skandar suddenly realized he was going to have to leave for the Earth Trial on the same day Kenna was having her mutation investigated at the Stronghold. What if they didn't let her out? He swallowed. "Kenn, I don't want to leave you, but—"

Kenna chuckled. "I'll be fine, Skar. You'll only be gone for a day or something. Don't worry."

"To be fair to him, Kenna," Bobby said, looking mischievous, "it *was* only yesterday that you destroyed the Nomad Tree."

"Oh yeah," Kenna mumbled awkwardly.

"Can't wait to see what you've destroyed by the time we get back!" Bobby crowed.

Kenna threw her head back and laughed, a sound so free that Skandar couldn't help but believe everything was going to be okay.

KENNA

Happiness

KENNA SMITH WAS STARTING TO REMEMBER
what happiness felt like.

*Happiness was Skandar's smile whenever he saw her. It was
the reassuring pulse of the unicorn-rider bond round her heart
and the brush of Goshawk's wings against her cheek.*

*Happiness was possibility. The possibility of training as a
Hatchling. The possibility of being accepted. The possibility of
belonging somewhere at last.*

*Happiness was the tug of the earth mutation round her
arm, the beginnings of power. It was tracing fingers along her
wounded palm and remembering she was on the Island at last.*

*Happiness was dreaming. Dreaming of a future with
a quartet of her own. Dreaming of a treehouse to call home.*

Dreaming of no more dreams because they'd already come true.

All these thoughts cheered Kenna as she made her way down inside the Eyrie's wall the week after she'd toppled the Nomad Tree. It had been scary at the time, especially followed by the pain of her first mutation. But now the whole episode seemed sort of . . . funny. As Bobby had said, everybody had hated that tree anyway. The tree that recorded failure.

Kenna unlatched Goshawk's stable door, and the wild unicorn hissed quietly—in welcome or in warning? She wasn't certain. Girl and wild unicorn regarded each other warily. Goshawk lowered her transparent horn protectively, skeletal ribs moving visibly under her anxious skin. Kenna turned both palms upward as if to say, *I won't hurt you. I won't cause you more pain.* Kenna understood that—for now—this was a dance she must do whenever they encountered one another. But she was willing to learn the steps.

Kenna didn't know what it was like to have an uncomplicated bond. She didn't know if any other rider felt the fear climb up their throat as they looked into the endless pits of their unicorn's eyes. She didn't know if any other rider felt death's icy chill each time they reached out to touch their unicorn's neck. And she was sure no other rider was haunted by two ghosts: the ghost of a destined unicorn crying in the Wilderness and the ghost of a rider who'd never made it to the Hatchery door.

Kenna suspected she and Goshawk were the only ones troubled by such things. Sometimes she was proud of her forged bond: that she was discovering its power and its limits all on her own. At other times she was terribly afraid of its capacity to isolate her—just as Erika Everhart had warned. But she was trying not to think about Mum. She wanted to pretend, for now, that she could be happy at the Eyrie with Skandar. And if she pretended hard enough, perhaps—in time—it would become reality.

Kenna reached into her pocket and pulled out the single green Jelly Baby she'd stolen from Skandar's stash.

She held it up at Goshawk's eyeline, and the unicorn snorted, putrid black smoke swirling round Kenna's vine-punctured wrist. She was used to the smell of wild unicorn magic now; it didn't bother her as it did the others.

Slowly Kenna placed the sweet on her palm so it covered the hole made by Goshawk's horn. The wound still hadn't healed. She understood now that it never would.

"Come on, Gos," Kenna coaxed. "Scoundrel eats them, and you don't want to be outdone by that show-off, do you?" She took one step forward, arm outstretched.

With a flash of bloodstained teeth Goshawk snatched the Jelly Baby from Kenna's palm.

"Yes, Gos!" Kenna cried. "You did it!"

Goshawk rumbled happily back and lifted one bat-like wing as though giving permission for her rider to come closer. Pure joy exploded in Kenna's heart, and at last it was safe to wind her arms round Goshawk's neck, honey-colored feathers brushing her arm.

"We'll be fine, Gos. You'll see."

Later, as she returned to Instructor O'Sullivan's tree-house, she stopped on a high platform to look out over the twinkling lanterns of the Eyrie, their light reflecting off the armor wrapped round the tree trunks. She often stopped here because it allowed her to catch a glimpse of one particular view.

The round window of her brother's treehouse shone out like a welcoming beacon from the cluster of others nesting in the nearby branches. Kenna loved to gaze at that window, even if she'd only left Skandar and his quartet a few moments before. Seeing its warm light reminded her that there—past only a few swinging bridges and a couple of rickety ladders—was Skandar. Because *he* was her home. And now she could visit anytime she liked.

CHAPTER FOUR

The Earth Trial

"HOW MANY TIMES DO I HAVE TO TELL YOU?" Agatha said harshly. "The focus of my sessions this year is battle magic. *Not* Mender magic."

"But—"

"Do I really need to remind you that it is *vital* that you pass the Chaos Trials? That the responsibility is on your shoulders—skinny as they are—to bring spirit magic back to the Island?"

Skandar sighed. "I know." Of course he hadn't forgotten the bargain he'd made with Commodore McGrath as a Hatchling. If he completed his Eyrie training, the Hatchery door would no longer be barred to spirit wielders like him—like Kenna. But Kenna wasn't really a spirit wielder anymore, was she? That was the whole reason he wanted to learn more about being a Mender.

"Let's get back to it, then, shall we?" Agatha put her instructor voice back on to indicate that they weren't discussing Menders any longer. Skandar promised himself he'd badger her later.

It was mid-September, and this was Skandar's last spirit training before the Earth Trial in the morning.

"Now I'm going to demonstrate something with Arctic Swansong. I think you'll like it." Agatha rode her white unicorn out into the middle of the water training ground, her instructor's cloak blending in with Swan's back. She was very keen on doing demonstrations, because she was only allowed to use magic when teaching Skandar. That was the deal Rex had struck with her.

"I want to show you what we're working up to this year." Agatha summoned the pearly white of the spirit element into her palm, and it grew brighter until her body glowed with it. Beneath her, Arctic Swansong was doing the same—his wings shimmering white, sinewy bones visible as the power spread. Whatever the pair were doing was taking an incredible amount of energy.

Then, suddenly, there were two of them.

Skandar blinked, yet they were still there: two Agathas and two Arctic Swansongs drenched in spirit magic. Scoundrel shrieked in confusion, and Skandar couldn't tell which were the real ones until the magic faltered and the doppel-gängers disappeared.

Agatha smirked at the look of wonder on Skandar's face as she trotted Swan back toward Scoundrel.

"How did—There were two of you," Skandar spluttered.

"Well observed," Agatha said sarcastically.

"Can you teach me now?" Skandar asked hungrily. He was thinking about all the ways there being *two* of him would be extremely helpful during the Chaos Trials.

"Do not be arrogant. I am an extremely skilled spirit wielder, Skandar. Duplication requires immense power and concentration. And first you must understand that what you are doing is accessing another rider's psyche through their bond. You are making them see what's not really there—manipulating their mind."

"Okay," Skandar said impatiently. He didn't really understand what she was saying but wanted her to carry on.

"So we will start small. You'll learn how to make another rider hear your voice in their ear. It's called spirit speech."

Skandar half wondered if Agatha was joking.

Seeing his doubt, she explained, "It's an old spirit wielder distraction tactic. Very useful in battles. I'll show you."

Agatha trotted Swan all the way over to the blue pavilion opposite. "What am I supposed to be doing?" Skandar yelled, but she raised a finger to her lips and summoned the spirit element to her palm.

Skandar huffed in irritation.

When you make that face, you look constipated.

Agatha's voice was so clear in his right ear that Skandar looked over his shoulder to see if she'd crept up on him. But no. She and Swan were still three hundred meters away. The hairs on the back of his neck stood up.

Your turn, Agatha said, and Skandar jumped. Her voice had moved to his other ear.

They practiced for over an hour. Agatha told Skandar that he had to summon the spirit element and then focus on what he wanted her to hear. They weren't doing full sentences, just individual syllables. Skandar got increasingly frustrated as Agatha shook her head over and over to indicate she hadn't heard anything. It didn't help that Scoundrel was bored and kept firing lightning bolts from his horn.

Then—when Skandar was most annoyed with himself *and* Agatha *and* Scoundrel—he thought, *Argh!*

This time, Agatha's hand flew to her left ear. "OUCH!" she yelled back. "Not so loud!"

She rode Swan over, wisps of brown hair flying around her face in the breeze. "Well, now we have something to work with. But, Skandar"—her tone was no longer teasing—"you must be careful with the volume. There were spirit wielders who used to scream into their opponents' ears back in the day. It was strongly frowned upon; it can really affect someone. Remember to fight the darker side of your element."

Skandar felt horrible. "I'm so sorry! Did I hurt you?"

Agatha chuckled. "You're all right, little spirit wielder. Don't worry."

Skandar spent the rest of the session summoning spirit weapons on command: spirit saber, spirit bow, spirit axe, spirit javelin, spirit mace.

"You're getting quick with those," Agatha observed at the end of the session. She *almost* smiled.

Skandar decided to take advantage of her good mood. "Aga—

"Instructor Everhart," she corrected.

"The reason I want to know more about being a Mender is because—"

"You want to bond Kenna to her destined unicorn—the dapple-gray that kept interrupting our training sessions last year."

Skandar was stunned.

"I've seen you in Scoundrel's stable practically every night. Did you think I wouldn't work it out?"

"Kind of!" Skandar spluttered.

Agatha rubbed her mutated cheeks in frustration. When they'd first met, Skandar had thought they were scarred, but now that he had a skeletal spirit mutation on his own fore-arm, he could hardly believe he'd missed hers. "How many times have I told you how dangerous those dreams are? How you need to wait until you're more experienced? And if you *are* going to ignore me, at least have someone with you to wake you up. A few nights ago, you only stopped shouting out in pain when I banged on Scoundrel's stable door."

"Have you been checking on me?" Skandar felt a bit pleased.

Agatha looked shifty, as though she didn't want to admit it. "I have trouble . . . sleeping." She sighed. "I know you're worried about your sister. So am I. But she already has a bond to Goshawk's Fury."

"The Island still hasn't approved her training! And now there's the whole Nomad Tree thing—"

"Indeed. Last I heard, Kenna's wild magic poisoned it at the roots. Personally, I don't think it's a great loss, but then I've never been particularly sentimental about trees."

"But what about the rest of Kenna's mutations? And what if she ends up less . . . human, like the Weaver?"

"The fact remains—she *has* a bond, Skandar."

He hesitated. He hadn't talked to Agatha about separating Kenna from her wild unicorn yet. If he was honest, he was ashamed of how badly he wanted Goshawk out of the picture, and he wasn't sure what Agatha would think.

He decided to chance it. "What if I could separate Kenna from Goshawk and then mend Kenna's bond to her destined unicorn? Wouldn't that be safer for her?"

Agatha was looking at him very intently. "That is *quite* an undertaking for a Fledgling spirit wielder."

Skandar's heart was hammering. "Can it be done? Can a forged bond be broken?"

The air seemed to vibrate between the two of them.

"I do not know," Agatha said finally. "But I think it's much more complicated than breaking and making bonds, don't you? Were you thinking of *killing* Goshawk? Because the last time someone started murdering wild unicorns, it went rather badly, as I recall."

"No!" Skandar cried, horrified. "Of course not!"

"That's just as well, since no one has been able to find the pieces of the bone staff."

Skandar was now scrabbling around for something else to keep the conversation going—and then it hit him.

"What if I didn't have to *break* Kenna's bond with Goshawk? What if I just bonded her to the dapple-gray unicorn . . . as well. Like the Weaver. Erika had two bonds, didn't she? And she never got wild mutations; maybe it would help!"

Agatha's mouth curled into a snarl. "Never. Suggest. That. Again." Swan loomed very large next to Scoundrel, and the black unicorn skittered sideways.

"Why not?"

"Are you really asking me that?" Agatha exploded at him. "Did I not tell you that Erika *fled* to the Mainland to try to escape her wild unicorn's anger? Did I not recount its fury at how my sister prioritized her bond with Blood-Moon's Equinox?"

"But Kenna wouldn't do that!" Skandar protested. "She'd love them both!"

"Tell me—given the choice, which unicorn is the Island going to let Kenna train in the Eyrie? Which unicorn would be more likely to be accepted as a qualifier into the Chaos Cup? Because it's not going to be a wild one, is it?"

Skandar's mind filled with images of Goshawk's Fury banished to the Wilderness, consumed with rage and bitterness as Kenna raced her dapple-gray round the Chaos Cup course.

"We only have one soul, Skandar," Agatha said quietly. "No rider can love two unicorns with their whole soul. No rider can treat them equally—especially not on an Island that hates wild unicorns. I will *not* let you assist history in repeating itself."

"Okay," Skandar murmured. "I'm sorry. I didn't think."

Unexpectedly Agatha reached a hand over Swan's wing and placed it on Skandar's armored shoulder. "Forget this. If all goes to plan, Kenna will start her training in the Eyrie on Goshawk, and she'll learn to control her magic. And I *will* teach you more about mending one day. But for now you must concentrate on the Chaos Trials. Promise me!"

"I promise," Skandar said. And he meant it. For now. "Instructor Everhart?"

"Forking thunderstorms, what is it now?"

Skandar's mouth twitched—she sounded like Mitchell. "You know we have to collect these solstice stones in the trials? I was wondering—"

"About spirit stones?" Agatha raised one wiry eyebrow.

Skandar waited.

"Spirit stones certainly were used in the Chaos Trials—there used to be a Spirit Trial, too. But they're all gone now. Destroyed by the Silver Circle."

Skandar frowned. "Rex Manning said the stones are indestructible."

Agatha shrugged. "Before last year, everyone thought killing a wild unicorn was impossible. If the Silver Circle wanted to get rid of the spirit stones enough, I expect they found a way. Believe me—as a person they wanted to get rid of, *I'd* know."

The Fledglings woke in the middle of the night, struggled with their armor in the dark, and tightened girths round sleepy unicorns. They flew in a line behind three of the Eyrie instructors: Webb, Anderson, and Everhart. In the moonlight, Skandar watched Fourpoint give way to the earth zone's bountiful farms, which turned to moorland, then rolling hills, and finally to mountains. He focused on the beating of Scoundrel's wings, the rhythm of his snorting breaths, the clink of chain mail beneath his boots. In the calm, he tried to forget saying goodbye to Kenna the night before and his worries about the trial ahead.

The thirty-six Fledgling unicorns gathered at the foot of a mountain just before dawn, awaiting instructions. Two teams of healers had assembled—one for riders and one for unicorns—which made Skandar feel even more nervous.

Instructor Webb cleared his throat importantly. "This year the Earth Trial will be a race to the top of the zone's most challenging mountain."

Whispering broke out among the Fledglings. Flo started muttering to herself beside Skandar. "Please not the Restless Mountain, please not the Restless Mountain, please not—"

"The Restless Mountain." Instructor Webb gestured to the towering peak on their left. "This mountain is alive with magic. According to those who have reached its summit, it is almost as though the mountain doesn't want to be climbed. Expect the ground to shift beneath your feet, the paths to transform into dead ends, the trickling streams to become torrents without warning."

"But surely we can just fly our unicorns to the top?" Amber's piercing voice rose from the crowd—she was a member of the Peregrine Society like Skandar, and he'd been thinking exactly the same thing.

"Flying is forbidden in this trial. We instructors will be patrolling the air around the mountain. If you are caught flying, your earth stones will be confiscated. Understood?"

"Yes, Instructor," the Fledglings mumbled.

"This trial will test endurance, perseverance, and teamwork. All skills that Chaos riders require to triumph in the Cup. But here no good will come of fighting other riders. Focus on keeping your unicorns under control and following the right path. Rider and unicorn will need to trust each other to succeed. Each rider will receive an earth stone. To keep it, your whole quartet must reach the top of the Restless Mountain *with their earth stones* by sunset. And, importantly, there will be a reward for the first quartet to reach the summit."

Skandar could see Bobby fidgeting, desperate to get going; Falcon kept turning to snap at her boots.

"I don't really like heights," Mitchell confessed to Skandar in a whisper.

"But you're a unicorn rider!" Skandar exclaimed. "You fly!"

"It's different," Mitchell mumbled. "It's different standing on something you could fall off."

"But you could fall off Red anytime!"

"Oh, thank you, that really helps," Mitchell snapped.

"Please come to collect your earth stones," Instructor Webb called; he was immediately mobbed by the quartet closest to him—Sarika, Gabriel, Zac, and Mabel—as he opened a green drawstring bag that had been attached to his Bhadresha saddle.

Instructors Anderson and Everhart had green bags too. Agatha ignored the quartets approaching her and made a beeline for Skandar's.

As Agatha handed Skandar his green solstice stone, she whispered sharply into his ear, "Watch your back. Don't try to go after other people's stones. And if you think another quartet is hunting you, hide."

"But this is the Earth Trial," Skandar protested.

"Nobody's going after each other, are they? Isn't our main worry keeping the unicorns under control?"

Agatha's eyes were flinty. "Don't be a fool, Skandar. The Chaos Trials turn riders ruthless—that's the point of them. People get greedy. Yes, the earth element is supposed to be the nice one, but that doesn't mean you can let your guard down. Everyone is going to want that reward for finishing first. Do you understand?"

She released him as Instructor Anderson came past, handing out backpacks with supplies—raincoats, blankets, water, snacks, and a compass. There was also a map to the summit that Mitchell cradled to his chest. "Thank you," he whispered to nobody in particular.

Skandar studied the other groups of Fledglings, wondering if they felt as scared as he did. At least he had Bobby, Flo, and Mitchell to face this with. The riders in broken quartets—where one, or in some cases even two, of their number had been declared a nomad in the past two years—had been forced to team up with other broken quartets to make groups of four. He glanced over at Ajay and Smoldering Menace, who'd been added to Albert's old quartet: Marissa, Ivan, and Aisha. He looked very awkward.

"Solstice stones must be attached to your armor and visible at all times," Instructor Anderson shouted.

The clinks of green solstice stones attaching to breastplates echoed around the riders.

"We'll be watching," Agatha warned. And Arctic Swansong, Moonlight Dust, and Desert Firebird took off and began to circle the mountain.

Mitchell hesitated. "Do we . . . ?"

"Yes! Go!" Bobby shouted, and the quartet galloped their unicorns toward the trees lining the Restless Mountain's base.

The Fledglings dispersed throughout the dense thicket. Once they were sure they wouldn't be overheard, Skandar, Bobby, Flo, and Mitchell huddled their unicorns together to look at the map.

"This looks like the most direct route." Mitchell ran his finger along the paper and then checked his compass.

"Can we just go?" Bobby said impatiently. "What if the other quartets are further ahead already?"

"Bobby, this trial isn't about winning," Flo said. "It's about making it to the summit . . . alive." Her brown eyes were wide and terrified.

"It's just a mountain, Florence," Bobby said dismissively.

"It is NOT just a mountain," Flo snapped, quite unlike herself. "It's the *Restless* Mountain. I grew up in the earth zone, remember? I've heard the stories."

"What stories?" Skandar asked nervously.

"This mountain is *alive*. It doesn't want us to climb it. What are the instructors thinking, setting this challenge for a bunch of Fledglings? My parents have always forbidden me and Ebb to come anywhere *near* here."

"Superstition," Mitchell scoffed.

"Mitchell," Flo said indignantly, "that is exactly what you said about truesongs last year, and look what happened. That bard was right about *everything*. Even Kenna."

"Not necessarily," Skandar mumbled. He refused to believe that the truesong foretold that Kenna would be the Weaver's successor. Having a forged bond like their mum didn't mean Kenna had to *become* like her.

A bird squawked loudly. Everyone jumped—except Bobby, who rolled her eyes at them. "Restless or not, we have to climb this piece of rock or we lose our earth stones. Flo can tell us horror stories about the mountain on the way up."

But Flo never got the chance, because soon they were in a horror story of their own.

Everything was fine until they left the thicket. The unicorns had *generally* been behaving, although Red had started dragging the tips of her hooves over rocks, spraying sparks everywhere. They'd also been forced to take a detour when Falcon had spotted a hare and Bobby hadn't managed to stop her from chasing it. Despite that, Mitchell was excited when they reached a narrow rocky gorge, its jagged sides towering up on either side of them. Especially when he spotted the stream trickling down the slope ahead of them.

"This is definitely the shortcut I identified!" he announced, brandishing the folded map triumphantly, as all four unicorns drank from the clear water. "If we follow the stream to its source, it'll take us higher."

"Shortcut? I'm in." Bobby pushed Falcon forward. The

gray unicorn picked up her hooves very high as she entered the water—wet meant muddy.

"Let Red go first," Mitchell whined. "I'm the one who knows the way."

Flo, on the other hand, was clutching at the front of her Martina saddle as though it might save her.

As they splashed higher, Skandar noticed caves cut into the rock on either side of the stream. Their entrances were dark yawns, with sharp stalagmites and stalactites guarding the entrances like incisors. The unicorns had spotted them too. Scoundrel's eyes flashed to red, and Blade was hissing into the openings. With great ceremony, Red turned and farted magnificently into the gloom of the nearest cave, as though warding off evil spirits.

At first Skandar thought it was just the unicorns messing around, but then—out in front—unflappable Falcon skittered away from the cave on her right. Her shriek echoed hauntingly back and forth between the towering sides of the gorge.

"I genuinely think there's something in there." Bobby's voice was serious.

"Other Fledglings?" Mitchell's hand went protectively to his solstice stone.

"Oh no!" Flo muttered from behind Skandar, and a chill went down his spine.

Scoundrel and Blade caught up with Red and Falcon.

"Should we—" But Skandar didn't manage to ask his

question before a gray creature crashed out of the nearest cave and slammed into Falcon's flank.

Bobby reacted instinctively as Falcon roared with rage, summoning the air element and throwing a tornado at the creature so it was catapulted sideways. It looked like it had been carved from the cave itself, its mouth a swirling black void.

"Watch out!" Flo yelled.

There were more of them.

Skandar watched—with a combination of horror and wonder—as the stalactites hanging from several cave entrances began to drop like candle wax, each blob of rock morphing until it resembled the gargoyle-like creature Bobby had just taken out with her tornado.

"Forking thunderstorms!" Mitchell swore as a gray monster grabbed Red's tail, its grip firm even when the red strands ignited.

"They're stalignomes!" Flo shouted, springing to action. "Earth elementals! You've got to hit them with sheer physical force! Fire or water won't do it. Try air or earth attacks!" Blade kicked out sand jets from his front hooves, hurling the closest creature back into its cave.

"What happens if they get to us?" Bobby asked coolly, blowing her brown bangs aside to eye up her next target.

"Umm, they just sort of smash and smash until you stop moving. If they can get their arms round your neck, they suffocate you. . . . That's what my dad told us when we were little, anyway." Flo's voice quivered, her palm glowing green.

"And you didn't think to mention murderous rock creatures *before* we entered an enclosed space surrounded by caves?" Bobby grunted, as another creature collided with her sand shield.

"You're the one who wanted to get going!" Flo yelled. Silver Blade flapped his wings menacingly, and she sent a torrent of glass shards at the nearest rock creature.

Skandar copied Flo and summoned the earth element into his palm, sending a stream of sharp flints toward the creature hurtling straight for Scoundrel's left leg. The bond was suddenly filled with Scoundrel's confidence in Skandar, and a fierce protectiveness—all rebellion forgotten—as they faced the danger together.

On his other side, Bobby and Mitchell teamed up, throwing down tornadoes to sweep the stalignomes back into their caves as soon as they formed from the stalactites.

Then, somehow, a stalignome got past them and fixed its jagged arms round Scoundrel's glossy neck. He reared up furiously, and Skandar knew he needed something big to dislodge it. He summoned the spirit element, magnifying the earth element already inside the bond. An impressive mace burst into Skandar's hand, and he swung it like a baseball bat, right at the mountain creature. With a satisfying clunk, it soared into the air and hit the side of the gorge fifty meters above.

Scoundrel shrieked with relief, the bond filling with love for his rider.

Skandar stroked the unicorn's sweaty neck. Perhaps he was beginning to understand Instructor O'Sullivan's words: *Show your unicorn why they should do as you say, why they should fight with you. Show them what your future together will look like.*

There was a rumbling like thunder. A rattle of pebbles colliding.

"ROCKFALL!" Mitchell yelled. The riders pushed their unicorns into a gallop, splashing upward through the mountain stream. Boulders, soil, and tree roots were falling behind them like sheets of rain, getting closer. Skandar could feel Scoundrel's desperation to fly out of the gorge and away from danger. But they couldn't. They'd sacrifice the earth stones of everyone in the quartet if they broke the rules.

The noise of the rockfall behind Skandar was so loud that he barely heard Bobby's whoop of relief, as Falcon disappeared through a narrow gap between the rocks. Red's flaming tail disappeared next, then Blade's silver one. Scoundrel followed his friends without hesitation. They'd made it. They'd survived. Then—

SPLASH.

Boy and unicorn were underwater. Submerged. Scoundrel roared at the unexpected dunking, but it only sent bubbles bursting from his mouth. Skandar grasped Scoundrel's neck, as the unicorn pumped his wings and drove them upward.

They broke the surface, both heaving in glorious breaths of air. A crystal-blue waterfall cascaded into the plunge pool they'd landed in. Six other heads—three unicorns, three riders—bobbed about nearby. They swam to the side of the pool and heaved themselves up onto its rocky edge. The unicorns followed, shaking out their wings.

"I'm sorry," Skandar said, once they were all wrapped in blankets. "I think I caused that. I smashed that stalignome into—"

"It wasn't your fault," Mitchell reassured him. "We should have listened to Flo."

"Yes, you should have," Flo said, although she sounded more resigned than annoyed.

"I'm sorry, Flo," Bobby said in rare apology. "This is the Earth Trial—I shouldn't have tried to take the lead. I want to hear every nightmarish bedtime story you've ever been told about this killer mountain."

Flo grinned. "Once upon a time . . ."

And all four of them collapsed into relieved laughter.

CHAPTER FIVE

The Restless Mountain

AFTER THEIR UNINTENTIONAL SWIM, THE quartet continued to make their way up the Restless Mountain. Mitchell, Bobby, and Skandar listened carefully to the tales Flo's parents had told her about the tricks the mountain might play on a wandering child—or indeed a Fledgling unicorn rider. And, sure enough, they encountered some of them as morning became afternoon.

When they began to get thirsty, the mountain springs dotted around the path would sparkle invitingly in the September sunshine, before freezing over as soon as one of the riders approached. It took all the fire magic Mitchell and Red could muster before the thick ice returned to liquid form.

By the middle of the afternoon, the map stopped making sense. At first, not even Mitchell could work out what was happening. It was Bobby who eventually spotted part of the mountainside morphing in shape, changing the direction of the path they were following. This discovery sent Mitchell into a rage, and Flo managed to grab the map from him just before he ripped it to pieces.

Without a useful map, all they could do was climb higher. Skandar wasn't sure whether it was a good sign that they hadn't spotted any other quartets for a while. Were they very far ahead? Or had their route through the gorge slowed them down?

"This really is extremely unsafe," Mitchell moaned, eyes half-shut as he waved toward the severe drop on one side of them.

"We must be almost at the top," Skandar said, trying to be reassuring.

"I don't want to be at the top, Skandar!" Mitchell snapped. "I don't like heights, remember?"

"How long do you think we have before sunset?" Flo asked from behind Scoundrel, sounding exhausted.

"Don't think about that! We just have to keep going— come on!" Bobby called from in front. But as Skandar glanced toward Falcon, he saw an enormous chunk missing from the path ahead of her gray legs. Then the air around the gap shimmered and it looked solid again. But Skandar knew better. If Falcon took another step, she'd plunge through the hole and be forced to fly, losing the whole quartet their earth stones.

"Bobby!" he yelled. "STOP!"

The urgency in his voice made Bobby pull sharply on her reins.

"The path isn't there," Skandar called. "Just ahead of Falcon's hooves! It isn't real!"

"Oh, well, that's just fantastic," Mitchell groaned, as the air around the gap flickered.

Bobby squinted down. "That was close," she breathed, after the unicorns had jumped across the gap. "Thanks, spirit boy."

"We'll have to be more careful," Flo said, her voice shaking.

Then—when they were all deliriously tired, thirsty, and irritable—things got even worse. The quartet turned a bend, and Dusk Seeker was blocking the narrow path ahead of Bobby and Falcon. But Alastair wasn't alone. Meiyi and Rose-Briar's Darling appeared above them on the steep crag to Skandar's right. Kobi and Ice Prince moved into position at the rear of the quartet.

"I would say it's nothing personal," Alastair snarled, green eyes narrowed. "But I'd be lying."

"Spirit wielders—especially ones with a mini-Weaver for a sister—do *not* belong in the Eyrie," Meiyi shouted angrily, her mutated lips glowing like burning embers.

"Your special treatment has gone on long enough," Kobi said roughly.

Skandar's quartet were completely trapped—with Alastair, Meiyi, and Kobi on three sides and a sheer drop to their left. There was a moment of stillness; time seemed to slow. . . . Then the air exploded with elemental magic.

Alastair sent a sand blast at Bobby's face, but she was ready with a defensive tornado to blow it off course as Falcon snarled at Seeker. Meiyi rained down flaming arrows from her higher ground, so Skandar and Mitchell both had to summon shimmering water shields above their heads while Scoundrel and Red teamed up, blasting jets of water from their horns right at Briar. Kobi's frosted eyelashes flashed as he swiped at Flo with an ice sword—Blade was doing a good job holding him off, though, rearing up at Prince with flaming hooves.

"You're not supposed to be attacking people during the Earth Trial," Flo called to Kobi, as his sword melted.

Skandar's mouth twitched into a smile; was Flo really scolding Kobi mid-battle?

"You do realize you've lost your air wielder? You must be as rock-headed as everyone says!" Bobby shouted at Alastair, blasting strands of electricity toward Seeker. Skandar thought the taunt was also a warning for the rest of her quartet—where *was* Amber? And would her arrival tip the balance of the fight?

Then the enemy trio changed tactics. Dusk Seeker and Ice Prince scrambled up to higher ground to join Rose-Briar's Darling. Confused, Falcon, Red, Scoundrel, and Blade turned on the narrow path to face them, tails hanging over the sheer drop.

It was a mistake. The trio's palms all glowed yellow, and they blasted gale-force winds right at the quartet. Skandar felt Scoundrel being forced back by the gusts, his hind hoof scrabbling for footing on the path's outer edge.

"The wind's too strong!" Flo called.

"Don't let your unicorns take off!" Mitchell warned, as he struggled to raise his ice shield against the wind. Red's feathered wings were half out, as though preparing to fly them to safety.

"Kobi! Get him under control!" Alastair shouted angrily, as Ice Prince roared and water streamed from his mouth, distracting the other two unicorns.

"I say we make a break for it." Skandar kept his voice low. "Kobi's struggling with Prince. We haven't come all this way to get eliminated by flying now!"

"And let them get away with this?" Bobby said through gritted teeth, switching shields as they were battered by the wind.

"It's not about that, Bobby! We don't have to win this battle," Flo called, as Blade stumbled dangerously close to the edge. "We go on three. One. Two. Three!"

Falcon turned up the rocky path first, then Red, then Scoundrel—

"Argh!" Skandar's stomach lurched as Scoundrel's back hoof slipped over the mountain's crumbling edge.

"Skar!" Flo cried, trying to halt Blade, but she was powerless to stop him from thundering after the rest of his friends.

Scoundrel's black wings snapped out, as he tried to balance himself. His foot scrabbled for a safe piece of rock as howling laughter echoed above them.

The storm the trio had brewed was battering Scoundrel's whole body, and Skandar could feel his panic. Even so, the unicorn seemed to sense how important it was not to fly.

"You can do it, Scoundrel," he murmured, flooding the bond with reassurance.

And finally, muscles straining, Scoundrel managed to drag his hind leg back up onto the mountain path.

A second later, they were galloping after the others, trying to put as much distance between themselves and the angry shouts coming from the enemy riders. Scoundrel hurtled round the narrowing mountain track at breakneck speed, and—after a seemingly endless series of terrifyingly tight bends—it was clear that Kobi, Alastair, and Meiyi had given up.

Skandar slowed Scoundrel to a walk and tried to spot Falcon or Blade or Red. Had he taken a wrong turn? Then

Skandar looked over his shoulder, and his whole body flooded with fear.

A wild unicorn stood on a rocky overhang behind him.

And it had a rider.

The Weaver was unmistakable in her black shroud, the skeletal white stripe shining down her face. Wisps of her graying hair flew around her sallow haunted features. The rotting unicorn wasn't moving; its bone-splintered knees were motionless, its red eyes fixed ahead as black fumes swirled around its ghostly horn. The smoke clung to the Weaver's shroud, and she looked even less human than she had two years ago.

Mother and son held each other's gaze. Skandar's storm of emotions had him paralyzed.

Terror. Would she try to kill Scoundrel? Had she attacked his quartet already?

Fury. She'd tethered Kenna to a wild unicorn. The wrong unicorn. Her own daughter.

Confusion. Why was his mum here? He felt oddly drawn to her, despite everything.

The Weaver blinked.

You are in my way, Skandar Smith.

The whispered words sounded in Skandar's left ear. He turned, half expecting to see the Weaver right beside him.

But Erika Everhart was still up on the jagged rock, her shroud billowing in the wind.

She was using spirit speech.

You are in my way.

The words were louder this time, an unspoken threat of violence in them.

"We need to go!" Skandar choked out, unsure if he was speaking to Scoundrel or himself.

They galloped higher up the mountain's side. Skandar kept glancing over his shoulder, expecting the Weaver to follow, expecting . . . something. But he carried on riding, heart thundering, until he lost sight of the wild unicorn on the rock.

Scoundrel rounded another bend, and finally Skandar saw Falcon, Blade, and Red halted just below the summit. Bobby, Flo, and Mitchell were shouting his name in different directions.

"Nice of you to join us," Bobby said, clearly annoyed at having to wait.

"You didn't fly, did you?" Mitchell checked. "Flo said Scoundrel lost his balance."

"No. I—" Skandar croaked, looking over his shoulder again.

"Are you all right?" Flo stared at him. "You look like you've seen a ghost."

"I think she's gone," Skandar rasped. His hands were shaking on the reins, and Scoundrel launched a bubble of concern into the bond.

"*Who's* gone? Did Amber catch up with you?" Mitchell leaned round in his saddle to look down the path.

"What's wrong, Skar?" Flo asked.

Skandar took a shaky breath. "The Weaver. Didn't you pass her . . . ?" He trailed off as the others exchanged confused looks.

"I didn't see anyone," Bobby said first. "Where was she?"

"Back there!" Skandar jabbed a finger. "Sh-she whispered in my ear—spirit speech."

"What was it that you thought she said?" Mitchell asked, his voice matter-of-fact.

Skandar swallowed. "She said, 'You are in my way.' Twice!"

Flo took a deep breath and then another one—like she always did when she was worried about what she was about to say. "Skar, this mountain plays tricks, remember? She might have been an illusion, or—"

"She was real," Skandar said stubbornly. But even as he said it, the doubts poured in. Why would the Weaver be here? Why hadn't she attacked?

"Can we please just finish the trial before we work out if Skandar's imagining things?" Bobby said impatiently.

"I'm not—" Skandar protested.

But there was no stopping the air wielder now. "The reward!"

Hardly waiting for them to follow, Bobby and Falcon led Red, Scoundrel, and Blade round the last steep bend. Finally the sky opened up above them and they spilled out onto the Restless Mountain's rocky summit.

"Well done, Florence!" Instructor Webb wrung Flo's hand. "Another of my earth wielders safely through."

"Are we first to finish?" Bobby demanded. "Where's the prize?"

"Oh dear, no." Instructor Webb chuckled. "It's been almost eight hours! I'm afraid you're one of the last." The earth instructor did not miss the look of absolute horror on Bobby's face. "But, no matter, that was never the *main* objective of this trial. You have all done yourselves proud by finishing together."

Skandar barely registered the congratulations. He couldn't get the image of the Weaver out of his head, get the sound of her voice from his ear.

"I am going to KILL that Threat . . . Trio," Bobby muttered, as the unicorns flew back down to the mountain's base.

Most of the other Fledglings were milling around the healer tents, chattering on logs as the sun began to set, or eating snacks from their backpacks. Some of the unicorns had even started to doze round a campfire.

As soon as the quartet landed, healers buzzed around them to check the riders and unicorns for injuries. Still preoccupied with the Weaver, Skandar silently fed Scoundrel a whole packet of Jelly Babies to thank him for getting them through the trial.

Nearby, Niamh was surrounded by a circle of other Fledglings. ". . . and there was a green ribbon across the entrance to the summit, and four solstice stones hanging from it!" She sounded delighted, her strawberry-blond ponytail swinging as she told the story.

"The reward was *four* spare stones?" Elias asked, removing his helmet. While Gabriel had stone curls, this earth wielder's hair had become tightly packed sand grains when he'd mutated—and he styled it like a sand sculpture atop his head.

"One of each element." Niamh opened a freckled white fist to reveal a shining stone—Farooq, Art, and Benji did the same.

"That's clever," Mitchell observed, as the healers moved on. "Did you see? They've each chosen the stone corresponding with their weakest element."

Bobby turned away from Niamh's group in jealous disgust.

Skandar now understood how valuable winning the Earth Trial had been, and it finally distracted him from the Weaver. "Niamh has a spare fire stone, so that means she doesn't even need to get through the Fire Trial. She could fail it, and still pass Fledgling year?"

Mitchell nodded.

"We should have gone faster!" Bobby moaned.

"At least we have our own stones." Flo tapped the green gem on her armor.

"That might not be enough," Bobby argued, sounding uncharacteristically anxious. "We *need* to become Rookies.

My little sister's taking her Hatchery exam this year; imagine if she comes to the Island and someone from my quartet's just been declared a nomad. I'll never hear the end of it. The *shame*!"

"She might not *pass* the Hatchery exam, though," Mitchell said, regarding this worried Bobby as he might a cornered tiger. "Not everyone is destined for a unicorn."

"Oh, she'll pass. Isabel is *perfect*," Bobby spat. And Skandar couldn't work out whether it was jealousy or pride in her voice.

There was a commotion as Instructor Webb landed Moonlight Dust, followed by eight other unicorns. Four of them were the Threat Quartet. The other four—Naomi, Divya, Mateo, and Harper—Skandar didn't know very well. Neither quartet had earth stones attached to their armor. Other Fledglings had noticed this too, and were pointing at the riders as they dismounted.

Bobby danced a jig on the spot. "The Threat Quartet failed the trial!"

"Do you think their unicorns flew?" Flo wondered.

"Shh," Mitchell said. "I'm trying to listen."

The eight riders had surrounded Instructor Webb and were all talking at once.

"It isn't fair!" Amber said, the star mutation on her forehead crackling wildly. "I wasn't even involved in the attack!"

"There *wasn't* an attack." Alastair protested. "Naomi's

making it up. She clearly *dropped* her stone, and now she's embarrassed and trying to blame—"

"I'm not making it up!" Naomi cried. "I was attacked!"

"ENOUGH!" Instructor Webb roared, and there was a stony silence. "Kobi, Alastair, and Meiyi, Instructors Anderson and Everhart spotted you attacking other quartets from the air."

"They attacked *us*!" Bobby called out, enjoying every moment of this.

"And us!" Zac shouted. "I almost lost control of Ghost, thanks to that lot!"

"There we have it. And attacking other quartets in the Earth Trial means you forfeit your stones."

"You didn't tell us that at the beginning," Meiyi complained. "You just said fighting wasn't necessary; you didn't say we'd lose our earth stones!"

"The trials test more than your ability to follow the rules," Instructor Webb replied. "They test your understanding of the elements. And you clearly have no appreciation of the fairness and friendship underlying the earth element. You left one of your own quartet behind. Amber was waiting for you just below the summit—for hours."

"Yes *exactly*," Amber purred. "It would be *super* unfair if I lost my stone too."

Instructor Webb shook his mossy head. "I'm sorry, Amber. One of the keys to this challenge was teamwork, and your quartet failed miserably."

"So can we have *our* stones back?" Harper asked. "Since we were attacked unfairly?"

"I'm afraid not," Instructor Webb said. "You should have been better at protecting each other from attacks. Even"—he glanced disappointedly at the Threat Quartet—"surprise ones."

At sunset, Instructors Webb and Everhart began collecting all the solstice stones.

Agatha approached Skandar, leading Arctic Swansong.

"Hello, Swan." Skandar reached out to touch the unicorn's nose. He could just about make out the spirit blaze: a fraction lighter than the rest of the unicorn's head.

Then Swan tried to bite Skandar's hand. Agatha howled with laughter and rewarded him with a sugar lump.

"Did you really just feed a unicorn allied to the *death* element a sugar lump?" Mitchell said.

Agatha shrugged. "Nowadays he gets what he likes." She recorded that the quartet had one earth stone each and dropped them into her green bag.

"I saw the Weaver," Skandar blurted before Agatha could move on.

"What?" Agatha snapped, her eyes darting to him.

"You *think* you saw the Weaver," Mitchell corrected bossily.

"She was real," Skandar said, a little too loudly. "She was on the Restless Mountain during the trial and she—spoke to me."

Agatha rubbed her translucent cheeks and frowned. "I don't see why the Weaver would expose herself like that. Why would she be at a trial?"

"I saw her," Skandar said forcefully.

"What did she say to you, then?" Agatha asked, clearly still skeptical.

"You are in my way, Skandar Smith."

Agatha's frown deepened.

"The Restless Mountain plays tricks," Flo insisted. "Maybe it was trying to get Skandar to leave?"

"Instructor Everhart, are you finished?" Instructor Webb called loudly. "All solstice stones must be returned to the Stronghold immediately."

Agatha flinched and lowered her voice. "I'm inclined to side with Florence on this one, Skandar. I don't see why the Weaver would put herself on that mountain for all to see—you Fledglings were crawling all over it." But Skandar thought his aunt sounded unusually upbeat, as though trying to mask her concern.

Agatha patted Scoundrel's neck, and his snort broke the tension. "I think you should all focus on what comes next. Mark my words, fighting for the stones will *not* be against the rules in the Fire Trial. You all need to watch your backs—especially *you*." She pointed at Skandar aggressively, then left with a swish of her white cloak.

"Always such a ray of sunshine, your aunt," Bobby observed.

"Shh," Skandar said. "Do you want *every*one to know I'm related to the Weaver?" The Island knew Agatha was Erika's sister, but nobody outside the quartet was aware that Skandar was the Weaver's son—at least, nobody but the Secret Swappers.

On the flight home, Skandar tried to stop thinking about the Weaver. They'd made it through the Earth Trial! They were all one solstice stone closer to becoming Rookies, and his bond with Scoundrel felt a little more secure.

Mitchell started talking about how he couldn't wait to tell his father—Ira—that he'd passed the Earth Trial. "He said he wouldn't write to me beforehand. He's agreed not to put so much pressure on me," he explained. "But now I can surprise him with this excellent news!"

Skandar started composing a letter in his head to his own dad. Maybe he'd even draw a quick sketch of the quartet with their stones, so Dad could get excited about watching the Air Trial at the end of the year. By the time Scoundrel landed outside the Eyrie's colorful entrance tree, Skandar was much calmer.

He should have known it wouldn't last for long.

CHAPTER SIX

Hatchery Heist

IT WAS CLEAR SOMETHING WAS WRONG AS soon as the Fledglings entered the Eyrie. People were huddled together, holding whispered conversations when they'd usually have been asleep. Skandar, Bobby, Flo, and Mitchell settled their tired unicorns in their stables, and as they approached their own treehouse—passing clusters of restless riders on swinging bridges—they were surprised to find the squadron leader *and* flight lieutenant of the Peregrine Society sitting against the metal door.

Skandar rushed over, a feeling of dread descending. "Rickesh? Prim?"

"Skandar, finally," Rickesh breathed, as both he and Prim stood up.

"What is it? What's wrong?" Skandar asked desperately.

The Preds glanced at each other. "You haven't heard yet?"

"We've been doing the Earth Trial! Is it Kenna?"

Rickesh's face was grim. "Earlier today, Instructor Manning gathered the whole Eyrie to explain . . ." He hesitated, running a hand across his wave of white-tipped hair.

Prim took over. "Commodore Kazama has been keeping it a secret for months. Rex thought it was time we all knew."

"Knew WHAT?" Mitchell and Bobby demanded at the same time.

"The Hatchery is empty," Rickesh said, voice hollow. "There are no unicorn eggs left. For this year, for the next. For thirteen years. Instructor Manning said every storage level had been emptied when he and the Commodore went to check the damage to the Hatchery's side."

"An entire generation of unicorn riders, lost," Prim finished, flaming eyebrows flaring.

Mitchell was first to recover, wanting details. "But when was this? How long have the eggs been missing?"

Skandar's heart pounded. He had guessed the answer.

"June. Nina and Rex discovered they were gone after the summer solstice. But they think it must have happened—" Rickesh glanced at Skandar.

"Right after the Weaver bonded Kenna to her wild unicorn," Skandar finished for him.

"It was the only time the Hatchery was left unguarded,"

Prim said quietly. "The riders were starting to evacuate. The Grins were leaving the Island, remember? Everyone was."

"*All* the eggs are gone? Even for next summer solstice?" Bobby's voice was hoarse with panic, which scared Skandar even more. "This can't be happening."

"No wonder Nina hasn't been herself," Flo said. "Why didn't she say anything?"

"Maybe she didn't want to worry everyone," Rickesh said grimly. "Thank goodness for Rex. Now that he's told the Eyrie, it won't be long until the whole Island knows and can actually help! But, Skandar"—Rickesh's voice was suddenly urgent—"you need to find Kenna. She's . . ." He hesitated. "It's common knowledge that she was with the Weaver in June—the *Herald* reported it. People are starting to say she must have been involved."

"But she helped *save* the Island!" Skandar was indignant. "She was with us on the Divide." Though, he couldn't help thinking how little he knew about Kenna's time with the Weaver *before* that day.

Rickesh held his hands up defensively. "There's no point getting annoyed with *me*. Especially when Prim and I have been guarding your treehouse from riders trying to interrogate Kenna. She's not even here, but we caught three Rookies about to break in."

"Is it that bad?" Flo whispered.

"It's worse," Prim replied bluntly.

"Where's Kenna?" Skandar demanded, already moving toward the nearest ladder.

Bobby's face was pale. "Yes! Kenna's got to know where the Weaver's hidden the eggs, right? She was with her in the Hatchery just before!"

"She *doesn't* know!" Skandar said angrily, even though he'd just had the very same thought.

"We need to check whether she's safe first, Bobby," Flo said firmly.

"Last I heard," Rickesh murmured, "Kenna was hiding out at Instructor O'Sullivan's treehouse."

"Thank you," Skandar said to Rickesh and Prim. "Thank you for being here."

The quartet climbed so fast that there was no time to talk, and once they'd passed under the flowery arch leading to the instructors' treehouses, it became very clear where Kenna was. A thirty-strong group—from Hatchlings to Preds—was gathered outside Instructor O'Sullivan's blue treehouse, banging on the windows. As Skandar prepared to rush over, Kenna emerged through the door—Instructors O'Sullivan and Anderson shielding her as riders shoved closer, shouting questions.

"What's the Weaver's plan with the eggs?"

"Is she going to make more wild freaks like you?"

"You're a unicorn thief! That egg was never yours to take!"

Skandar had never felt fury like this. How *dare* they turn on his sister like this?

Instructor Anderson clearly felt the same. "I suggest you all get out of here before I declare every single one of you a nomad! Do I make myself clear?" The flames around his dark brown ears billowed; he was angrier than Skandar had ever seen him.

There was a moment when the riders looked like they might risk it, but then they dispersed, muttering feverishly.

A white-faced Instructor O'Sullivan glanced up at the quartet in front of the platform's central trunk. "GET OUT OF— Ah, Skandar, I'm glad you're here. We're moving Kenna to Instructor Everhart's treehouse for now—riders are more afraid to come near it. The instructors have all been summoned to an emergency meeting with Commodore Kazama, so if you could stay . . ."

But Skandar had already thrown his arms round Kenna, whose sobs were shaking her whole frame.

"She's mine, Skar. Goshawk's mine. She was going to be alone without me. Her egg was about to be sent to the Wilderness. I didn't steal her; I *chose* her." Kenna sounded half-distraught, half-furious.

"It's okay," Skandar whispered. "I'm here now."

Much later that night, Agatha returned from the Commodore's meeting. She didn't look at all surprised to see Skandar's quartet inside her treehouse. Ignoring them, Agatha made a beeline for Kenna, who was sitting on a sheepskin-covered chair by the fire, the light flickering over the vines at her wrist.

Agatha kneeled and put both hands on Kenna's shoulders, looking her right in the eye. "Do you know anything, Kenna? Anything at all about Erika's plan for those eggs?"

The desperation in Agatha's voice made Skandar feel sick. This was bad. Really bad.

Kenna shook her head vigorously, her eyes welling with tears.

Agatha dropped her hands from Kenna's shoulders, clenching her scarred fists in frustration. "But you were with Erika for weeks! You must have seen something suspicious."

Bobby stood up, her expression more serious than Skandar had ever seen it. "Please, Kenna. Isabel—my little sister—is supposed to try the Hatchery door this year. I don't care if you lied before, okay? Just tell me what you know! We're friends, aren't we?"

Skandar understood that Bobby was worried about her own sister, but he wasn't going to let her accuse *his*. "Kenna doesn't know anything! She wasn't *at* the Hatchery when the Weaver stole the eggs."

"It wasn't necessarily the Weaver," Mitchell piped up. "We're just assuming—"

"Of course it's Erika," Agatha snapped. "It's always her."

"What's Nina saying?" Flo asked, trying to defuse the tension. "Has she been looking for the eggs?"

Agatha slumped into the other chair by the fire. "Every day and night for the last three months. She and Rex thought they could find the eggs before anyone realized they were gone."

"But there must be hundreds!" Bobby was still frantic. "How did the Weaver move them? They'd be obvious, wouldn't they?"

"Apparently not. Though, now Nina will be able to enlist more people for the search. Perhaps she'll even widen it beyond the Island, if the Mainlanders are willing to cooperate."

"A wider search is bound to work," Mitchell said. "The eggs have to be *somewhere*—they're naturally indestructible. Surely if every sentinel on the Island is searching, they'll be found eventually."

"The problem is, finding them 'eventually' could be too late," Agatha replied. "I don't know what Nina was thinking, keeping it secret for so long. Never thought I'd be saying this about a silver, but thank the five elements for Rex Manning."

"What if the eggs *aren't* found in time?" Bobby demanded. "Will the Island turn destined riders away? Send Mainlanders back home with nothing?"

Agatha started to pace in front of the stove. "That's not the only risk. Do you really think it's a coincidence that right after Erika forged a bond for Kenna, she carried out the biggest heist in Island history?"

Skandar's breath caught. "Before Kenna, she'd never

actually forged a bond to a wild egg for anyone—except herself."

"Exactly," Agatha said darkly. "Now she knows she can do it. And other Islanders are making that connection too—the Council and the Silver Circle especially. Because of Kenna, they know what the Weaver is capable of creating—especially after the incident with the Nomad Tree. We're not talking about pathetic false bonds this time—mere puppets. We're talking about riders allied to all five elements, harnessing the might of wild unicorn magic."

"Do you think she's already done it? Is it already too late?" Flo asked fearfully.

Agatha shook her head. "Forged bonds can only be made at the summer solstice—when the eggs are mature and ready to be hatched. There's time."

"B-b-but," Mitchell stammered, "if they're not found, that's about fifty Weaver-made wild riders next solstice!" Mitchell didn't mask his fearful glance at Kenna.

"And those fifty unicorns will never get to bond with their destined riders!" Bobby cried.

"Do you think the eggs are in the earth zone?" Skandar asked suddenly. "Should we tell Nina I saw the Weaver there?"

"Enough," Agatha said, sounding tired. "We need to keep things in perspective. From what I know of the Weaver's own forged bond, she's had it for so long now that it's weakened her power. The wild unicorn has claimed a lot of her strength. Skandar, you yourself told me that she seemed very frail in the Wilderness two summers ago, once you unraveled her false bond with New-Age Frost."

"I suppose," Skandar murmured.

"And from what Erika and I read all those years ago, it takes an enormous amount of power to create even *one* forged bond."

"That's true." Kenna spoke up for the first time since Agatha had arrived. "After she forged mine, she was exhausted. She could barely stand."

"There you go," Agatha crowed. "If the Weaver is that fragile, I'd be surprised if she was able to forge more than a couple of bonds to the stolen eggs next solstice—let alone fifty."

"But what if she's got stronger?" Skandar protested. "You're just guessing."

"I am," Agatha accepted. "But since I'm older and wiser than you, we're going to take my word for it. IN the meantime"—she raised her voice as Mitchell *and* Bobby tried to interrupt—"we have bigger problems. Kenna isn't safe in the Eyrie. Not with all this suspicion around her link to the Weaver."

"Look, I'll go now and tell Nina I've got nothing to do with the Weaver," Kenna said. "It'll all calm down again. It's just the shock that the eggs are missing, isn't it?"

"I'll go with you." Skandar turned to Agatha. "Kenna isn't leaving the Eyrie—she belongs here with me. She and

Goshawk had all those investigations—she's close to having her training approved."

"But, Skar, don't you think that might have changed—" Flo started to say, but she was interrupted by two sharp knocks.

Agatha swept to the door and opened it a crack. When she returned, there was something in her hand.

"What is it?" Skandar asked, as Agatha silently handed him a letter. The others crowded round to read over his shoulder.

Agatha—the Council and the Silver Circle voted only moments ago on Kenna's future. I tried to delay it, but there was a push for a decision following her mutation, the Nomad Tree, and now the news of the missing eggs.

Kenna and Goshawk's Fury are to be separated and kept under constant watch—the Silver Stronghold and the prison are both being discussed. Kenna will be interrogated about the eggs and about any part she may have played in their disappearance.

The Council and the Circle wish to prepare for a future in which the eggs aren't found, and the Weaver begins to create other riders like Kenna. They wish to prepare for a world in which the Weaver creates fifty forged bonds every year and establishes a new generation of riders allied to all five elements. Therefore they believe it is unsafe and inappropriate for Kenna to train in the Eyrie. As Commodore, I am bound to support them in protecting the Island.

Commodore Kazama

On the back of the letter were a few more hastily scrawled lines.

Tell Kenna and Skandar I'm sorry—part of the reason I delayed breaking the news about the eggs was because I knew the Island would immediately turn on Kenna. I was hoping for more time. I was hoping for better.

Sentinels will come for her in the morning. Do as you see fit and I will protect you.

Nina

The whole treehouse reverberated with shock.

Finally Kenna spoke. "But I was supposed to train as a Hatchling. I was supposed to live here with Skar!" Her brown eyes searched his desperately.

Skandar wasn't ready to give up. "I'll come with you tomorrow when the sentinels arrive. We'll go to Nina, to Rex—tell the whole Council you've got nothing to do with the eggs."

"I'll come with you too, Kenna," Flo said strongly. "I'm a silver. Rex will listen to me."

"I'll come with you," Mitchell said shakily. "And I'll speak to my father. He knows lots of influential people—even some of the Council."

"Well, if we're all going," Bobby huffed, "I'll come as well. If Kenna doesn't know where the eggs are, then somebody needs to make sure all the 'important' people start searching and don't get distracted by pointless witch hunts."

Skandar felt his heart swell with love. His friends were the absolute best. Together, he knew they could persuade the Island authorities that Kenna was harmless.

But then Agatha spoke. "If we wait to see what happens—if you let them take you, Kenna—I cannot promise that you or Goshawk's Fury will ever walk free on this Island again."

The weight of Agatha's words hit Skandar so hard he felt winded. His mind flashed with images of Kenna behind prison bars, where he'd never be able to get to her.

"Nina wrote *do as you see fit*," Flo murmured. "Instructor Everhart, what did she mean?"

"I believe"—Agatha swallowed—"I believe the Commodore meant I should help Kenna hide. Help her run."

Mitchell frowned. "Won't that put you and Swan at risk?"

"When Nina says she'll protect me, I trust her. That note isn't just a courtesy—it's a warning. It's giving me time to get Kenna out of the Eyrie while I still can."

"But isn't there a way that Kenna . . . ? Can't we . . . ?" Skandar trailed off, out of ideas.

Agatha shook her head gently. And with that simple movement, the Smith siblings' dreams shattered into a thousand pieces.

Skandar swallowed back tears, as Kenna closed her eyes tightly for a long moment. Her shoulders rose and fell; then she turned to Agatha. "So you're saying Gos and I need to get out of the Eyrie?"

"You need to go right now."

"*Where* is she supposed to go?" Skandar asked desperately, unable to put on as brave a face as his sister.

"Wildflower Hill?" Flo suggested. "My parents would never turn Kenna over to the authorities."

Skandar smiled at her gratefully.

"That's too obvious," Agatha countered. "They'll search anywhere Kenna has a connection. Skandar has a Shekoni saddle; it's one of the first places they'll look."

"The Wilderness?" Bobby suggested.

"Absolutely not," Agatha and Skandar said forcefully.

"All right, sorryyy, only trying to help."

"How about you all listen to me for a second?" Agatha growled. "After being the Executioner, I managed to escape the Silver Circle and went on the run. I avoided arrest for quite a few years. Not because I was hiding, but because I was *being* hidden. By the Wanderers."

"I've never heard of them," Mitchell announced.

"Of course you haven't. They're very secretive. They reject the Island's traditional ways. Which is why I think they'll help Kenna."

"Fancy joining up with these edgy rebels, Kenna?" Bobby said playfully. Given how worried she was about her own sister's future, Skandar knew it must have been extremely hard for Bobby to stop asking Kenna about the eggs. She nodded at him, as if to say, *You're welcome for now, spirit boy, but we'll talk about this later.*

Kenna didn't smile. When she spoke, her voice was full of anger. "It doesn't really sound like I have a choice, does it?" She glared down at her wild mutation. "What is *with* this Island, hating people who're different? What's so bad about not being the same as everyone else?"

"I've asked myself that question many times," Agatha muttered.

Mitchell was already planning. "I'm sorry to point out the obvious, but how are we going to actually find these 'Wanderers' in the middle of the night? I've never even read about them." He looked as though this was a personal insult.

Without answering, Agatha walked to the opposite end of the treehouse and rummaged through a storage chest carved with an intricate pattern of daggers. After a few moments, she came back with four objects dangling from cords wrapped round her hand. When Skandar peered closer, he realized they were wooden whistles, smaller than the plastic recorder he'd learned to play at school but bigger than the stubby silver whistles the instructors used in training. They were carved in the shapes of four different birds.

"Take these." Agatha handed them clumsily to Skandar. "The cuckoo is the one you need to get the attention of the Wanderers at this time of year."

Flo pointed over his shoulder. "That one's the cuckoo."

"First Instructor O'Sullivan with her fish. Now you with your birds," Bobby teased. "Life really is full of surprises."

"Do you *ever* stop talking?" Agatha asked incredulously.

Bobby shrugged. "Not usually."

Skandar handed the cuckoo whistle to Kenna, who hung it round her neck. "I still don't get how a bird whistle is going to help us find the Wanderers," Kenna said. "Can't you just tell us where they live?"

Agatha shook her head. "The Wanderers move round the zones with the elemental seasons. And it's possible they've changed their earth base since I was with them. The cuckoo represents the earth element—the Wanderers gave me the whistles as a gift so I could always find them again. When you get into the earth zone, follow the fault line and blow."

"But the *Weaver* might be in the earth zone!" Skandar protested. "What if she—"

"Skandar," Agatha snapped, "the Weaver has stolen all the contents of the Hatchery. I doubt that what you saw on the Restless Mountain was real. And I *highly* doubt that she will come out of hiding to attack a group of Fledglings, when she has a larger plan afoot. *However*, I will inform Nina—after Kenna is hidden with the Wanderers—so that the Commodore can search that blasted mountain. All right?"

Skandar nodded, satisfied for now.

It was about three in the morning, when they climbed through the now-deserted Eyrie. As Kenna turned away to fetch Goshawk, Skandar saw her look out through the shadowy armored trunks, her shoulders shaking with sobs. He'd only seen her this devastated once before—the day she'd failed the Hatchery exam. Skandar moved to go after her, but Flo pulled him back.

"I think Kenna just needs a minute on her own," she said quietly. And as his sister's form disappeared, all Skandar could think about was the idea he'd kept to himself all summer. Was there a possibility of reuniting Kenna with her destined unicorn? She'd be a spirit wielder like him, but she wouldn't look like the Weaver's successor. She wouldn't be like the new generation of wild riders the Island feared Erika Everhart was making.

"Kenna's not going to have to hide forever, right?" Skandar asked his friends desperately as they saddled their unicorns.

"Of course she won't," Flo said, giving Skandar a small smile of reassurance.

Mitchell looked thoughtful. "The Weaver must have been planning to steal the eggs for a long time. But she needed an enormous distraction to do it, and she needed to keep a low profile. Kenna told Skandar back in June that it was the Weaver who helped the Silver Circle discover how to kill wild unicorns—though they didn't realize the information had been planted by Erika herself. The Island destroying itself was the perfect cover for the Weaver to remove the eggs at the summer solstice. Though she must have had help moving them to . . . wherever they are now."

"Who on the Island would actually help her do *that*, though?" Bobby said.

Flo was fixating on the worst-case scenario. "Say Agatha is wrong, and the Weaver *does* have enough power to forge bonds with all the eggs ready to be hatched on the solstice. That's fifty riders with forged bonds like Kenna's."

"And if those eggs aren't found, it won't only be fifty riders—will it?" Skandar said. "The Weaver has every batch of eggs for the next thirteen years. That's an entire generation. She could start her own Eyrie."

"Or take over ours," Mitchell said ominously.

As the sun rose over the earth zone, Skandar felt a bit ridiculous. They'd ridden through Fourpoint, then passed through the earth zone's farms and along the edges of lavender, thyme, and rosemary fields as quietly as possible, terrified of being spotted. Now they were out on the rougher moorland with its patches of heather and mossy rocks.

Kenna blew the cuckoo whistle over and over again.

And there was absolutely no sign of the Wanderers.

Bobby was finding the whole thing quite funny—or at least pretending to. Every so often, she'd mimic the cuckoo's call—"COO-koo"—in response to the whistle, only to be shushed nervously by Flo. Then Mitchell would start a bout of tutting, skeptical that anyone was actually going to find them in the dim light of the morning—let alone the Wanderers he was half convinced Agatha had invented.

"Kenn, I don't think you have to blow the whistle the entire way," Skandar suggested. His ears were starting to hurt.

"What if the one time I *don't* blow it is when they're actually listening?" Kenna was in a surprisingly good mood considering she was now on the run. Skandar thought he knew why. Down at the stables, they'd had a swift argument about whether Kenna should *ride* Goshawk out into the earth zone. Just like when they were growing up, Kenna had prepared all her comebacks. She'd insisted that they'd get caught if she had to walk; that she'd have the whole quartet to help if anything went wrong; that she knew what summoning magic felt like now so she wouldn't do it by accident.

"Gos looks just like the others from a distance," Kenna had argued. And—as usual—she'd won.

Goshawk would end up stronger than other wild unicorns, more adept at flying—that was Agatha's theory based on the Weaver's experience with a forged bond. But looking at Goshawk walking beside Scoundrel, she could never be mistaken for a *bonded* unicorn. Her horn shone transparent in the first light of the day; her palomino coat was dull and thin, the bones in her skeleton occasionally poking through. Skandar knew Kenna had a connection with her, but whenever he looked at Goshawk, all he wanted was for her coat to be dapple-gray not palomino; her horn solid not transparent. For her to be bonded not wild.

Flo—ahead on Silver Blade—pointed to a colorful mound in the distance. "There's Wildflower Hill!"

"What's Wildflower Hill?" Kenna asked Skandar quietly, thankfully taking a break from the cuckoo whistle.

Skandar was just about to start telling his sister about Flo's family home when a lone rider on a white unicorn seemed to melt out of the hillside a little way ahead.

Instinctively the quartet closed round Kenna and Goshawk, hiding her from view. They all had their left hands on the reins, their right palms up, ready to summon elemental magic at the first sign of trouble. Skandar tensed as he watched the rider lift his hand and—

"Wait a second." Bobby narrowed her eyes, as the rider trotted toward them. "Don't we know him? Isn't that—"

"Albert!" the quartet exclaimed together.

The boy grinned as he slowed his unicorn to a halt. Skandar couldn't believe it had taken him so long to recognize Albert and Eagle's Dawn. Albert had been one of the first riders Skandar had spoken to when he'd arrived at the

Eyrie. But then, during their Hatchling year, Albert had been declared a nomad.

"Hello, you lot!" Albert waved to the quartet, Kenna and Goshawk still hidden. "Long time, no see!" His light pink cheeks dimpled, as Eagle's Dawn shrieked to the other unicorns in welcome.

"Albert," Mitchell spluttered. "You look *really* different."

It was true. Albert had grown his blond curly hair long, and it was tied in a ponytail at the nape of his neck with a piece of brown leather. His thin frame had filled out—his shoulders wider, his arms muscled—and he was wearing a faded purple tunic that suited him much better than the all-over black of the riders' uniforms. Then there was his mutation. All the joints on the fire wielder's hands glowed like hot coals, smoke rising from his knuckles. It made him look quite threatening.

"So are you in league with these Wanderer people, then?" Bobby got straight to the point as usual.

Albert nodded. "I'm one of them. And I was out riding when I heard the cuckoo's call. Who sent you? Is something wrong?" His blue eyes flicked to the white spirit blaze on Scoundrel's head, which Skandar had covered with black polish while Albert had been in the Eyrie.

"We need your help," Skandar blundered. "It's my sister, Kenna. Well . . . you'll see."

The quartet parted their unicorns, and Kenna rode Goshawk's Fury toward Eagle's Dawn along the fault line.

Skandar waited for Albert's horrified reaction, for the look of revulsion to cross his pale white face. But it never came.

"It's wonderful to meet you both. The Wanderers have heard all about you." Albert then raised his voice to include everyone. "Follow me!"

Kenna and Goshawk fell into step beside Eagle, and Albert began to explain how the Wanderers moved round the zones with the seasons. Kenna asked question after question, and Skandar smiled for the first time in a while.

"Albert's barely looking at her wild unicorn," Mitchell said in awe. "I mean, we're all *kind of* used to Goshawk now, but he didn't even blink! He used to be so scared of everything when he was at the Eyrie."

"And he used to fall off a lot," Bobby recalled.

Flo had a small smile on her lips. "He's found where he really belongs. Like us. We're like—like four birds on a branch." Stretching out, she draped her arms round Skandar's and Bobby's necks. Blade turned his neck to give her a withering look, as if to say, *What do you think you're doing?*

Skandar laughed, pleased that everything was feeling a bit more hopeful. "Or peas in a pod?"

"No, no, no. No peas. No birds," Bobby scolded. "Flo, you've got to be less *soppy* about these sayings. Go for the shock factor—a picture that'll really stick in someone's mind. We're like four maggots in a flesh wound. That would be better, you see?"

Flo looked a little bit ill at the thought.

They rode for another hour. Scoundrel was still so tired from the Earth Trial that he didn't have the energy to misbehave. The group of six unicorns snaked round hills and through tunnels, and now they were skirting the base of one of the smaller mountains. Skandar thought it was unsurprising that nobody could find the Wanderers without help.

"I can't believe we're back in the earth zone," Mitchell muttered, his eyes flicking around as though afraid there might be more stalignomes about to pounce. Skandar was feeling extremely jumpy too, though he was more worried about the Weaver appearing than vicious earth elementals.

Then, finally, Eagle's Dawn disappeared into one of the caves cut into the mountain's rocky side. Kenna looked over her shoulder, shrugged, and rode Goshawk after Albert. Skandar had no choice but to follow her into the dark.

Typical, Skandar thought. Kenna had never been afraid of anything, and it looked like she wasn't going to start now.

CHAPTER SEVEN

The Wanderers

RIDING INTO THE CAVE AFTER ALBERT AND Kenna, Skandar was plunged into darkness.

"I hope this isn't an ambush," Mitchell whispered as Red came up behind Scoundrel. Skandar was glad of the glow from his friend's flaming hair.

Albert chuckled. "Look up in three seconds, and things will seem a lot . . . brighter."

"Well *that's* not cryptic at all," Mitchell muttered irritably. "Just because he has a cool ponytail now."

"Whoa!" Kenna's cry of amazement echoed around the cave walls.

"Leaping landslides," Flo breathed, the silver in her Afro glinting in the new light.

Skandar looked up. The cave ceiling was glowing a deep ethereal blue, pulsing and twinkling like stars in the night sky. Even the unicorns were fascinated.

"How's it doing that?" asked Mitchell, who'd gone from irritation to wonder in seconds.

"Glowworms," Albert replied cheerfully. "They're bioluminescent. It's one of the reasons the Wanderers chose this cave network as their earth season home."

"Beautiful," Flo breathed.

"Did you know glowworms are carnivorous?" Bobby said loudly.

Flo sighed. "Did you *have* to tell me that?"

Bobby pointed to herself. "Truth-teller. Can't help it."

"Are all your elemental homes this great?" Skandar heard Kenna ask.

"Absolutely." Albert winked, and Kenna grinned. "But the Glowing Caves are definitely the flashiest."

"See," Mitchell whispered as they continued under the blue glow, "he's cool! How?!"

"*You're* cool," Skandar protested.

"Don't be ridiculous, Skandar." Mitchell sighed, then suddenly became more animated. "Jamie is, though— definitely. I don't know why he wants to spend time with me, to be honest."

"Because you're great," Skandar said, though he was unsure what Jamie had to do with Albert or glowworms.

They rode so deep into the belly of the cave network

that Skandar felt like they were being swallowed up. When the way ahead finally widened out, lanterns—balanced on rocky ledges—added to the light of the glowworms, and all at once there were people and unicorns everywhere.

Skandar spotted two women on rope swings having an animated conversation. There were people grooming unicorns, all wearing non-elemental colors: purples and pinks, oranges and browns, grays and creams. Unicorns dozed in cave crevices, their wings fanning out over the rocks. A group of teenagers was submerged in a steaming pool and called out as they passed:

"You found them!"

"Nice one, Al!"

One of them was definitely Charlie, rider of Hinterland Magma, who'd been declared a nomad last year.

There was a roaring fire ahead, sending its smoke out into the sky through a large gap in the cave roof. People were sitting round it on smooth stones, but the low murmuring of their voices petered out as they watched the Eyrie riders approach.

A woman stood waiting for them. She had a stillness about her that demanded attention, and they all found themselves dismounting instinctively. As the fire lit her tall frame, Skandar noticed she had the most unusual amethyst-colored eyes—he couldn't tell whether it was a mutation or not—and a sharp white bob with severe bangs like Bobby's. When she spoke, her voice had a lilt that sounded like she'd learned to sing before she could speak.

"You are welcome here, young riders." She opened her arms wide. "My name is Elora. The Wanderers call me their Pathfinder—it's how they address the one they choose to lead them." Elora inclined her head to Albert. "I am grateful to you for answering the cuckoo's call."

Albert's ears turned pink. He looked extremely pleased. "This is Kenna." He pointed. "And her brother, and Flo, and Mitchell, and Bobby."

The way Elora nodded gave Skandar the feeling she knew about them already.

"What do you seek from us?" the Pathfinder asked. But at the same moment, Skandar spotted a young wild unicorn out of the corner of his eye heading right for the fire. Elora must have seen it; the transparent horn was practically glowing. Why wasn't she moving? Whipping his head round, Skandar realized there were five wild unicorn foals in the cave, their already rotting bodies lit by the blue glow above.

"Watch out!" Skandar cried. His friends turned too and started to reach for their unicorns' saddles, preparing to face the threat.

"All is well," Elora said, her calm voice cutting through Skandar's panic.

"What do you mean?" Mitchell spluttered. "There are wild unicorns in this cave. WILD UNICORNS!"

"I am aware," Elora said, a smile dancing around her

lips. "They won't hurt us. The Wanderers have long been friends to the wild unicorns. We reject the notion that they are monsters."

Mitchell made a sound of disbelief in his throat, and Kenna raised an eyebrow in his direction.

Elora continued. "Do you have any idea how hard it is for a wild unicorn foal in the Wilderness? Their immortality crushes down on them the minute they are cast out into the world, alone. And the older wild unicorns are competitive for territory and won't always accept them until they can prove themselves. They cannot kill each other, of course. But that doesn't mean they don't inflict pain and suffering. The young wild unicorns often flee to the zones. We are here to heal their wounds as best we can, and to offer them shelter until they are strong enough to join a herd."

Kenna's face was full of wonder. Skandar felt it too—he'd experienced the complex natures of the wild unicorns before. He understood exactly why Agatha had sent them here.

"The wild ones never stay very long, but we do our best. The Wanderers have been looking after wild unicorn foals for generations, so that many of those we cared for now lead herds of their own. It means they respect us, and we trust them not to harm us."

"But you make it sound like the wild unicorns are organized. Like they have alliances. Even feelings," Mitchell said.

"Well, of course they do." Elora laughed softly. "Haven't you realized yet that unicorns are far more intelligent than we are? Isn't that the whole idea behind the trials you are currently facing? Your unicorns have reached the age when they've discovered that you might not always be right. That they do not have to follow you without question. Now *you* have to be worthy of *them*. The wild unicorns are no different."

Bobby was unusually quiet, staring at Elora as she continued speaking. "Sometimes the wild foals even form deep connections with particular Wanderers. We'll show you. Noah?"

A dark-haired boy—a couple of years younger than Skandar—stepped into the fire's glow. At the same time, one of the smallest wild unicorns looked up from the bloody meat it was eating and moved toward him.

Skandar and Scoundrel were both on edge as the wild unicorn's ghostly horn pointed directly at the boy. At any moment Skandar felt sure the wild unicorn was going to attack. But Noah reached out and stroked the foal's midnight-black coat, avoiding an open wound halfway down its neck. The wild unicorn shook out its ragged wings happily, the way Scoundrel sometimes did, and Noah laughed, throwing his arms round the foal's neck.

Their love for each other was beautiful, and terrifying, and . . . impossible.

Instinctively Skandar put a palm on Scoundrel's shoulder

and summoned the spirit element. He wanted to double-check whether the boy *had*, in fact, been destined for this unicorn—perhaps he was a lost spirit wielder or had avoided trying the Hatchery door. Skandar wanted something, anything, to explain the wild unicorn's behavior.

But there was nothing. No colorful hint of a potential bond shining from his chest. No broken link splintered around his heart.

The wild foal turned suddenly to stare at the spirit magic in Skandar's palm, taking a step forward. Skandar shut his fingers, quickly extinguishing the white glow. He'd forgotten wild unicorns were drawn to spirit wielders.

Noah and the foal moved away toward other wild unicorns and Wanderers grouped peacefully together.

"*How?*" Bobby managed to say first.

Elora chuckled softly. "In truth, we're not entirely sure ourselves. We think of it as two kindred spirits finding each other—the wild unicorn recognizing something familiar in the human it forms an attachment with, and vice versa."

"But there's no bond between them—nothing?" Mitchell half turned to Skandar for confirmation.

Elora answered. "Not as the Island understands a bond. No."

Skandar was reminded of the story the First Rider had told him down in the tomb last year, about the friendship he'd built with a wild foal that had called him across the waves: about how she'd shared her magic with him. She'd become the Wild Unicorn Queen—and he, the Island's founder.

The wild unicorns were here before us all—don't forget, the First Rider had told Skandar. *They are woven deep within the elemental fabric of this place.* He thought about the Earth Trial suddenly—the stalignomes, the disappearing paths—and how the riders had been forced to fight against the elemental magic of the zone rather than with it. Meeting the Wanderers, he wondered for the first time—was that the kind of rider he wanted to be?

Flo spoke up then. "Who are you all? I mean, how does someone become a Wanderer?" She glanced sideways at Kenna, who was still transfixed by the group of wild unicorns.

"There is no such thing as a typical Wanderer. But we all reject the traditional ways of the Island. Some of us have bonds but were declared nomads, some of us used to have bonds, others never have. We welcome everyone here."

"Will you help us?" Kenna had pulled Goshawk into the firelight so that it reflected off the unicorn's transparent horn. "The Commodore, the Council, the Silver Circle—they're all afraid of what I am."

"People do unthinkable things when they're afraid," Elora said sadly.

"Can I stay here?" Kenna asked in a small voice. It was the second time Skandar had heard her ask that on the Island. The first was when she'd begged Commodore

Kazama to let her stay in the Eyrie. This time the answer was different—and simple.

"Of course you can stay. Stay for now. Stay for a while. Stay forever. Whatever you need," Elora said easily, gesturing for Kenna to sit on a smooth stone by the fire while Goshawk joined the other wild foals, bellowing low in greeting.

Skandar felt his heart squeeze with emotions he hadn't felt for a long while. The gratitude and relief that comes when people offer help and don't want anything in return. Once, back in Margate, the boiler had broken, and it had almost been Christmas and they'd had to call out an emergency plumber. It was one of Dad's bad days, so Kenna and Skandar had stood shivering in scarves and multiple pairs of socks, afraid of how much it was going to cost. They'd watched the stranger leaning on the table, writing out the bill. Kenna had taken it—Skandar craning to see—and all he'd written was *Merry Christmas* followed by a smiley face with a Santa hat. To this day, Skandar still remembered the plumber's name.

There was a sudden flurry of activity: more Wanderers rode into the cave, and others emerged with rods and baskets of fish, before a team prepared them to be grilled on skewers. As they readied the food, Skandar's eyes were drawn to some of the Wanderers' Hatchery wounds. They had the central circle from their unicorn's horn, and the five lines snaking up their fingers, but they'd also inked decoration in different colors. He spotted tiny birds flying across palms, flashes of flowers round fingers, and one rider had a wave crashing over his scar.

Everyone sat round the fire talking, telling stories and laughing, and Kenna settled by Skandar. "I think I'll be all right with them—just for now," she said, staring at her fish skewer.

"I wish I could stay with you," Skandar murmured. Not one person had treated Scoundrel differently from the other unicorns. He hadn't realized how they'd become so used to being the outsiders.

"Me too," Kenna said sadly. "Are you sure you can't?"

"The Chaos Trials *are* important," Skandar said, sounding like he was trying to convince himself. "I need to get through them if I'm going to bring spirit wielders back to the Island."

"I suppose," Kenna said, her expression unreadable. "Well done for the Earth Trial by the way—Agatha told me. I guess we all got a bit sidetracked by the whole *Kenna's getting arrested* thing. When's the fire one?"

Skandar shrugged. "It'll probably be November or December. But, Kenn, I'm going to talk to Nina. I'm going to get you back to the Eyrie as soon as I can."

"Me *and* Goshawk," Kenna corrected.

"Yeah," Skandar said quickly. "And if you're not back in the Eyrie by the Fire Trial, I promise I'll come to visit you straight after so we can make a plan—I have all the bird whistles, so I can find you in every zone." He chuckled. "They're a lot closer than Margate."

A shadow passed over Kenna's face. He plowed on—feeling a little like he didn't know her as well as he once did, that the years they'd spent apart were ten not two. "If you don't want to stay here, we can find another option."

"No," Kenna said firmly. "I like the Wanderers. Nobody has looked at me like they think Goshawk is going to eat them—which is a nice change. Anyway, like you said, hopefully Nina will let me come back to the Eyrie. And maybe I'll learn some magic here?"

"Definitely," said Skandar, trying to sound less upset about them being apart.

"You're going to have to lie to Dad, you know," Kenna said, sighing.

"What d'you mean?"

"You'll have to say I'm still at the Eyrie with you."

Skandar nodded wearily. They were telling Dad so many lies already—he didn't know anything about Kenna being bonded to a wild unicorn. And he'd been shocked when Skandar had written to him about being a spirit wielder—something Robert Smith had never heard of. There was no sense worrying him even more.

"What's that noise?" Mitchell asked.

"It sounds like music," Flo said, cocking her head to the side.

"I LOVE THIS SONG!" Bobby yelled, and started to

dance wildly in front of the fire, swiftly joined by a large group of Wanderers.

Skandar grinned at Kenna. "Dad loved this one! They always used to play it on—"

"Race Day," the Smith siblings said in unison.

Kenna grabbed Mitchell by the hand. Skandar took Flo's, pulling her up.

"Too-Ra-Loo-Ra . . . ," Bobby sang, swinging a Wanderer round on each arm.

"How do they even have this?" Skandar yelled to her, as he and Flo joined the frenzied dancers. Even Mitchell was laughing as Kenna kicked out her legs in time with the beat.

Bobby pointed, mid-swing. "Contraband Mainland radio. The signals must reach this far! TURN IT UP!" she called.

"The Wanderers really seem to like illegal things," Kenna shouted over the music, and Bobby roared with laughter.

Kenna reached for Skandar and Flo then, and swung each of them on opposite elbows. Flo was laughing uncontrollably, and Skandar noticed that her eyes were glistening with happy tears. The sight made his stomach skip with joy, and he fully understood what Flo had meant last year when she'd wished that they could both just be ordinary. Not a silver and a spirit wielder at all. Maybe then they could always have fun like this. Maybe then he wouldn't have to worry so much.

"Kenna! Skar!" Flo cried, tipping her face upward.

Hundreds of fireflies had joined the dance, their little golden lights bobbing and swirling round the dancers. Skandar realized too late that he'd stopped concentrating on his feet. He tripped.

And Kenna caught him.

As he regained his balance, the music swelled. Skandar took hold of Kenna's hands, and they were leaning back and spinning each other around as fast as they could, both grinning so much Skandar's cheeks ached. He didn't care that he was dizzy and sweaty and Goshawk's burn on his thumb was hurting—he didn't want to let his sister go. He wanted this song to last forever. A song from the Mainland that linked them to who they'd been before.

Kenna must have seen something in his face because she stopped their spinning, the other dancers still moving in a frenzy around them. Somehow, the party faded just for a moment as the siblings tried to say everything they were feeling with one long look.

They'd done this a lot when they were younger. It wasn't mind reading exactly—though they'd loved to pretend it was. It was more like what happens when you grow up with someone and you share their hopes and dreams; their best moments and their worst. Skandar and Kenna had perfected *the look* all those times they'd soundlessly agreed on how to tackle Dad's bad days, or wordlessly accepted that neither of them were going on a school trip they couldn't afford, or silently pretended they were completely fine that

Dad was missing their parents' evenings again. Somehow, all those silent looks between them meant that sometimes they could tell better what the other was feeling if they said nothing at all.

Skandar understood that Kenna was afraid and didn't want him to go. That him leaving her here reminded her of being left on the Mainland without him.

Kenna understood that Skandar was scared and he didn't want to leave her. But he was worried that if he stayed here, the spirit element—and Kenna—might be hunted forever.

"We *are* going to be together again, though," Kenna said finally. "As riders."

"Soon," Skandar said, making a promise he was determined to keep. No matter what.

"Too-Ra-Loo-Ra, Too-Ra-Loo-Raaaa . . . !" Bobby careered past them at the head of a snaking conga line.

Kenna was dragged in, but Skandar suddenly felt lightheaded and horribly sad. "I'm going to sit down!" he called, as a new song began.

Skandar found himself next to the Pathfinder, who was watching the fireflies pulsing alongside the dancers. Elora turned her unsettling amethyst eyes on him.

"Your sister will be safe here. She can stay as long as she likes."

"We're grateful," Skandar murmured. "Agatha said you helped her before?"

"Agatha has a good soul, though she does not believe it,"

Elora said sagely. "She has kept all our secrets."

Skandar wanted to ask *what* secrets but knew that would be rude. So instead he said, "The fireflies? Are they doing that because of elemental magic? And the hot springs—is that earth magic or . . . ?"

Elora's gaze intensified. "This Island is awash with magic, Skandar. But it doesn't always look how you'd expect, or come from a bond, or have any use in a battle. The Island is always speaking, but nobody listens anymore."

"Do you mean like the truesongs?"

Elora shrugged. "In part. But there is no magic bringing the fireflies here, or influencing the birds who wake us in the morning, or keeping the cave warm in the coldest months. That is all about understanding the Island we live on. And there are no elemental tricks to keep the wild unicorn foals coming back either—our only secret is that we are kind to them when nobody else is. And they remember that forever."

Skandar decided to ask a question that scared him. "Do you think the Island will ever accept Kenna as she is?"

"I do not know," Elora said honestly. "What I do know is that the Island has forgotten that there are more important things than winning. That sometimes the best people to lead us are the quieter ones—with good hearts—rather than those who battle to win at any cost."

Skandar sighed. He was still struggling with where his original dream to become a Chaos rider fitted in all of this.

It was unsettling to meet people who rejected everything he'd wanted so badly growing up—a place at the Eyrie, perhaps even in the Chaos Cup one day. Was Elora right? Had the Island lost its way?

Elora must have noticed the confusion flickering across his face. She put a hand on his shoulder. "Change is always possible if you want it enough. Your quartet, for instance, gives me hope." She gestured to Mitchell, who was dancing with Kenna. "A boy taught to hate difference dances with a girl bonded to a wild unicorn." She gestured to Bobby leading the conga line. "A girl ruthless enough to win her Training Trial still prizes teamwork." Finally she gestured between Flo and Skandar. "And just a few minutes ago I saw a silver and a spirit wielder dancing under the fireflies. If that's not a good sign for change, I don't know what is."

Skandar, Bobby, Flo, and Mitchell stayed in the Glowing Caves that night. Around midnight, the radio was switched off, and the Wanderers began to bed down in deep hollows carved into the rock. Mitchell was skeptical that the hollows would be comfortable, but they turned out to be lined with spongy moss and knitted blankets.

As the Wanderers quieted, Bobby leaned over to peer into Skandar's hollow. "Ey up!"

"Oi!" Skandar protested, as she shoved him sideways and joined him in the small space; they sat cross-legged next to each other.

"You have to talk to Kenna before we leave," she said.

"Of course I will."

Bobby tutted. "I mean *really* talk to her, Skandar! About the eggs."

Skandar pulled at a tuft of moss by his foot. "She says she doesn't know anything."

"Argh! Can't you see? You've got a blind spot when it comes to Kenna! She was with the Weaver for *weeks*! Logically, she must have an idea where these eggs are."

"Logically? You sound like Mitchell," Skandar muttered. "I trust her, okay?"

"You don't understand," Bobby said, picking at her purple nail polish. "You and Kenna are so close. Kenna *literally* crossed the sea to join you. Me and my sister, Isabel, we're not like that—we didn't even say goodbye properly when I left for the Island. We fought all the time. I wanted unicorns to be *my* thing—Isa was always trying to muscle her way in. Frankly, I was thrilled to get a break from her for a couple of years."

"You hardly ever talk about her," Skandar said gently. "How come?"

"How could I?" Bobby half laughed. "You and Kenna have this epic sibling story. I didn't know *how*. But now Isa won't even get to try the Hatchery door if she passes the exam. And I always thought—"

"You always thought she was going to become a rider," Skandar guessed.

"Exactly. Isabel Bruna is practically perfect in every way—of course she'd be destined for a unicorn. And these past two years I've been thinking I'd try to be a better sister to Isa when she came to the Island. To *share* this whole unicorn thing with her." Bobby sighed heavily. "Basically, sharing a room with Flo Shekoni has rubbed off on me. But without the eggs, I might never get the chance to make things right."

Skandar took a deep breath. "I'll talk to Kenna again. I can't promise it'll help, but I will."

Bobby nodded. "You're a good 'un, spirit boy." Then she climbed back into her own hollow.

Skandar waited until the inhabitants of the cave were asleep, then carefully tiptoed toward Scoundrel snoozing nearby. He wanted to check on Kenna's destined unicorn.

Scoundrel watched him approach, and Skandar wondered if the unicorn was weighing up his rider's performance in the Earth Trial, deciding whether he deserved to get what he wanted.

The black unicorn blinked, made a small squeaking noise, and lifted his wing, the feathers sparking slightly at the tips. Scoundrel let a relieved Skandar snuggle up to his side, chomping playfully at a clump of his rider's brown hair and breathing warm air into his ear. Then, just as Skandar's eyelids were drooping, Scoundrel ignited a patch of moss and playfully blocked the water element in the bond, watching in curious fascination as his rider had to stamp it out with his boot. As they eventually drifted off to sleep, the bond was still humming with Scoundrel's lighthearted mischief, though Skandar made his tired brain focus instead on Kenna's dapple-gray unicorn.

Skandar was sitting cross-legged on hard ground. He was someone else. He was wearing shorts, his knees visible. Kenna? No, they were more tanned than his sister's. A jolt of confusion went through him. How had he got here? This wasn't Kenna. He tried to see the person's face, separate their dream presences. And as soon as he'd thought it, Skandar was sitting beside a boy with wavy brown hair and bright blue eyes. He must have been a couple of years older than Skandar.

Then—far too quickly—Skandar found himself standing. He was back in a body. A different body. His hands were dark brown with neon-pink nails. Skandar tried to get himself out, and for a moment he was beside her. A teenage girl, her black hair in long braids that fell to her shoulders. But as soon as he'd seen her face, Skandar was already looking through someone else's eyes. There was something heavy resting on his nose. He lifted a hand to his face and realized he was now wearing glasses, but as soon as he'd touched the rims, Skandar was looking at an old man, not the girl at all, and then he was struggling to breathe, struggling to escape from the man's body. From all the bodies. He was hopeful, so hopeful it hurt, it hurt so much he couldn't breathe—

Skandar gasped, the pain from the dream waking him. Then Scoundrel hissed softly because the Pathfinder was staring down at them.

"Was that a Mender dream?" Elora asked curiously. "I've heard about them, but I've never seen one."

Skandar was still groggy from the pain of the dream. "There were three people. That's never happened before. Usually I just find Kenna and then her dapple-gray. It was so confusing. I couldn't stay out of their bodies, I lost myself, I—" Skandar realized he was speaking aloud, but understanding had already dawned in Elora's purple eyes.

"Kenna has a destined unicorn on the Island, doesn't she? It's still wild?"

"Yes," Skandar admitted.

"And you're a Mender?"

"I just check on her unicorn sometimes. I was too late to mend her bond; the Weaver had already forged her to Goshawk's Fury. Not that I know how to actually do the mending yet, but if I could . . ."

"You do not plan to break Kenna's bond with Goshawk?" Elora's voice was suddenly severe.

"I—" Skandar didn't know how to say he'd been thinking about it since June.

"Skandar," Elora said seriously, "nobody knows the effect breaking a forged bond has on the rider. It could hurt Kenna. It might even kill her."

"That's what I've been trying to find out!"

"Listen to me," Elora said forcefully. "You are not going to be able to find out for sure. Believe me, I spent years researching it at the Silver Stronghold."

"At the—" Skandar broke off. "Are you a *silver*?"

Elora nodded. "After the Weaver killed twenty-four unicorns on a single day, a few silvers were asked to research ways to stop further attacks. We had theories about an exchange—could the forged bond be released if the human's true unicorn was found, and the wild unicorn's true rider identified too? Not a breaking, but a replacing. Not a forging, but a remolding. Perhaps destiny would win out over the forged bond and allow each rider to be united with their own true unicorn. I'm assuming these are the theories you've heard? Why you're dreaming of Kenna's unicorn? We too thought about trying to locate the Weaver's destined unicorn—though we didn't get far, since her identity was unknown at that time."

"But Blood-Moon's Equinox was already dead," Skandar blurted. Elora had mistakenly assumed he'd already heard this theory about an exchange. But this was all new information. Information he was desperate for.

"Exactly. Nobody was ever able to test the exchange theory, or any of the others. We locked up all the spirit wielders, after all." There was shame in Elora's voice, but Skandar hardly registered it.

"So you're saying that if I find Goshawk's true rider, then I might be able to exchange—"

"No," Elora said forcefully. "What I am trying to tell you is that you need to forget all this. You should not be trying to change Kenna and Goshawk so that they fit the Island's mold. You must learn to accept her as she now is, not who you wish her to be." She turned away. "Try to get some sleep."

Skandar's mind was still whirring when he smelled breakfast. The Pathfinder didn't understand. Of course *he* accepted Kenna, but the Island was never going to, and he didn't want her to have to hide with the Wanderers forever. She wanted to train in the Eyrie with him.

When it was time to leave, Kenna pulled Skandar into a hug. "I hate this."

"Me too," Skandar mumbled into the side of her head. "I just got you back."

"Are you sure you can't stay?" Kenna asked again, pulling away to look at him.

"I wish I could. But I have to talk to Nina. I've got a plan, Kenn. I promise." New hope filled him. A bond exchange. Could it really work?

Kenna sighed. "I guess in the meantime I'll just have to make friends with that Albert guy. He's quite good-looking, really."

Skandar let go of her, spluttering. "What do you mean? Albert? What?"

"Oh, calm down." Kenna rolled her eyes, and Skandar couldn't remember whether she'd done it her whole life or she'd copied it from Bobby. *Bobby.* He'd promised.

"Kenn?" Skandar asked, not sure why his voice was shaking. "You know the eggs? You're certain you don't know anything that could help find them?"

"If I knew, I'd say, Skar." Kenna's voice was sad.

"That's what I thought," Skandar said, not wanting to dwell on this when he was leaving.

"Come and get me soon, okay?" Kenna said, giving him another hug.

"I'll be back before you even miss me," Skandar said. "Be careful of the mutations."

"I'll be fine." Kenna stepped back, and the movement felt like a pain in Skandar's side.

A few minutes later, Elora walked the quartet to the mouth of the Glowing Caves. "Best of luck with the Chaos Trials. Some parting advice, for what it's worth: fight for the stones, Fledglings, but don't lose yourselves along the way."

As they rode away from the Wanderers, Skandar tried to crush his feelings of guilt. He was leaving Kenna behind again—with a wild unicorn and a forged bond. Instead, he focused on the plan that was forming in his mind as he rode.

If the theories Elora had spoken about were true, maybe he really could exchange a single forged bond for two destined ones. Kenna could be bonded with her own dapple-gray unicorn. And Goshawk's true rider—if Skandar could find them—could be bonded to her. Then maybe the Eyrie would let Kenna come back, and he wouldn't have to worry about the effects of the forged bond or the four wild mutations she still had left. And wouldn't this save two wild unicorns from dying forever?

He shivered as he remembered the haunted look on the Weaver's face—the toll of tethering herself to a wild unicorn. Was it so wrong that he didn't want his sister ending up like that?

Skandar glanced sideways at Flo, Bobby, and Mitchell and he knew he could no longer do this alone.

It was time to talk to his quartet. And then go straight to the Commodore.

KENNA

Hope

KENNA SMITH WAS DARING TO HOPE.

Hope was Albert making her laugh. It was being treated like she was a person, not a monster. It was companionship round an open fire and unicorn foals snuggled up to Goshawk.

Hope was learning. Learning a new way of a life with the Wanderers. Learning she was allowed to be herself. Learning to listen to the beat of the Island's magic.

Hope was the joy of those who loved the wild foals, the meeting of kindred spirits. It was imagining herself safe here for a while and sleeping soundly under Goshawk's musty wing.

Hope was believing. Believing that there was still a path back to the Eyrie. Believing that Skandar would come for her. Believing that their childhood dream could still come true.

A week or so after Kenna arrived with the Wanderers, Elora invited her to train with the riders for the first time. As she rode Goshawk out into the late-September sunshine of the earth zone, she put her shoulders back and sat up proudly on her unicorn's bony spine. Nobody here cared that Gos was wild. Nobody here cared that their bond was forged, not destined.

The Wanderer riders lined up in front of Elora and her unicorn, Silver Soldier. Kenna still couldn't believe that the Pathfinder was an earth-allied silver, just like Flo Shekoni. When Kenna had found out, it had made her heart sing. Elora had given up all that power and rejected the traditional ways of the Island. The same Island that was currently hunting her and Goshawk. And now, beginning her training under Elora's amethyst gaze made Kenna feel more hopeful than ever. The Wanderers trusted her. A *silver* trusted her.

Kenna spotted Eagle's Dawn, who was setting the edges of her white wings on fire at random, the smoke making the nearest Wanderers cough. Albert looked embarrassed as he attempted to summon the water element to put them out.

"Is she okay?" Kenna asked, as she slotted Goshawk into line beside Eagle. Smoke was now circling menacingly round the fire unicorn's horn.

Albert shrugged. "She's three. It's a thing. She's realized that she is wayyy more powerful than I am. But don't worry about that! It's your first-ever training session! Be excited!"

He grinned at her, and she smiled back—smiles came more easily now. After Skandar had left her on the Mainland, she'd practically forgotten that her mouth had corners.

"We have a new rider with us today," Elora announced. "Please make her feel welcome."

Kenna blushed as the other riders waved and called out in welcome. Nobody wore armor like Skandar did, and they dressed in whatever colors they chose. They were all different ages—anywhere from about fourteen to at least seventy years old. They had mutations of different elements, from diamond eyes to curls of flowers. Not one of the unicorns had a saddle like Scoundrel. Their bare coats shone out in colors of deep red or iron gray or snowy white.

"Perhaps a demonstration of what we're all working up to?" Elora said.

"You're going to love this, Kenna," Albert whispered. "The Eyrie doesn't know about it. You'll have to keep it a secret when you go back."

One of the oldest Wanderers rode out to join Elora and Silver Soldier in front of the line. The mountain behind them cast sharp shadows onto the unmown field. Kenna had spoken to the man round the fire last night. He was an air wielder called Otto; his gray unicorn was Screech-Owl's Strike.

Both riders dismounted and stepped away from their unicorns. Kenna couldn't help but feel disappointed—she'd been hoping to see some magic.

When the riders were about ten paces in front of their own unicorns, they each raised a palm so that Kenna could see their Hatchery wounds clearly. Elora's palm was decorated with leaves in green foliage; Otto had inked golden wings on either side of his circular wound. Behind the riders, Soldier and Strike reared up, front hooves sparking as they pawed the air. Elora closed her violet eyes first; then Otto mirrored her.

"What are they—" Kenna tried to ask Albert, but he shushed her gently.

"You'll see. Just wait."

And then something impossible happened. Their palms lit up.

Otto swept his yellow palm up and down as he turned in slow circles. Gusts of wind grew stronger every second. And then the birds came—swallows and chaffinches and swifts and wrens and robins. The birds called to each other in blissful song as they played, swooping and diving in the breeze swirling around the rider.

Elora moved her hand so that the green glow of her palm was facing the ground beneath her feet. Then, right before Kenna's eyes, the grass began to grow wildly around her boots, the shoots gaining in height until they reached Elora's hips. Flowers sprouted within the grass—roses and dahlias and hydrangeas and orchids and lilies—until the Pathfinder was at the center of a bouquet she'd created.

The other Wanderers were clapping, but Kenna just

stared in complete shock. Elora and Otto had been able to summon magic without being in physical contact with their unicorns. The possibilities were unbelievable. If she could learn this, then she'd have an advantage over the other Hatchlings once she returned to the Eyrie. She might even win the Training Trial!

Kenna couldn't keep her thoughts to herself. "How did you do that? Can you teach all of us? Even me, with Goshawk being . . . different?"

Elora closed her hand and stepped out of her flowery cocoon; Otto let the wind drop, and his birds soared off over the mountain in one feathery cloud.

"Of course you will be able to learn this, Kenna," Elora reassured her. "Goshawk is allied to all five elements—in many ways her magic is more closely aligned with the Island's fundamental nature than other unicorns'."

"But doing magic without touching her—how is it possible?" Kenna pushed.

"It is all about listening. Feeling the hum of the elements under your feet. Understanding the change of the elemental seasons. It is believing. There has never been a limit on a rider's access to their unicorn's magic. It is about confidence and trust. After all, your bond encircles your heart, does it not? Why should physical contact with a unicorn matter if you are joined in life and magic?"

Kenna's excitement was spilling over. "In battle you would be unstoppable. Your unicorn could summon elemental magic and you could be somewhere else using it and—"

Kenna stopped. The Pathfinder's purple eyes had hardened. There were noises of disapproval from the other Wanderers.

"We never use our magic in battle, Kenna Smith," Elora said firmly. "Wanderers do not wield the elements that way. It is a rule that you must abide by should you wish to stay here."

"Never?" Kenna asked in a small voice. "Not even if you were being attacked?"

"Even then," Elora confirmed. "We are privileged to access the raw magic of the elements the way we do. We do not abuse them or use them to do harm. Do you understand?"

Kenna nodded quickly, though her mind lurched toward her mother.

Erika Everhart had always talked about life like it was a war. Like Kenna had to battle the whole world just to be herself. But what if she didn't have to fight at all? What if she was just allowed to live?

CHAPTER EIGHT

Soul-Shine

IN THE WEEKS SINCE RETURNING FROM THE Wanderers, Skandar had spent most of his time being interrogated about Kenna's whereabouts. The Eyrie was full of rumors about him once again, whispers following him around. But—despite being summoned to Council Square for questioning practically every day by members of the Council of Seven, the Silver Circle, and high-ranking sentinels—Skandar *still* hadn't been able to speak to Commodore Kazama about Kenna.

Now Skandar was inside the large, official-looking treehouse on the air side of the square. He was sitting in front of the Justice Representative from Nina's Council. And she was asking the same question everyone else was: "Where is your sister?"

"I don't know."

"Where were you the night your sister disappeared?"

"Wildflower Hill," Skandar answered easily.

Flo's parents had told everyone that the quartet had spent the night of Kenna's disappearance with them. Skandar was pretty certain the Shekonis' influence was the only reason he hadn't yet been hauled off to the prison.

"Has your sister contacted you since she disappeared?"

"Nope. Just like the ten other times you've asked me," Skandar said through gritted teeth. "Can you please just take me to the Commodore? I need to speak to her."

The Justice Representative tutted—she had large green eyes behind her glasses, though her long black bangs hid them from sight whenever she wrote in her notebook. "Commodore Kazama has no time to be speaking with the likes of . . ."

"Spirit wielders?" Skandar guessed.

The Justice Representative coughed awkwardly. "The Commodore is currently mobilizing the search of the Island."

Skandar knew about Nina's big search, of course. He'd read her rousing speech printed in the *Hatchery Herald* for those who'd missed it down at Element Square. It had been full of assurances that she would leave "no stone unturned" in her mission to return the eggs to the Hatchery.

Thankfully, Skandar was released from the Justice Representative's room a couple of minutes later to find Bobby, Flo, and Mitchell waiting outside on a wooden bench. He wasn't the only one who'd been called in for questioning today—the whole quartet were under suspicion.

Skandar squeezed onto the end of the bench next to Flo, and his friends immediately stopped talking. It had been happening a lot these last few days—ever since he'd shared his plan for Kenna and Goshawk.

"It's okay," Skandar said with a sigh. "I can guess what you were talking about."

"Skar, it's just that"—Flo paused as she touched him on the arm—"won't Kenna be really upset if we suggest this? I'm worried she doesn't want her destined unicorn, that she's set on Goshawk."

Mitchell looked doubtful. "But a forged bond can't possibly feel the same as a true bond. Kenna has never had a true bond, so how could she know what she's missing? I think Skandar's plan makes perfect sense—two wild unicorns saved from immortal death! Two riders with their destined unicorns."

"But *how*," Bobby said impatiently, "are we going to exchange one forged bond for two destined ones? How are we going to find the mystery rider originally destined for Goshawk? And Skandar doesn't even know how to mend bonds! It sounds like a lot of wasted effort, and *I* think we should be concentrating on the missing eggs!"

Skandar was finding this all very disorienting. The quartet had almost always agreed on their plans before now, especially when it came to something this important.

"Look," he said quietly, "we don't have to agree on anything definite right now. It's not like I can go to visit Kenna yet. All I want to do is try to convince Nina that Kenna isn't a threat and mention the *possibility* of a bond exchange. Meanwhile I'll use Mender dreams to try to find Goshawk's destined rider."

"And I can search the libraries and work with Craig on finding information about forged bonds. The Weaver can't be the only one who's ever tried it," Mitchell added. He looked sideways at Skandar. "I still can't believe you were doing research behind my back, with *my* favorite bookseller. I feel very betrayed."

Bobby rolled her eyes.

"I suppose it would be good if Kenna didn't have to have any more mutations," Flo said.

"Skandar Smith?"

A sentinel stopped by the bench, mask glinting. "The Commodore will see you now."

"Now?" Skandar said, completely surprised—he'd been trying to see Nina for days.

"Don't question it!" Mitchell hissed.

Skandar gestured to his friends. "Can they come too?" But the sentinel shook his head sharply and marched off.

"Good luck!" Flo called to Skandar, as he jogged after the guard.

The sentinel didn't go far along the corridor of the air treehouse before turning into the Council of Seven's chamber. Skandar half expected the Council to be occupying their tornado-shaped thrones, but the room was completely empty.

The sentinel marched right up to Nina's lightning-bolt throne and gestured for Skandar to join him.

"Sit!" he commanded.

"S-sorry?" Skandar spluttered.

"Sit on the throne—it will take you to the Commodore. Hold on tight."

Skandar did as he was asked, feeling very awkward on the ceremonial chair. The sentinel disappeared round the back, and Skandar started to wonder if this was some kind of joke, when—

"WAAAHHHH!"

The entire throne was propelled upward at great speed. Skandar just had enough time to glance down and see crisscrossed metal legs unfolding upward beneath the chair, before he disappeared through a hole in the chamber ceiling. The throne came to an abrupt halt, jolting sharply.

Skandar had been half expecting to see open sky, but instead he seemed to be inside a small treehouse built on top of the Council chamber. He spotted the spiral windows first—matching the air element symbol—and then he noticed the Commodore rising from her desk in the center of the room.

"Hello, Skandar." Nina waved him down from the throne and guided him toward two yellow-striped armchairs by the windows, the low table between them littered with copies of the *Hatchery Herald*. That morning's headline read:

CHAOTIC BUT IN CONTROL: KAZAMA BEGINS ISLAND-WIDE SEARCH.

Nina sighed, following Skandar's gaze. "I think that's about as nice as they're going to be about me for now." She looked more tired than when he'd first met her three years ago. Skandar knew he was supposed to look at the Commodore and want to *be* her—that was what the Chaos Cup was all about, wasn't it? But there was so much stress in her every movement that he wondered whether it would be a job he'd actually want.

Nina sank into a striped armchair and twisted a ring round her thumb. Skandar noticed it change color from red to burnt orange—it didn't look like jewelry from the Island.

"It's a mood ring," Nina explained. "Do you remember them from the Mainland? They're supposed to change color based on your mood. I mean"—she chuckled—"now I understand that the color changes with my temperature, but back when I was little, it was the closest thing I had to magic."

"And you still wear it?" Skandar asked curiously.

"It reminds me of who I was before all this." She gestured to the luxurious wallpaper shining with golden-beaked birds. "I'm sorry about the way you had to enter, Skandar. These are the Commodore's private quarters— every element's Council chamber has them for when one of their own wins the Chaos Cup. It's the best place for us to talk without being overheard—while the throne is up here, nobody else can enter."

"Thank you for seeing me."

"I also apologize for the questioning you've had to go through." Nina grimaced and ran a hand through her cropped black hair. "I have to at least *look* as though I'm concerned about Kenna's whereabouts. The others on the Council, they . . ." She hesitated. "They're ruled by their prejudice, I'm afraid. They don't see a child when they look at Kenna; they see only the Weaver."

"I know," Skandar said quietly.

"Is she safe? You don't have to tell me where she is, but is she being looked after?"

Skandar's throat closed up with nerves. "She is safe, but I—I want her to come back to the Eyrie. We need to be together."

"I understand that, Skandar," Nina said kindly, "but bringing her back to the Eyrie before we find the eggs is far too risky. Even the riders *within* its walls won't tolerate that. And the wild bond is a problem—that's what Rex and I were torn about. Wild unicorn magic doesn't heal;

what if Goshawk hit another rider during training?"

Skandar hid his permanently injured thumb inside his hand and took a shaky breath. This was his chance. "What if there was a way to bond Kenna to her destined unicorn? Could she come back to the Eyrie then?"

The Commodore said nothing for a moment. Then she spoke, her voice laced with concern. "Kenna would be allied to spirit? She would have two unicorns? Like the Weaver did before Blood-Moon's Equinox died?"

"No, no. Kenna wouldn't be bonded to Goshawk anymore, so she wouldn't be anything like the Weaver. She'd be just like me," Skandar said hurriedly.

"I think that would be easier." Nina frowned, remembering. "We spoke about this on the Divide back in June, this *mending* of bonds—have I got that right?

Skandar nodded, trying not to get his hopes up.

Nina's expression was more curious than wary. "Practically, how would it be done?"

Skandar's heart soared. The Commodore was listening to him! "I don't know how to do it for sure yet. And I know I can't risk breaking the forged bond because it might hurt Kenna—and, of course, killing a wild unicorn obviously isn't an option."

"No, absolutely not," Nina said, her tone sharp.

"But," Skandar rushed on, "I already know which unicorn was destined for Kenna. And if I can find Goshawk's destined rider too, then it might be possible for me to exchange one forged bond for two destined ones. That's the theory anyway."

Nina's light brown face was thoughtful. "Where did this theory come from? Agatha?"

Skandar shook his head. "A rider called Elora—she used to research this kind of thing at the Silver Stronghold." As soon as he'd said the Pathfinder's name, Skandar wished he hadn't. Did Nina know Elora had joined the Wanderers? Would she guess that Kenna was with them?

"Elora Scott? I've heard of her. One of the only silvers ever to leave the Silver Circle. The last silver earth wielder before Florence Shekoni." Nina stared out the window as a unicorn flew past the high treehouse. "And this *exchange* would mean both those wild unicorns—Kenna's dapple-gray and Goshawk—they would become bonded?"

"Exactly!"

"And both the riders would be spirit wielders?"

"More than likely," Skandar admitted. "But there's still my bargain with Aspen McGrath. If I get through the next three years of training, the Island is going to bring back the spirit element anyway, isn't it? And they could live in the Eyrie until then, couldn't they?" Skandar was sure Nina could hear the desperation in his voice. This sudden separation, after seeing Kenna every day for the last couple of months, was almost worse than when she'd been back on the Mainland.

Nina leaned forward in her chair. "How would you find

Goshawk's destined rider? That seems to be the priority, since all the other pieces are in place."

"Because I'm a Mender," Skandar explained, "Scoundrel and I have these dreams together. We can identify people and unicorns who were supposed to be destined for each other but missed their chance. I can try to dream Goshawk's rider, but obviously the next problem would be finding them in real life. They could be anywhere, on the Island or the Mainland."

Nina's mouth twitched. "And that's where you'd need my help, I suppose."

Skandar nodded.

Nina sighed heavily. "You must understand that my focus is finding the missing eggs."

"Of course."

"But if you can get me a description of Goshawk's destined rider—"

"I could draw them from the dream!" Skandar interrupted.

"Excellent—if you can do that, then I can work with the Island sentinels and the Mainland police to find them. It helps that we know they must be the same age as our current Hatchlings. Goshawk was supposed to be hatched the summer solstice just passed, correct?"

"That's right," Skandar said, elated. "Goshawk's rider has to be thirteen or fourteen. And if I do it? If the exchange works, Kenna can come back to the Eyrie?"

"I will try my best to make that happen," Nina said, rising from her chair. She sounded so certain, so like a Commodore, that Skandar felt much calmer than he had in days. Bobby shouldn't worry so much—Nina was going to fix everything.

"Commodore Kazama," Skandar said, once he was sitting back on the lightning throne, "you said Kenna was only part of the reason you kept the egg theft a secret. What was the other part?"

Nina looked defiant. "This Island is completely irrational when it comes to the Weaver. We treated her like our greatest threat and she became it. Villains do not become infamous because they wish it—it takes our terror to feed them. I didn't want to give the Island more fuel for their fear of the Weaver. How will we ever defeat her if we are all so afraid?"

Skandar nodded, Nina's words making sense. "So why did Rex decide to tell everyone?"

Anger flashed briefly across Nina's tired face, as she reached for the throne's lever. "Power," she said. "Nobody ever thinks they have enough."

And she pulled, sending Skandar plummeting back to the Council chamber.

A couple of weeks later, Skandar was sleep-deprived, feverish with frustration . . . and late for dinner. Something had happened to his Mender dreams. He couldn't understand it—even a month ago, he'd found it so easy to dream of the dapple-gray unicorn. But now he kept being thrown through three, sometimes even four, different human bodies—just like the dream he'd had at the Wanderers' home. The images were so foggy it was impossible to focus on even one face. And although he willed himself to stay asleep, the terrible pain always woke him too soon and without the first clue whether any of the blurred faces might have been destined for Goshawk's Fury. Nina's offer of help was useless without him being able to draw the wild unicorn's true rider.

There was palpable excitement in the Trough when Skandar finally arrived on that last evening of October. While he was spooning chickpea curry into his bowl, he tried to eavesdrop on the riders around him, but he couldn't make sense of what they were saying. Flo, Bobby, and Mitchell were up on one of their usual dining platforms, and Skandar climbed a ladder to join them.

"So what you're saying is I *can* go to all of them?" Bobby was asking as Skandar reached the platform.

"I don't see why not, though I doubt many people do." Mitchell looked thoughtful. "But then, *nobody* is as competitive as you."

Bobby beamed at this, although Skandar wasn't sure Mitchell had meant it as a compliment.

"Well, I think it would be better if we skipped them," Flo said, sounding a bit panicked. "Can't we just hang out at the treehouse together?"

"What are you all talking about?" Skandar asked, sitting down.

"The dens have announced the order of their dances," Mitchell explained. "The posters went up before dinner."

"Oh," Skandar mumbled. As far as he knew, he *was* technically allowed into the water den. But given that the other water wielders had previously banished him from the Well, he wasn't keen to go anywhere near it.

"People are already asking each other, even though the dances aren't until December," Bobby said. "You can invite one person to your own elemental dance. But I need to do it tactically to increase my chances of getting to all four."

"You're trying to go to *all* of them?" Skandar checked.

"Yes, she is." Flo sighed, exasperated. "It's not very sensible because they go on all night and they're back-to-back. Well, there's a break on the winter solstice."

Bobby wasn't listening. "Okay, so I've already been invited to the Well Dance."

"When?" Flo spluttered. "The posters have only been up for twenty minutes!"

"A water Rookie asked me as we came into the Trough—he seemed nice enough. Don't be surprised, Florence. I'm popular, gorgeous, and Commodore material. But I still need earth and fire invitations, so *you*"—she jabbed at Flo with a rolled-up *Hatchery Herald*—"can invite me to the Mine Dance."

"Sorry, Bobby. I don't want to go to any of the dances," Flo said quickly.

Bobby looked annoyed but didn't question it. "Fine. Then, Mitchell—"

"No! Absolutely not," Mitchell said forcefully. "I'm asking Jamie to the Furnace Dance." He paused. "Look, I know what you're all thinking. It's unorthodox; people might not be okay with it; maybe I should just ask someone else. But there's nothing in the rules saying I can't bring a non-rider to my dance."

"Well, that just ruins everything," Bobby huffed. "I hope you have a *brilliant* time." She went back to flipping through the newspaper.

"I just hope Jamie says yes," Mitchell said nervously.

Flo squeezed his arm. "Of course he will." She turned to Skandar. "Skar, you're not interested in going to the dances, right?"

Skandar was startled. A buried memory of a school disco surfaced. He hadn't had anything to wear or known any of the songs. He remembered how the embarrassment had mixed with the suffocating smell of the smoke machine and made his eyes water. If a den dance was anything like that, he wanted nothing to do with it.

"Erm, no, I don't think dances are my thing either," he said firmly.

Flo looked delighted. "Oh, great! Let's get snacks from

Fourpoint. We could get those hot dog things again—with mayonnaise, right?"

Skandar tried to smile at her, but it didn't reach the corners of his mouth.

"You look tired," Mitchell scolded him. "I know you haven't been sleeping in our room at all—your hammock is always empty when I wake up."

"The Mender dreams still aren't working, are they?" Flo asked, her voice low.

Skandar shook his head. "Everything is so fuzzy. And I can't stay asleep because of the . . ." He stopped before he said *pain*. "I'm going to talk to Agatha again at spirit training tomorrow. I need to see Kenna, explain what's happening."

Bobby pointed at the metal feather on Skandar's—now very patched—green jacket. "Isn't it the first Peregrine Society meeting tomorrow night?"

Skandar was shocked she'd used its real name—she usually called it *that stupid bird club*. "Yeah, during the Fire Festival. Rickesh has finished recruiting now. Why d'you ask?"

"Nina still hasn't found the eggs." She pointed to the *Hatchery Herald*. "I've been checking every day, and *nothing*. I was thinking you could start searching in your meetings."

Skandar felt the guilt hit him. Bobby was worried about her sister losing out on her destined unicorn on the next

summer solstice. The whole Island was terrified by the prospect of a new generation of riders allied to five elements and
loyal to the Weaver. But if Skandar was honest, right now
he cared a lot more about getting Kenna back to the Eyrie.
The Commodore would find the eggs, wouldn't she? What
the Commodore couldn't do was reunite Kenna with her
destined unicorn. *That* was his job.

"I'll definitely ask the other Grins," Skandar promised
Bobby, his guilty conscience spurring him on. "We can fly
fast and far, hopefully cover a lot of ground."

"Thanks, spirit boy."

"Where does he keep going?" Agatha fumed down on the
Fledgling plateau late the next afternoon. Spirit training
hadn't exactly gone to plan, because Skandar was missing a
spirit *unicorn* to train on. He'd made the mistake of leaving
Scoundrel to hunt animals around the Eyrie's wall after the
rest of his quartet had left for the Fire Festival—and now
he'd disappeared again.

"If I knew that," Skandar snapped, "I would have found
him. The only clue I have is that whenever Scoundrel comes
back, he's always coated in dust."

"Dust?" Agatha frowned, as they trudged back up the
hill, Arctic Swansong walking majestically beside them.
"Maybe it's just a Fledgling thing, testing boundaries?"

"None of the other unicorns are running away," Skandar
muttered.

Agatha peered sideways at him. "You look dreadful. Are you worried about the Fire Trial?"

"We don't even know what it is yet."

"You *should* be worried about it."

"Oh, great, thanks," Skandar said, but took advantage of the way the conversation was going. "What I'm actually worried about is my sister. I need to see her."

"How many times do I have to tell you it's too risky? What if you're followed?"

"But—"

"Everyone is looking for her right now. *Everyone.*"

"I need to tell her what's going on. What my plan is!"

"And what exactly *is* your plan?"

Skandar hesitated. He hadn't told Agatha about the bond exchange yet. He was too worried she'd tell him it was impossible.

"I don't know," he said, trying to be vague. "I'm sure being a Mender could help."

"We've talked about this. Kenna already *has* a bond," Agatha said. "And you're not ready for fully fledged mending yet—it's dangerous. I don't have many responsibilities as your aunt, but keeping you *alive* probably falls within the job description."

"What about all the other lost spirit wielders?" Skandar argued, trying to keep her talking. "Don't you want to teach me how to mend their bonds? So we can bring them back to the Island one day?"

"One day, yes." Agatha sighed. "You're turning into a proper little rebel, aren't you?" She eyed him curiously. "You seem to think I'm some kind of expert on Menders—but they were rare, even when the spirit element was legal." She paused. "I do remember seeing an interesting detail once, if you promise you'll drop this for a while?"

Skandar nodded eagerly.

Agatha started gesturing with her hands. "So, you've had your Mender dream and you've identified a rider and their destined unicorn. Next, the Mender must verify in real life whether the match they've seen in the dream is a true one. And there's a very easy way to tell."

"What is it?"

Agatha raised her wiry eyebrows. "Soul-shine. The bones of the wild unicorn begin to glow first—the color of their allied element—and then the rider's bones do the same as they approach each other. Only spirit wielders can see it—just like with bonds. *I* saw it once." Her voice was full of wonder. "I watched a Mender bring an earth-allied partnership together on the edge of the Wilderness. The green glow was beautiful."

Skandar glanced down at his spirit mutation, the bones and tendons in his arm visible in the last light of the day. His thoughts went immediately to Kenna and her dapple-gray unicorn—would their bones shine bright white when he finally brought them together?

"Listen to me, Skandar," Agatha said, as they continued

to walk. "Kenna is safe with the Wanderers for now. *Please* don't do anything . . ." She paused, searching for the right word.

"What?" Skandar asked, trying to sound innocent.

"Idiotic," Agatha finished harshly.

Skandar was still imagining soul-shine when he arrived on the Sunset Platform later that first November evening. Scoundrel had returned to the Eyrie's hill about an hour after his non-training session with Agatha.

Typical, Skandar had thought, brushing dusty debris from Scoundrel's coat. *You come back for the elite flying squad, but not for an actual training session.*

But Scoundrel screeched so happily when they landed on the Eyrie's highest platform that Skandar had to admit it felt wonderful to be back with the Grins—even amid all his worries. He waved to Marcus and Patrick, but they were having some kind of friendly arm wrestle, their unicorns—Sandstorm's Orbit and Hurricane Hoax—lurking disinterestedly nearby.

"What are these ridiculous Rookie boys fighting over now?" Adela—now a Pred—asked Fen, who was adjusting Eternal Hoarfrost's saddle.

"If Patrick wins, Marcus has to call him *Bolt* forevermore."

Adela's smoking ringlets crackled. "But doesn't Marcus have an entire right arm made out of sandstone? His earth mutation?"

Fen nodded.

"You don't stand a chance, sweetheart!" Adela purred.

Patrick groaned. "But *Bolt* is my *perfect* nickname—Hoax and I are fast, *and* we're air-allied, you see?"

"Just give it up, mate," Marcus said, not unkindly, as Patrick's arm wobbled.

Just then, Flight Lieutenant Prim landed Winter Wildfire, and Amber came soaring toward the platform on Whirlwind Thief. Squadron Leader Rickesh and his unicorn, Tidal Warrior, still hadn't arrived.

A new Nestling rider was next to land on the platform—identifiable by the two wings decorating the arm of his red jacket. Clearly nobody had told him the Grins weren't keen on anything to do with the elements. They preferred to focus on speed alone.

"Hi!" Skandar said, as the boy unstrapped a folded wheelchair from his unicorn's back and lowered himself into it. "Congratulations on making it into the Peregrine Society!"

The boy looked relieved he was in the right place. He was clearly a water wielder; his sandy hair was trapped inside ice spikes that pointed upward from his scalp. "Hi, I'm Liam." He pointed to his unicorn. "This is Coastal Crusader."

"I'm Skandar."

"I know," Liam said, grinning. "You're kind of . . . famous? And your sister—"

"Right," Skandar groaned.

"I'm not supposed to be wearing this jacket, am I?" Liam whispered, glancing over at the other Grins. "Urgh, sometimes it sucks being a Mainlander."

"Tell me about it," Skandar said. "Here, I'll hide it in my saddlebag."

"Really?"

"Sure." Skandar was quite excited about the prospect of having another Mainlander among the Grins. He wondered if Liam had any Chaos Cards he might want to swap. But thinking about the Mainland reminded Skandar of his promise to Bobby.

Rickesh had just landed on the platform, and the rest of the Grins were drifting toward their squadron leader. Skandar suddenly felt nervous. Would the Grins even *want* to search for the eggs? They prided themselves on being disconnected from the Island—a law unto themselves. For a moment, he hesitated. But the worry on Bobby's usually carefree face flashed into his mind—and he knew he couldn't let her down.

"All right, Skandar?" Rickesh gripped his shoulder in welcome. "You've been down to Council Square a lot recently, I hear. I hope they're treating you okay."

"They'd better be," Fen growled, making a fist with her snowflake-covered knuckles. "Let me know if those sentinels are giving you any grief, and I'll show them what real pain feels like."

Flight Lieutenant Prim cast a concerned look at Fen.

"You really are terrifying, you know that?"

"No, honestly, it's fine," Skandar said quickly. "But I, er, I was wondering about our meetings."

"What about them?" Rickesh swept his hand through his wave-mutated hair, interested.

Skandar swallowed. "Would we maybe be able to use them to search for the missing eggs—you know, since we can fly so fast and far and everything?"

Every single Grin was listening now—all dressed in rider black, all staring at him.

He rushed on, his voice rising with nerves. "And imagine if the Grins *do* find the eggs. We'd be heroes, wouldn't we?"

There was a pause, then—

"Well, I'm in," Patrick said abruptly, easily won over by the prospect of fame.

"I can't believe I didn't think of that! Let's do it!" Rickesh crowed.

"Really?" Skandar asked, shocked.

Red-haired Prim looked less pleased. "What about our plans, Ricki? We've mapped out the whole year already—our last one at the Eyrie."

"This is more important," Rickesh countered. "It's a whole generation of riders, Prim." He cocked his head very slightly, as if to say: *Get on board, Lieutenant.*

"If the Commodore can't find them, I don't see how *we* would," Amber muttered to Marcus.

Rickesh heard her. "*We* are the best of the best!" cried the squadron leader.

Patrick whooped. "Bring on the glory!"

Amber groaned.

"Mount up!" Rickesh said. "And don't worry. After our search tonight, we'll still welcome Liam in the usual way."

Liam looked panic stricken, so Skandar reassured him there was no scary initiation to worry about. They'd only be roasting marshmallows.

It was fun at first, flying and diving at high speed if they saw anything unusual on the ground below. Although every time Skandar dived for something that turned out to be a false alarm, Amber sniggered at him and he felt panic rising in his chest. Maybe Bobby was right? Maybe Nina *wasn't* going to find the eggs?

When darkness truly fell, the Grins had to accept that they wouldn't be finding the eggs that night. Back on the Sunset Platform, Prim, Marcus, and Fen began to prepare a fire, and Patrick started pestering Rickesh for marshmallows.

Rickesh batted Patrick away, as the younger rider poked him with a toasting twig. "One more thing, before we officially welcome Liam and Coastal Crusader. This year I'm starting a new tradition! The Grins will go to one den dance together—to celebrate as a squad. A fun night that doesn't involve flying."

Prim raised a flaming eyebrow. "A *convenient* new tradition, since our squadron leader loves showing off his dance moves."

Skandar was horrified. "But why?" he spluttered. "The Grins don't care about the elements; we don't even go to the festivals."

Rickesh chuckled. "You make it sound like I'm sending you to your death, Skandar! Anyway, the den dances actually go against elemental separation. You can invite anyone you want into your den for one night—in many ways it aligns with our philosophy."

Prim laughed. "You have absolutely no shame."

Rickesh grinned. "I think most of us can get into the Well Dance." He turned to Liam. "I'm sorry, as a Nestling you're too young—next year. But as for the rest—I'm a water wielder, so I can take Prim, and Fen can take Patrick."

"Gross," Fen and Patrick said in unison, though fairly good-naturedly.

"Adela, isn't your girlfriend a water wielder?"

She nodded, brushing her fingers through the smoking coils of her hair.

"Okay, so that leaves . . . Marcus?"

"I've got a few options," he said, absentmindedly flexing his sandstone arm.

"That's what I thought." Rickesh sounded pleased. "So that means, as an honorary water wielder, Skandar can take Amber."

"WHAT?" they both shouted from opposite sides of the fire.

"I know you two don't always get along."

"Understatement of the century," Amber muttered.

"But you're Grins. That takes priority over whatever this"—he gestured between them—"is. The Peregrine Society is attending a dance together. It's happening. Don't fight it—you might even have a nice time."

Skandar struggled to enjoy his marshmallows after that. He didn't want to take Amber to the Well Dance, even as part of a group. They'd formed an uneasy truce by the end of Nestling year—but they weren't friends. It would be so *awkward*, and he was already dreading telling his quartet.

Back at the treehouse, Skandar was surprised to find his quartet still awake—and gathered round the noticeboard. Then he spotted a new red piece of paper pinned up. "Is that about the Fire Trial?"

"We just got back from the festival and it was here!" Mitchell said, sounding flustered.

Flo made room for Skandar next to her, and they read.

> Fire is a ruthless, destructive element that burns
> fiercely. Therefore, in this second trial, the key
> is conflict. One in four will be missing a fire
> stone, so they only succeed if they steal from

another. It's every Fledgling for themselves: loyalty means nothing now.

The way to win is for another rider to lose out—fire consumes its fuel as it burns. And in its brutality, it will reward those who take more than they need. A reward that may make all the difference in lighting the way ahead.

"Every Fledgling for themselves," Mitchell murmured. "That must mean the Fire Trial isn't quartet-based. Though, of course, *we'll* all work together, won't we?"

"I don't want to steal from another rider!" Flo whimpered.

"If you're given a fire stone at the start, you won't necessarily have to," Mitchell said reasonably.

"How will they choose who goes into the trial without a stone?" Skandar wondered.

"I bet one person in each quartet won't get one." Bobby turned to Flo. "And if it's you, Florence, you *will* have to steal if you want to pass the trial. Don't forget, other riders will come after our stones too. We have to be prepared," she said darkly. "Do you want to get the blackboard, Mitchell, or shall I?"

Mitchell looked delighted as he retrieved it from behind the bookcase. "Let's write a list of all the Fledglings. That way we can narrow down potential targets. Maybe we could even team up with some of the stronger riders?"

Skandar suddenly remembered Elora's parting words as they'd left Kenna in the earth zone: *Fight for the stones, Fledglings, but don't lose yourselves along the way.*

And as Mitchell started to write up the names and elemental weaknesses of their fellow riders, Skandar wondered whether they were starting to lose themselves already.

CHAPTER NINE

Alliance Fever

FOR THE NEXT SIX WEEKS, LIFE WAS VERY strange for the Fledglings in the Eyrie. Everyone was sizing each other up as potential allies—and targets—for the Fire Trial. Training became more competitive, as riders tried to show off their strengths and get chosen by the more powerful alliances. Fierce negotiations were undertaken. The Fledglings had got it into their heads that the support of their own quartets was not enough—to survive the ruthless Fire Trial with a stone, you needed other riders watching your back too.

Skandar knew how important it was that he pass the trial. As a result, he'd rationed himself to three Mender dreams per week—though they were still getting him nowhere. He was convinced that the number of bodies he was thrown between was increasing, but the pain woke him before he could make sense of the blurred faces. The rest of the time, he tried to focus on training for the upcoming trial and navigating Scoundrel's rebelliousness.

In mid-December, the morning of the Fire Trial arrived. Skandar was waiting for Flo. He'd woken earlier than usual, climbed quietly down the rungs of the tree trunk, and was now half dozing on the blue beanbag, trying not to think about the trial starting at sundown.

"Breakfast?" Flo asked Skandar in a whisper as she joined him in the living space. This was how it had been since the Earth Trial. Bobby and Mitchell often skipped going to breakfast to maximize on sleep, but somehow Flo and Skandar always ended up agreeing to go to the Trough together.

"I can't believe it's today." Flo fiddled nervously with a thin circlet of silver fixed to her red jacket's lapel—the symbol of the Silver Circle. Last year she'd refused to go to meetings, but now—with Instructor Manning in charge—Skandar noticed that Flo trained with the silvers more often and would go to Rex for advice when Blade was hard to control.

Inside the Trough, Skandar was barely awake as he filled his plate with eggs, bacon, tomatoes, toast, and sausages. He stifled a yawn as Flo passed him a bottle of mayonnaise across the long serving table.

"Skar, you look exhausted."

"Don't worry, the Fire Trial will wake me up," Skandar joked.

Flo winced. "I wonder if sleepsong would work on a person," she murmured.

"Huh?" This happened sometimes with Flo and Mitchell—they forgot he hadn't been born on the Island and didn't know all its ways.

"Oh!" She half turned on the ladder up to one of the dining platforms. "My mum sometimes asks the bards to sing her sick unicorns into a long sleep. It helps them heal."

Skandar's mind whirred as he climbed. He knew Flo had meant that *he* needed more sleep, but could this sleep-song thing work on unicorns and riders together? If he and Scoundrel were forced to stay asleep, surely that would help him make out the face of Goshawk's destined rider in their Mender dreams?

As they reached a platform nestled in the top branches, Skandar decided that as soon as the trial was over, he would speak to Jamie about sleepsong. Perhaps his parents could help?

This table had become Skandar and Flo's favorite— partly because Flo liked to watch the birds flying in and out of their nests, but mostly because they could avoid—

"What will it take, Flo?" Romily jumped onto the plat- form, her face slightly pink and very determined. "There has to be a way to convince you. The alliances I've built for the

Fire Trial are guaranteed to get you to Rookie year."

"What it will *take*," Flo said patiently, "is you allowing the rest of my quartet to join your alliance. But I told you that at training yesterday."

"We'd happily ally with Bobby or Mitchell. You know we can't take everyone, Flo. It makes the alliance too unstable." Romily glanced at Skandar, who was pretending to concentrate very hard on squeezing mayonnaise over his breakfast. "We've got space for one of them if you join us." She smoothed her feathered head nervously—thanks to her mutation, she now had plumage instead of hair.

Flo crossed her arms over her chest. "No deal. It's all of us, or none."

"The four of you don't stand a chance in the Fire Trial alone," the air wielder protested. "Listen—"

"I said no."

Romily held up her hands defensively, as though Flo had shouted at her, and left. Skandar felt smug. You didn't mess with a silver—even one as kind as Flo Shekoni.

"Everything all right?" Rex Manning was climbing up to a table of Preds nearby, who were waving him over. Unlike the other instructors, he often ate with the trainee riders and was already so popular that Skandar thought there might be fights soon over who got to sit with him.

Flo said she was fine, but Rex clearly knew her well enough to hear the strain in her words. "It happened to me during my trials too," he reassured her from the ladder, somehow managing to balance a full tray effortlessly on one palm. "Staying true to your friends is definitely the best way to go. Good luck, both of you!"

"Thanks, Rex." Flo flashed him a smile but was still gloomy. There were four more interruptions to their breakfast, each rider ignoring Skandar and offering Flo various incentives for her support during the Fire Trial—from mucking out Blade's stable for the rest of his life, to several different den dance invitations. Skandar sat silently through the heated conversations until he and Flo were alone again.

"Why is everyone trying to push for alliances so late in the day?" Flo said. "When I was younger, I would have been so happy that all these people wanted me on their team." She laughed. "But now that everyone's asking, it's actually quite stressful."

Skandar fiddled with a fallen leaf. He knew why Flo was really saying no. She didn't want him to be left out. Every rider who'd offered an alliance to Flo—or Mitchell, or Bobby—had only done so on the basis that Skandar, the spirit wielder with a wild-unicorn rider for a sister, wouldn't be joining.

"You can't blame them for trying to ally with a silver." Skandar shrugged. "You and Blade have the most powerful magic."

"Hardly," Flo mumbled through a mouthful of cold toast. "Bobby won the Hatchling Training Trial, and Amber won the Nestling Joust; by comparison, my results have been pretty average. And Blade's magic has been even harder to control since we became Fledglings—I don't know how I'd manage without Rex's help."

Skandar winced at the mention of Amber. He still hadn't told anyone he was taking her to the Well Dance. He plowed on. "People are bothering Bobby, too. Believe me, you're a lot nicer to them than she is." He took a deep breath. He had to say it. Flo couldn't put herself at risk for him—if she was declared a nomad, then she wouldn't just be kicked out of the Eyrie. Because Blade was a silver unicorn, the Circle would take over Flo's training, and force her to live inside the Stronghold for the next few years.

"Look, Flo, I'm so lucky to have you as a friend"—he hurried on, heat filling his cheeks—"but I won't blame you if you want to ally with a bigger group for the Fire Trial. You heard what Romily said; we might be at a big disadvantage just the four of—"

Quick as a flash, Flo picked up a mushroom from her plate and threw it at him.

"Oi!" Skandar burst out laughing. "What was that for?"

"Being ridiculous," Flo announced, sounding like Bobby. "I *want* to be allied with you three for the Fire Trial. I know some quartets have split up and chosen a strong alliance over staying with their friends—but that's not us. *We* stick together."

"But—" Skandar started, but Flo held another mushroom threateningly in the air.

Skandar laughed again. "Okay! Sorry!"

That afternoon, the Fledglings flew over the fire zone. The nervous feeling in Skandar's stomach was made worse as he spotted the silver flash of sentinels searching the outer parts of the zone—for the eggs, yes, but no doubt for his sister, too. Skandar concentrated on the landscape instead, as they followed Instructors Anderson, Manning, and Everhart through the skies. The unicorns soared over clusters of Joshua trees between large rocks and spiny cacti. Then they pushed onward over the desert proper, and in the distance volcanoes rose, magma glowing like fiery threads through the terrain below.

Skandar was hoping that the instructors might avoid the volcanoes altogether, but instead Desert Firebird, Silver Sorceress, and Arctic Swansong started to make their descent and landed on the flat volcanic plateau ahead. The sun's warmth faded as it began to set below the horizon, and Skandar tried to convince himself he was glad for—rather than terrified of—the hot magma bubbling below the surface.

The instructors waited for the Fledglings to gather in a large round crater known as the Lava Bowl, which—according to Mitchell—filled with red-hot fiery liquid when the nearby volcanoes were active. As the quartet landed, it soon became clear that the other riders and unicorns were gathering in their alliances. Skandar's stomach did a nervous flip on seeing Romily's nine-strong group, with a broad mix of elemental abilities.

"Some of them were top ten in the Training Trial *and* last year's joust," Mitchell said fretfully. "Lots of them have even left members of their own quartets behind."

It wasn't just Romily's alliance that looked formidable. Kobi, Alastair, and Meiyi had teamed up with another quartet: Ajay, Marissa, Ivan, and Aisha. Skandar felt sick—had his quartet made a huge mistake in going it alone?

There was one rider completely on her own. Amber Fairfax sat on Whirlwind Thief's chestnut back, chin stuck out defiantly.

"Do you think we should ask Amber to ally with us?" Flo whispered, as they moved further into the crater.

"Have you lost your mind?" Bobby hissed. "Amber Fairfax will turn on us the first chance she gets."

"She *did* free Scoundrel for me last year, remember?" Skandar said, hardly believing he was considering this.

"Adding another air wielder to our group wouldn't be the worst thing in the world." Mitchell was still looking at the other alliances. "Though, does it *have* to be Amber?"

"I'm asking her," Skandar said firmly.

"Don't come crying to me when she murders us and leaves our bodies for the crows," Bobby said.

"It would be quite difficult to cry to anyone once the crows had eaten us," Mitchell pointed out.

"Oh, shut up, Mitchell."

Skandar had only walked two steps when Amber turned sharply in her saddle and narrowed her eyes, her star mutation crackling threateningly on her forehead. "Don't you dare, spirit wielder," she growled.

Skandar took another step. Whirlwind Thief bared her teeth at him.

"Amber—"

"No, absolutely not."

"You don't even know what I'm going to ask!"

"Yes, I do." She flipped her chestnut hair to one side so she could eyeball him. "I'm not joining your pathetic excuse for an alliance. And before you start feeling sorry for me, you should know that unlike *you* I've been asked to join a bunch of different riders. I've *chosen* to do the Fire Trial alone. There are lots of advantages."

"Suit yourself, then," Skandar snapped. "Go it alone. We were only trying to be nice."

"Well, don't," Amber said coldly.

Skandar hurried back to the others; Bobby looked delighted that he'd returned without Amber.

"She doesn't want any allies," he explained quickly, as Instructor Anderson started to speak.

"Like fire magic, this trial is straightforward. You will enter the trial area at sundown, and one in four of you will not have a solstice stone. To pass, you *must* have a red fire stone displayed on your armor at sunrise—the end of the trial. If you end up with more than one fire stone, you will be permitted to swap any spares for the elemental stones of your choice."

"*That* wasn't in the instructions," Mitchell muttered.

"Remember that the Chaos Trials can sometimes be as much about tactics as they are about fighting alongside your unicorn," Instructor Anderson warned, flaming ears flaring. "If you choose to go after another rider's solstice stone, they may well retaliate later on."

Skandar saw riders shifting their unicorns closer. Whispered discussions started all over the clearing.

"Some of these alliances are one hundred percent going to break down," Bobby whispered to Skandar. "I can't see the Threat Quartet sharing *any* solstice stones they manage to steal—especially if they're able to trade them in."

"They failed the Earth Trial, remember?" Mitchell said, overhearing. "At the very least they'll try to steal fire stones so they can trade them in for the earth ones they need."

"And *we* need to stay away from them," Flo said nervously.

"We can't stay away from *everyone*," Bobby snapped. "One of us isn't going to get a fire stone. If we all want to be Rookies, we have to fight."

The three instructors moved among the Fledglings, each holding a red drawstring bag. Skandar watched Instructor Manning give out glassy blood-red stones to the quartet standing together in front. Gabriel took one, then Mabel, then Zac, then—

"Are you serious? No stone?" Sarika cried. Rex moved away, apologizing profusely.

Sarika burst into tears, her flaming fingers covering her brown face.

Earth wielder Gabriel put an arm round Sarika's shoulder. "We'll get you a stone; we'll work together."

Arctic Swansong blocked Skandar's view, and Agatha slammed a fire stone onto his breastplate with a clunk. Its glass sides—etched all over with fire symbols—reflected the dying light of the sun.

"There you go," Agatha said gruffly. Then she handed a stone up to Flo and another to Bobby, who snatched it.

Mitchell looked grim. "You haven't given a stone to any of the fire wielders, have you?"

"Sorry, Henderson." Agatha looked genuinely apologetic. "You'll have to steal one for yourself. The rest of you—*especially* you"—she pointed at Skandar—"watch. Your. Backs."

Next, Instructor Anderson flew Desert Firebird above the crater and threw flames at the volcanic rock below. The fire exploded and moved in an enormous circle, crackling like a firework fuse. For a moment, the flaming line disappeared behind the volcanoes, but then it swept back toward them in an arc.

Instructor Manning jumped into action. "You must stay within the circle at all times!" he warned. "Leave the circle, fail the trial. And your stones must always be visible on your armor. You must *not* conceal them, or I'm afraid we'll have to disqualify you."

The blazing line sped toward the Lava Bowl, closing the fiery ring.

The sun sank out of view. When Skandar saw it again, the trial would be over.

"GO!" Agatha shouted.

The Fledglings galloped out of the crater, and scattered as quickly as they could. Some unicorns flew toward the shadow of the largest volcano—deep within the circle—while others galloped away into the darker pockets that were unlit by the smoldering threads of magma.

Bobby and Falcon took the lead, heading for a giant volcanic rock. The others followed, and—as Scoundrel reached it—Skandar saw it was a good choice: the rock towered above the unicorns, casting shadows for the quartet to hide in. The four riders encouraged their unicorns to lie down behind the rock so they could talk half-covered by their wings.

"Here's the situation," Bobby whispered, "Mitchell needs a fire stone. We have to help him steal it *without* having ours stolen in retaliation." She seemed exhilarated, rather than terrified like the rest of them.

"Roberta, that really is very kind of you."

Bobby rolled her eyes. "I told you, I can't have one of my quartet being declared a nomad before my sister gets here. She'll never let me forget it."

"But we just need *one*, for Mitchell," Skandar said, glancing at Flo snuggling unhappily against Blade's silver wing. "We don't need to steal any spare stones—it's greedy and it's too risky."

"I agree," Flo said quickly. "But how are we supposed to choose a target? It feels horrible."

"Everyone out there"—Bobby pointed to the magma-filled plateau—"is asking themselves that very same question. And I'd bet my last jar of Marmite that they're plotting to take out Skandar right now. No offense," Bobby added.

Mitchell still looked worried, but he spoke clearly. "Niamh is the logical target. She's been given a fire stone for this trial, but her quartet won the Earth Trial, remember? *She* got the spare fire stone."

Skandar was nodding. "So if we take hers, she'll still pass the trial."

"I like Niamh, though," Flo murmured. "I can't imagine attacking her."

"If you'd rather go for riders we don't like," Mitchell mused, "Amber would be a good target. She has no allies."

"Plus," Skandar muttered, "if I stole her fire stone, Amber probably wouldn't come to the Well Dance with me anymore."

Skandar didn't realize what he'd said until he saw Bobby, Mitchell, and Flo staring at him open-mouthed.

"You asked Amber?" Flo said, her voice tiny.

"I didn't want to!" Skandar cried. "But the Peregrine

Society are all going to the Well Dance together, so Rickesh said I *had* to bring Amber because I'm an honorary water wielder!"

"This is a joke—right, Skandar?" Mitchell asked desperately.

"No! I didn't get any choice! The Grins are all going together so I had to—" Skandar stopped mid-protest, watching Flo wriggle out from under Blade's wing.

"I thought you said you didn't want to go to the den dances, Skar?" Flo's eyes filled with tears. "We were going to get snacks and stay in at the treehouse. Did you just forget about that?"

Skandar hesitated. "I— They— The Grins are all—"

"I get it," Flo choked out. "You want to hang out with your other friends. That's fine."

Guilt was making Skandar's heart race. "But we can hang out at the treehouse on the other den dance nights! I only said I'd go to the Well—"

"That's not the point!" Flo interrupted him. She mounted Blade "I— This, the stones, it's all too much. You can all go and attack people without me. I want to be on my own."

"Don't be ridiculous, Flo!" Mitchell said. "You can't go! What if *you* get attacked?"

Flo's face was suddenly severe. "I'm a silver. We'll see how far they get." And she sounded so angry—so unlike herself—that Skandar's stomach turned over as he watched

Silver Blade disappear into the fiery darkness.

"Floundering floods," Bobby cursed, grabbing Skandar's leg. "Get down, will you? Are you *trying* to give away our hiding place, as well as losing us a quarter of our alliance?"

"I have to say, Skandar," Mitchell hissed, "I've not had much experience at all with this friend stuff, but even *I* wouldn't have chosen Amber over Flo."

"I didn't choose!" Skandar yelled. "It's a Peregrine Society thing."

"But you *did* choose," Bobby said, sounding furious. "You didn't have to go with the stupid bird group at all. What were they going to do? Kick you out because you already had plans? There was a choice, Skandar, and you made the wrong one. You've lived with Flo for two and a half years. You *know* she's shy and unsure of herself sometimes. She was really excited that you wanted to hang out with her at the treehouse. She's already bought hot dogs!"

"I was excited too—"

"Ditching her isn't exactly showing her that, is it, though? Flo always thinks she likes people more than they like her, which I've told her a million times is ridiculous, but now *you* go and do this?"

It was only then that they realized they'd been talking far too loudly.

Four elemental attacks hit their rock at once. Flames erupted at its base; an ice spear rebounded; lightning lit up the night; and flint missiles hit the volcanic surface like bullets. Scoundrel, Red, and Falcon panicked, flapping their wings and rising from the ground. Skandar just had time to grab on to his saddle and pull himself up before another barrage began.

Skandar flung up a shining white spirit shield to deflect a fork of lightning, but—with the dark and the elemental debris—he couldn't even make out the Fledgling rider who'd attacked him.

"It's the spirit wielder!" Was that Ajay, on Smoldering Menace?

"Grab his fire stone!" Another voice—it sounded like Ivan, on Swift Sabotage, but Skandar couldn't be sure.

Mitchell and Red were battling someone on Skandar's left. Mitchell was shooting fire arrows from a flaming bow, but his attacker wasn't letting up. Fireballs kept exploding nearer and nearer to Red's legs.

"Coming through!" Bobby yelled, and then Falcon was rearing up in front of Scoundrel, the fire illuminating her perfectly braided mane as Bobby let rip.

A cyclone flew from Bobby's palm, growing as it gathered the elemental debris from the battle around them. Once it was big enough, Bobby directed it toward the Fledglings ahead. Then she fired a lightning bolt into the middle of the cyclone, electrifying the storm.

Skandar, Bobby, and Mitchell's attackers had no choice but to flee.

"You're welcome," Bobby said, pretending to blow out her glowing yellow palm.

"We need to get out of here!" Mitchell shouted, smoke pouring from Red's nostrils in spirals.

"Toward the volcano?" Skandar said, hoping they'd find Flo on the way. But even as he suggested it, he could see Fledgling unicorns rearing up on the magma-threaded rocks, elemental magic flashing in the darkness as they roared into battle. All interested in one thing. Survival.

Bobby voiced exactly what Skandar was thinking. "How do we get past that lot?"

But he didn't get a chance to reply, because—in three strides—Scoundrel had taken off without Skandar giving any kind of command.

"I guess we're flying, then," Bobby called to Mitchell.

Skandar looked down to see Red and Falcon take off too. "I hope you know what you're doing, Scoundrel," he warned.

They were spotted multiple times from below. At one point, Meiyi and Rose-Briar's Darling sent a fire blast right at Scoundrel's stomach, trying to ground him. At another, Elias and Marauding Magnet tried to knock them off course with a gust of gale-force wind.

Eventually Scoundrel, Falcon, and Red managed to land safely in the shadow of the largest volcano in the valley.

It was much quieter here, though there was still the

unsettling sound of a lava lake bubbling away within the inner crater of the volcano. Smoke and ash filled the air, making it hard to see much at all.

"We hadn't actually agreed on the flying plan, you know," Mitchell said, all prickly.

"It wasn't me!" Skandar protested. "It was Scoundrel. Take it up with him!"

"Keep your voices down—and get in here," Bobby ordered, gesturing toward an opening at the volcano's base.

"Watch out for salamanders!" Mitchell hissed, halting Red at the dark opening and dismounting. "And whatever you do, don't step on one!"

"What's so scary about salamanders?" Bobby said, thumping to the ground. "Aren't they just tiny lizards?"

"They're fire elementals living deep in the zone. I've only ever seen them in captivity—in displays for the Fire Festival and things. They're highly hazardous."

The cave was just big enough to fit all six of them. For a moment they were silent—listening to the vibrations of the active volcano, the snorts of their unicorns, and the elemental battles in the distance.

"Who attacked us?" Skandar whispered. "I couldn't see properly through the smoke."

"I couldn't make them all out." Mitchell wiped ash off his cheek. "But Niamh and Snow Swimmer were there."

"Did you get her fire stone?" Bobby asked excitedly, peering at Mitchell's breastplate.

Mitchell shook his head. "Niamh's had gone. Someone had already stolen it."

"Well, that's more disappointing than a duck-sized dragon." Bobby jerked her chin pointedly in Skandar's direction. "Wish *Flo* had been here for that one."

"What am I going to do?" Mitchell choked out, ignoring Bobby. "If I don't get a fire stone, I'll fail. Who knows whether I'll be able to get a spare in any of the later trials! And then I won't be allowed back into the Eyrie, and you're the only friends I've ever—"

"Chill, Mitchell," Bobby interrupted. "We'll get you one; we just need to widen the net a bit."

"We need to find Flo first," Skandar insisted.

Skandar saw Bobby raise an eyebrow, but she conceded. "Two objectives, then. We find Flo. We find Mitchell a fire stone. Got it?"

The boys nodded.

Bobby stood up and walked forward purposefully. "What the—" Something four-legged had scuttled out from under her boot and began to glow bright red, lighting up the cave.

Mitchell had frozen in horror. Skandar and Bobby were watching—half-fascinated, half-disgusted—as the lizard-like creature's veins set on fire from within. Then its entire body—legs, head, and tail included—melted like molten rock, until it was a glowing orange pool on the ground. Black smoke began to rise off it in thick plumes.

"Well, Mitchell," said Bobby, "I don't know why you were making such a fuss about—"

"RUN!" Mitchell yelled. "The smoke is poisonous!"

Skandar didn't need telling twice. He grabbed Scoundrel's reins, and they all exploded out of the cave.

"That, Bobby," Mitchell wheezed once they were a good distance away, "was the perfect example of what not to do when you see a salamander."

"I didn't see it!"

"Is it dead?" Skandar asked, looking back at the fumes billowing from the cave.

"Oh, the *salamander* will be absolutely fine. If they're touched—for example by a *foot*"—he glared at Bobby—"they melt defensively and let off noxious gas. Once they've knocked out anything living within a few meters, they re-form and scuttle off."

"No need for a lecture," Bobby grumbled. "Two objectives, remember?"

As they rode up the volcano's slope, Skandar kept expecting to see the silver sheen of Blade through the swirling smoke. But as they climbed higher toward the lava lake, there was no sign of Flo or her unicorn.

Mitchell coughed through the black ash that was lifting from Red's hooves. "I think most riders all the way up here must be hiding to protect their stones."

Skandar thought Mitchell was right. They hadn't been attacked in their search for Flo—the smoky outlines of other Fledgling unicorns appeared and disappeared like specters in the red glow from the lake.

"I don't know how much longer I can be up here," Bobby moaned, her brown bangs plastered to her sweaty forehead. "It's too hot."

They were very close to the lava lake now; veins of magma smoldered under the unicorns' hooves as they walked. Scoundrel kept hissing, sparks escaping between his teeth—Skandar could tell that he wanted to fly away from the fiery orange mass writhing inside its crater.

Then they heard a scream.

Flo's scream.

CHAPTER TEN

The Fire Trial

AT THE SOUND OF FLO'S SCREAM, BOBBY sprang into action, gathering Falcon's reins. "If anyone hurts her, I will *make them pay*!"

Flo screamed again, and then yelled in terror, "She's here! She's inside the trial!"

And Skandar knew exactly who Flo was talking about.

Without a second thought, Skandar, Bobby, and Mitchell galloped their unicorns toward the panicked cries. For a moment, the smoke around the lava lake cleared, and Skandar saw Flo and Blade silhouetted against its hellish glow.

Scoundrel, Falcon, and Red crashed toward them.

"She was here, Skar," Flo said as soon as he reached her. "The Weaver."

She was shaking from head to foot. Bobby pushed Falcon closer to Blade so she could take Flo's hand over their unicorns' silver and gray wings.

"I saw her through the smoke on the other side of the lake," Flo croaked. "I think she was looking for someone. But when I screamed, she flew her wild unicorn off the crater."

Fear gripped Skandar's heart. Had the Weaver been looking *for him*?

"Are you sure it was the Weaver?" Mitchell asked, sounding desperate for Flo to change her mind.

"If you want proof," Flo said, her voice shaking again, "look down there."

They rode their unicorns right to the edge of the lava lake, the volcano quivering under their hooves. As it gurgled like a hungry monster, Skandar saw the proof Flo had promised.

The Weaver had lost her shroud. He watched the tattered black material burn at the edges, before being slowly pulled into the belly of the fiery beast.

"We need to stop the Fire Trial right now," Flo said determinedly. "It's not safe! The Weaver could be anywhere!"

Bobby looked very unhappy about this idea. "Didn't you say the Weaver flew off? Maybe she's gone?"

Skandar sensed that the others were waiting for him to say something. "Whatever the Weaver's doing, I won't let her hurt our chances of all becoming Rookies. Mitchell needs a fire stone—and if we stop the trial, we won't be able to get him one."

"Flo?" Bobby asked hopefully.

"Fine. But as soon as we're out, we tell the instructors."

"Deal," Bobby and Mitchell said together.

The quartet found a deep crevice in the side of the volcano and decided to use it as a base. They worked in pairs—Bobby, Flo, and Skandar taking turns to go with Mitchell—so that they were only risking one stone at a time. When she was left behind with Skandar, Flo only spoke when absolutely necessary and avoided looking at him directly. The den dance argument was clearly not forgotten.

On one occasion, Bobby and Mitchell came back shaken. They'd been about to creep up behind Kobi and Meiyi, who'd broken off from the rest of their allies and were sheltering near a rock stack. As Bobby and Mitchell had summoned elemental magic into their palms, Kobi and Meiyi had opened fire on a group ahead of them. Mateo, Naomi, Divya, and Harper had been completely ambushed—abandoned by their spooked unicorns, and trapped between the rocks and Kobi and Meiyi's relentless elemental attacks.

"They surrendered," Bobby reported. "Actually put their hands in the air and let those snakes take the stones right off their breastplates!"

"But only Meiyi needed a fire stone. Are you telling me they took *three* from Mateo's quartet?" Flo was outraged.

"They needed the extras to swap for earth stones," Mitchell reminded her miserably.

"Also, they're awful," Bobby added, for good measure.

As the faint twilight before dawn punctured the inky sky, riders started to get more frantic. Skandar and Mitchell watched as Elias and Marauding Magnet swooped down on Gabriel and Queen's Price, launching a volley of flint missiles. Despite the defensive efforts of Gabriel's allies, Elias managed to stretch out his arm as he flew past and grab Gabriel's red solstice stone from his armored chest.

When morning started to break, Mitchell became so reckless that he abandoned the shelter of the volcano completely. Skandar, Bobby, and Flo each tried to go with him, but he wouldn't let them. "The last thing we need is one of you losing your stone now."

But Mitchell's last-ditch attempts weren't fruitful, even though Red was doing as he asked and soaring down at every potential target they could find. The Fledglings that were out in the open didn't have fire stones. The ones who did were staying hidden until sunrise.

"How long do you think we have?" Mitchell asked desperately when he returned to his quartet empty-handed again.

As though in answer, there was a whooshing sound and the flaming circle of the fire ring extinguished itself. The sun had risen. The Fire Trial was over.

Unicorns and riders climbed out from camouflaged

craters, crept out from behind black rocks, and emerged from round the side of the nearest volcano. Everyone looked completely exhausted and extremely dirty.

Mitchell had managed to hold it together until they dismounted. "I can't believe it," he said, his voice hollow. "My father is going to be so disappointed, and what will Jamie think? Will he even want to go to the Furnace Dance with me now? A fire wielder failing the Fire Trial. Pathetic."

Flo pulled him into a hug. "You're not pathetic, Mitchell! It wasn't fair. I'm sorry—I shouldn't have left you at the beginning." They both descended into sobs.

Bobby—who was not a crier—tried to be upbeat. "Look, there's no need for all this fuss. We've got two more trials to get Mitchell a fire stone, for goodness' sake!"

"Exactly," Skandar said, trying to meet Flo's eye.

The sorry-looking quartet made their way back to the Lava Bowl, where healers were waiting to check them for injuries and the instructors stood by to record the results.

There was more crying here, too. Skandar spotted Walker sobbing alone on the ground, as well as Sarika in floods of tears as she tried to apologize to Romily for stealing her stone.

"Aren't they friends?" Bobby murmured to Skandar as they dismounted.

Skandar sighed. "They *were*."

As he looked around at the distressed Fledglings, Skandar remembered what Elora had said all those weeks ago.

What I do know is that the Island has forgotten that there are more important things than winning.

What about friendship? Skandar thought. *What about loyalty?* If losing sight of all that was the price for becoming a Chaos rider, did he really want to pay it? When his training was done, was this really the kind of person he wanted to be?

"Oh great. Amber's still got her fire stone." Bobby peered over at Whirlwind Thief.

"Let me at that spirit wielder scum!" Suddenly Alastair was right in front of Skandar, the tall boy being unsuccessfully restrained by Meiyi and Kobi.

"You took my stone! I know it was you!" Alastair shouted, spittle flying toward Skandar's face.

"What are you talking about?" Skandar asked, confused. "I didn't attack you. I never even saw you!"

Alastair's arms were flailing out toward him. "Liar! I know what I saw. You shouldn't even *be* in the Chaos Trials. There isn't even a *trial* for your element. You're illegal. You should be locked up." Escaping his friends for a moment, he tried to grab the blood-red stone from Skandar's armored chest.

"That"—a familiar voice sounded, loud and clear—"is quite enough of that."

Agatha rode Arctic Swansong right at Alastair, and the presence of the fully grown spirit unicorn was enough to make him back away from Skandar. He spat on the ground for good measure before slinking off. "Spirit scum."

Agatha ignored this and dismounted from Swan. She pulled out a clipboard and unclipped the red bag from her saddle, ready to collect the quartet's solstice stones.

"Why does Alastair think you took his stone?" Flo asked. It was the first time she'd looked directly at him since the trial had ended. "You didn't, did you?"

"No! I've got no idea what he's on about. Flo, are you—" But he was interrupted by Agatha.

"All right?" she asked Skandar, her eyes raking him—he had the feeling she was examining him for injuries. "Half-way through and still alive. Excellent. Give me your stone, then; I'll record it."

"The Weaver was inside the trial!" Flo gasped out, as though the information had been boiling up inside her. "I saw her this time."

Agatha paled slightly. "Is this true?" When she asked the question, she looked directly at Skandar, as though he was the only one she trusted.

Skandar nodded. "We saw her shroud burning in the lava lake. She was definitely there." He half expected an apology from Agatha for not believing him about the Weaver the first time, but he didn't get one. Agatha rubbed her mutated cheeks.

"What is Erika playing at?" she said, half to herself.

"I think she was searching for someone," Flo said, glancing at Skandar. "She was looking out over the zone when I saw her."

Agatha seemed even more concerned. "I'll tell the Commodore. Give me your stones, quickly."

Skandar, Bobby, and Flo handed her their fire stones. But when Agatha looked expectantly at Mitchell, he hung his head.

"It'll be all right," Skandar said. "We'll fix this."

Mitchell nodded glumly. But Skandar felt sick as Agatha scrawled an *X* next to his friend's name.

"It'll be all right," Skandar said again. But it was mostly to reassure himself.

The days between the Fire Trial and the den dances were very strange. The Fledglings avoided each other—preferring to go to bed early, dodging the usual evening activities like chatting round the campfires in the fire quadrant or sitting by the moonlit pools in the water quadrant. Everything felt horribly awkward. When Skandar confessed this to Marcus at a Peregrine Society meeting, the earth wielder sighed sympathetically. "What do you expect, Skandar? The trials are different every year, but I'm guessing you've just had fire so you've all tried to take each other out? True colors have been shown. We were exactly the same—it feels like you can't trust anyone."

"Which you can't," Fen said, overhearing. "It's every rider for themselves. That's what the Chaos Trials are all about."

"Do you think that's right, though?" Skandar asked, as he mounted Scoundrel to prepare for their latest egg search.

"Should they really make us do this to each other?"

Fen shrugged. "Doesn't matter. That's what it takes to stay in the Eyrie. To become a Chaos rider—maybe even the Commodore. You either want that enough, or you don't."

Skandar immediately thought of Kenna. It wasn't just about being a Chaos rider for him. Every year he stayed in the Eyrie was a year closer to the spirit element being legal again, and—if he mended Kenna's bond—closer to her becoming a real rider too. He'd already decided he was going to visit Kenna for Christmas in a week's time—though he wasn't going to tell Agatha, because he knew she'd try to stop him. Skandar was hoping to have some progress to share with his sister by then. And that had a lot to do with Jamie.

When the blacksmith had come up to the Eyrie after the Fire Trial to check Scoundrel's armor, Skandar had asked him all about sleepsong. Immediately practical, Jamie had talked to his mum, and she'd agreed to visit the Eyrie the evening before the den dances began. Skandar was hoping she'd be able to put him and Scoundrel to sleep for long enough that they could dream of Goshawk's destined rider.

The afternoon before Jamie's mum arrived, Skandar, Bobby, Mitchell, and Flo landed their unicorns on the Fledgling plateau for water training. Since the Water Trial was next, these sessions would outnumber all the others for a while.

Nobody seemed particularly cheerful as they lined up

in front of the water pavilion. Flo had been even quieter than usual all week. And although she was talking to Skandar, she wasn't *really* talking to him. They were polite to each other, but hadn't once been to breakfast together since the Fire Trial. Skandar still waited for her every morning, but she never appeared. He'd taken to obsessively drawing blurry dream faces in his sketchbook instead and missing breakfast altogether.

Bobby had a copy of the *Hatchery Herald* resting over Falcon's neck, clearly trying to read the whole paper before the start of the session. Skandar knew she was scanning it for news of the missing eggs. Whenever he returned from a Peregrine Society meeting, her face fell when he told her they'd found nothing.

Mitchell kept muttering to himself, not even telling Red off when she set fire to her mane over and over again. Finally Bobby snapped. "You do realize newspapers are flammable, right? What's up with you?"

"If you must know, I'm nervous."

"About what? *You're* not going to be put in an unnaturally long sleep."

"No, but I am going to have to meet Jamie's mum. I'm worried she won't like me."

"Why do you always think people won't like you?" Skandar asked. "You shouldn't be so down on yourself."

"Skandar, I wasn't convinced that my own father liked me until last year. *He* was supposed to be guaranteed—so I treat the rest of humanity as a complete unknown."

"But you've already met Jamie's parents," Flo said, confused. "In the spirit den last year."

"Yes, but"—Mitchell was clearly flustered, the flames in his hair getting brighter—"not as his, you know, romantic interest. We're going to the dance together!"

"Romantic interest?" Bobby spluttered. "You sound like you're from the 1800s!"

Mitchell ignored this. "And Jamie's mum is a very well-respected bard. What if she asks me about the Fire Trial? Which I *failed*, by the way!"

"You've got nothing to worry about," Flo said kindly. "I'm sure Jamie's mum will love you as much as we do."

"What do you mean *we*?" Bobby said, and Flo kicked her in the shin.

Instructor O'Sullivan asked the Fledglings to pair up. Skandar and Bobby went together, and Falcon and Scoundrel faced each other across the waterlogged grass.

"Today's session is all about the malleability of the water element!" Instructor O'Sullivan called from Celestial Seabird's back. "I want one rider in the pair to throw a large amount of water, perhaps a strong water jet or *small* wave— I'm looking at *you*, Kobi." The water wielder sniggered in response. "And the other rider will meet their partner's water magic with their own and try to *mold* it into something useful to attack with. I'm thinking swords, spears, maces—"

"What about a bow and arrows?" Art called—it was no

secret that the bow was their favorite weapon.

Instructor O'Sullivan chuckled. "Art, if you and Furious Inferno can mold a bow from Niamh and Snow Swimmer's water attack before it hits you, you can stay in bed all day tomorrow."

"Seriously?" Art asked eagerly. "I can skip training?"

The instructor inclined her head, her swirling eyes amused.

As the Fledglings quickly discovered, molding weapons from fast-flying water was even harder than it sounded.

The problems Bobby and Skandar were having were different from each other, but equally frustrating. Falcon was doing anything possible to avoid getting wet, and so—every time Skandar and Scoundrel sent water jets toward her—she froze them before they could reach her.

"Falcon!" Bobby cried. "We're supposed to be making a weapon out of *moving* water! This is cheating!"

Skandar's problem was that—like many of the other Fledglings—he was too slow. He'd begin to manipulate Bobby's water in the air, feeling for the shape of his favorite saber, but the attack would hit him before he knew it. He *and* Scoundrel were wet through. Scoundrel wasn't finding this fun, and kept trying to attack Falcon instead.

Skandar readied himself with another water attack to throw at Bobby, but she waved at him to stop and rode over.

"I think drowned rat is definitely one of your worst looks."

"Cheers," Skandar grunted, trying to stop water from dripping into his eyes from his bangs.

"Look, spirit boy." Bobby was suddenly serious. "Are you sure about this sleepsong thing tonight?"

Skandar was completely taken aback. Bobby was never one to shy away from risky situations. It would usually have been Flo warning him off, but she was barely speaking to him.

Bobby sighed. "I've heard you yelling out in your Mender dreams. It sounds bad, Skandar. Like you're in a lot of pain. I know you're playing it down, because you want this for Kenna, but it could be really dangerous. Like *death* dangerous."

"Jamie's mum is going to be there. You're all going to be there! If anything goes wrong, then you can just throw something to wake me up," he joked.

Bobby barked out a laugh. "All right. If you say so. But you've got to be careful."

"I will. I promise."

Bobby seemed satisfied and went back to chucking water at him, but Skandar felt spooked. He'd been so focused on seeing a clear face he could draw for Nina that he'd pushed Agatha's warnings about the Mender dreams aside. But how painful was it going to get if he couldn't wake up?

Jamie met the quartet by Scoundrel's stable that evening once all the other riders had left the wall.

"When my mum gets here, if she says anything about a bard portrait, just ignore her," Jamie said, looking stressed. "My picture is supposed to be hung in the Song School because I sang my truesong earlier this year—I've been avoiding her since she asked."

"What's the Song School?" Skandar asked.

"It's the bard equivalent of the Eyrie. Been trying to avoid it my whole life," Jamie said, untangling a knot in Red's untidy mane.

"I—we really appreciate your help with this, Jamie," Mitchell said softly, and the blacksmith smiled at him.

"We'd better fetch her from the Eyrie entrance," Jamie said, sighing, but—as he and Mitchell turned to leave—a woman with long sandy hair, a floor-length magenta dress, and an infectious smile came marching toward them.

"Hello, sweetheart!" She folded Jamie into a hug.

"Mum!" Jamie protested, his voice muffled. "How did you even get in here?"

"I have my ways. Never underestimate the power of charm." She let go of her son, but immediately grabbed Mitchell's hands so enthusiastically that his glasses almost flew off.

"Mitchell! My goodness, Jim-Jam, he's even more handsome than I remember. And clever too, I hear."

The flames in Mitchell's hair were billowing so much that Skandar thought he might set fire to something. His face was a mixture of embarrassment and delight.

Bobby was stifling a smirk. "Jim-Jam?" she mouthed at Jamie, who shrugged, unbothered.

Jamie's mum rushed over to them. "So lovely to see you again, Skandar and Flo. And to meet you, Bobby. You *must* all call me Talia."

Skandar overheard Jamie say to Mitchell, "See, I told you she'd like you!"

"Do you think I should have asked her more about herself? Or said something funny? I'm actually *not* very funny, though, so that may not have worked."

"Stop," Jamie said, half laughing and taking Mitchell's hand. "You don't need to be funnier or cleverer or braver. You're Mitchell, and that's why I like you."

Mitchell's wide smile was quickly followed by a slight frown. "I mean, I'm very smart already, so I'm not sure how I'd actually get *cleverer*."

Jamie burst out laughing. "See, you are funny!"

"Erm . . . that wasn't actually a joke."

"Well, Jamie refusing to sit for his bard portrait is a little embarrassing for me," Talia was explaining to an awkward Flo. "I'm a battlesong specialist at the Song School, you see." She touched a hand to one of her dangling earrings—two musical notes crossed like dueling swords.

"But I'm not a bard." Jamie kept his tone level. "And I'm busy. I'm blacksmith to a Fledgling rider this year, Mum. Do you have any idea how much work that is? New armor tailored to the particular elemental trial every season."

Skandar felt guilty. He'd been so wrapped up in his own problems that he'd barely noticed how much Jamie had been up at the Eyrie fitting Scoundrel's armor. He'd put it down to Jamie wanting to spend time with Mitchell.

"Jamie really is the best blacksmith around," Skandar said hurriedly. "I don't know what I'd do without him."

"Well, that may be so, but we'd better focus on the main event," Talia said, scrutinizing Skandar. "A Mender, well, well. *Such* a long time since the bards have helped one of your kind."

"So you know about Menders?" Skandar asked, trying to steady his nerves.

"Oh yes," Talia said, her eyes distant. "Bards remember many things that the Island would prefer we forget." She blinked, looking round at the quartet huddled by Scoundrel's stable. "Gosh, you all look very stressed. Jim-Jam has told me all about the Chaos Trials. I must say, they sound terrible."

"They are," said Flo flatly.

"Well, there's absolutely no need to be worried about sleepsong. I'm very used to singing for injured unicorns." She put a hand on Skandar's shoulder. "In we go."

Skandar attempted to send a volley of reassuring emotions into the bond as he and Talia entered Scoundrel's stable. The trouble was, *Skandar* was now feeling nervous. Had Talia just said she'd only sung for injured *unicorns*? He was beginning to think he should have talked to Agatha first.

Scoundrel squeaked anxiously once the bard kneeled in the straw. Skandar slipped him a red Jelly Baby, and then popped one into his own mouth for courage. This was for Kenna.

"Wait!" Flo called urgently. "For drawing the rider!" She handed Skandar a pencil and his sketchbook, turned to a blank page.

"Thank you," he managed to croak. His quartet and Jamie all leaned over the stable door, worry on their faces.

"Settle yourself how you usually would when you sleep in Scoundrel's stable," Talia instructed. "Under his wing? Yes, that's good. Do not be alarmed if I enter the trance state before you do."

Skandar tried to make himself relax as Scoundrel's dark wing cocooned him. It was a bit difficult—he wasn't used to having an audience when he slept.

"See you on the other side, spirit boy," Bobby said, and all his friends put in earplugs to block out the sleepsong.

Skandar jumped as—without warning—Talia opened her mouth and began to sing, elemental magic dancing around her whole body. He'd been hoping to talk to her more about the dreams, to explain . . . Had she said *she'd* be entering a trance too? But the notes drifted through Skandar's mind, the magic taking its sleepiest forms around them—embers extinguishing, the gentle patter of rain, a warm breeze blowing in his face, the soothing smell of lavender—and he found himself getting drowsy, his mind clearing of all thoughts—except one that lingered a little longer than the others: *You need to wake me if it gets really bad*, he tried to say. *You need to wake me if I start shouting out.* But then even that thought was gone and Skandar and Scoundrel were fast asleep and dreaming.

Skandar looked out through eyes that were not his own. He was searching for someone, and he felt both excited and terrified. Skandar tried to pull himself from the body that didn't belong to him—tried to see the face—but as soon as he thought it, he was sent into another, sitting cross-legged on the ground. The stranger's hands were pulling up grass and throwing it into the wind, watching it catch and fly out over a cliff.

Who are you? *Skandar thought it so hard his chest began to ache.* I want to see you.

Suddenly he was sitting next to the cross-legged person, but disappointment crashed over him as the face of the stranger blurred and there was no chance he could make out any features. Skandar's chest started to sear with pain—he'd usually wake up at this point, but the sleepsong was giving him more time. He tried something different. He reached for the stranger's hand, noticing a birthmark on one knuckle, and although there was no physical contact, the outline started to become clearer. The face of a boy appeared. A boy with blond hair, startlingly gray eyes, and constellations of freckles across his white cheeks. A boy about the age of an Eyrie Hatchling.

There was a strong tug, and Skandar's own bond shone from his chest. He knew that Scoundrel was calling him to switch places, about to show him the boy's destined unicorn.

Skandar traveled along the bond and became the creature. This wild unicorn did not feel like the others he'd dreamed himself into. There was no misery or pain. There was confusion. There was anger. There was bloodlust, for sure. But there was also something completely impossible . . . a tiny pinprick of joy. Something was making this wild unicorn happier than the others. Something was making its immortal life worth living.

Then pain filled Skandar's head. He was struggling to breathe, and he knew he was way beyond when he'd usually wake himself up. But he was not waking, he was drowning. And he was trapped in the wild unicorn's body, its mind. The pain was too much to bear, too much even for him to cry out. He was going to die here. He had pushed it too far.

Kenna, *he thought desperately.* I can't leave her again. I can't leave her for good.

As his sister's face burst into his mind, Skandar found he was himself again.

He was looking at the wild unicorn ahead of him.

And in the last flash of the dream he knew for sure. It was Goshawk's Fury.

Skandar woke up to a world of pain. He was vaguely aware of lots of people inside the stable talking to him all at once—saying the earplugs had failed, that they'd slept too, that they were so sorry they hadn't woken him. But Skandar only had one thing on his mind. He reached for the sketchbook by Scoundrel's leg, and started to draw everything he could remember of the blond boy with the flint-gray eyes.

Bobby, Flo, and Mitchell were now kneeling by him, supporting his weight as he added freckles and the birthmark on the boy's hand. Skandar wiped something from his nose—blood?—but he didn't stop until he'd finished the drawing.

Finally he dropped the pencil and stared down at the sketch, exhausted.

The cross-legged boy from the dream stared out from the paper.

"Goshawk's destined rider," Skandar croaked to his unicorn. "We did it."

And then Scoundrel started to shriek in distress as Skandar lost consciousness, the darkness claiming him.

KENNA

Doubt

KENNA SMITH WAS BEGINNING TO DOUBT.

Doubt was posters of Kenna's face plastered on tree trunks. It was Albert spotting sentinels hunting her on the edge of the zone, and no longer feeling safe among friends.

Doubt was confusion. Confusion about her place among the Wanderers. Confusion about who she was becoming. Confusion about the future she wanted.

Doubt was the fury of Goshawk in her mind. It was the battle to balance her wild power with the Island's peaceful song, and dreading the next mutation, and the next.

Doubt was disappointment. Disappointment every morning to find that Skandar had not arrived in the night. Disappointment every afternoon that he had not arrived in the

morning. Disappointment every evening as another day ended
without her brother—the one person who knew Kenna well
enough to remind her who she was supposed to be.

The evening before the Wanderers moved on to the
fire zone, Kenna and Albert sat with their feet dangling in
one of the cave's steaming rock pools. The elemental season
had changed from earth to fire some time ago, but Elora
had worried about moving Kenna with so many sentinels
searching for her.

Then finally, when the patrolling Wanderers spotted
sentinels flooding the water and air zones instead, they
packed up their belongings. They would travel at night to
avoid anyone who might be looking for the missing eggs or
the girl with the wild unicorn. It didn't help Kenna's anxiety
about leaving the place she'd called home for the last couple
of months or so.

"What if someone sees me on the way to the fire zone?
Sees Gos?" Kenna worried.

Albert fiddled with the end of his blond ponytail—a
habit Kenna had noticed whenever he was feeling uneasy.
"It'll be fine," he said, trying to reassure her. "The sentinels
have rotated their search, and we're going in the dead of
night. Anyway, we always stick to remote paths that the rest
of the Island has long forgotten."

"It isn't fair." Kenna sighed, jerking her foot so it splashed
up some of the warm water. "I haven't done anything! The
Island is treating me like a criminal. Though I don't know

why I'm surprised—the Eyrie practically treated *you* like one, too, when they kicked you out."

Albert shrugged. "They treat all nomads that way. I didn't fit in with what they thought a Chaos rider should be. And I suppose they were right. Mine and Eagle's fire magic wasn't very well controlled. And I had a lot of problems with my balance!"

"Then they should have taught you, like the Wanderers have," Kenna fumed. "Not smashed your pin into a thousand pieces."

Albert grinned at her exaggeration. "Just the four pieces, Kenn."

Kenna froze.

Albert looked horrified with himself. "I didn't mean to call you that. I'm sorry. I—I know that's what your brother calls you."

Kenna took a deep breath. "You know what? It's fine. It isn't like Skandar has even bothered to come back to get me, is it? It's nice to hear my nickname, actually."

Albert's cheeks turned the same red as his mutated knuckles. "I'm sure he'll come soon."

"I'm not," Kenna said vehemently. "I think he's perfectly happy in his precious Eyrie, pretending his problematic sister doesn't exist." Anger rose so quickly in her throat—so far beyond the depth of her own emotion—that she almost choked. *Goshawk*, she realized. The bond filled with their combined rage. Her vision blurred with the force of it, and for a moment her whole world was in shadow. Then she blinked—and it was over.

If Albert noticed, he didn't say anything, and instead moved the conversation on to music they'd both liked growing up on the Mainland. He offered her a square of the chocolate that his parents sent him religiously every month. He said he couldn't live without it. Quite a few of the Mainlander Wanderers still communicated with their families via communal post trees back in Fourpoint—unlike Kenna, most of them were not being hunted by the authorities.

But she never understood why Albert wanted to talk about the Mainland with her, why he hung on to it the way he did. Perhaps he missed it? He talked about his older brother a lot—talked about the trips they'd been on before Albert had left; how he was training to be a vet; how they'd watched the Chaos Cup together on TV. But Kenna was doing her best to forget it all. She wasn't sure what her future looked like, but she knew for certain it wasn't back there—where she'd only been able to see unicorns on a screen.

So she tuned Albert out, nodding in the right places without really listening. Instead, she thought about something else he'd said and let doubt spread through her like a sickness.

I didn't fit in with what they thought a Chaos rider should be.

If kind, thoughtful, fire-allied Albert had been rejected by the Island, how was Kenna ever going to belong?

CHAPTER ELEVEN

Fairfax Flees

SKANDAR WOKE TO THE SOUND OF BOBBY telling him he was an idiot.

"I hate to say I told you so— Wait, actually, I don't. I *told* you this would happen. And did you listen? Of course not. Fatal dreams were *no concern* for the *invincible* Skandar Smith, until—oh yeah. You ALMOST DIED!"

Skandar blinked into bright sunlight.

Bobby stopped mid-rant. "Oh. You're awake." She peered at him, face softening. "You're in the healer treehouse—you've been unconscious all night. Are you . . . okay?"

Memories started flooding back. The dream. The blond boy. Goshawk.

"My sketchbook"—Skandar looked wildly around,

hammock swinging—"where is it? I drew Goshawk's destined rider! Where—"

"Calm down. We told the instructors you'd had some kind of spirit wielder accident, and they all seemed to believe that—apart from Agatha, who is proper mad at you, by the way. Then we went straight to Council Square last night and refused to leave until Nina saw us. Mitchell put the drawing into the Commodore's hand himself."

"He did?" Relief flooded Skandar's painful body.

"Of course." Bobby shrugged.

"Did Nina say anything?" Skandar asked hungrily.

"Not yet." Bobby rubbed her tired eyes. "We thought we'd lost you for a minute there, spirit boy."

He swallowed, propping himself up on an elbow. "I can't believe I actually managed to draw the boy's face. It worked!"

Bobby had a sad smile on her face. "You're not always the sharpest needle on the cactus, Skandar, but you really do love your sister, don't you? I wish I'd—" She broke off, clearing her throat.

"What?" Skandar frowned.

"The last time I saw my sister, do you know what I said to her? 'Don't you dare follow me, Isa. Not out of this room. Not out of the door. Especially not to the Island.' *That* was how I left. And the worst thing is, I can't even remember what we were fighting about." Bobby swallowed. "It's part of the reason why I want the missing eggs back in the Hatchery so badly. I have to do better. Isa is destined for one of those unicorns. I *know* she is."

Skandar reached for Bobby's hand and squeezed it. "Nina *will* find them. She's an air wielder like you."

"And what if she doesn't?" Bobby said seriously. "You have to talk to Kenna about the eggs when you see her on Christmas Day."

Skandar bristled. "I've asked her before, remember? She doesn't know anything."

"Look, I'm a big fan of the badass that is Kenna Smith, but, Skandar, have you ever even *considered* that she might be lying?"

"She's not," Skandar insisted. "She wouldn't lie to me."

Bobby sighed. "If you say so, spirit boy." Then she changed the subject. "You know, you looked so ill when the healers brought you up here, I was worried you might not make it to the den dances. How rubbish would that have been?"

"Oh yeah," Skandar said sarcastically. "That would have been terrible."

The four den dances happened around the winter solstice: two before and two after. Skandar had heard that they lasted all night, with different element-themed food and entertainment arriving throughout the evening to keep the revelers going—there was even a hearty breakfast for those who managed not to fall asleep before dawn. Since the den dances sounded much better than the disastrous disco he'd gone to at school, Skandar might have been excited—if he wasn't so worried about what the dances might do to his friendship with Flo. She'd been slightly more friendly since he'd almost died during the Mender dream, but they still weren't back to normal. And she became more distant again with the arrival of the first dance—the Furnace Dance.

After dinner that evening, the atmosphere inside the treehouse was about as frosty as the weather outside it, and with Bobby upstairs getting ready, the rest of the quartet lapsed into a heavy silence. Flo was sewing a patch on her jacket to cover a scorch from the Fire Trial. Mitchell was doing some last-minute reading on the history of the den dances. Skandar scratched away in his sketch pad.

After Flo announced abruptly that she was going to bed—three hours earlier than usual—Skandar turned to Mitchell. "I can't stand this!"

"What do you mean?" Mitchell asked. "I'm having a perfectly lovely evening—very peaceful so far, I think I'm fully prepared for the Furnace Dance now. Ask me anything." He brandished his book at Skandar, who grimaced. "You're *not* having a lovely evening, then?" Mitchell asked, more gently.

"It's Flo. She's still not . . . we're still not like we were before."

"Look," Mitchell said kindly, "have you talked to her?"

"I don't know how!" Skandar said, throwing his hands over his face. "What should I say?"

"She's your friend," Mitchell said. "You just need to explain that you're sorry you chose the Grins over her. Have you even *said* sorry?"

"I—I've tried, but it's . . . scary." A couple of times Skandar had started to apologize, wanting desperately to make things right, but Flo always found somewhere else to be or someone else to talk to. It made Skandar even more afraid to speak up. What if he lost Flo? He didn't know what he'd do if she didn't want to be his friend anymore.

"It is scary," Mitchell admitted. "But you're two of the bravest, kindest people I know. You can work it out."

Nerves jangled in Skandar's stomach. "But what if I say sorry and it's not enough?"

"Then you'll have to think bigger." Mitchell shrugged. "Meanwhile you can distract yourself by polishing my shoes for tonight."

"Oh great, thanks!"

"You're welcome."

It was easy to get swept up in it all. An hour later, Mitchell was dressed and fretting, convinced that Jamie was going to be wearing something much cooler than him. When Bobby emerged, dressed in a red jumpsuit, Mitchell was still asking Skandar—"But is my shirt *too* red, though?" Luckily, there was no time for him to dash back up the ladder to change again, because the blacksmith marched through the treehouse door at that exact moment.

"You look very dashing," Mitchell blurted at Jamie, who was dressed in a dark red suit—red trousers and an open red blazer—with a casual white T-shirt underneath.

Bobby raised both eyebrows. "Not bad, blacksmith bard."

But Jamie didn't seem to notice. He strode over to Mitchell with an easy smile, took his arm, and led him out into the cold night. Neither of them looked back. Bobby skipped after them to meet the fire wielder who'd asked her to the dance.

Now alone, Skandar began to pace. He didn't even want to go to the stupid Well Dance tomorrow night! He stopped abruptly. Wait. *Did* he have to go? Could he take Amber into the den and then *leave*? Nobody could stop him from doing that, right? Then he could come back and spend the evening with Flo instead! *Think bigger*, Mitchell had told him.

Brain whirring with the beginnings of an idea, Skandar went out in search of some water wielders who didn't mind being late to their dance.

Twenty-four hours later, Skandar's plan was in place and he was waiting for Bobby. Thank the five elements *she* would be heading into the Well Dance with him. He tugged nervously at his new blue shirt as he sat on one of the beanbags. He wasn't used to buying clothes, and he'd sort of panicked—it had pearls for buttons.

"You should brush your hair more often." Bobby made him jump as she sprang off the bottom rung of the tree trunk. "You look . . . all right."

"Er, thanks?" Skandar said, unsure whether this was a compliment. "You look nice too." And he meant it.

Bobby was wearing a blue dress with long sleeves and a wide white collar. She did a spin, and the skirt caught the air. "Just so you know, dancing is how I get through parties. I take it extremely seriously."

"Get through?"

"I like parties. But sometimes all the people bring on my panic attacks. Dancing helps."

There was a knock at the door.

"That'll be Hayden," Bobby said. She didn't sound particularly excited about going to the dance with this Rookie.

"Umm, it might actually be—"

Amber Fairfax was standing in the doorway. She was wearing one of the sparkliest dresses that Skandar had ever seen; it was short and aquamarine, with every edge frosted in tiny diamonds. She had her chestnut hair up in a high ponytail, fixed with yet another band of sparkles that brought out the star mutation crackling on her forehead.

A strange look passed over Amber's face as Bobby answered the door, but it quickly turned to a sneer when she was greeted with: "Are you trying to blind people with that outfit, Fairfax?"

"Your dress is *distressingly* old-fashioned, Bruna."

"Hello!" It was Hayden. The Rookie had just arrived on the treehouse platform, completely unaware that he was walking into a war zone.

"Who are you?" Amber asked rudely, her upturned nose in the air.

"This is *Hayden*," Bobby said slowly, as though Amber was a toddler. "He's taking me to the dance. Come on, Hayden. Let's go."

"We're all going the same way, aren't we?" Hayden piped up, though his smile had dimmed slightly at the exchange between the Fledglings.

Bobby sighed dramatically.

Amber kicked the treehouse door.

Skandar was very relieved he was going to leave the dance almost as soon as it began.

Hayden led the three Fledglings across swinging bridges and down ladders. He had brown, tightly curled hair and was much taller than Skandar, with veins that flowed like rivers—they shone bright blue along his pale white skin.

Hayden jumped to the forest floor, and Bobby batted him away as he tried to help her down.

"Not a good start, Hayden. Keep your hands to yourself."

Blushingly returning his hands to his pockets, Hayden led them onward, deep into the water quadrant of the Eyrie. Skandar was very glad someone knew where they were going.

"What's the name of Bobby's unicorn?" Hayden asked when the girls had fallen behind to hurl insults at each other.

"Falcon's Wrath."

"That's it! Air unicorns with bird names often do well, you know? Just like water unicorns with river names—mine's Oxbow's Revenge."

"Interesting," Skandar said vaguely. He'd heard theories like that on the Mainland, too.

"Do you think you could put in a good word for me?" Hayden's eyes shone hopefully.

Skandar frowned. "I mean, she's not exactly friendly. She's very well groomed, sure, but last time I tried to touch her nose, she practically chomped my whole hand off."

"*Bobby* did?"

"No, what? Falcon's Wrath."

Hayden laughed loudly. "I don't want you to put in a good word with a *unicorn*. I heard a rumor Bobby's trying to go to all the den dances, which is totally cool, but I was hoping she might actually give me a chance."

"Oh, yeah, I guess I can do that," Skandar blundered. This was excruciating.

"Thanks, man. Appreciate it."

Skandar was still trying not to imagine what Bobby would do to him if he tried to play matchmaker, when he noticed a crowd up ahead. He spotted Kobi—who was wearing a blue bow tie and awkwardly looking down at his shoes—along with a couple of the other water-allied Fledglings: Niamh, adjusting a crystal necklace that set off the ice spikes at her ears; and Mariam, wearing a blue glittery headscarf.

On reaching them, Skandar realized that the crowd was standing round a large pond. They'd come past quite a few ponds on their way through the water quadrant, but this one was among the largest. A frog croaked loudly from a giant lily pad.

Rickesh stood at the water's edge—metal feather displayed prominently on his blue jacket, Prim's arm hooked through his. Something about seeing the squadron leader and flight lieutenant made Skandar feel calmer.

"You won't get wet," Rickesh was explaining to the non-water wielders in the crowd, running a hand through his wave of hair with a flourish. "Anyone for a demonstration?"

"Why do you *always* have to be the center of attention?" Prim teased. "You should have been an air wielder."

Rickesh shrugged theatrically, then stepped off the edge of the pond. He heard some of the non-water wielders gasp. But there wasn't even a splash. Instead, he rose up triumphantly on a tree stump—fist in the air. Along with the first smaller stump, several more rose out of the murky water, forming steps up to a thicker, hollow stump right in the center of the pond.

"Don't try that if you're not a water wielder, folks!"

Rickesh winked very obviously at Skandar. "Unless you fancy a swim." Then he offered his hand to Prim, and they danced nimbly up the half-submerged steps before disappearing inside the central stump.

"Let's partayyyy, Peregrines!" Rickesh's voice echoed against the wood as the hollow stump disappeared again under the surface of the pond.

Hayden went next, stepping off the edge of the pond to trigger the appearance of the den's entrance. He held out a hand to Bobby—who didn't take it.

"Wait!" Amber called, her voice a command. "Skandar won't be able to do that—we need to climb in with you!"

Skandar and Amber followed Hayden and Bobby over the wobbling stumps, and they just about managed to squeeze into the hollow trunk together.

"Cozy," Amber said with a smirk, as Bobby tried to elbow her in the side.

"Going down!" Hayden yelled. And—like with the entrance to the spirit den—Skandar gripped the handles inside the trunk as they whooshed downward.

The inside of the Well sparkled beyond a waterfall curtain. Skandar followed Amber through a gap in the streaming water and couldn't help but stop and stare at everything. An impressive unicorn ice sculpture dominated the center of the den, rearing on its back legs and baring its teeth. Its rider had their Hatchery palm facing outward, fingers curled round a shining stone, while a giant wave swept around them both. The walls glittered with ice crystals, like the ones on Kobi's eyelashes. And where they weren't glittering, Skandar could see colorful fish and odd-looking aquatic creatures swimming past, oblivious to the riders inside. He wondered whether this was where Instructor O'Sullivan's fish ended up once she'd nursed them back to health.

Elsewhere, den dance guests used rods to hook floating snacks out of miniature wells lit up in different shades of blue. It reminded Skandar of hooking plastic ducks for prizes with Kenna at Deal Carnival years before. He was particularly interested in taking a turn at the well offering up enormous slices of chocolate cake, although he'd definitely follow that with the giant frozen Popsicles hanging from the ceiling. Skandar suddenly felt a pang of guilt. How could he be here enjoying a party? His sister was hiding out deep in the zones, unable to return to the Eyrie.

Bobby and Hayden were queuing for ice skates, and Amber watched intently as Bobby glided effortlessly onto the ice rink. It was the shape of a blue droplet, glowing brighter as more people joined the water wielders' version of a dance floor. Amber snorted as Hayden clung to the edge, trying to wave at Bobby, who was already doing spins, the skirt of her blue dress fanning out around her. A group of bards skated right by her, singing an upbeat melody.

Rickesh approached, half dancing to the music. "Fen's in position. I'll take you up."

"Right," Skandar said, nerves filling his stomach. "Amber?"

"You know you don't have to stay by me the whole time, right? It's *super* cute, but—"

"I'm leaving," Skandar said, cutting her off. "I wanted to get you in here, but I have to go."

Amber cocked her head. "Why are you so random, Skandar Smith?" Then she flicked her hair and waved him off like an irritating gnat.

Skandar followed Rickesh, passing hot spring pools with steam rising so thickly that the waterfall curtain disappeared from view.

"May I speak with you a moment?" A woman in a cerulean mask appeared at Skandar's shoulder, blocking his exit. Without waiting for an answer, she guided him away from Rickesh and toward one of the glittering walls.

The steam cleared as they faced each other, and one glance at the woman's hand told Skandar exactly who this was. The Commodore's mood ring glowed bright blue on her thumb.

"Commodore Kazama?" Skandar whispered.

"Hello, Skandar. I hope I didn't startle you—the mask helps me keep a low profile."

"How did you get in on your own?" he spluttered. "You're not a water wielder."

"Ahh, but I am the Commodore," Nina said, eyes dancing mischievously. "And what's the point of being in charge of the Island if I don't get to go to all its parties?" She lowered her voice. "I've shared your drawing of that boy with the Island and Mainland authorities. And Rex even allowed me entry to the Stronghold to check the names of the lost spirit wielders. Though I didn't tell him *why*, of course.

"Unfortunately, none of the lost spirit wielders on the Island matched your drawing, so we think he's most likely a Mainlander. The police started their investigations this morning—some of my advisers were already liaising secretly with them."

"About searching for the missing eggs?" Skandar guessed.

"Agatha told me you saw the Weaver at the Fire Trial, but I think there's a strong possibility she's on the Mainland." A troubled look flashed in Nina's eyes. Skandar's breath hitched at the thought of wild unicorn foals hatching there, maybe even near Dad. Nina noticed. "Don't you worry about that. Finding Goshawk's rider should be a lot easier. We have a fairly short list of possible names from the Stronghold records, and your drawing is excellent—I don't think it'll be long."

"Really?" Skandar's heart burst with hope. "You really think they'll find him?"

"I think it's very likely," Nina said, smiling. "Then we'll talk about what comes next, all right?"

"Skandar, we've got to go!" Rickesh called from over by the waterfall.

"You're leaving? A party?" Nina sounded appalled. "But why?"

Skandar grinned. "Something more important came up—well, some*one* actually."

"Well, then. Off you go." The Commodore melted back into the crowd.

Once Rickesh had got Skandar out of the Well and wished him luck, Skandar sprinted along the swinging walkways back to his own treehouse.

Flo was nestled in a beanbag by the fire, balancing a book in one hand and a stack of Custard Creams in the other. She choked on her cookie in shock when she saw him. "Skar! What are you doing back here?"

"Umm . . ." Skandar's voice was half an octave higher than usual. "I came to see you."

"But what about the den dance?" Flo asked, clearly confused.

"I was wondering if you wanted to go for a walk."

"A walk? But it's freezing outside."

"Please," Skandar croaked. "I want to talk to you."

But once they were on their way, Skandar found it hard to say anything to Flo at all. His heart was hammering, and he could barely look at her as he led her back the way he'd just come. Their breaths clouded the chilly December air.

As they reached the denser trees of the water quadrant, Flo spoke up. "Skandar, this is getting silly now."

"I promise we're almost there. Can you shut your eyes?"

Her deep brown forehead crinkled in a frown, but she did as he asked. Skandar couldn't help but take that as a good sign. They walked a few more unsteady steps, and then Skandar snapped a stick *very* loudly with his foot, to signal they'd arrived.

"Okay, you can open your eyes now."

Flo blinked in the lantern light. And then her eyes widened in wonder. "Skar, it's snowing! How is it *snowing*? Did you do this?"

He shrugged—still nervous, hands deep in his jacket pockets. He'd brought Flo to a tiny clearing within the water quadrant, ringed by some of the tallest pine trees in the Eyrie. It was open to the sky—perfect for Skandar's idea. Flo had been so excited when it'd snowed in their first year, since it was very rare on the Island. And so—with Rickesh's and Fen's help and a bit of elemental magic— he'd filled the tiny clearing up with snow and asked if Fen could conjure some snow clouds, just for tonight, before she headed to the Well.

Skandar stared at the ground, not brave enough to look at her, and blurted, "I'm so sorry. I don't know why I didn't just say no to the Grins in the first place. You're my best friend. I always want to stay in and eat snacks with you, but I'm a complete idiot and—" Finally, he raised his head.

And a snowball hit him square in the face.

Flo was grinning from across the clearing, eyes full of joy and mischief. "You *are* an idiot." Skandar dodged another snowball, though it still hit his shoulder.

"I just wish you'd talked to me about it first." Flo threw a third snowball, and this time Skandar ducked and it clanged off the armored trunk behind him. "But I forgive you, Skar." This time she crunched toward him through the freshly fallen snow.

They sat down next to each other, and made patterns with their heavy black boots until Flo started to speak. "I think the reason I was so upset was because I'm always the one everybody assumes will be fine, the one who won't make a fuss. Growing up, if there was a limited number of people to pick for a team or invite to a party, I was always the one who didn't make the cut. Not because people didn't like me, but because they didn't like me *enough*. And they knew I wouldn't make drama about it, and I'd still be friendly to them the next time I saw them—just the same as before. Everybody wins, right?"

Flo took a deep breath. "When I was younger, my actual *friends* would tell me about fun stuff they'd done together on the weekend without me, and I'd think, *Don't you realize I have feelings too, even if they aren't as loud as yours?* But when I got to the Eyrie and met you, all that changed. I felt like I belonged with our quartet."

"You do!" Skandar protested.

She continued. "Then Bobby wanted to go to all the dances, and Mitchell was planning on asking Jamie, and you—you just forgot about our plans like they didn't mean anything, Skar, and I was the one left out. Just like the old days, the days I thought were over. I convinced myself that you'd all got sick of me and you'd found people you wanted to be friends with more. I thought, *Of course I like Skandar more than he likes me. Of course he's more important to me than I am to him. Why would he even remember our plans?* I felt so stupid for forgetting that I'm Flo, the one people don't think they're hurting because I never seem to mind. But I did mind, Skar. I minded a lot."

"Flo, I'm so sorry—and I'm so sorry people treated you that way," Skandar said quietly.

He couldn't imagine *ever* forgetting about Flo—even for a moment. She was the first person he looked for when he stepped into the treehouse. The first person he looked forward to seeing in the morning. The first person he wanted to tell, well, anything.

"That wasn't what was going on with me at all," Skandar continued. "I wanted more than anything to stay at the treehouse with you and *not* go to that dance—I just got all mixed up and did what everyone else expected instead of what *I* really wanted. Instead of the *right* thing. And I'm so sorry it took me so long to say sorry properly. I was scared you'd never forgive me. That you wouldn't want to be my friend anymore."

Flo smiled at him then, though the corners of her mouth still seemed a little sad. "I'll always be here for you, Skar. Nothing will ever change that. Trust me."

"I do, Flo. I really do."

Then she tipped her face up to watch the falling flakes of snow, their tiny shadows dancing against the armored trunks. "And, just for the record, this was a pretty good apology."

Midway through their making snow angels, shouts echoed through the Eyrie.

"Did you hear that?"

Flo sat up, snow caught up in her hair. "Do you think something's happened?"

At more shouting, they both stood—just in time to see Lightning's Mistake gallop by, flanked by silver-masked sentinels.

"Was Nina at the Well Dance?" Flo asked, frowning.

"Oh yeah, I forgot to tell you . . ." Skandar trailed off. Someone had just dropped to the ground by a nearby tree, sobbing.

"Is that—"

"Amber?" Skandar was two steps ahead of Flo already, rushing to the air wielder's side. "What's happened?"

Amber's freckled cheeks were extremely pale when she finally answered, not looking at Skandar. "My father is out. He's out of prison."

Shock vibrated through him. "Simon Fairfax? You mean— What? How?"

"The Weaver broke him out—him, Joby Worsham, and Elise Hissington. Three of her spirit wielder followers. Some of the sentinels at the prison turned—they helped her."

"Did anyone see the Weaver? Did they follow her? Find the eggs?" Skandar asked. His breaths were shallow, panicked. *Sentinels* had helped Erika? It suddenly felt like his mother was everywhere, gaining on them all.

Amber shook her head. "Nobody saw anything until it was too late. The three prisoners were all in high-security cells. The Justice Representative was in his office but didn't hear anything." Then Amber turned to face Skandar fully, looking furious and devastated at the same time. "Why does my father always have to ruin EVERYTHING?" she yelled.

"I actually went to *visit* him in prison." She laughed harshly. "I didn't tell my mother—she doesn't even let me mention him. But I wanted to meet this man, who I'm naturally supposed to love or whatever. I suppose I wanted to try to understand him, or myself, or . . ."

"And did you?" Skandar asked gently.

"No," Amber scoffed. "He was just this sad man sitting in a cell. I felt sorry for him, I guess. But he's a stranger. That's what people with ordinary parents don't understand. I felt all this pressure to feel something for this guy—but I didn't. Although, he promised me he'd left all the Weaver stuff behind. That when he got out of prison, he'd come to apologize to my mother and maybe we could get to know each other properly. He said we could go and get something to eat together one day. . . . Obviously he lied. Obviously."

"I'm so sorry, Amber," Skandar said sincerely. Erika Everhart's painted face flashed into his mind. Although he couldn't tell Amber why, he knew exactly what it felt like to be disappointed by a parent. By someone who should have loved you, and instead made you feel like you meant nothing to them.

"Forking thunderstorms, I hate being a Fairfax!" Amber tore at the earth with her sparkly blue fingernails. "Did you know that the Fairfaxes actually used to live next to the Everharts?"

"Really?" Skandar said, trying not to give anything away. Only his quartet and Agatha knew he and Kenna were Everharts, as well as Smiths.

Amber choked out a laugh. "My family living next door to the Weaver's. Super-cozy spirit wielders together. And the treehouses are still there for everyone to see."

Skandar's mind was spinning. He'd never thought about the Everhart treehouse. Never imagined that Agatha and Erika's family home might still be standing.

"And now," Amber raged on, "just when I was starting to have friends in the Peregrine Society—when people were starting to forget my connection to my dad and the Weaver—*everyone* is going to be talking about Simon Fairfax's escape. And they're going to stare at me, and, worst of all, some of them might even feel *sorry* for me."

"The Grins won't be like that," Skandar tried to reassure her.

"I guess." Amber sniffed. "And my quartet already hate me."

"You can always come and hang out at our treehouse."

"Of course you can," Flo said kindly.

Amber snorted. "I'm sure Bruna would *love* that. And Henderson—I was awful to him when we were younger."

"They'll come round. They're pretty accepting of outsiders," Skandar said, smiling crookedly at Amber. "And I think Bobby actually enjoys arguing with you. It would provide her with endless entertainment."

Amber hiccupped. "Really?" Then she frowned. "Why are you always so nice to me, Skandar?"

"We have more in common than you think."

There was a beat of silence.

"Not our dress sense, I hope." Amber's eyes raked over Skandar's blue shirt. "Those pearl buttons are vile."

"They really are," Flo agreed.

And all three of them burst out laughing.

CHAPTER TWELVE

Christmas Chaos

AT DAWN ON CHRISTMAS MORNING, SKAN-
dar rode alone into the fire zone. He blew the eagle-
shaped whistle, and its cry rang out along the fault line
as the rocky terrain turned to desert sand beneath Scoundrel's hooves. Skandar felt cheerful. Not even the prison
breakout could dampen his high spirits. It was Christmas
Day, and he was finally going to see his sister again! He
was going to tell her about his plan for the bond exchange,
and couldn't wait to see her face when he told her Nina
had basically promised that Kenna could come back
to the Eyrie if he succeeded. There was just one thing
bothering him—that pinprick of joy he'd felt in Goshawk
during the Mender dream. Whenever he remembered it,

the tiniest drop of doubt entered Skandar's mind. What if Goshawk didn't want her own destined rider anymore? What if she wanted Kenna instead? And what if Kenna felt the same?

No. He couldn't think about that. The den dances were over, and things between him and Flo were back to normal—when they'd gone to breakfast together the previous morning, she'd even made him promise to wear his armor. "Just in case, Skar, please." Okay, so the Weaver had broken her key allies out of prison, and she still had an entire Hatchery's worth of eggs hidden somewhere, but the whole Island—and even the Mainland—was now looking for her. Surely the eggs would be found soon?

"Skandar!"

Eagle's Dawn galloped toward them, sand flying up from her hooves. Scoundrel fell into step beside the white unicorn, Albert directing them off the fault line.

"Kenna was hoping you'd come today! I've been keeping a lookout," he said, grinning as Skandar removed his helmet. "Thought it'd be better that it was someone you recognized. Lots of sentinels out here recently."

"Searching for the eggs?" Skandar guessed.

Albert hesitated. "Yes . . . and your sister. Especially with that prison breakout last week."

"Is Kenna all right?" Skandar asked anxiously.

"She's settled in well," Albert said, pulling on Eagle's rein to turn in the opposite direction. Scoundrel shrieked impatiently as he followed. "Although . . ." Albert hesitated.

"What?"

"Kenna puts on a brave face, is all I'm saying. She seems fine when she's riding Goshawk or helping out with chores or learning about the Island. But sometimes, when she doesn't think anyone's watching, it seems like there's a lot going on in her head. Anyway, she'll be really happy now. She's been desperate to see you ever since you left."

As Albert counted Joshua trees under his breath, Skandar basked in how magical the zones were. It was hard to wonder at them when he was fighting for his place at the Eyrie during the trials. But right now, it felt deliciously impossible that just a couple of days ago he'd been in the snow with Flo and now he was in a hot, dry desert. Elemental magic really was very cool.

"It's through those two there," Albert announced, and the unicorns passed between the trees, their branches shaking green fists at the pink morning sky.

Skandar's jaw dropped. A small lake glistened ahead of them, nestled between the sand dunes. It was surrounded by greenery—lush palm trees, spiky cacti, and emerald bushes adorned with colorful desert flowers. Unicorns—bonded and wild—had their horns bowed and were drinking from the sparkling blue water. He spotted Goshawk's palomino coat among them.

Albert saw the amazement pass over Skandar's face. "It's a desert oasis. It's fertile because of the fresh water. I'm pretty sure I learned about them in Geography lessons back on the Mainland."

Skandar laughed. "I'd completely forgotten about *Geography* lessons!" It was strange how little he thought about his life back on the Mainland. Before it became all about Scoundrel's Luck and his quartet and being a spirit wielder.

"This is the biggest oasis in the whole fire zone desert," Albert explained. "But it's basically impossible to find unless you've got a guide. Come on, I'll take you to Kenna."

Skandar dismounted—chain mail clinking—and Scoundrel trotted down to the watering hole to drink with the others.

Like the riders in the Eyrie, the Wanderers slept in hammocks at their fire zone home. Under the dense leaves of the palms, the sleepers were protected from most weather—the biggest danger was probably falling coconuts.

"Kenna's hammock is over there." Albert pointed. "I'll see you later. Oh, and merry Christmas by the way!" He held something out to Skandar.

"Is that a *Mainland* chocolate bar?"

"Just a little something." Albert shrugged. "I thought it might remind you of home."

"Albert, I don't have anything for you!" Skandar panicked; his backpack was full of presents for Kenna, but no one else.

"You being here will make Kenna happy." Albert smiled. "That's enough for me."

Skandar made his way through the palms, and spotted his sister. He would have recognized Kenna's sleeping form anywhere. It made him want to laugh and cry at the same time. Things were so different now, it was disorienting. Sometimes, he still felt like the scared little boy nobody had expected to become a unicorn rider. And other days, he could scarcely remember being that Skandar at all.

Kenna stirred in her hammock. "Skar?" she said sleepily, propping herself up on one elbow. "Is that really you?"

"Hey, Kenn! Happy Christmas!"

Kenna still looked groggy as she sat upright on the hammock's edge. "You came, then," she said. "Finally."

Skandar felt a swoop of guilt in his stomach. "I wanted to come earlier, but Agatha kept saying I might put you at risk. And I've had the Fire Trial, and the den dances—"

"Dances?" Kenna said, her eyes sharpening. "Oh, I wouldn't have wanted to get in the way of you going to a *dance*." Her voice dripped with sarcasm. "You abandoned me with the Wanderers—a bunch of complete *strangers*—and then left me alone with them for months. I haven't seen you since September!"

"Don't you like it with the Wanderers? Albert said you were settling in."

Kenna stood up abruptly, hands on hips. "That's not really the point—is it, Skandar?"

Hearing his full name was like an iron bar across the chest. She hardly *ever* used his full name.

Kenna took a deep breath, one hand gripping the nearest palm tree. "Look, I'm really happy to see you, I am. I just thought you'd come back for me much sooner than this. You promised you'd come after the Fire Trial, and I've really missed you, Skar. I've liked living with the Wanderers, but I'm supposed to be training in the Eyrie. Everyone here has either rejected that way of life or *been* rejected from it. But I haven't even had the chance to try yet. It's not how I wanted things to go."

"I'm sorry," Skandar murmured. "I should have just ignored Agatha. I should have come sooner."

"So when are we leaving? Now?" Kenna asked hopefully.

"We can't go back to the Eyrie yet, Kenn." Her face crumpled, and Skandar felt like a piece of his heart was breaking off. He hurried on. "But I do have a plan. I want to tell you all about it—hopefully it won't be long until everything's sorted out."

Kenna roughly wiped away the tears on her cheeks. "I guess the prison break didn't help. I shouldn't have got my hopes up just because . . ." Then much more brightly—*too* brightly—she added, "I'm sorry, I shouldn't take it out on you. I know you're trying your best. But sometimes Goshawk gets in my head, and—" Kenna stopped herself.

"What d'you mean?" Skandar asked, uneasy. "Are you already sharing emotions?"

Kenna shrugged. "Kind of. Well, not the good ones. But some of the older riders here said it's really advanced to be sharing emotions with my unicorn already." She changed the subject sharply. "It's Christmas. Let's do Christmas. Did you bring presents?"

Skandar struggled to smile. From his Mender dreams he knew what it was like to share a wild unicorn's emotions—did his sister have to deal with that all the time?

Kenna chuckled as Skandar opened up his bag.

"I see Albert already got to you," she said. "Honestly, that boy and chocolate—it's a sickness."

Kenna loved her presents without distinction or exception. She treated the leather-bound book on Island history with just the same excitement as the round jousting shield Skandar had bought from Battle Bargains. The Smith family hadn't always had the money for presents, so it was the giving—not the present itself—that counted. Unwrapping something from a person who loved you, and knowing that—if they could—that person would have given you the world.

For Skandar's present, Kenna—with help from a Wanderer called Otto—had carved a piece of black onyx into the shape of a unicorn's head. She'd even painted a white stripe down the front to show that it was Scoundrel.

"It feels a bit weird doing this without Dad, doesn't it?" Kenna said as they sat side by side, presents filling the hammock.

"Oh! I brought Dad's Christmas card for us!" Skandar remembered.

The card had Rudolph the Red-Nosed Reindeer on the front, which prompted Skandar to tell Kenna about the helicopters that flew Mainlanders from Uffington to the Mirror Cliffs being named after Santa's reindeer. She found this hilarious, her howls of laughter setting Skandar off too. Eventually, they pulled themselves together and read it.

Dear Skandar and Kenna,

Happy Christmas! Hope you and the unicorns are doing well—counting down the days until the end of the year when I can visit! I'm missing you two, that's for sure. But work is good, and one of the neighbors keeps coming round with mince pies—Maggie from number thirty. So it's not all bad. Send me more drawings soon, Skandar! I don't even know what your unicorn looks like, Kenna—I'm no good at imagining from descriptions.

I'm running out of space. Love you both! Dad x

ps Kenna—some of your friends came round asking for you, wanting to make sure you got their messages. Write back to them, will you, sweetheart? I know you've got your new life with your unicorn now, but they only want to hear from you.

"Do you reckon Maggie fancies Dad?" Kenna giggled, trying to grab the card.

But Skandar wasn't thinking about his dad's love life.

He wanted to give Kenna her last present.

"Kenn?" he said, passing her the drawing he'd been working on for weeks. "I need to talk to you about my plan for getting you back to the Eyrie."

Kenna looked down at the page from Skandar's sketchbook. It was a drawing of a dapple-gray unicorn soaring down from the Eyrie. There was a girl with brown hair and brown eyes on its back, a look of joy on her face as she shot a ghostly white arrow from a glowing bow. Skandar thought it was one of his best-ever sketches—perhaps because he'd poured all his hopes into it.

But Kenna looked very confused. "This isn't Gos, though."

"It's your destined unicorn, Kenn," Skandar said. "The one you met in the Wilderness last year."

"I know it's the dapple-gray," Kenna said shakily, "but I'm bonded to Goshawk's Fury, so why—"

"I think there's a way for me to safely bond you to your *destined* unicorn. *This* one." He pointed at the sketch. "All I need is to find Goshawk's destined rider—and I know that seems like a long shot, but I've already managed to draw him from a Mender dream. The Commodore's searching the Mainland for him!"

"Wait, what?" Kenna was on her feet now, the drawing still in her hand.

"And Nina said you can come back to the Eyrie when you have your true bond—and then, as long as I complete my training, you'll be able to be a proper spirit wielder in a couple of years. Although, I reckon Agatha might secretly let you start early."

Skandar stopped, reading the expression on his sister's face. It was pure rage.

"How can you even *think* about doing this to me and Goshawk? You're my brother! You're talking about *breaking* our bond. I love Gos—you know that!"

"Not breaking—"

"You're just like all the rest of them!" Kenna shouted. "You *hate* that I'm different. You're trying to make me the same as everyone else!"

"Your mutation hurt you, Kenn!" Skandar said desperately, standing up too. "I know you love Goshawk, but you still have four mutations to go. What if they do permanent damage? And look at what the forged bond did to the Weaver! What it's *doing*. It's sapping her strength, draining her life away!"

"I'M *NOT* HER!" Kenna yelled. "I thought you would understand that, even if nobody else does!"

"I do. I know you're not. But this is the only way we can stay together."

"You could stay *here*," Kenna countered, tears streaming now. "I'm learning all kinds of magic with the Wanderers— you could too. What about that?"

Skandar was still trying to make her understand. "Goshawk wouldn't be wild anymore; she'd have her destined rider too—this boy I saw. A true bond is different from a forged bond."

"How do you know that?" Kenna shot at him. "How do you know what a forged bond feels like?"

"I know it can't be the same," Skandar said, pleading. "And giving up your bond with Goshawk is the only way Nina can get you back to the Eyrie. *Please* just think about this."

"If Goshawk is the price, maybe I don't want to come back to the Eyrie!" Kenna shouted, and she ripped the sketch of the dapple-gray in two before running out toward the sand.

"Kenn! Come back! Please!" Skandar called after her, but she didn't return. He stared at the two halves of the picture on the ground. He felt numb and frustrated and hurt. Had he really got this so wrong? He only wanted to keep Kenna safe, for them to be together again. He knew Kenna loved Gos, but how could she not see that a destined bond would fix everything?

A few minutes later, a familiar shriek broke Skandar out of his spiraling thoughts. Scoundrel came streaking through the palm trees, the bond twanging with the unicorn's panic. Then Skandar heard yelling.

It was coming from the watering hole beyond the trees, where an explosion of elemental magic was turning the sky an ominous red.

Skandar swung himself up into his saddle, and they crashed past groups of Wanderers. Skandar searched desperately for Kenna's face among them, but instead he spotted Elora thundering ahead on her unicorn's silver back, and followed her past the edge of the trees.

About twenty mounted sentinels lined the watering hole, silver masks glinting in the hot midday sun. They were slowly moving toward a rider and a unicorn. A wild unicorn.

Kenna and Goshawk were surrounded.

Fear gripped Skandar's heart. All he could think was that he needed to get to his sister. He gathered Scoundrel's reins—silently thanking Flo for insisting they wear armor today—but they'd barely moved one hoof forward before the sentinels attacked.

Streams of fire, water, sand, and lightning exploded from their palms toward Kenna and Goshawk.

"We need to help her!" he yelled at the Wanderers, who appeared to have frozen now that they were out in the open. "What are you waiting for?"

The look on Elora's face was of pure devastation. "We do not fight. That is not how we live." The Pathfinder was almost crying. "Do not ask me to wield my magic in battle."

Skandar didn't understand what she was talking about, but he knew he didn't have time to argue. If the Wanderers weren't going to join him, he'd fight the sentinels from the air so he could reach his sister more easily. But in the few seconds it took Scoundrel to soar above the melee, the battle shifted.

Goshawk reared up at her attackers—eyes red, exposed bones catching the sunlight.

Kenna's palm glowed yellow, as she howled, "I'm so sorry, Elora!" A tornado escaped it, the swirling wind edged with tendrils of black smoke. The strength of the attack ripped armor from unicorns' chests and tore silver masks from sentinels' faces. The Wanderers shouted at each other to stay back, and Skandar could see that there was no point trying to save Kenna right at that moment.

Because it looked very much like she didn't need help.

Some sentinels had fallen from their unicorns and were groaning on the ground, but others were still attacking. Kenna screamed at them as she blocked with shield after shield that came effortlessly to her fingertips. "Leave. Us. ALONE!"

Then her palm glowed blue, and she launched a tidal wave of water at the sentinels directly ahead. The force smashed the sentinel unicorns backward, some overbalancing right into the watering hole. And as the smoky edge of Kenna's wave touched the water, dead fish started to float to the surface. Kenna was stronger than any of the Eyrie riders Skandar knew. She might even be more powerful than . . . No. He wouldn't even let himself think it.

The sentinels were in disarray. They clearly hadn't expected their target to be so powerful, and they hadn't counted on her friendship with the Wanderers either. Although they avoided attacking the sentinels directly, a team of Wanderers—accompanied by their own unicorns and a handful of wild unicorn foals—sprang to action to cause as much disruption to the desert landscape as possible. Elora was exploding the sand along the shoreline to make giant craters the sentinels had to avoid; tropical birds were swooping at the silver-masked soldiers, blocking their sight lines to Kenna; Albert and Eagle's Dawn were manipulating the watering hole so that it splashed and distracted Kenna's attackers, the pull of his magical current dragging sentinels further into the water.

Skandar and Scoundrel used the opportunity to fight their way forward. They were more united than they'd been for months; Scoundrel knew how much Kenna meant to his rider. Skandar threw javelins humming with electricity, flung three ice tridents down at a cluster of sentinels, and sent a flying fleet of diamond-headed daggers. Scoundrel blasted lightning strikes from his hooves and roared fireballs from his mouth. They were helped by some of the wild foals, who teamed up to attack the sentinels targeting the flying black unicorn. It was almost as though the foals were protecting the spirit wielder, and Skandar was reminded of his first fight against the Weaver—and the way the wild unicorns had saved him.

Before long, Scoundrel and Goshawk reared up tail to tail as the siblings continued to fight the barrage of attacks coming from the silver-masked riders surrounding them.

Skandar could sense an incredible energy coming from his sister. It buzzed and shimmered around her, like the air before a thunderstorm. And there was a darkness to it that made all the hairs on Skandar's neck stand up. Kenna was summoning element after element into her palm, flinging attacks indiscriminately without even looking at her targets. The shadowy edge to her magic was licking at palm trees nearby, the leaves curling to black. Her magic seemed, somehow, to make living things wither and rot—like they were mirroring Goshawk's own decay. Tears were streaming down her face. Then the colors began to blur, Kenna summoning them into her bond so quickly that the attacks mixed together: flame and ice, storm and rock.

"GET BACK!" The call came from both Elora and the sentinels—enemies suddenly united in their fear of the girl on the wild unicorn.

"Kenn! Slow down! They're retreating!" Skandar cried, but she didn't.

"Monster!"

"Witch!"

"Weaver!"

The fearful shouts of the sentinels reached Skandar's ears, and he hated to admit that he was afraid of her too. He'd guessed at her power when she'd brought down the Nomad Tree, but he hadn't fully understood it until now. Kenna was essentially untrained, but she was still more powerful than anything he'd seen of Erika Everhart. And she had been Commodore. *Twice.*

Then Skandar was terrified. Kenna didn't want to give

up her bond with Goshawk's Fury. But if nothing changed, the Island was never going to leave her alone. They would chase Kenna to the ends of the earth, because they were afraid. And when the Island was afraid—it hunted.

Kenna suddenly screamed mid-attack, water sloshing and hissing to the sand beside her. They were screams of pain this time instead of anger. The sentinels dropped back further, the Wanderers pressing their advantage and forming a protective wall between the attackers and the siblings. Albert called out in concern from Eagle's Dawn; Elora shouted Kenna's name.

Skandar turned, petrified in his saddle. Goshawk was rearing on her hind legs, a deep bellow in her chest and fury in her flashing red eyes. Kenna was clutching at her neck as ice spikes began to break through her skin like a nightmare necklace. Her second mutation. But it didn't stop there. Kenna's hands went to her ears, and she shouted in pain again as honey-colored feathers sprouted round both edges like ten elaborate piercings happening all at once. The sentinels were shouting in shock and revulsion.

"Kenn! Kenn! Are you . . . ?" Skandar threw himself from Scoundrel and pulled Kenna from her unicorn's back. Goshawk snarled at him, slime and blood around her mouth. Kenna's whole body was shaking in his arms as they collapsed to the ground. Skandar sensed the Wanderers moving in closer to surround them, piling up barriers of sand with their earth magic.

"I'm all right," Kenna croaked, sounding as though she was reassuring herself rather than him. "I'm all right." Her hand went up her right arm, checking the thorny vines, then to the ice spikes that surrounded her throat and finally to the feathers adorning the curves of her ears.

"Three," she breathed, as the siblings crouched behind the sand drifts. "Three mutations."

Kenna kneeled up a bit straighter. Instinctively she tried to tuck a strand of hair behind her ear, but the feathers got in her way.

"That's going to take some getting used to," she rasped, reaching up to stroke Goshawk's rotting nose.

"Are you sure you're okay?" Skandar asked again, voice shaking. How much time would the sand barriers buy them?

"I'm fine, Skar. I'm just exhausted—like last time, remember?" But even as she said it, her eyes drooped and she slumped more heavily against Skandar's side.

And that was the moment fifty new sentinels arrived.

Sand flew up as the armored unicorns galloped over the dunes toward them. Shouts of relief from the first sentinel group mixed with cries of alarm from the Wanderers. The air was soon thick with the tangy scent of all four elements. The Wanderers started to fall; Skandar could see at least five lying injured on the sand. They were still refusing to fight back directly; they were using magic to manipulate their surroundings, but avoiding direct hits on their opponents. And they were losing.

Kenna was barely conscious, the toll of the double mutation making her oblivious to the new silver-masked arrivals.

"Kenn!" Skandar shook her shoulder desperately. "We
have to get out of here!"

He spotted Albert gesturing at them through the
smoke. Wanderers were hoisting non-riders onto their unicorns' backs so they could make a break for it out of the
oasis. Screams and bellows erupted from between the palm
trees as sentinels searched for hiding Wanderers, and wild
foals broke cover. The unicorns' pungent blasts combined
with the acrid smell of smoke, as flames spread across the
camp and hammocks caught light.

Then suddenly Elora and Silver Soldier were right in
front of Skandar. Elora had a cut across her forehead, her
usually serene face haunted. "We need to leave. NOW! I've
already lost two Wanderers; ten more are injured. I'm not
losing any more. And I will not force them to use battle
magic."

"Kenna's barely conscious! I don't know if she can
ride!" Skandar called up from the ground, half supporting
his sister.

Elora dismounted and kneeled beside them. "Leaping
landslides," she cursed, as her eyes landed on the new mutations.

There was an explosion nearby, and suddenly sand was
everywhere—filling Skandar's mouth and stinging his eyes.
Coughing and spluttering, Skandar saw a sentinel on

an iron-gray unicorn approaching through the swirling grains. Scoundrel let out a rumble of warning in his chest, and Skandar flung out a hand to touch him—summoning the spirit element into the bond, sure an attack was seconds away. But instead, the sentinel dismounted and tore his mask from his face. Flames danced behind his eyes—a fire mutation. The flame-eyed sentinel tried to get to Kenna—but Elora and Skandar stood in his way.

"You're not going to get her out of here without my help," the sentinel shouted. Kenna's eyes fluttered open. She took in her surroundings: the shining sentinels, the scattered Wanderers, the destruction of the oasis home. And Skandar thought he saw something shift in her expression—a hardness in her brown eyes.

"I'll go with him," Kenna announced firmly, ice spikes glinting at her throat.

"He's a sentinel, Kenn. You can't trust—"

"I know him," she insisted. "He helped me at the Stronghold last year." She wobbled to her feet, and she let the flame-eyed man lift her onto Goshawk's back. Still exhausted, Kenna thrust her hands into the unicorn's straggly mane.

If Elora was confused by Kenna's willingness to go with the sentinel, she didn't show it. "Kenna, we will find you." To the flame-eyed man she said fiercely, "She is one of us, and I expect to find her safe and well once this is over."

The sentinel bowed his head and mounted his unicorn.

Skandar launched himself onto Scoundrel's back.

Elora's amethyst eyes were sharp. "Skandar, you cannot go with your sister."

Skandar tried to argue, but Elora held up a slender hand. "I need you to cause a distraction in the air. Blast elements, summon weapons, do anything you can. You are under the Eyrie's protection—I do not think the sentinels will try to harm you. The Wanderers will make a break for the desert, and Kenna will ride off with this sentinel in another direction. Agreed?" Elora fixed her gaze first on Skandar and then on the flame-eyed man.

Skandar didn't want to agree, but he couldn't think of a better plan. He looked at Kenna, still fighting to keep awake. "I don't want to leave you."

"You always say that," Kenna murmured sleepily. "But then you never stay."

"This will work," Elora insisted, mounting Silver Soldier. Then she spoke more quietly, so only Skandar could hear. "If you want to keep your sister safe, do not come looking for the Wanderers again. Everyone will be watching you. Especially once these sentinels report what they've seen today."

"But how will I know she's all right?" Skandar panicked. "I don't even know who that sentinel is!" He was thinking too of the blond boy who'd been destined for Goshawk. How would he convince Kenna to give up her forged bond if he didn't even know where she was?

"Send Agatha," Elora hissed. Then, more loudly: "Ten

seconds." And she rode Soldier back into the midst of the battle.

The flame-eyed sentinel replaced his mask and tethered Goshawk to his own unicorn.

Eight seconds.

"I'll fix this!" Skandar called to his sister.

Kenna looked at him with grief in her eyes. It was one of their long looks, the kind when Skandar could usually tell exactly what his sister was thinking. But right now he couldn't, and all she said was, "You can't fix this, Skar. But I don't blame you for trying. Remember that."

Six. Five. Four.

"I love you, Kenn!" Tears were rolling down Skandar's cheeks, and he didn't know why this goodbye felt different. He thought of Kenna's Christmas presents—left behind on her hammock—and for the first time in his life he wondered whether it might have been better if he'd stayed on the Mainland. If he'd given up his dream and stayed behind with Kenna.

Two.

But then Skandar mounted Scoundrel's Luck, and the bond sang in his heart, and he knew there had never been a choice. Ignoring the call of the Island, of his destined unicorn, had never been an option. Not really.

One.

Scoundrel reared on his back legs, flapping his great feathered wings. Boy and unicorn galloped toward the water of the oasis. He heard the sentinels shouting as they spotted the black unicorn with the white blaze: the brother of the girl they wanted to capture.

"Is she with him?" Skandar heard one of them shout, as the pounding of hooves on the sand behind him resounded in his chest. But before Scoundrel could even splash into the watering hole, they were airborne.

"Let's give them a show, boy," Skandar said through gritted teeth. He summoned the air element as they circled above the burning oasis and then unleashed spirit alongside it in the bond. Scoundrel's black horn turned to electricity, then his head, his neck, and the whole of his body. The sentinels pursuing them slowed in the air—many of them must never have seen a spirit unicorn turn to pure elemental magic before. For good measure, Skandar blasted lightning bolts from his palm, the air crackling and sparking around him.

Next, Skandar summoned the fire element, and Scoundrel's body turned from sparking electricity to roaring inferno. The flames making up the unicorn's outline licked round Skandar's armored legs, and he molded a fiery bow as more sentinel unicorns took off from the ground. His arrows rained down like smoking fireworks, and the sentinels were forced to summon shimmering water shields over their heads.

Skandar glanced over Scoundrel's wing and saw the Wanderer unicorns galloping away from the battlefield, fanning out into smaller groups to try to outride the sentinels. Scoundrel had soared too high for Skandar to make out Kenna, Goshawk, or the flame-eyed sentinel—all he could hope was that they were long gone.

The sentinels were getting braver again now, hurling elemental attacks through the air toward the flaming spirit unicorn. It was time to go. Skandar closed his palm, and Scoundrel's usual black color returned. Skandar and Scoundrel flew as fast as they could. And that was *very* fast—they hadn't been chosen for the Peregrine Society for nothing. They easily outpaced the sentinels, leaving the heat of the fire zone behind.

By the time Skandar glimpsed the Eyrie's trees, it was a frosty December afternoon again. He looked over his shoulder for his pursuers once more, but the sky behind was empty.

Skandar left Scoundrel in his stable before launching himself up familiar ladders. But he wasn't returning to his own treehouse just yet—he needed to speak to Agatha. Skandar hammered on her treehouse door, and she threw it open with an irritated grunt. When she saw the look of devastation on her nephew's face, though, her expression changed.

"You went to see your sister, didn't you?"

Skandar nodded, and then burst into tears.

KENNA

Guilt

KENNA SMITH WAS RIDDLED WITH GUILT.

Guilt was a burning oasis. It was wild foals fleeing from those who'd sworn to protect them, and the broken threads of fragile friendships.

Guilt was giving in. Giving in to the furious grip of the forged bond on her heart. Giving in to Goshawk's deep desire for destruction. Giving in to the wildness that lived in her soul.

Guilt was the Wanderers running from their home. It was thrusting the most peaceful people she'd ever met into battle, and a haunted look in amethyst eyes.

Guilt was shame. Shame that she had unleashed her power. Shame that she had shattered the one unbreakable rule. Shame that she had ever thought she could be safe.

After several days of frenzied riding through the zones, the flame-eyed man had left Kenna and Goshawk's Fury behind the shimmering sheet of a waterfall. That had been three nights ago. The relentless crash of the water into its swirling pool had sent Kenna into a kind of trance. Hours passed like seconds. Minutes passed like days. She didn't eat the food the man had left with her. She just sat—wrapped in a blanket—under the rocky overhang as the water rushed overhead and fell like a living curtain, shielding her from the world. A partition between before and after.

She let the guilt consume her, replaying the scenes at the oasis: black smoke rising from palm trees, screams of terror, fleeing wild unicorn foals. She made herself look again at the injured bodies on the sand: both the silver-masked ones she had put there and the Wanderers who had refused to fight back. She made herself remember the way she'd unleashed her own power to save herself, the way she'd felt it thrumming through her veins, the way she'd *enjoyed* feeling unstoppable. She made herself see again the fear on the faces of her foes *and* her friends—even the fear on her own brother's face as she'd called on the darker side of her elemental strength.

Was Skandar even looking for her? Had he really just returned to the Eyrie after all that destruction? Had he simply gone back to his treehouse, when she was out here all alone?

And she couldn't forget that Skandar wanted to separate her from Goshawk's Fury, that his grand plan was to bond the unicorn *she'd* chosen—the unicorn she loved—to a complete stranger he'd seen in a dream. Skandar wanted to change her. Was he staying away because she'd said no? Because he now believed she was a monster too?

Goshawk's Fury shifted a little closer to Kenna so that her wing was wrapped round her rider's body. In her less desolate moments, Kenna told herself that at least *something* good had come from the attack on the oasis. There was a closeness with Gos that had been missing before. Where Goshawk had felt only a hatred of the world and everything in it, there were now moments when Kenna sensed the unicorn's attention shifting toward her rider instead of herself. It felt like they were *sharing* emotions, instead of Goshawk just pummelling her own into the bond. When Kenna was feeling particularly upset or afraid, the flow of rage from Goshawk would falter—as though the unicorn was listening, checking to see if her rider was okay.

"Thanks, Gos," Kenna whispered, and stroked the edge of her honeyed wing. As she did, a feather dislodged itself and stayed in her hand. Sometimes it was easy to forget that Goshawk was dying every single moment. That she would carry on dying forever, even after Kenna was gone.

Kenna looked up suddenly. A swan's trumpeting call had reached her ears over the crashing of the water. It was insistent, repetitive. Goshawk was on her feet, ghostly horn pointing beyond the waterfall. The sound came again and again until Kenna could no longer ignore it. She edged round the side of the waterfall, the spray immediately soaking her hair and face.

There was no distressed swan in the plunge pool—but there *was* a silver unicorn circling, ridden by a woman with a wooden whistle pushed against her lips.

"ELORA!" Kenna cried out in excitement.

The Pathfinder stopped blowing the swan whistle and directed Silver Soldier to land behind the waterfall's drape. Kenna threw herself into the rider's arms as soon as she dismounted. She smiled as Soldier shook water from her great silver wings, Goshawk roaring in indignation.

"Thank the five elements I've found you," Elora breathed, holding Kenna at arm's length so she could see her face. "Has the sentinel gone?"

Kenna nodded; then questions exploded out of her. "Are you taking me to the others? Are you all gathered at your water zone home?" She hadn't realized how much she missed her life with the Wanderers until that moment.

But Elora shook her head. "I'm sorry, Kenna. The Wanderers are scattered across all four zones. The sentinels are hunting *us* now too. It's the best way to hide."

"So am I joining a smaller group?"

The Pathfinder avoided her gaze. "In a way. I'll be sending different Wanderers to visit you every day. To check that you're okay, to bring food, to keep you company. Of course, Albert has already volunteered."

Kenna swallowed, fear and anger constricting her throat. "Visit? So you're saying I'll be separated from the other Wanderers? I'll be on my own?"

"It's only for now." Elora tried to reach out a hand of comfort, but Kenna shrank away from it like a wounded animal. Goshawk hissed.

A few hours later Elora's *visit* came to an end. As Kenna watched Silver Soldier and Elora disappear through the waterfall's curtain, she felt sorrow and hurt and loss and guilt—but she also felt something else. Without the Wanderers, she was afraid.

Afraid of herself.

CHAPTER THIRTEEN

Birthday Surprises

AGATHA SPENT THE NEXT FEW WEEKS searching the zones for news of Kenna. When Skandar had explained what had happened at the oasis, Agatha hadn't seemed shocked by the extent of Kenna's power. In fact, she'd been most interested in the flame-eyed sentinel who'd broken ranks to help.

But as December became January, the lack of news made Skandar determined to do something. He kept voicing risk-filled plans to his quartet—like searching the zones for Kenna himself—and then snapping at them when they tried to dissuade him. He was in such a consistently foul mood that even Scoundrel's attempts to cheer him up through the bond didn't help.

One late-January evening, not long before the Water Festival, Skandar was drawing a sketch of the flame-eyed man in his notebook. Again. He'd latched on to the mystery of the sentinel's identity with a fervor that was usually reserved for Mitchell and his blackboard. The only distraction he allowed himself was checking the post trees for a letter from Nina. But there'd been no news of Goshawk's destined rider either.

Bobby appeared behind Skandar's shoulder, almost slipping on an abandoned letter to Dad. "How did Kenna say she knew this sentinel again?"

"He helped her at the Stronghold." Skandar rubbed out part of the man's face, trying to capture him exactly as he remembered from the oasis.

"Helped her *escape* maybe? I thought that was the storm."

"I don't know," Skandar said through gritted teeth. "I don't know who he is, or whether Kenna's safe with him. That's the whole— Argh!" He'd pressed so hard on the pencil that the lead had broken.

Flo came in and hung up her jacket by the treehouse door.

"How was the Silver Circle meeting?" Mitchell asked cheerfully—he'd been in an irritatingly good mood ever since he and Jamie had gone to the Furnace Dance together.

Flo pulled the green beanbag over to the fire. "Pretty pointless. Blade and I were supposed to be practicing switching between the elements with some of the older riders—for a silver unicorn, that's one of the hardest things to do. But they were all in an emergency meeting with Rex."

Skandar sat up. "What about?"

"Have they found the eggs?" Bobby asked.

Flo shook her head. "No. I'm sorry, Bobby. Apparently Rex has been having these crisis meetings ever since the prison breakout. And then when the sentinels came back from the fire zone . . . after they saw—"

"Kenna," Skandar finished for her.

"Exactly. He's asking them to describe what they saw. Nina has asked him to gather information about what a forged bond can do. How strong it is. They're trying to work out the threat we're facing if the Weaver succeeds in making more of them."

"Why don't they just ask *me*?" Skandar said bitterly. "I was there. I could tell them."

"Yeah, that's a good point," Bobby mused. "Why aren't *you* in trouble? You attacked a shedload of sentinels and stopped them from arresting Kenna." She sounded oddly proud.

Skandar had wondered the same thing. He'd been expecting to be hauled into Council Square ever since he'd got back from the oasis.

"My dad said Nina's protecting you, Skar—*and* Kenna,"

Flo said quietly. "She's insisting that they concentrate on recovering the eggs—rather than hunting a teenage girl with a wild unicorn."

Bobby sighed. "Nina's the best. They *should* be concentrating on the eggs. My sister deigned to write to me the other day, asking me what she should pack for the Island. What am I supposed to say?"

"I'm going to check if Nina's sent a letter," Skandar said, but he noticed the others looking at each other. "What?"

Flo took a deep breath. "Skar, do you think it's a good idea for you to carry on with this plan to find Goshawk's destined rider? You said Kenna was angry when you suggested it."

"And you don't actually know the effect this bond exchange would have on Kenna, or the boy," Mitchell added. "Or if it would even work. There are no books on it—Craig and I have both checked. It's a completely untested theory."

Skandar wanted to argue back, but he knew his friends had a point. Kenna and Goshawk were more connected than he'd realized—they'd done astonishing magic together. And he still didn't have the first idea how to *do* the exchange. But Skandar couldn't give up—his friends hadn't seen her mutating, hadn't seen her in pain.

"Elora was an expert on this stuff when she was at the Silver Stronghold," Skandar started to say, when—

BANG!

Agatha stood in the doorway, and her brown eyes scanned the room for Skandar.

"She's safe," Agatha rasped. "Elora's hiding her."

"And the flame-eyed sentinel?"

"Gone."

The knot in Skandar's chest loosened. Kenna was back with the Wanderers. They would protect her.

"Thank you, Ag—Instructor Everhart," Skandar breathed. But his aunt still seemed very worried. "What *aren't* you saying?"

Agatha looked like she didn't want to answer. "Elora is concerned about Kenna's mutations and what happens next. Two at once really took it out of her."

"What do you mean?"

Agatha swallowed. "Kenna has a fire and a spirit mutation to go. Elora is worried about them doing serious damage. The worst-case scenario being—"

"She doesn't survive them?" Mitchell guessed, his voice hushed.

"Nice to know I can count on you to keep everyone calm, Henderson," Agatha snapped sarcastically. "That is *not* what Elora said. She's just concerned for Kenna's future welfare."

"Well, that's the same as survival, isn't it?" Bobby said bluntly.

"Not necessarily." Agatha looked round at the quartet

hunched on beanbags. "I don't suppose you have any tea in this place, do you?"

"I don't think now is the right time for tea!" Skandar objected.

"Now is *always* the right time for tea," Agatha said, sounding so severe that Skandar was shocked into silence.

Skandar's mind whirred as he searched for the tea Flo had bought at the Fire Festival. Should he tell Agatha about his plan for Kenna's forged bond now? He'd hesitated before, in case she told him to stop, but if there was a possibility Kenna's next mutations might kill her . . . well, he had to be ready to act as soon as Goshawk's rider was found.

Once the tea was brewed, Agatha sat cross-legged by the stove. "Before we start worrying about Kenna's *survival*, let's get our facts straight." She took a sip of tea, then swore as it burned her bottom lip. "The Island is in panic mode, and of course nobody will listen to me. But the truth of the matter is that I know more about the forged bond than most people. Erika and I learned about forged bonds from an illegal book our father, Silas, had back when we were children and—"

Skandar interrupted before his courage failed him. "Ag—Instructor Everhart, Elora told me about a theory—a theory that you can remold a forged bond into two destined ones. I know which unicorn Kenna was destined for, and the Commodore has been helping me find Goshawk's true rider so . . . that could help keep Kenna safe, couldn't it?"

It was difficult to shock Agatha, but now shock flashed across her face. "You *have* been busy, little spirit wielder. I can't say I've heard of a theory like that—and I don't expect Kenna was keen on it, was she?"

Skandar wondered how Agatha had guessed he'd already told his sister about the plan.

"The Pathfinder is worrying unnecessarily about Kenna's next mutations," Agatha continued. "As far as I remember, nothing Erika and I read said anything about wild mutations causing harm—let alone death. I've told you that Erika originally wanted to forge a bond for me, so that we could be together if I wasn't destined for a unicorn. She wouldn't have wanted to hurt me. Not then. Not even now."

Once it was time for Agatha to leave, Skandar walked her out to the platform. Everything felt hopeless. He'd thought that once he'd plucked up the courage to speak to her about the bond exchange, she would—albeit reluctantly—at least give him an idea how it might be done. How was he going to save Kenna from the wild bond all by himself?

On re-entering the treehouse, Skandar found Flo and Bobby sitting in front of Mitchell's blackboard. The fire wielder was already writing something in chalk.

"What's all this?" he asked, as Flo patted the blue beanbag next to her.

Mitchell's voice rang out. "Welcome to Quartet Meeting Fifty-Three."

"I'm sure you make those numbers up," Bobby said.

Mitchell ignored her. "What do we know about Kenna's forged bond so far? Can we predict what will happen next? How advanced is the plan to find Goshawk's destined rider? How viable is it?" His looping writing filled the board with questions, and Skandar's heart swelled with gratitude. His friends cared about him. And now that they understood the danger Kenna was in, they were fully on his side.

He wasn't alone after all.

As the water season began, life for the quartet became a blur of late-night meetings, forged-bond research, and frustrating training sessions. The Fledgling unicorns became easily bored during training, testing their riders to breaking point. Falcon started blocking the element Bobby was summoning into the bond and swapping it for another. Skandar tried to help—it reminded him of Scoundrel in his Hatchling year, when they couldn't use the spirit element. But Bobby was too irritated and proud to take advice, and Falcon was just as stubborn as her rider.

Scoundrel and Red often played games during training, rather than taking part in the actual sessions. Skandar and Mitchell were left helpless as the red and black unicorns raced across the plateau or lay in the grass, seeing which of them could fall asleep quickest, or—the most annoying of all—as they decided to head back to the Eyrie, snapping up animal snacks on the way.

And then there was Blade. He was ejected from multiple

sessions because Flo was unable to control him. On one memorable occasion, he made it hail so strongly that multiple riders sustained heavy bruising. Back at the Eyrie, the only person who'd been able to console Flo—who hated hurting anyone—was her fellow silver Rex Manning. He told Flo horror stories of his own Eyrie days with Sorceress until she smiled again.

By March, all the Fledglings were on edge because there'd been no sign of the instructions for the Water Trial. So, amid the hours combing through the elemental scriptures for *anything* related to forged bonds, Mitchell was also memorizing all the challenges from previous Water Trials.

"Did you know that in 1927 the trial took place entirely *under*water?"

"No, Mitchell, I did not," Bobby would say, rolling her eyes.

"What about in 1989, when ten disoriented Fledglings flew out to sea?"

"Mitchell . . . if you don't stop, I swear I will—"

With all the frenzied training, and searching for eggs with the Grins, and waiting for news of Goshawk's rider, the weeks flew by. And one morning in late March—which also happened to be Skandar's birthday—the final day of the Chaos Cup Qualifiers arrived.

He began the day in Scoundrel's stable, tangled in a Mender dream.

Tall. Short. Freckled hands. Pink fingernails. Cropped hair.

Bald. Beaded braids. Standing. Sitting. Skinny. Broad. Muscled. Lanky.

The views from eyes that did not belong to Skandar snapped in and out of focus as he switched bodies over and over. They were all different, but they were all waiting for something. Skandar was desperate to escape the endless cycling through bodies, but he also wanted to understand. Why were they here? Together? He strained to pull himself out of the dream people—to look at them through his own eyes—but every time he tried to escape someone, another presence snatched him and he felt another jolt in his stomach.

He was staring at the sky, at rolling winter waves, at a forest. He was lying with his hands under his chin. He was sitting cross-legged on a clifftop throwing grass into the wind. Wait, *Skandar thought frantically. He was going to be sick; he couldn't see; he couldn't breathe—*

Skandar woke, panting. Agatha had said she'd throw Skandar in prison herself if he ever asked a bard for sleepsong again, so instead he combed painstakingly through the dream details. There was something familiar there. The views of the forest, sea, and sky were useless—they could have been a thousand different places. But . . . the last body he'd occupied had been throwing grass into the wind just like Goshawk's destined rider. Was the blond boy *with* all the other people who were in Skandar and Scoundrel's dreams? Were they all on the Mainland together?

With that thought, Skandar felt slightly more optimistic that the dreams might eventually prove useful, although a searing headache wasn't exactly the best birthday present. Breakfast didn't get off to a great start either. Since the news of Kenna's powers had spread, Skandar and Flo tried to eat early to avoid all the whispering about both him *and* his sister, but they were later today—partly because of the Mender dream, and partly because Bobby had insisted on presenting Skandar with a "birthday" emergency sandwich. The difference? She'd added Jelly Babies. Skandar had said he'd save it for later.

Many riders didn't bother to keep their voices down as the quartet entered the Trough.

"I heard his sister took out twenty sentinels at once."

"I heard he helped her escape."

"Well, *I* heard she's more powerful than the Weaver."

"I HEARD," Bobby said very loudly, as she piled her plate high with pancakes, "that if you don't shut up, Bobby Bruna will punch you in the face."

The Trough went very quiet.

"Thanks, Bobby," Skandar muttered.

"Well, it is your birthday." She winked at him.

They climbed up to their usual platform, but it was already occupied by a group of Rookies—including Hayden, whom Bobby had been avoiding since the Well Dance.

Bobby ducked. "Quick! Scram!" They made a detour for the nearest rope bridge.

"Is he . . . more annoying than a bogey in a burger?" Flo said hopefully.

"The student becomes the master," Bobby said, and Flo looked delighted.

As they made their way to an empty platform, Mitchell started on his usual rant about birthdays. "But I just don't understand what birthdays are really celebrating. Being born isn't an achievement, is it? And saying, 'Oh, congratulations, you've managed to make it through another year without dying' just seems depressing to me."

"Forking thunderstorms, Mitchell!" Bobby rolled her eyes. "Trust you to ruin birthdays."

"We don't take much notice of them on the Island really," Flo said. "Well, unless you're a double elemental like Nina. She's an air wielder who was born in the air season—it's supposed to be good luck."

"Nina doesn't need luck," Bobby said proudly. "Air wielder equals naturally fantastic. Did you know she has electric feet? Apparently, currents buzz and spark round her toes."

"Who did you hear *that* from?" Mitchell scoffed.

"It's why she loves dancing so much—just like me." Bobby sighed contentedly. "We're so similar."

Skandar was quiet. He'd already checked the post tree that morning and found a card from Dad. But, of course, there'd been nothing from Kenna. He was trying hard not to think about all the birthdays she'd made special for him back on the Mainland: the unicorn cakes she'd baked, the limited-edition Chaos Cards she'd given him after saving up for months. Knowing she was okay was all he really wanted for his birthday. He slumped down at the platform's table.

Bobby pulled out the chair next to him.

"Nope! No," Mitchell said loudly. "We cannot sit here."

"Er . . . why?" Skandar asked.

"This table is cursed. Don't sit there, Skandar!" Mitchell hissed, trying to pull him up.

"I have heard that actually," Flo said, taking a large step away from the chair.

"You cannot be serious?" Bobby spluttered.

"I'm deadly serious," Mitchell said firmly. "Every single Fledgling who has eaten at this platform since the trials started is missing a stone."

"But surely that's just a coincidence!" Skandar couldn't believe his fact-focused friend thought an inanimate object was cursed.

"Mitchell, *you* don't have a fire stone," Bobby said bluntly. "And you haven't sat here."

"Yes, I have. I came to lunch with Jamie after the Earth Trial, when he visited to repair Skandar's armor. I'm telling you, we sat at *this very table*."

"Don't be ridiculous," Bobby scoffed.

"I'm not eating breakfast here," Mitchell said, his voice rising in volume and pitch. "I'm down a fire stone! I can't risk losing out on water or air. It's bad enough that my father . . ." Mitchell stopped.

"Your father what?" Skandar asked. "I thought he was being more supportive this year."

"He was." Mitchell's eyes glistened. "He was until I messed up in the Fire Trial. He wrote to me after the den dances saying I wasn't trying hard enough. He said I should stop seeing Jamie because he was clearly distracting me from training." Mitchell took a shaky breath. "I thought he'd changed. I thought he was going to support me no matter what, but he obviously just . . . can't."

"Why didn't you tell us?" Flo asked gently.

The flames in Mitchell's hair billowed. "I suppose I was embarrassed. Father going back to his old ways felt like yet another failure."

"He's the one who should be embarrassed," Skandar said, getting up and giving Mitchell a hug.

Without further discussion, the quartet climbed to a different platform. As the others chatted, Skandar finally opened the birthday card from Dad, a lump forming in his throat.

> *To Skandar,*
> *Happy birthday! Can't wait to see you and*
> *Kenna in a couple of months.*
> *Love you, Dad x*

"Did you know Rex Manning is riding in the Qualifiers?" Mitchell asked Flo, as Skandar swallowed down tears.

He wished he could tell Dad how worried he was about Kenna.

Flo finished a mouthful, nodding. "He told me after air training the other day. It's exciting, isn't it? If Rex qualifies, he'll be the first silver in the Chaos Cup since the Treaty with the Mainland! And if Nina qualifies, she might become Commodore for the third time in— Skar, what's that?"

Skandar was staring down at a scribbled note in his hand.

"It was stuck to the back of my envelope," he murmured, holding it out over the table so they could all see it.

His name is Tyler Thomson. The Mainland police are still trying to locate him. N

"Goshawk's rider?" Flo guessed.

Skandar nodded. *Tyler.*

"*Still* trying to locate him," Mitchell said, frowning. "What's the holdup?"

"They have his name and description. I bet it won't be long now," Flo said brightly.

"Happy birthday, spirit boy." Bobby punched Skandar on the arm, and he smiled. It felt strange to get good news for once. But the rider having a name also made him more real. Tyler.

"Oh! I can't believe I forgot!" Flo cried, and pulled four tiny brown packages out of her pocket. She handed one to each of the quartet and kept one for herself.

"Umm . . . so I made these for us—from saddler thread. I know on the Mainland that you give presents on birthdays, but the only date I knew was Skandar's, so I thought I'd give them to you all today." She sounded nervous.

Skandar unwrapped the brown paper, and a bracelet fell out. It had been made with colored thread in all the elemental colors, but *Skandar & Scoundrel* was depicted in white. Next to him, Skandar saw that Bobby and Falcon's was the same, but with their names in yellow.

"You don't have to wear them if you don't want to," Flo added breathlessly.

"Did you *make* these?" Mitchell asked, slipping his onto his wrist. "I knew you were good at patching jackets, but this is highly impressive!"

Bobby was staring thoughtfully at the bracelet on her own wrist. "Why do I love it so much? It's the least badass thing I own."

"Thank you, Flo," Skandar said, pure happiness radiating through his entire body.

"Argh!" Mitchell squawked. A folded piece of paper had landed on their table.

Skandar looked up, trying to work out where it'd come from. Gabriel, Sarika, Zac, and Mabel were on the platform above, and Mabel—her frosted freckles flashing in the dappled light—motioned at Skandar's quartet to unfold it.

Mitchell's eyes widened as he straightened out the crumpled blue page. "Thank you!" he called up.

> Water is an adaptable, flexible element that flows
> where it pleases. Therefore, in this third trial,
> the key is choice. No one will begin with a water
> stone, so riders must decide whether to find their
> own path or bide their time and take what others
> have earned.
>
> There is no one route to success—water
> can give, but it can also take. And in its mercy,
> it will reward those who swim hardest against
> the current. A reward that may make all the
> difference in calming the seas ahead.

"Nobody starts with a water stone?" Skandar murmured.

"That must mean it's easy to get one." Mitchell sounded relieved.

"And there's another reward!" Bobby pointed at the lower part of the paper. "I bet we'll be able to get Mitchell his fire stone!"

"Yes, I'm sure we will," Flo said enthusiastically.

"How come Mabel's quartet had the instructions?" Skandar wondered.

"It was really nice of them to share them with us." Flo looked pleased.

Mitchell and Bobby glanced at each other conspiratorially.

"Niamh's quartet are doing the best. They've got loads of spare stones," Bobby said.

"That's exactly what I was thinking, Roberta. It wouldn't do us any harm to have them on our side. They have spare earth, water, and air stones right now."

Skandar watched, bewildered, as Mitchell folded the blue instructions into a paper airplane and passed it to Bobby with a nod.

"Perfect throw!" Mitchell applauded as Bobby landed it right where Niamh, Benji, Art, and Farooq were eating. Benji raised a winged eyebrow as he unfolded the page.

"It's scary when you two work together," Skandar murmured.

"You're trying to get Niamh's quartet to like us," Flo realized. "To be our allies?"

"They're doing better than we are," Bobby accepted bitterly.

"Do you think there's only one set of instructions for the Water Trial?" Skandar was suddenly starting to understand. "Do you think who we share it with is a kind of test?"

"It's the Chaos Trials, Skandar," Mitchell said feverishly. "*Everything* is a test."

CHAPTER FOURTEEN

Bait

LATER THAT MORNING, IT WAS A RELIEF TO leave the Fledgling unicorns munching on meat snacks in one of Fourpoint's side streets. Falcon and Blade in particular had been a nightmare on the journey into the capital for the Chaos Cup Qualifiers. The two unicorns had fallen out for some reason, and Flo and Bobby struggled to get them to fly in the same air space—let alone walk through Fourpoint side by side.

Jamie met the quartet by the blacksmith forges and fell into step beside Mitchell and Bobby. Everywhere was packed and in full party mode for the Qualifiers. But Skandar couldn't help but feel a bit detached from it all. *Tyler.* Nina had almost located Goshawk's rider, but what if Kenna still felt the same about the wild unicorn? What if she chose to be an outcast while Skandar was fighting so hard for the spirit element to belong? What would he do then?

"Are you okay, Skar?" Flo asked quietly.

"I'm not sure," he told her with a weak smile. "It's all just a lot, isn't it?"

"It really is."

"This year feels harder than the others," Skandar admitted.

"It's Fledgling year, so I guess that makes sense."

"No, I don't mean the Chaos Trials. It's harder with Kenna here. It feels bad to say it, but when she was on the Mainland, at least I knew she was safe. At least I could make plans for us to be together on the Island one day. At least I could dream that everything would be okay. But now she's here—and everything isn't all right, is it? I don't know what she wants. I feel like I don't even know her anymore."

"Of course you do." Flo stopped and put a hand on Skandar's shoulder. "You know her better than anyone else."

Skandar thought of Kenna wielding her wild magic at the oasis, of the look she had in her eyes sometimes that he didn't recognize. "I used to. I think she changed a lot when I abandoned her to come here."

"You didn't abandon her, Skar," Flo argued. "What choice did you have?"

"I could've stayed," Skandar admitted. "I could've ignored Agatha when she came to Sunset Heights."

"Would Kenna have done that for *you*?"

Skandar swallowed. "I don't know." Flo had landed on the exact thing that he was afraid of. Perhaps Kenna *wouldn't* have left him with Dad, all alone, like he had done to her. He was afraid of the brother that made him. Deep down, he feared that Kenna's forged bond was all his fault.

"I think she would have gone to the Island without you," Flo said stubbornly. "I think she wanted to be a unicorn rider just as much as you did—maybe even more."

But Skandar was never going to know for sure.

Flo started pointing things out, clearly trying to cheer him up. Unlike at the festivals, riders were dressed in their own elemental colors today, so there was a mixture of red, blue, green, and yellow in the crowd that made everything seem more exciting. The outside of the arena was surrounded by colored tents, too—some belonged to healers, others to blacksmiths, others to saddlers. Skandar spotted the orange tarpaulin of Shekoni Saddles flapping in the breeze.

"Come on!" Bobby urged, as they pushed through the crowds to the closest arena entrance. "I heard the loudspeaker announce the next qualifier—Nina Kazama *and* Rex Manning are racing."

When they eventually found five seats together, the race had already started. Mitchell took it upon himself to remind everyone how the Qualifiers worked, ignoring Bobby saying "We *know*, Mitchell" every few words.

"This is the final day of the Qualifiers, and it's the only

one open to the public. There were four other days before this, with multiple shorter heats to filter riders out. They have those first because of the number of competitors—technically, the Chaos Cup is open to anyone Rookie age and over."

"Although, Rookies and Preds hardly ever qualify," Jamie added. "They usually spend a few years training at elemental yards before they try out. Nina's an exception to that—she entered right out of the Eyrie. Right, Mitchell?"

Mitchell had been staring at Jamie while he was speaking, a big goofy smile on his face. "Oh, yes, yes that's correct," he continued, slightly flustered. "And—er—there are four final qualifiers today. Twenty-five riders in each, like the Chaos Cup. The six fastest go through from each heat, plus one Wildcard chosen from across all four races."

"Wildcard?" Skandar asked.

Flo answered this time—leaning round Bobby, who was glued to the screen as sky battles exploded along the course, the unicorns racing onward. "A Wildcard is a rider chosen by the Qualifier Committee. It's usually someone who has a tough qualifier but performs so well they might have come top six if they'd been entered into a different one. The committee look at all the rider times, their overall performance, that kind of thing."

"Isn't your dad on the committee?" Mitchell asked.

"Yes," Flo said proudly. "They have a saddler, a blacksmith, a—"

"NINA'S IN THE LEAD!" Bobby yelled, and Skandar turned his attention to the big screen in front of them.

The crowd was suddenly on its feet as the unicorns flew down the final straight of the course. Nina Kazama was half-turned in her Shekoni saddle, lightning bow in hand, firing arrow after arrow at the riders behind her. Her chestnut unicorn, Lightning's Mistake, was pumping her wings and occasionally kicking out backward with her own bolts of electricity. Watching their teamwork, Skandar couldn't imagine Lightning *ever* disobeying Nina as a Fledgling.

"Nina's balance has always been absolutely on point," a commentator said appreciatively over the loudspeaker.

"But here comes Rex Manning and Silver Sorceress on her inside shoulder. This is the first time the young silver has decided to enter the Chaos Cup Qualifiers, and he has flown a remarkable race," another commentator added.

"Oh my goodness! He's going to qualify!" Flo squealed.

But it wasn't over yet. As Lightning and Sorceress soared over the arena, elemental magic exploded in the air above the crowd, the debris falling and scattering spectators. It was unusual for battles to continue so late in the race—most riders abandoned magic at this point and raced for the finishing arch.

"Why isn't Nina just going for the win?" Bobby called out.

"It looks like she's trying to take out Rex!" Mitchell replied.

"But why?" Flo looked very conflicted. She was close with Rex, but her father was Nina's saddler.

Skandar had an idea why. He remembered what Nina had said when he'd asked why Rex had broken their agreement to keep the missing eggs a secret: *Power. Nobody ever thinks they have enough.*

Perhaps the Commodore had decided that she wanted to take Rex out before he got any more power. And Skandar supposed that a sky battle was the only acceptable way to do it.

As the unicorns swooped toward the arena's sand, Nina sent a water jet from her palm that was so strong the sound of it hitting Rex's armored shoulder was audible even above the roaring crowd. Rex managed to stay in the saddle—just—and recovered quickly enough to summon a javelin with flames so wild his whole body disappeared in its smoke.

"Careful, Rex," Flo murmured. "He's letting his silver magic take hold."

The commentator echoed Flo's words. "It looks like that javelin has lost more than it's gained for Rex Manning. He doesn't look entirely in control."

Rex launched the javelin at Nina, but he was too slow— Lightning's Mistake had landed, a split second ahead of Silver Sorceress. Lightning galloped under the arch and Nina raised her fist in triumph. The crowd cheered their current Commodore, but they went even wilder for Rex and Sorceress. Skandar didn't join in. So far, Rex had seemed fairly harmless, but Skandar couldn't help wondering whether, if a silver won the Chaos Cup, Kenna would ever be safe again.

"Well, Declan, this race really has been something," the commentator shouted. "Rex Manning and Silver Sorceress qualify very comfortably for the Chaos Cup—the first silver for many, many years. I think he could be a real contender—"

"And Nina Kazama," the other commentator interrupted, "is now in with a chance of winning the Chaos Cup for a third time and making Island history once again. She was the first Mainlander to win—but could she also be the first-*ever* rider to be Commodore three years in a row?"

Inevitably Skandar thought again of the only other rider and unicorn he knew of who'd had that chance: Erika Everhart and Blood-Moon's Equinox.

Skandar was still watching Rex and Nina down on the sand when five members of the Council of Seven sprinted toward them.

"What's going on?" Jamie asked from the other side of Mitchell.

"Has something happened?" Flo said.

Nina looked like she was giving orders now; Rex and Sorceress left the arena at full gallop.

"Flo?" Skandar turned to her. "Maybe we should ask your dad what's happening."

The five friends fought their way back down the steps and through the impatient buzz of a crowd clearly wondering why the next qualifier hadn't started.

Flo stepped through the entrance of the orange tent. "Dad?"

Olu Shekoni was talking to a couple of other saddlers, who nodded goodbye as the quartet and Jamie entered. Olu pulled Flo into a hug, as though relieved.

"What's wrong?" Flo wiggled to get out of his arms. "I'm fine!"

"Mr. Shekoni, do you know what's happening?" Skandar asked. "They haven't started the next qualifier."

Olu cleared his throat, looking very serious. "It's the Silver Stronghold. Thirty sentinels started attacking from the inside this morning. A rebellion. Apparently they were shouting about taking destiny into their own hands. Saying they were no longer satisfied being second-best to Chaos riders."

Skandar was reminded of Erika Everhart's words to him in the Wilderness two years ago, when she was trying to persuade him to fight by her side: *Destiny be damned.*

"They've joined the Weaver, haven't they?" Skandar guessed.

Olu nodded. "The rebel sentinels that were caught confirmed as much. The Weaver's *new generation* was all they could talk about. But they're refusing to reveal the location of the eggs. Apparently lots of them are claiming they helped her on the solstice last year."

"So the sentinels *have* been caught?" Mitchell asked hopefully.

Olu grimaced. "Not all of them. Are your unicorns in Fourpoint?"

The quartet nodded as one.

"Then fly back to the Eyrie right now. Jamie, I suggest you head back to the forges. Fourpoint is going to be in chaos when this news spreads."

They left the tent, and all Skandar could think about was getting Scoundrel out of the capital. But there was another surprise waiting for them. Craig was standing by the quartet's unicorns, bun bobbing wildly as he looked out for their returning riders.

"You're here, thank the five elements."

"We know about the sentinel rebellion," Mitchell said, mounting Red.

But the bookseller was shaking his head. "No, it's not that. Skandar, I've found something out about forged bonds. Completely by chance, I stumbled across an ancient volume that mentioned it just once—uncensored, would you believe it? All the references to the spirit element were still in!"

"Craig, I'm so sorry but we really have to get out of here as quickly as we can," Flo apologized, her voice shaking. There were shouts in the distance.

"Skandar, the book said that forged bonds can only be made with a person who was *destined* to be a rider. It can't be just anyone—do you understand?"

The words filtered into Skandar's brain. "That means the Weaver's new generation would have to be made up of people who were destined for a unicorn. Who missed their chance at the Hatchery door?"

"And what is the biggest group of people that applies to?" Craig asked. "Which group has been barred from the Hatchery door for years?"

Skandar's jaw dropped. "The lost spirit wielders."

"Precisely," Craig said darkly.

The quartet didn't say a word until the unicorns were safely in their stables.

"Skar." Flo reached him outside Scoundrel's door. There was a look of horror on her face, and Skandar knew she was thinking the same thoughts he was.

"The Weaver said I was in her way," Skandar murmured. "Back at the Earth Trial. *You are in my way, Skandar Smith.*"

"What?" Mitchell and Bobby said, joining them by Scoundrel's door.

"Don't you see?" Flo was practically in tears. "If the Weaver is targeting the lost spirit wielders, then the biggest threat to her plan, the only other person who can give them a unicorn, is Skandar! He's a Mender!"

"I can give them more than a unicorn," Skandar said seriously. "I can give them their *destined* unicorn." His hands were shaking. "No wonder she wants me out of the way."

"So you're saying the Weaver has been coming to the trials because . . . she's trying to *kill* Skandar?" Mitchell asked, appalled.

"If that's true, she hasn't tried very hard," Bobby scoffed.

"She hasn't tried very hard *yet*!" Flo turned to Skandar. "You can't take part in the rest of the trials, Skar. If that's where the Weaver's targeting you, it's too dangerous!"

"But then he won't have a water or air stone," Mitchell said automatically.

"What does it matter!?" Flo cried, Blade bellowing as he felt his rider's distress. "He won't have a *life* if the Weaver kills him!"

Nobody said anything for a long moment.

Skandar was first to speak. "Flo, I *have* to get through the Chaos Trials. If I give up now, spirit wielders will be barred from the Hatchery door forever. Kenna will never be free. I'm not letting the Weaver win."

He started to pace, Scoundrel's eyes tracking him. "I think it's the lost spirit wielders I've been seeing in my Mender dreams. Erika must be holding them somewhere until the summer solstice."

"But how does she know who the lost spirit wielders are?" Mitchell asked.

"The records in the Silver Stronghold," Flo answered immediately. "The rebel sentinels could have been passing names to the Weaver for months."

Skandar took a deep breath. "I think that's why the Mainland police can't find Tyler. I saw him in a dream this morning—I think the Weaver has taken him for her plan. I don't know where, exactly—but he's with her already." Saying it out loud made Skandar's stomach flip.

He thought about the pain of Kenna's mutations, the wild unicorn's anger in her head, the risk that she might not survive the wild magic. They couldn't let the Weaver inflict that upon more innocent people—more spirit wielders whose destined unicorns were still waiting for them in the Wilderness.

"We can't let the Weaver get away with this," Skandar insisted. "It's not just about Tyler and the other lost spirit wielders she's gathering, or the fact that they'll be a fighting force allied to five elements. What about Bobby's sister? And all the others like her who might be destined for those missing eggs? We have to keep trying—we have to help Nina find them." Skandar stopped, guilt filling him. "I'm so sorry," he said to Bobby. "I should have taken the missing eggs more seriously from the beginning. I've been so focused on Kenna that I—I didn't listen to you properly."

"I get it, spirit boy. But finding the eggs will help both our sisters. It'll take us to Goshawk's destined rider, *and* it'll mean my sister gets her destined unicorn this solstice."

"And it'll stop the Weaver from creating her new generation," Skandar said firmly.

"But can't we tell Nina that the Weaver is after you during the trials, Skar? She might be able to catch her and protect you at the same time!" Flo still sounded tearful.

"I'll tell Nina what we know," Skandar promised. "You're right, catching the Weaver would solve a lot of our problems."

"It's just unfortunate that you have to be the bait," Bobby observed ominously.

Shards of evening light illuminated Commodore Kazama and Lightning's Mistake as they landed on the Sunset Platform the following evening. It had been Nina's idea to meet at the Eyrie's highest point—Skandar suspected it was to keep him out of Council Square during the aftermath of the Stronghold rebellion. According to Jamie, rumors were going round that Kenna had been working with the rogue sentinels. That disturbed Skandar, making him think of the flame-eyed sentinel. Had *he* joined the Weaver? And if so, could that mean Kenna still had something to do with Erika Everhart? He'd tried to squash the thought. Kenna was with the Wanderers; Agatha had told him that.

"Are you all right, Skandar?" Nina asked, approaching. She was dressed like any other rider, in black clothing and a blue jacket for the elemental season. The jacket had obviously been repaired many times: there were patches in multiple shades of blue, lightning bolts stitched over the worst scorches, and one large rip was even covered by a square of chain mail. Skandar thought it must be the same one she'd worn throughout her Eyrie training.

"Where's Scoundrel?" Nina prompted.

"He, umm, he's gone off for a bit," Skandar said awkwardly. "He keeps disappearing. Fledgling unicorn thing, I think."

Nina looked confused. "Then how did you get up here?"

"Turns out you *can* actually climb up to the Sunset Platform. I wouldn't recommend it, though—took me about an hour." He brushed a few leaves out of his hair. "There's something I need to tell you."

Boy and Commodore sat cross-legged on the platform as though they were waiting to toast marshmallows with the Grins. Nina listened intently as Skandar spoke.

"You believe the Weaver is hunting you?" she asked when he was finished.

"I'm the only one who can bond the lost spirit wielders to their destined unicorns. I'm an alternative for them. The Weaver must know that, somehow." Skandar took a deep breath. "I'm assuming the police haven't found Goshawk's destined rider?"

Nina shook her head. "He's been reported missing. I think you're right. I think Tyler is already with the Weaver. Here on the Island or—" She threw a hand in the air.

"What about the Mainland?"

"The authorities there haven't found a thing either."

Skandar couldn't help feeling relieved. All those Mainlanders, *Dad* included, were unprotected—unprepared for riders wielding all five elements for evil. At least there were *bonded* unicorns on the Island. At least they had a chance.

"I'll keep dreaming, keep trying to work out where the Weaver's holding the spirit wielders," Skandar promised. "Have the rebel sentinels said anything about the eggs?"

"Not yet. Rex—Instructor Manning—has them all under arrest. It doesn't look good for him as the new head of the Silver Circle." She looked up sharply. "Don't repeat that, please. That was . . . indiscreet of me."

"I won't."

Nina sighed. "I think it's being up here; I almost feel like a young Peregrine Society member again, Lightning and Sorceress racing side by side. Things were easier then."

"Wait . . . was Rex Manning a *Grin*?" Skandar asked, surprised. "He's never said!"

Nina rotated the mood ring on her thumb. "Oh, yes. Rex and I were close friends at the Eyrie, though at first I found him a bit intense—he was always more serious than me, more diligent with his training, more quietly competitive. But once we were both chosen for the Peregrine Society in our Nestling year, he lightened up—flying let him forget some of his worries, I think."

Skandar knew exactly how that felt.

"We actually had a laugh together—he loved talking to me about my childhood on the Mainland. Then, at the end of our Rookie year, it was time for the outgoing squadron leader to choose who would take over her role. I think Rex assumed it would be him—he rode a silver, after all. But I was chosen instead. I asked him to be my flight lieutenant; foolishly, I thought he'd like us to run the Grins together."

"But he wasn't happy?"

"He left the Peregrine Society," Nina said simply. "He didn't get angry, didn't even raise his voice at me. He just silently handed me his metal feather and told me he wouldn't be coming to any more meetings. We didn't speak another word to each other until I offered him the Silver Circle position last June. And now I don't know if it was the right—" Nina stopped herself. "That is, it hasn't been easy working with Rex this year. I hope perhaps one day he'll be able to see that winning together is even better than winning alone."

Nina mounted Lightning's Mistake. "Don't worry about the trials—if the Weaver shows her face, we'll catch her. And meanwhile, I'll do everything I can to find those eggs—and Tyler. We still have time."

"Thank you for helping me," Skandar said, meaning it. "I know it's a risk."

"Doing the right thing is always a risk." Nina smiled. "And we Mainlanders have got to stick together, right?"

"Can I ask you something?" When she nodded, he rushed on. "They tell us that to succeed at the Chaos Trials, that if we're going to have any chance of being Commodore one day, we have to win at any cost. But you don't seem like the kind of person who'd betray a friend for a solstice stone." This thought had been on Skandar's mind since the Fire Trial.

"Do I not?" Nina murmured, sadness flickering behind

her eyes. "The truth is, Skandar, you have no idea what I did to get where I am today. But I'll give you a piece of advice. Never let anyone tell you who you need to be. There are many kinds of Commodore, just like there are many kinds of spirit wielder. Wouldn't you agree?"

CHAPTER FIFTEEN

The Water Trial

IN THE WEEK BETWEEN THE QUALIFIERS
and the Water Trial at the beginning of April, Skandar, Flo,
Mitchell, and Bobby spent a lot of time in airborne Quartet Meetings. Mitchell had decided, given that their main
focus was now locating the eggs and lost spirit wielders, that
it was no use wasting any free time they had *not* looking for
them. Skandar felt glad to be doing something construc-
tive, rather than sitting around worrying about Kenna or
the small problem that his mother wanted to murder him.

The quartet had come up with elaborate routes across
the Island, both in the air and on the ground, which also
included sweeps right round the edge of the cliffs. Bobby
had stopped mentioning that Kenna might know where the

Weaver had hidden the eggs, though sometimes Skandar felt the accusation hovering unspoken in the air between their unicorns' wings.

Meanwhile, Nina stepped up her own search for the eggs again, requisitioning the entire fifth year of the Eyrie—the Preds—to join the teams. They were often spotted flying beyond the boundaries of the Island itself—dipping over the sea, perhaps imagining the Weaver had hidden the eggs on some sort of barge.

Between training and searching, there was also regular tea with Agatha. She seemed to find Craig's discovery about the forged bond disquieting.

"So Erika's idea to forge me a bond would never have worked?"

"If you weren't destined for a unicorn, not even Erika Everhart could have got you one," Mitchell replied.

"She was wrong," Agatha murmured. "Impossible."

"Wasn't Erika, like, fourteen at the time?" Bobby said. "My sister turns thirteen in April and she might *think* she's cleverer than everyone but—"

"My sister was a genius at fourteen," Agatha interrupted sharply—and Skandar changed the subject.

All the same, Agatha continued to insist that the Weaver simply didn't have the power to forge fifty bonds. But Skandar knew that the number of people in his dreams was multiplying every time. Why would the Weaver gather the lost spirit wielders now, only to make them wait years for a unicorn? Meanwhile, the idea that the Weaver was hunting him had taken root in Skandar's mind, and his nightmares were filled with a black-shrouded rider chasing him across the Wilderness.

April arrived, and the Water Trial with it. Given everything he had to worry about, Skandar didn't quite feel mentally prepared to undertake the third of the four Chaos Trials.

The Fledglings followed Instructor O'Sullivan to land on the edge of the Lake of Shoals—the largest fish-filled lake on the entire Island. Celestial Seabird looked ghostly in the half-light of the morning.

Bobby yawned from Falcon's back. "Why do so many of these stupid trials start at sunrise?"

Skandar knew Bobby had it much worse than the rest of them—she always got up early to groom Falcon to perfection.

"Fledglings!" Instructor O'Sullivan called. She was flanked by Instructors Anderson and Everhart. "Welcome to the Water Trial. Many of you will have read the single page of instructions that was circulated, but I will add to those details now."

The Fledglings fell deadly silent—even the unicorns were quiet. Perhaps the unicorns had begun to understand the importance of the trials, even if their training sessions still bored them.

"This trial is designed to test problem-solving, logic,

and determination. No Fledgling will receive a water stone at the outset. But each quartet will be assigned three clues—one each for the fire wielder, earth wielder, and air wielder—and each unique clue will reveal the location of one water stone."

"Clues? Logic? Problem-solving?" Mitchell was practically bouncing up and down with excitement in his Taiting saddle. Red Night's Delight hissed at him.

Instructor O'Sullivan's whirlpool eyes spun dangerously. "The water wielders among you will not receive a clue to begin with. But the stones you help the rest of your quartet collect will each contain part of a *final* clue that will point you toward a water stone of your own."

Bobby stuck her hand in the air, although she started speaking immediately. "What about the reward? The instructions specifically said there was going to be a reward!" A few other Fledglings made noises of agreement.

Instructor Anderson laughed, the fire around his ears flickering. "Yes—if a quartet works together to solve the final clue, they are rewarded. Not only will they find a water stone, but also one *spare* solstice stone, which may help them get closer to completing their set."

Skandar exchanged an excited glance with Mitchell. Finding him a fire stone suddenly seemed a lot more possible.

"The trial will begin at sunrise," Instructor O'Sullivan announced. "By sunset you must have reached the finish line at the first branch of the delta. We'll hand out your clues now."

As usual, Agatha made her way to Skandar's quartet first. A frown formed a groove in her forehead. "The most dangerous stretch of this trial is the last two hundred meters. You can't fly to the finish—there's not enough space to land—but that's exactly where the riverbanks narrow, forcing all riders close together."

Mitchell looked confused. "But why would it be dangerous? This trial's all about solving clues!"

"Don't be naive, Henderson," Agatha snapped. "Riders are getting desperate. Some of them won't even bother searching for their clues—they'll just lie in wait near the end so they can steal other people's stones. That's what I'd do, anyway."

"Is this the reason you come to every trial?" Bobby asked Agatha. "So you can warn us we're going to be attacked? I mean, it's getting pretty obvious at this point."

Agatha stroked Arctic Swansong's neck. "It's easier for me to attend the trials than for the other instructors. My only student is here." She pointed at Skandar.

"Oh." Bobby had the decency to look apologetic; Flo looked mortified.

Agatha reached into a blue-cloth bag; the contents clacking. "Here are your clues."

She handed a scallop shell first to Flo, then to Mitchell, then to Bobby. The outsides were plain white except for a number—one, two, or three—but the inside had words scrawled in neat blue handwriting.

Just then, the shadow of Lightning's Mistake—flanked by a dozen sentinels—soared over the Fledglings. Many whispered excitedly that the Commodore had come to watch. But Skandar and his quartet knew better; the Commodore had come to *patrol*.

"I highly doubt Erika will try anything with Nina here." Agatha pressed a map of the water zone into Skandar's hand. "But in any case, watch yourselves." The gruffness was missing from her voice as she turned away, and it made Skandar more nervous.

"Put that shell back in your pocket," Mitchell urged Bobby. "We don't need to worry about *our* clues yet. They're numbered for a reason. Let's focus on yours, Flo, and *don't* say it out loud—someone might steal the stone before we can get there."

On their unicorns' backs the quartet passed round Flo's shell, reading the words hidden on the inside curve. *Trees bewail rivers' betrayal.*

"That isn't a real clue," Bobby hissed. "It's a riddle! If I'd known how many riddles I'd have to solve as a unicorn rider, I might've stayed on the Mainland."

Instructor O'Sullivan shot a blast of water into the brightening sky, and the instructors took off after it so they could circle high above the zone. The Water Trial had begun.

Unlike at the beginning of the Earth or Fire Trial, the Fledglings didn't rush off. Most remained huddled in their quartets, poring over their clues. After all, nobody had a stone to steal just yet.

Mitchell was mouthing the clue silently, over and over. But in the end, it was Flo who came up with the first step toward a solution.

"When I think *bewail*—wail—I also think crying," she whispered. "So what if the trees in my clue are trees that cry?"

"Trees don't cry!" Bobby scoffed.

"Not actual tears, no—but the name," Skandar whispered excitedly. "Weeping willows! Flo, that's brilliant."

"Yes!" Mitchell crowed, and they all shushed him.

"Hate to break it to you," Bobby murmured, "but this is the water zone. Weeping willows are basically the native tree. I can see five from here."

Skandar looked out over the Lake of Shoals, and, sure enough—at multiple points on the reeded bank—willows bowed their cascades of leaves toward the water.

"We need to work out the rest of the clue, and fast," Mitchell said through gritted teeth. "Every rider has a unique clue, but that won't stop people from stealing our stones if they come across them by accident."

It didn't help their nerves that every now and then a cheer would go up from a quartet nearby, and they'd gallop off or launch into the air.

Bobby was getting increasingly agitated. "Can't we try to solve it on the way?"

"On the way to where?" Mitchell asked sarcastically. "The clue is the thing that tells us where we're going."

It was, Skandar knew, Bobby's worst nightmare. He tried to give her a reassuring smile, but she was threading Falcon's mane compulsively through her fingers and taking deep breaths. Skandar moved Scoundrel closer to Falcon and put his hand out for Bobby to grip on to while she breathed through her panic attack.

"Ouch!" he said, as she squeezed very hard.

She wheezed out a laugh, and Skandar grinned at her.

Once Bobby's breathing was even again, Skandar decided to unfold the map Agatha had given them. He traced his finger along the river, stopping at the place where they'd found the dead wild unicorn at the beginning of last year. An image of that riverbank came into his mind—the view of the water ahead broken up by a little island, home to two weeping willows.

Wait. He checked the map against his memory, and there it was—a tiny dot sitting on the crossing of two rivers. *Betray. Double-cross.*

"I think I've got something!" Skandar said, no longer bothering to keep his voice down. Other than Romily, Elias, Mariam, and Walker, they were the only quartet left by the lake.

"*Rivers' betrayal*—on the map here there are two rivers

crossing over each other *twice*—if you double-cross someone, you betray them, right?" He looked at Flo for confirmation.

She nodded encouragingly.

"So the rivers cross here and here." He pointed to the
map. "And between the two crossings there's this tiny island
near where we had our picnic. Don't you remember? It has
two weeping willows."

Bobby was already gathering up Falcon's reins. "That's
good enough for me, spirit boy."

Flo beamed. "Excellent."

"Seriously impressive," Mitchell said, pushing his glasses
up his nose.

They decided to risk flying, hoping most other Fledglings were solving their own first clues rather than trying to
steal just yet. Mitchell used his trusty compass to navigate
through the skies, Red's scarlet tail leading the way.

It was a secluded spot, enclosed by wild bushes and
undergrowth. Dismounting from their unicorns, the quartet stared out at the two willow trees where the rivers
crossed.

"I'm not even sure there's enough space for a unicorn to
land on that island," Skandar said warily.

"Falcon and I can do a dive or something," Bobby volunteered.

"No, you can't," Flo said urgently. "It's too exposed—
you'll be seen from miles away."

Bobby crossed her arms. "How then, dearest Florence, would you suggest we get to that island?"

But Flo was already slipping off her blue jacket, her boots, her socks, then lifting her T-shirt over her head.

"Has she lost the plot?" Bobby whispered to Skandar. "It's April!"

"Umm, Flo," Mitchell said, "what exactly . . . ?"

Flo stood on the river's edge in a bright blue swimming costume, Blade shining at her side. She looked amused at the expressions on her quartet's faces. She put a hand on her hip, and—in a perfect imitation of Bobby—said, "Are you honestly telling me that you came to the *Water* Trial without swimwear? Amateurs."

They all burst out laughing.

"Shh! Shh!" Flo insisted once she'd stopped giggling. "I'm going in, okay? Try to keep Blade here. He might panic when he sees me in the water." She handed the silver unicorn's reins to Skandar. Blade's eyes turned to swirls of molten lava, as if to say: *Stop me from doing what I want? I'd like to see you try.*

Flo waded out until the water was deep enough for her to start swimming. Skandar, Bobby, and Mitchell watched as her black-and-silver cloud of hair bobbed further and further from the shore until her body resurfaced again on the tiny island. For a moment Flo disappeared between the two willow trees—their trunks bowed toward each other like an old married couple.

There was a sudden noise behind Skandar. A snapping twig, a rustle of leaves.

"What was that?" Mitchell looked over his shoulder.

Skandar turned. Two sentinels flew over, circling low. Skandar felt his heart rate slow—surely the Weaver wouldn't risk doing anything with Nina's guards so close.

Bobby's eyes remained fixed on the island.

Mitchell looked into the undergrowth once more. "Probably just a rabbit."

"She's only gone and done it!" Bobby whispered, snapping Skandar's attention back to the river.

Flo re-emerged from between the trees and held a fist up in triumph, the blue solstice stone catching the early-morning light. Skandar wanted to cheer, but he knew they shouldn't give away that they'd found their first stone. Instead, he, Bobby, and Mitchell did a silly silent victory dance on the edge of the riverbank.

Flo pulled herself out of the water, dripping wet and shivering uncontrollably.

"Th-th-there's a t-towel in m-my b-b-bag," she managed to say as she hugged her arms round herself.

Skandar leapt into action and held it up for her. "Do you want—"

In answer, Flo practically hurled herself into the towel, teeth chattering, and somehow Skandar ended up with his arms wrapped round her too.

"Th-thanks, Sk-Skar," she said—and he let go, cheeks flaming.

"That was totally badass!" Bobby crowed.

Skandar thought about how Flo never believed she was brave, and yet she'd been willing to swim out into the unpredictable currents of the water zone's rivers in the freezing cold. He wished she could see herself like they all did.

Once Flo was dry, the quartet sat on the riverbank and looked at her water stone. As the trial instructions had promised, it had come with the first word of the clue Skandar would need to find his own. A metal chain was looped round its blue belly with a tag that read: *Lily*.

"Well, that's one down," Bobby said, getting up. "Two more to find. Mitchell, let's have a look at your stupid clue. You're next, aren't you?"

"Oh, I solved mine the moment Agatha handed me the shell," Mitchell said casually.

He tossed it down to Bobby, who seemed unsure whether to be annoyed or pleased. "I thought you said we weren't supposed to look."

"It was for your own good. We're supposed to solve the clues in a particular order, and I didn't want any of you to get ideas about skipping ahead."

Bobby turned the shell over in her hands. Skandar and Flo came to look at it with her. The blue writing read: *Might makes light with shell closed tight.*

"Well, I've got nothing," Bobby said. "You?"

Skandar and Flo shook their heads.

Mitchell looked rather pleased with himself. "*Might* made me think of *muscle*, which can also be spelled *m-u-s-s-e-l*. Some mussels make pearls—which I believe is what *light* is referring to, since pearls sort of shine—inside their shells. Easy. There's a freshwater pearl farm in the water zone."

The other three stared at him.

"That was even harder than mine," Flo murmured.

Skandar was shaking his head in wonder. "Mitchell, that's really brilliant."

Bobby ruffled Mitchell's flaming hair. "A genius walks among us."

Skandar thought it might have been the nicest thing she'd ever said to him.

The quartet navigated along the winding riverbanks, occasionally passing the treehouses of the zone's residents—linked together by bridges stretching over the blue ribbons of water. At one point, they spotted Mateo, Divya, Harper, and Naomi from a distance. But both quartets ignored each other, too intent on seeking out their next stones. Eventually Skandar, Bobby, Flo, and Mitchell arrived at the pearl farm. Hundreds of floating buoys were dotted across the surface of a small lake, underneath which—Mitchell informed them—were nets that housed the mussels.

"How are we supposed to find the stone among all those?" Bobby asked, frustrated. Skandar thought she was probably worrying about finding her own solstice stone, like he was. It was already past midday.

"I'm not sure," Mitchell murmured. "The stone could be right at the bottom of the lake. The unicorns could probably dive with us on their backs, but I'm worried they'd get tangled in the nets."

"There's no way Falcon is going into that water—is it even clean? I don't think she'd ever forgive me."

"Wait!" Skandar had spotted something glinting in the sunlight. "It's there! I can see it!"

He pointed at a buoy about a quarter of the way out into the lake. The stone flashed in a makeshift nest balanced on top of it, like a rare bird's egg.

Mitchell gathered his reins. "Excellent! I'll fly over on Red, reach down, and grab it."

"Shouldn't Skandar get it?" Bobby said quickly. "He's quicker at flying—it's the kind of thing he does in his bird club."

Mitchell looked disappointed. "I suppose that's best."

Skandar hesitated. He knew that the trials were trying to teach them what being a Chaos rider meant—that they should triumph at any cost. But after his conversation with Nina, he was beginning to question whether that was who *he* wanted to be. And right now, all Skandar wanted was to be a good friend. He knew Mitchell and Red could get the stone if they were given the chance.

"No, I think Mitchell is the best one to get it. It's his stone," Skandar said aloud.

Red Night's Delight looked very pleased with herself as Mitchell took off from the bank. Her tail burst into flames over the water, so for a moment she looked like a phoenix.

"So much for keeping a low profile," Bobby muttered.

Red flew low, approaching the buoy—so far, so good. Mitchell reached down to grab the stone and then—

Missed. Red had swerved sideways, heading for a jumping fish.

"C'mon, Mitchell," Bobby said through gritted teeth.

Red turned sharply in the air, her great wings sending ripples across the water beneath her. Mitchell stroked her blood-red neck, encouraging her. The pair tried again, soaring low, back toward the buoy. This time, Mitchell let his arm hang down so that it was almost touching the water, and he stretched out his fingers for the stone. Red was keeping steady, he was there; his hand closed over the precious blue prize, and—

A greenish-gray arm shot up out of the water, the fingers—or perhaps claws—closed round Mitchell's wrist. He cried out in shock, but the creature did not loosen its grip. Skandar watched in horror as the lake monster pulled Mitchell out of his saddle and into the water.

Red shrieked in alarm as soon her rider's weight was missing from her back, searching for him with blazing red eyes.

"Help!" Mitchell's head bobbed above water. "It's still got me!" He thrashed and splashed, trying to dislodge the creature's iron hold on his wrist.

Red was dive-bombing the water—her head half-submerged, trying to get Mitchell to grab on to her—but the creature was strong and kept pulling him downward.

Scoundrel shrieked in distress to his fire-allied best friend, and she bellowed back. Unicorns knew that the one thing not to do was let their riders fall.

Skandar didn't hesitate. He gathered up Scoundrel's reins and the unicorn took off, body arching over the lake in three strides as his wings extended outward. They hurtled through the air like a black bullet toward Mitchell, who kept trying to break the surface of the water. When they reached him, Skandar got one look at the relief on his face before Mitchell disappeared underneath the water again— one arm flailing upward.

Scoundrel did exactly what Skandar needed, as though reading his rider's mind. The black unicorn hovered on strong wings right by Mitchell's arm, and Skandar grabbed his wrist—the only part of himself the fire wielder had managed to keep above the surface.

Skandar immediately felt the pull of the creature in the opposite direction, and he held on to the front of his Shekoni saddle with all his might. For a brief moment he thought of trying to use elemental magic, but the water was too choppy—he was afraid of hurting Mitchell.

There was only one thing for it. Bracing his whole weight against his saddle, Skandar encouraged Scoundrel to pump his wings so they could pull Mitchell up and out of the water. The unicorn strained, all his muscles tensing.

Slowly, Mitchell's head, then neck, then whole body was lifted into the air.

Unfortunately, the lake creature came with him.

"I can't get it off!" Mitchell cried, a slimy claw still clamped round his other wrist. "I feel like I'm going to split in two!"

Then Red Night's Delight soared toward the creature dangling from her rider's arm. She was usually a rather mild, fun-focused unicorn—but not today. Not when some kind of water demon was attempting to kill her beloved rider. Red did not bother with an elemental blast. She resorted to pure violence—skewering the monster with her horn right through its slimy chest.

The creature let out a bloodcurdling wail before releasing its grip on Mitchell's arm.

For a second, Skandar was relieved—until he realized he was holding Mitchell's entire weight with one hand. But Red was on the case. She dislodged her horn from the monster's chest, and it dropped back into the water with a splash. Then she hovered beside Mitchell, so he could scramble back into his saddle. His tawny skin was very pale as Scoundrel and Red flew side by side back to shore.

Mitchell slid from Red's back as soon as she landed and

collapsed onto the bank. The others gathered round him, trying to check that he had no serious injuries. Skandar examined his arm, Flo wrapped him in a towel, and Bobby offered him one of her emergency sandwiches—at which point he vomited a lungful of lake water in her direction.

When Mitchell had regained enough strength to sit up, he croaked, "I think that was an undine."

"For goodness' sake, Mitchell—it doesn't matter what it was!" Bobby looked very pale herself. "It almost killed you!"

"I can't wait to tell Jamie I saw one. They're really rare. They feature in old bard songs quite frequently. Water elementals that guard the pearls; some say they're seals but . . ." He trailed off, losing his train of thought.

There was a long silence. "What are we going to do now? I don't fancy fighting that lake monster for the stone it stole." Skandar shivered.

"Nobody's going back in there," Flo said, more forcefully than usual. "Let's move on to Bobby's clue."

"We can't do that!" Bobby was on her feet. "It means Mitchell will be down two stones and we won't be able to solve Skandar's clue! There's no way we'll all make it through the Chaos Trials. We can't be separated!"

And then the earth jolted on its axis because Bobby Bruna was crying.

Flo was up on her feet first, reaching out. "It's all right, Bobby. It's okay."

Bobby wiped angrily at her tears. "The reason I—I want

us to pass the Chaos Trials isn't really about me making sure I still have a full quartet when my sister"—she corrected herself, fresh tears rolling—"*if* my sister gets here." She hiccupped. "I know I always talk like I don't need you lot, like I'm the most popular one—which I am, by the way. And I know I can get any friend I want. But I need *you*. I hated branching out last year. Nobody understands me like you do—you even know about my panic attacks, you help me through them, you *get* all of me. I can't go through being split up again. I don't want to lose any of you—even Mitchell." She gave him a watery smile. "But now we're already down a fire and water stone and—"

Finally Mitchell wobbled to his feet, a look of confusion on his face. "Roberta Bruna, what *are* you talking about?"

He opened his fist, the fist on the same arm the undine had grabbed.

Bobby's mouth fell open. Flo gasped. Skandar whooped.

A blue solstice stone shone in the center of Mitchell's palm.

KENNA

Loneliness

KENNA SMITH WAS HOPELESSLY LONELY.

Loneliness was the indifference of birdsong in the morning. It was sleeping in late so there were fewer hours to bear, and eating standing up so she wasn't sitting alone.

Loneliness was pain. The pain of magma seeping through the creases of her skin. The pain of knowing nobody could hear her cry. The pain of her fourth mutation pushing her further beyond the Island's version of acceptability.

Loneliness was not knowing what to say when her visitors came. It was talking about the weather and the trees, when all she wanted to do was scream: Please stay. Don't leave me!

Loneliness was waiting. Waiting all day for her brother. Waiting so long she knew that if he ever came, she'd be unable to speak for anger. Waiting until she no longer cared.

Kenna sat on a rock with her knees pulled up to her chin, watching the water falling from a great height and churning in its plunge pool. She had not slept properly in days, and she was trying to tire herself out by listening to the rhythm of the water. But all she could think about was her new mutation.

And the nightmare that there was still one more to go.

The day Kenna had mutated for the fourth time, she'd woken alone. Well, she supposed she was never truly alone now—she should be thankful for Goshawk in her head, in her heart. But sometimes the anger from Gos weighed so heavy on her soul that she struggled to get up in the mornings. Some days she understood Dad better than she ever had before. It made her want to hug him. It made her terrified for herself.

But on the day of the mutation, Kenna had risen with the light bleeding through the waterfall curtain. She'd felt inspired to work on her magic with Goshawk and to follow the training schedule she'd devised. Each morning, she focused on one of the four legal elements—fire, earth, water, or air—trying to improve Goshawk's responses in the bond. She learned to control the shadowy edge that sometimes entered her magic, so that she didn't poison the water. She didn't tell any of her Wanderer visitors about *this* particular part of her training—not even Albert.

Kenna reserved the spirit element for the afternoons.

Every afternoon. She could remember much of the content of *The Book of Spirit* Dorian Manning had given her when she'd been imprisoned in the Spear. And she was *good* at the spirit element—she knew she was.

The white glow came easily to her palm, and though it was tinged with that same smoky edge as all the other magic she summoned, she could tell that this should have been her allied element. She could summon spirit swords in the blink of an eye and brandish pearlescent maces bigger than her own head; she knew she'd be able to trick her opponents by imagining weapons that didn't quite exist, just like the book had explained. And she was certain that if there'd been someone with a bond to break, she could have done that, too.

On the day of the mutation, she'd been on the edge of the waterfall's plunge pool—trying to get a flaming bow to balance in her hands—when her fire magic had surged. She still didn't know whether it had been Goshawk pushing more magic through the bond or simply that the time for the mutation had come. The bow had grown in size, the black smoke round its edges thickening and spreading so that the plants round the waterfall withered and died. Kenna had tried to shut her palm to stop the flow of magic completely. But Goshawk's whole mane and tail had ignited—along with every bedraggled feather left on her wings—and she'd roared columns of glowing ash toward the water as though she was trying to put the fire out just as Kenna was.

Then the pain had started. Just as at the oasis, Kenna's other mutations had flared up first as if in warning—the thorns prickling up her right arm, the ice spikes slicing at her throat, the feather points re-piercing her ears—and then came a new searing pain at her left wrist.

She'd made the mistake of looking at it. Liquid fire had broken through every crack in her skin, the bubbling threads snaking all the way up to the crease in her elbow. Her left arm had burned so hot that she had no longer been able to remain on Goshawk's back, and she'd thrown herself into the waterfall's pool, thrusting her arm into the cool water, and it had dulled the pain a little. Though if a doctor had asked her in that moment how she would have rated her pain on a scale of one to ten, she wouldn't have known how to answer. It had been on a different scale altogether.

All Kenna could think was that nobody was here. Nobody was going to tell her everything was going to be okay. The waterfall crashed on—oblivious to the desolate girl soothing her molten arm in its waters.

Then Goshawk's Fury had approached the edge of the plunge pool, smoking red eyes fixed on her rider. Looking back, Kenna had felt the tiniest vibration of the wild unicorn's fear. Gos had been worried about her—and that, more than the pain, had finally made Kenna burst into tears. Happy tears. Lonely tears. Because she'd wished so much that there'd been someone to tell. About the mutation. About Goshawk caring. And that someone was Skandar.

Kenna examined the threads of magma in her arm, and a tiny brown wren landed on the same rock Kenna was sitting on. Its round body bobbed up and down with its short tail, the occasional dot of white flashing on its feathers as it cocked its head to look at her. Returning its beady gaze, Kenna was suddenly aware of the fluttering of its tiny beating heart—the blood racing around the bird's body, vibrating with its own melody.

She reached out a hand toward the bird. It was still singing, unafraid of the shadow of the stranger's arm moving across the sunlit rock. Kenna opened her fingers wide and then started to close them—very slowly—the songbird's frantic heartbeats thundering under her skin.

There was a sudden splash from the plunge pool, and in that moment Kenna realized what she was about to do. She withdrew her hand quickly, shaking with horror—had that been Goshawk's influence? Or had that all been her?

Kenna wasn't sure she knew anymore.

CHAPTER SIXTEEN

Cheated

THOUGH MITCHELL HAD MANAGED TO hold on to his solstice stone during the undine attack, the metal tag with the clue word had been lost. Skandar's heart sank when he realized. Even if they found Bobby's water stone in time, would they be able to work out where Skandar's was with only two words out of the three? All they had so far was *Lily*.

The quartet rode back into the dense thickets along the riverbank. Once they were satisfied they'd gone far enough, Skandar, Flo, and Mitchell huddled their unicorns round Falcon, and Bobby pulled out her scallop shell.

At that exact moment, all the hairs on Skandar's neck stood up. He couldn't explain it—he could just feel a presence. Then a twig snapped, and there was the unmistak-able sound of something moving through the undergrowth. Scoundrel growled.

"There's definitely someone following us," Skandar hissed.

Flo followed Skandar's gaze between the shadowy trunks. "Do you think it's the Weaver? Why hasn't she attacked?"

"Well, don't *encourage* her," Bobby said.

Instinctively, all four riders backed their unicorns into a protective circle—facing outward, palms glowing the color of their elements.

They waited. And waited.

"Maybe it was another quartet?" Mitchell whispered.

"Forking thunderstorms, there's nobody there," Bobby said dismissively. "Can we please concentrate on *my* stone now? We only have until sunset!"

"I want to get out of here!" Flo whispered. "Skar might be in danger."

"Let's all just calm down," Mitchell said, though he still looked shaken. "Bobby, hold the shell in your palm. Nobody say the clue out loud, just in case that was another quartet trying to steal our stones. Once we've solved the clue, we'll leave immediately."

Skandar read the words on Bobby's shell and couldn't make any sense of them at all: *The gilled guild wears wares ewes use.* Was it something to do with fish? Sheep?

But Mitchell and Flo were giving each other a significant look, hopeful smiles on their faces.

"Please tell me you two aren't just grinning at each other like idiots for no reason," Bobby groaned, shoving the shell back into her jacket pocket. "I hate these riddles. Fighting, I can do. Words? Hate them."

"We know where to go," Flo said quietly. "Not exactly, but the general area. Come on."

Skandar was pleased to leave that part of the zone behind. He still couldn't shake the feeling that they were being followed. A couple of times he could have sworn he heard hoofbeats behind them—until he realized that it was Scoundrel's own feet, hitting rocks along the river path. Skandar was so wound up, not even the shape of the Commodore's unicorn passing overhead could settle him.

"You're a bit jumpy, spirit boy," Bobby said, riding Falcon beside Scoundrel, more cheerful now that they were going somewhere. "Only one trial left after this, eh? Is your dad coming?"

"What?" Skandar asked, distracted. "Oh. Yeah. Dad's really excited."

"*You* don't sound very excited," Bobby observed.

"No, I am. I just . . . Dad keeps asking me about Kenna's Training Trial, and I'm so sick of lying to him about *everything*." The words burst out of Skandar so easily; he hadn't realized he'd been keeping them coiled up inside.

"Maybe try to focus on the future?" Bobby suggested.

"That's what I do with my panic attacks. I fast-forward to the moment after they've finished, and imagine that I'm breathing easy again. So, come on, picture what it's going to be like. You've passed your Pred year in the Eyrie—the spirit element is no longer illegal. Your brilliant friend Bobby Bruna has just won the Chaos Cup—"

"Ha, ha!"

"Don't interrupt, I'm doing a thing here. The Divide lights up for seven new spirit wielders, including Kenna and a dapple-gray unicorn. Your dad is invited to watch—because I'm the new Commodore and I said so. Everyone is happy and the Weaver has been defeated and we all live happily ever after."

Skandar was speechless. Bobby had just described everything he wanted.

"I don't know if Kenna will give up Goshawk's Fury," Skandar said in a quiet voice. "Even if I *do* manage to work out how to remold the wild bond into two destined ones."

"You were pretty handy at all that bond stuff with Aspen McGrath two years ago," Bobby said, shrugging. "And nobody told you how to fix her bond with New-Age Frost. You'll work it out. You're smart—sometimes."

"Oi!" Skandar said.

She winked at him. "Hey, maybe you could show Kenna the glowing-bones thing you told us about?"

"Soul-shine?"

"Yeah. If she sees her dapple-gray glowing for her, their

souls recognizing each other, don't you think that might persuade her? And if she sees Goshawk's Fury glowing for Tyler, too? It's not every day your skeleton glows for your destined unicorn, is it?"

Skandar chuckled. "You know, I think you're right."

It was only afterward that he realized Bobby had distracted him so much, he'd completely stopped worrying about being followed.

After a while, they began to see boats on the river. They were long and narrow, propelled along by a person standing on the back with a long pole. Some moved at an impressive speed, while others were weighed down by piles of goods— everything from bags of apples to stacks of furniture.

Further on, the riverside thickets thinned out. Voices filled the air, and the networks of wooden treehouses became more bustling. The delta had widened, and throngs of Islanders were stepping out of boats or climbing across gangplanks to reach wide floating platforms that housed stalls. Sellers haggled loudly. Children chased each other in and out of bobbing kayaks. Skandar realized this had to be the famous floating market.

Despite being mid-trial, Skandar couldn't help feeling excited to see the market up close. Now that they were in the bustle of the crowd, the quartet spoke freely about Bobby's clue as they tied their unicorns to metal rings along the bank.

"The only part of the clue that made sense was the

wares part. *Wares* means 'goods,' things to buy," Mitchell explained.

"We both thought of the floating market—it's the most famous place for shopping on the whole Island—but that's about as far as we got." Flo frowned. "We hoped it might be clearer once we arrived, but it's so busy." Flo didn't like noisy places—she found them overwhelming, after growing up on peaceful Wildflower Hill.

"The gilled guild wears wares ewes use." Bobby had taken out her scallop shell again. "Aren't ewes female sheep? Maybe we're looking for something made of wool?"

"That could be useful," Mitchell said, trying to mask the surprise in his voice. Bobby looked delighted and stepped onto the nearest wooden platform, the others chasing her into the crowd.

They'd entered the market near the food stalls. Skandar spotted Fred's Frothing Fish Sticks, and the sizzling smell of butter melting made his stomach rumble. Each stall had its own floating platform, tied to the next with algae-stained ropes, so shoppers had to jump between them. The quartet tried to keep up with Bobby, leaping from platform to platform until they reached the stalls full of blankets, cushions, Chaos Cup T-shirts, and anything else made of cloth or fabric.

Bobby soon ran out of steam, circling back to them. "There is *so* much wool. Where are we supposed to start?"

Flo looked up at the sky. It was obvious from the sun's

position that it was late afternoon—they only had a couple of hours before sunset.

"*Gilled guild.*" Mitchell murmured. "Fish have gills, and a guild is a group of people, isn't it? Does this group wear woollen clothing? But why *fish*?"

"Kipper Knitters!" Flo exclaimed. She'd been scanning the nearby stall signs, and now she was grinning her face off.

"Come again?" Bobby said, bewildered.

In answer, Flo took Bobby's arm and pulled her toward a stall a few platforms down.

"Sorry! Excuse me!" Flo called politely, as they swerved round groups of people. Mitchell and Skandar wobbled across platforms after them.

Flo stopped outside a stall selling knitwear of every imaginable color. They were the kind of sweaters to put on in the dead of winter, that feel like wearing a warm hug.

"What? I don't see—" Bobby started, but Flo interrupted her.

"Look at the name!"

THE KIPPER KNITTERS' CLUB. Their symbol, sewn onto every sweater, was two crossed knitting needles with fish tails at their ends.

Mitchell began to laugh, while Skandar waited for Flo to explain.

"See," Flo continued, "fish have gills. A kipper is a type of fish, and the people that knit these sweaters call themselves a club. Like a guild! *G-I-L-L-E-D. G-U-I-L-D.*

And all the clothes they *wear,* their wares, are made of wool! Sheep! *Ewes!*" She was beside herself with excitement.

Bobby eyes raked over the sweaters piled on the stall's table. "Say you're right about these Kipper Knitters. Where's my stone? Are we supposed to go through all those?"

"Why don't you try inside that blue one?" Skandar suggested, feeling desperate to contribute something, even if it was probably a silly idea. "That sweater is water element blue, right?" The stall owner inclined his head as if to confirm. Skandar hoped he wasn't expecting them to buy it.

Bobby dashed up to the table—as quick as a spark—and pulled the blue sweater from the bottom of the stack, toppling the others. Flo followed and started gathering them up under the stall owner's steely gaze.

There was a loud clink—and then a cheer from Bobby, as she hurled herself under the table to retrieve an object that had fallen from inside the folds of the blue sweater.

"I've got it!" she crowed. "I've got it!" The glassy sides of the water stone glinted in the afternoon sun. She showed it excitedly to Flo, and then hugged her.

The stall owner shook his head disapprovingly. "Fledglings," he said, sighing, before starting to refold all the sweaters.

"Does it have the metal tag with the clue?" Skandar couldn't hide the desperation in his voice.

Bobby nodded and showed the boys the word on the metal tag.

Bridge.

"*Lily* and *Bridge*," Mitchell said. "I'm sure I've seen . . ." He took out the map of the water zone and sat down cross-legged to study it right in the middle of the crowds of shoppers.

For some reason, Flo was having an animated conversation with the owner of the Kipper Knitters' Club. He seemed to have cheered right up. There were now more customers—a man was holding a purple sweater against his small son, a lady in a blue hooded cloak was examining a woolly hat, and then there was Flo. Skandar watched as she searched in her pocket for something, handed it over, and was given an emerald sweater in return.

"You've still got a sweater in your hand," Bobby said, as Flo rejoined them.

"I bought it!" Flo shrugged off her blue jacket and pulled the sweater over her head. "As a memento of the trial, but also because I'm still *freezing*."

Mitchell looked up from his map. "You want a memento of a time when you had to swim in a freezing river, I was almost drowned by an undine, Bobby cried for possibly the first time ever, and Skandar is almost certainly being followed by the Weaver?"

Flo shrugged. "I just like us being together."

Bobby sniggered. "Yeah, Mitchell, don't be so negative."

"Okay, okay, I'm sorry," Mitchell said, rubbing his eyes. "It's just, we haven't solved Skandar's clue, it's getting late, and honestly 'Lily Bridge' is not an awful lot to go on. There are about a hundred bridges, and does it mean near water lilies or lily flowers? They're very different!"

"Can you see Lily *Pad* Bridge?" Flo asked brightly. "The stall owner said that's the first one that came into his mind when I told him we were looking for a Lily Bridge."

Mitchell searched the map feverishly. "Yes! Yes, it's here! It's on the way to the finish!"

Flo grinned. "Sometimes people can be more helpful than maps."

"Let's go and get our reward!" Bobby cried. "And Skandar's water stone, of course," she added sheepishly.

The quartet had no choice but to fly to Lily Pad Bridge. Mitchell reckoned they had less than an hour to reach the Fourpoint end of the delta. As Scoundrel soared above the blue river threads below, Skandar spotted other Fledglings doing the same. He wondered how many of them had found their stones—and how many were planning to lie in wait on the final stretch to steal what they hadn't earned.

"Hey! Is that Whirlwind Thief?" Bobby called over the pounding of Falcon's wingbeats.

Sure enough, Amber—all alone—was soaring to the quartet's left.

"Do you think she's all right?" Flo yelled.

"Don't get any closer," Mitchell warned, as Red shrieked to Thief in greeting. "She might try to steal our stones, especially if her quartet has abandoned her again." His hand went to his breastplate to check his own blue gem.

Skandar ignored this, and moved Scoundrel to the left so he was in shouting distance of Amber. After all, *he* didn't have a stone for her to steal yet.

"Are you okay?

"What?" Amber called over the wind, the star mutation on her head crackling.

Skandar made a thumbs-up gesture, the wind making Goshawk's permanent burn sting. "Are you all right?"

An actual smile broke across Amber's face. She put a thumb up and then pointed at her own metal breastplate, where a solstice stone shone.

Then she shouted, "See you at the end, loser!" But it sounded so cheerful, Skandar didn't take the *loser* bit to heart.

Lily Pad Bridge was easy to spot, even from the air. The water on either side of it was covered in green discs of varying sizes, each one boasting a flower of pink or white. Dismounting, Skandar was the first to rush onto the bridge, hoping that it would be easy to spot the blue stone that he needed.

But there was no nest on the bridge like there had been on the buoy—only bare wooden slats.

"It's in the water!" Bobby cried, before Flo was able to shush her. The rest of the quartet joined Skandar on the bridge, and Bobby pointed over the side. Sure enough, there was a twig-woven nest resting on one of the larger lily pads right under the bridge. Skandar couldn't see the stones—his view was blocked by the lily's white flower—but he knew exactly how he was going to get them.

Skandar launched himself onto his stomach. "Grab my legs!" he called to the others. "Lower me over the side. It's not that far down; I think I'll be able to reach it."

"Not without some kind of anchor," Flo said, and rushed back to Silver Blade. She summoned the earth element to her palm and shot several vines toward Lily Pad Bridge. Bobby got the idea immediately and grabbed them, then started to fix them round the slats of the bridge and then Skandar's ankles.

With the vines fastened to the bridge, and his friends holding each of his ankles, Skandar crawled to the very edge of the planks and started to lower himself over the side. Scoundrel let out a shriek of concern from the bank, and Skandar tried to fill their bond with as much reassurance as he could muster.

It didn't take long before his whole body was hanging over the edge, then his legs. He could hear his friends straining above. He could almost touch the nest; he was so close, and then—

He had it. He grabbed the whole thing off the lily pad and then yelled to Mitchell, Flo, and Bobby to heave him back up to the bridge.

"The extra stone! It's fire! Flaming fireballs, thank you!" Mitchell cried, as soon as Skandar was safely back on the slats. He grabbed the red solstice stone out of the nest and hugged it to his chest; then he was hugging Skandar and Flo—and Bobby too, who grumbled, "Get *off* me, Mitchell!"

Skandar looked back at the nest for a glimmer of glassy blue.

"Skar?" Flo asked tentatively. "What's wrong?"

He pointed wordlessly at the nest. The water stone was gone.

With the sun sinking in the sky, the quartet rode their unicorns toward the beginning of the water zone's delta. Agatha had been right about how the land between the rivers narrowed toward the finish. Once they turned the last bend, Skandar could feel the eyes of the Fledglings hidden among the vegetation lining the banks. They might have avoided the Weaver during the trial, but they couldn't escape this. The blue stones on his friends' armored chests seemed to shine as bright as beacons—Mitchell's blue *and* red stones even more so. Skandar tried not to look at his own bare breastplate. He felt cheated. They'd solved all the clues, they'd worked as a team, and yet he'd never got his water stone. Perhaps that table in the Trough really was cursed?

Bobby was still obsessed with the missing solstice stone. "But which Fledgling would have taken the water stone and not the fire stone?"

Flo sighed. "Maybe someone who already had all the fire stones they needed and was trying to be kind."

"Kind?" Bobby exploded. "Florence, these are the Chaos Trials. Nobody's being *kind*."

Mitchell cleared his throat nervously. "We have a decision to make. We have two choices: either we gallop to the finish as fast as we can, or we try to battle another Fledgling to steal their water stone for Skandar."

"No," Skandar said immediately. "I'm not having you risk your own stones. There's a third choice: you ride to the finish, and I can try to get a stone for myself."

"I'm not leaving you out here alone with this lot," Bobby said, eyes narrowing at the Fledglings waiting to pounce. "You don't have a stone to steal, but you're a spirit wielder, and some of them are *not* your biggest fans."

"And there's the Weaver . . . ," Mitchell added ominously.

"I agree," Flo said. "We're not leaving you, Skar."

Skandar understood what his friends were offering, what they were prepared to risk for him. But he wouldn't let them do it. "We ride for the finish together."

"There's only one trial left," Mitchell warned.

"I know," Skandar said determinedly. "But we've got a brilliant air wielder in our quartet." He smiled at Bobby. "There's been spare stones in every trial so far; I think we stand a good chance of winning a reward in the next one too."

Bobby grinned. "You can count on it, spirit boy."

"Okay," Mitchell said. "I'll count down from ten, and then we gallop—"

"Can you please just count down from three?" Bobby begged. "We haven't got all day!"

Mitchell sighed. "Fine. Three."

Skandar gathered his reins and poured one single desire into his bond with Scoundrel: *Get me to the finish as fast as you can, boy. I trust you.*

"Two."

The four riders bent low in their saddles, armor creaking, making themselves as streamlined as possible.

"ONE!" Mitchell shouted, and the unicorns exploded forward onto the sand of the final stretch.

Elemental magic blasted from the riverbanks on both sides—fire jets, lightning arrows, and hailstones. An entire diamond axe clanged off Scoundrel's chain mail, and the black unicorn shrieked with rage. Unicorns and riders exploded toward the quartet—too many to count.

Quickly surrounded, Skandar, Flo, Bobby, and Mitchell fought facing outward in a tight diamond. Skandar could barely see who was attacking them through the magic—although he was fairly certain the diamond axe had belonged to Alastair.

When the cloud of elemental debris cleared, Skandar saw Kobi throwing an ice spear at Mitchell, who created a flaming shield just in time to melt it. Old Starlight whipped sand into the air, as Mariam molded a small tornado and threw it toward Flo and Blade. Flo's hand glowed green as she quickly threw up a glass shield to block it—though it wobbled dangerously in the wind. Marissa looked half-crazed as Demonic Nymph reared up and water exploded from the unicorn's hooves toward Bobby, who swiftly took down her lightning shield to avoid getting electrocuted and replaced it with a sand one that easily absorbed the blast.

Skandar realized quickly that nobody was attacking him, which—given how his life on the Island had gone so far—was fairly unusual. The reason was clear: He had no stone to steal. It would be a waste of energy when the sun was starting to set. But it meant he could help his friends get to the finish.

Unnoticed by the brawling Fledglings, Skandar summoned the spirit element. The colored bonds of his fellow riders flashed brightly around their unicorns. He wanted to neutralize the magic of those attacking his quartet. Skandar sent thin tendrils of spirit element from his palm into Mariam's bond, then Kobi's, then Marissa's. All their attacks snuffed out, and they looked around in bewilderment.

In the moment it took them to reignite their palms, Skandar spoke urgently to his friends. "In five seconds, Marissa, Kobi, and Mariam are going to look over their shoulders. They're going to be confused. When that happens—you gallop to the finish."

"What—" Mitchell started to ask.

"Trust me."

The cinnamon smell of the spirit element surrounded Skandar as he summoned it back into the bond. Scoundrel was working with him—his wing tips starting to glow as he concentrated along with his rider—and just as Kobi's palm turned blue again, Skandar focused harder than he ever had in his life on the exact words he wanted each of the attackers to hear.

I'm behind you, Kobi.

I'm behind you, Mariam.

I'm behind you, Marissa.

All three looked over their shoulders, and then back at Skandar. Marissa even rubbed feverishly at the lenses of her blue glasses, as if to clear her vision. He could tell their brains were struggling to work out what was real.

Blade, Falcon, and Red burst away from the other unicorns, using the split-second opportunity to make a break for the finish.

And now for Skandar's own escape. He swept his arm up and down, creating a shining spirit shield that grew brighter and brighter until it blurred his and Scoundrel's outlines completely.

I'm coming for you, he thought—loudly this time—and he heard Mariam scream.

I'm coming for you—Kobi yelped in fear.

I'm coming for you—Marissa called for help.

Then Skandar dropped the shield, and with the attackers terrified he let Scoundrel take over, galloping after his friends and toward the finish.

Instructor O'Sullivan clapped as Scoundrel reached

the sandbank where the wide river branched into the delta, though her face fell when she saw that Skandar didn't have a water stone attached to his breastplate.

Several minutes later, Bobby and Mitchell returned from fetching slices of lobster pizza from one of the tents on the riverbank beyond the finish. All four of the unicorns were eating bloody meat nearby, as ravenous as their riders after the long day. Bobby was regaling them all with gossip from the pizza queue as they munched hungrily.

"So the Hapless Quartet—"

"Don't call them that, Bobby," Flo scolded.

"Fine. Mateo, Divya, Naomi, and Harper have no stones so far, remember? But this time they managed to solve the three scallop-shell clues *and* the last clue."

"Oh, that's good," Skandar said through a mouthful.

"No, no." Bobby wagged her finger. "Because someone stole their first water stone, and then the Threat . . . Trio? Anyway, they stole the rest just before the finish."

"Apparently, Amber solved her water clue on her own, and left the rest of her quartet to it," Mitchell added.

Skandar had guessed as much when he'd spotted the stone on her armor.

Bobby started counting on her fingers. "Gabriel's quartet got all theirs. Niamh's quartet, *of course*, got all theirs and a spare fire. Ooh, and Mariam managed to steal one from Aisha in the end—I thought *they* were friends. Awkward. Walker never found his . . ."

Agatha approached to collect their stones. Skandar practically hid behind Mitchell as he proudly handed over his fire and water stones.

"You're all square then, Henderson," Agatha said approvingly, dropping them into her blue bag.

"Skandar?" Her eyes flew to his empty breastplate. "Where's your water stone? You must have one if Henderson got his fire stone. You solved the last clue."

Skandar shook his head. "It was gone by the time we got there."

"That's preposterous," Agatha scoffed. "Who would take the water stone but leave the fire stone?"

"Told you," Bobby chimed in.

Skandar was getting irritated. It was bad enough that he was now going into the final Chaos Trial one stone down. Bad enough that Dad might attend the Air Trial only to watch his son become a nomad. "Look, I don't know who took it, but this is the situation I'm in, okay?"

Seething, Agatha turned on the rest of the quartet. "Well, if there's a water stone to be won in the Air Trial, then you lot had better help. You owe him." To Skandar she said, "I saw how you used spirit speech to distract their opponents out there. It was well done."

"Thank—"

She didn't let him finish. "Any sign of Erika?"

The casual way Agatha said her sister's name always surprised Skandar. He recovered quickly. "We thought we heard someone following us, but we never saw them."

Agatha grunted. "Nina must have spooked her. You probably heard another Fledgling. I'm glad you're safe," she added, briskly.

Skandar thought it might have been one of the most emotional things Agatha had ever said about him. But before he could respond, she'd already stomped away, white cloak billowing out behind her.

As the quartet headed back up to the treehouse later that evening, Skandar found his exhausted mind wandering. He thought of Kenna, of how at the beginning of the year she'd hung out with him here with his quartet. But now a future with them side by side felt so distant. He was haunted by the Goshawk he'd dreamed of—a wild unicorn's joy—and the fury on his sister's face when he'd suggested separating them.

"It is an ABUSE of your position, Rex. An *absolute* breach of trust!" Instructor O'Sullivan's voice rang out, and Skandar spotted the blue-cloaked instructor outside his quartet's treehouse just ahead. Then five silver-masked sentinels marched out of the open door.

"What's going on?" Skandar demanded, looking from Rex to the sentinels now flanking him.

"What were they doing in our treehouse?" Bobby glared at the sentinels.

Instructor O'Sullivan's whirlpool eyes swirled dangerously at Rex. "Would you like to tell them? Or shall I?"

"Persephone, be reasonable. We're talking about confidential information paramount to the Island's security. It isn't appropriate for Fledglings to be involved. We don't want to unsettle them."

"Perhaps you should have thought of that before you *broke into their treehouse*," Instructor O'Sullivan said, seething.

The young head of the Silver Circle addressed the quartet, voice earnest. "Solstice stones are going missing. When the first one disappeared, we put it down to a counting error. The second time, we became concerned, but the third? Well, there appears to be a thief at work."

"Aren't they just pretty stones? What have they got to do with Island security?" Bobby asked, at exactly the same time Flo said, "Did they get stolen from the Stronghold itself? Did the rebel sentinels take them?"

Rex winced—the betrayal of the rebellion still raw. "No. We believe it's happening during the Chaos Trials. Only I have access to where the stones are stored. A thief operating *inside* the trials is the only explanation. Therefore, I thought it prudent to search this treehouse." Rex sounded very formal, electricity sparking in wild tendrils over his cheekbones.

"And how many other treehouses have you searched?" Skandar said venomously. "Let me guess. Just *one* other?"

"Instructor Everhart understood the gravity of the matter and was very cooperative."

"I bet she wasn't," Mitchell muttered.

"After all," Rex continued, "Agatha and I have become great friends since I reunited her with Arctic Swansong. And I assure you, we put everything back exactly how it was."

Skandar felt confused. Was he supposed to be grateful that they'd searched *gently*? But Rex was being so reasonable, it felt impossible to stay angry.

"The truth is," Rex said, his green eyes imploring now, "I am *responsible* for the stones. I've been the head of the Silver Circle for less than a year, and this is my fault. I didn't know what else to do. And now I'm afraid I'm going to have to ask you all to empty your pockets. Just so we've covered every possibility."

"That will NOT be happening," Instructor O'Sullivan said, fuming. She looked angrier than Skandar had ever seen her.

"I . . ." Rex hesitated. Nobody moved. "Yes, perhaps overzealous. If you'll excuse me." He sounded tearful as he turned to leave.

"You didn't answer my question before," Bobby said loudly. "Why are you so worried that the stones are missing?"

"You don't understand," Rex said.

"Adults always say that!" Skandar's anger ignited again. "How about you talk to us, instead of accusing us? Ask us about the stones, instead of breaking into our home? You never know, we might actually be able to help!"

"You are completely right, Skandar. Next time I will do just that. I *will* ask you. I am sincerely sorry to—"

Skandar interrupted him, wanting the young silver to understand, desperate for him to avoid his father's mistakes. "Honestly, I don't care if you search my treehouse for the stones: today, tomorrow, whenever. I don't even care if you search my pockets. You won't find anything. Just because I'm a spirit wielder doesn't mean I'm guilty, Rex."

Skandar expected Instructor O'Sullivan to tell him off for using the instructor's first name. Instead she turned to Rex, the full authority of the Eyrie in her voice. "Skandar is being very generous, but I certainly care if you search any more treehouses *or* pockets. I suggest you get your henchmen out of the Eyrie, right now."

"I am trying to protect the Island, Persephone. We still haven't found the eggs, and now the solstice stones—"

"Maybe so, but being afraid never gives you the right to use your power for wrong. And this was *wrong*, Instructor Manning."

"I truly am sorry," Rex said to them all, a blush creeping right up to his blond hairline as he left the platform.

Bobby peeked inside the treehouse door and gasped. "He said they'd left everything exactly as it was—but look at my Marmite—they smashed the jar!"

Flo rushed over to her distraught friend, looking about as confused as Skandar felt. This was quite unlike Rex.

"As if I didn't have enough to worry about with the eggs still missing," Bobby raged. "It'll take me weeks to get another one sent over from the Mainland."

"I'm sorry, I really am." Instructor O'Sullivan's voice was grave as she looked toward the treehouse. "The Eyrie is supposed to be a sanctuary for young riders. This should never have happened."

"Rex is under a lot of pressure. I get it. It's okay," Skandar mumbled.

But Instructor O'Sullivan shook her head. "It is not. Mark my words, I will not forget what he did here tonight. And neither should you."

Half an hour later, the quartet was settled with mugs of fire zone tea.

"Did you notice?" Bobby said. "Rex didn't answer my questions about the *actual* deal with these solstice stones. Why's he so worried about them going missing?"

"I was thinking the same thing," Mitchell muttered. He had—predictably—pulled four books down from the bookshelf and was already turning pages feverishly.

"If Rex realized the stones were going missing a while ago, surely Fledglings would have noticed too, especially if it was happening during the trials?" Flo said.

Skandar's confusion was replaced with an epiphany so sudden that it felt like he'd been zapped by the air element. "What if riders *did* notice, but just blamed it on each other? We're all stealing from each other anyway."

"What do you mean?" Bobby asked.

"Leaping landslides," Flo breathed. "The Fire Trial!"

"Exactly!" Skandar was on his feet now. He turned to Bobby. "Remember after the Fire Trial, Alastair was convinced I'd taken his fire stone. There was so much smoke and debris in the dark, maybe the Weaver managed to steal it without Alastair realizing it was her? We know she was there—Flo saw her!"

"And during the Earth Trial!" added Flo. "Kobi, Alastair, and Meiyi swore that they didn't take that stone from Naomi. We didn't believe them because they'd tried to attack us! But what if they were telling the truth?"

"And during the Water Trial," Bobby said, cottoning on, "Skandar was convinced someone was following us. What if it was the Weaver? What if *she* took his water stone?"

"And left the fire one because she'd already stolen Alastair's!" Skandar cried.

"So were we wrong? Is the Weaver just trying to steal stones and *not* kill you?" Flo asked hopefully.

"I think it's probably both," Skandar said quietly.

"MITCHELL!" Bobby said loudly. "We're having a fairly important epiphany here; would you care to join us?"

Finally Mitchell looked up from his book. Skandar knew his friend well enough to tell there was bad news coming. "Turns out solstice stones *are* more than just pretty rocks," Mitchell croaked. "And I think I know why the Weaver wants them."

"Oh, so you *were* listening," Bobby said accusingly.

The fire wielder pointed at the open book in his lap. "This is about historic Island wars. Apparently, solstice stones were used as a power source for years, all the way back to the First Rider. They can store a rider's elemental power."

"You're saying solstice stones are like"—Bobby paused to think of the word—"elemental batteries?"

Mitchell nodded gravely. "According to *Waging War and Winning*, riders used them as a source of strength to give them an edge during battle. It was common for riders to carry one stone of each element for maximum effect. They'd fill the stones with their own power before they went out to fight."

"How did they get the power out of them, though?" Bobby asked.

Mitchell had the answer to this, too. "If a rider holds a solstice stone over their Hatchery wound, the elemental power stored in the stone combines with their own."

Skandar remembered something. "There's a statue in the Well of a rider with a stone in his hand, but I didn't realize it was a *solstice* stone. That has to be the same thing!"

"So the Weaver has an earth, fire, and water stone." Bobby counted on her fingers. "It's pretty obvious she's trying to collect a set, don't you think? Just like us."

Dread settled like cement in Skandar's chest. "The Weaver's going to use the stones to forge all those bonds.

She's going to use the power ancient riders channeled into them."

"That's what I'm guessing," Mitchell said, starting to pace. "That may well get her the energy she's lacking."

Flo was frowning. "Something doesn't feel right. The Eyrie lets us fight over these solstice stones. They don't even tell us to be careful with them. What if we accidentally unleashed an ancient rider's power mid-battle? Surely the instructors have checked that the solstice stones we use in the Chaos Trials are empty of power?"

"I hadn't thought of that," Mitchell admitted.

"Batteries without juice?" Bobby sounded optimistic.

Flo nodded. "Maybe the ones the Weaver has stolen are empty?"

But Skandar was already shaking his head. "Even if that's true, can't the Weaver just fill the stones up with her own power before the solstice? Before she forges the bonds?"

There was a long silence as the quartet took this in.

Bobby was the first to fight back against Skandar's pessimistic conclusion. "But Erika doesn't have all the stones!" Bobby insisted. "She doesn't have air or spirit. Maybe she needs all of them for this to work? Why else would she risk getting captured at every trial?"

"Agatha did tell me all the spirit stones were destroyed," Skandar remembered, feeling slightly better.

"See!" Bobby pointed at him. "Only three out of five, then."

Skandar knew Bobby was just guessing, but he desperately wanted to believe she was right. Wanted to hold on to the hope that even if the eggs weren't found, the Weaver's plan would fail.

CHAPTER SEVENTEEN

The Air Festival

AS THE APRIL DAYS GREW WARMER, THE summer solstice started to feel horribly close. Perhaps emboldened by her performance in the Qualifiers, Commodore Kazama made clear that she would be preparing for the Hatchery exam to take place as usual; she appointed a new president of the Hatchery, ready for the eggs' return and the hatching ceremony on the summer solstice. She gave interviews about the widespread search effort—and when forced to talk about the worst-case scenario, she insisted that the Weaver would have to show herself on the solstice to forge the bonds. The Island would be ready for her. Skandar wasn't sure whether the Commodore was putting on a front to avoid mass panic, but he—like everyone else—wanted that to be true.

But Nina's calm resolve couldn't distract from the reports in the *Hatchery Herald* that people were going missing. A blacksmith's daughter had gone on a hike in the water zone three weeks ago and never come back. A librarian's boyfriend had gone out to buy dinner from Island Tacos and never returned. Skandar suspected the Weaver had targeted Mainlanders first so she didn't alert the Island, but now—with the rebel sentinels on her side and the summer solstice approaching—she was gathering lost spirit wielders from among the Islanders, too.

The quartet had three major worries about the impending Air Trial: Skandar was down a water stone; the Weaver might use the trial to get an air stone; and the Weaver might *also* use the trial to kill her Mender son.

Agatha had lots of opinions when Mitchell shared his theory that the Weaver was hoping to rely on power stored inside the solstice stones. Some more reassuring than others.

"Of course the stones don't have power stored in them anymore, Henderson," Agatha said, after she'd settled down with a fire zone tea beside the stove. "You think the Eyrie would let Fledglings throw them about if they still contained the power of ancient riders?"

"I told you!" Flo punched the air in a very un-Flo-like gesture.

"But how can you tell?" Mitchell spluttered. "There's nothing in the Eyrie libraries."

Agatha shrugged. "Solstice stones went out of fashion very soon after the Chaos Cup started—they're banned from the race, and so carrying one became associated with weakness." She took a sip of tea. "But you can tell a solstice stone is empty fairly easily. Hold it in your palm, summon the element matching the stone, and if the symbols etched on it glow—but the rest of the stone doesn't—then you're safe."

"So if the whole stone glows, that means it's full of power?" Mitchell checked.

"Correct," Agatha said. "Try it before you start the Air Trial if you like—I guarantee that all you'll see are glowing air spirals. Oh, actually, using them as a power source is *also* banned from the Chaos Trials. So maybe don't try it."

She raised an eyebrow at Bobby, who scoffed, "As if I'd need any extra elemental power."

"But if they don't have power inside, why does the Silver Circle lock them up after every trial?" Skandar asked.

"Rex said at the beginning of the year that they were sacred symbols of the Island's power. Maybe it's just that?" Flo said.

"The Circle does like locking things up," Agatha said, pointing to herself. "And your other theory is that Erika is going to fill the stones with her *own* power?"

"Yes," Mitchell said quickly.

Agatha locked her heavy gaze on Skandar, and he couldn't help but notice the fear flickering behind his aunt's usually impenetrable eyes.

"That's possible," Agatha accepted. "I filled a stone once—no, Henderson, I do not want to go into why." She held a finger in the air as Mitchell opened his mouth to speak. "But I will tell you it wiped out my elemental magic for about a week. It takes a huge amount of energy to fill a stone."

"Shouldn't we get Rex to cancel the Air Trial?" Flo asked. "Surely we should try to make it as hard as possible for the Weaver to get an air stone—just in case."

"Absolutely not. Skandar is down a stone—what if the Eyrie just skips straight to Rookie re-entry and he's declared a nomad? Like I've said a thousand times, I just don't think Erika is strong enough to manage the bonds—even if she fills a full set of stones."

But Skandar had seen the fear in Agatha's face, so it was very hard to believe her.

Mercifully, news from the Wanderers about Kenna arrived at the very end of April—the night before the Air Festival. Agatha had barely got through the treehouse door before Skandar was ripping the paper out of her hand and reading it for himself.

> K is safe & well. 4th is fire. Magic
> growing stronger every day. Wants

to see S. We will make CC day safe.
Swallow zone. 5th will not be long. PF

Skandar read it several times before looking at Agatha for clarification.

"Elora says you can see Kenna on the day of the Chaos Cup—I expect the Wanderers think it'll be safe because most of the sentinels will be patrolling Fourpoint. She'll be in the air zone. They'll station lookouts, I suppose. I think it's foolish, but . . ." Agatha looked at the joy and relief that Skandar knew was plastered across his face. "But I suppose it'll be fine, since this time it will be a *planned* visit," she finished severely.

"Fourth is fire?" Skandar suddenly realized. "Does that mean Kenna's mutated again? And she's still okay?"

"Sounds like it," Agatha said, almost smiling. "What did I tell you? She'll be all right."

But despite this, the words of the note went round and round in Skandar's head while he lay awake in his hammock that night. *5th will not be long.* The final mutation. The spirit mutation. *Magic growing stronger every day.*

Stronger? Skandar worried in the dark. Kenna's power had been breathtaking at the desert oasis. What exactly did *stronger* look like?

The first of May dawned—warm and bright. Skandar made his way down the treehouse ladder to wait for Flo, and he couldn't help but feel a little more positive. He went out to sit on the platform and played absentmindedly with the bracelet she'd given him on his birthday. The sun was shining through the Eyrie's trees, the pines scattering the dappled light and making the spirit and water pins on his jacket twinkle. Skandar let himself feel hope for a moment. He was going to see Dad soon, even if he'd have to lie about his sister. And before that, he was going to visit Kenna at last. Elora had said she was strong. She had survived four mutations. Why not another? And Nina seemed very certain of finding the eggs. Even if the worst happened and the solstice passed, that didn't necessarily mean the Weaver was going to be able to forge more than a couple of bonds this year. She didn't have an air stone, and it was impossible for her to get a spirit stone. Perhaps everything was going to be—

"Skar, did you not see this?" Flo's urgent voice cut through the spring air. She was still inside the treehouse, the door ajar.

Skandar rushed back inside to see Flo standing by the noticeboard, and Mitchell, then Bobby, came thundering down the rungs of the tree trunk in their pajamas.

A yellow-dyed piece of paper was pinned to the board. The instructions for the last of the Chaos Trials had arrived.

Air is a powerful, unrestrained element that tears through the skies. Therefore, in this final trial,

the key is confidence. Every Fledgling must
begin and end their flight with an air stone, but
that is not enough to succeed.

Reaching the finish will require a true leap of
faith—air demands absolute commitment. And
in its intensity, it will reward those who speed to
the finish and dare to jump first. A reward that
may make all the difference in soaring through
the skies ahead.

Bobby cheered. "Yes! It's going to be a race!"

Mitchell was nodding. "Certainly sounds that way. It
says *tears through the skies* and *speed to the finish*. A Chaos
Cup–style race? Will the spectators be at the finish, do you
think?" Skandar knew he must be thinking about his father.
Mitchell had torn up the congratulatory letter Ira Henderson had sent after the Water Trial. "I need him to be my
father all the time, not just when he can boast about my
achievements," he'd said fuming.

"The instructions say there's another reward at the finish!" Bobby punched Skandar on the arm jubilantly.

"Ouch!"

"I'll get you that water stone, spirit boy!"

"You don't even know if there'll be one," Skandar said,
though he wanted to believe her. He didn't think it was
likely that any of the other Fledglings would hand over one
of their spare stones to a spirit wielder at the Eyrie entrance.

And after Rex's search of their treehouse, riders had become more suspicious of Skandar again. They trusted the dashing young air instructor. They did *not* trust the spirit wielder with a sister bonded to a wild unicorn.

"It's talking about jumping," Flo worried, pulling nervously at her sleeve. "That's the most worrying bit—*leap of faith*. Do you think that means there'll be obstacles on the course?"

"Awesome," Bobby breathed.

There was a different mood among the Fledglings at air training that day—everyone was being friendlier to each other, even the unicorns. Skandar wondered whether it had something to do with there finally being an end to the uncertainty of the Chaos Trials. When he said as much to Mitchell, he nodded. "Alliances aren't much good in a race. It's everyone for themselves. And we've all raced each other before—it takes the pressure off."

Bobby laughed from Falcon's back. "You two are so naive. Everyone is being nice to each other because lots of people are missing solstice stones. They're trying to cozy up to the more successful riders who might be able to save them."

Flo had been turning Blade in a circle to calm him but now joined in the conversation. "Bobby, I think you're being cynical. Why can't you just believe people are being nice?"

"Because look!" Bobby pointed over at Niamh, Farooq, Art, and Benji by the yellow pavilion. "That quartet are going into the Air Trial with bonus stones in all four elements. And who's riding over to say hello? Oh yes, Romily, who needs a fire stone. There's Walker and Marissa, both down a fire and a water stone, so absolutely bricking it. Aisha needs a water stone—there she goes. And, look, Gabriel's joining them—he needs a fire stone too. Point proven."

"It must be really depressing being you sometimes," Mitchell said.

Bobby shrugged. "Sometimes the truth *is* depressing."

A whistle was blown sharply, and Instructor Webb touched his mossy hair rather nervously. "Yes, yes. My congratulations to you on noticing that I am not the dashing young Instructor Manning. He has been called away on urgent Silver Circle business, and therefore you will be stuck with my slightly less perfect face for air training today."

Bobby cackled. "Since when did Bernard get so funny?"

Skandar chuckled. "And sarcastic."

Instructor Webb continued. "I suppose one could say that the earth and air elements are polar opposites. But it is important to remember that although you will need to channel the spirit of an air wielder to succeed, you will also require the other elements to battle your way through this final trial."

"Is he supposed to be telling us this?" Flo whispered.

"For goodness' sake, don't stop him!" Mitchell hissed. "The more information we can get in advance, the better."

Instructor Webb droned on, Moonlight Dust fidgeting

beneath him. "And, of course, with four stones to choose from as your prize, you will want to perform the best you possibly can."

"Did he say *four*?"

"One for each element, surely?"

Whispers exploded across the training ground, and Instructor Webb realized he'd said too much.

He cleared his throat. "Well, well. I suppose we should get on. How about flying some drills?"

Instructor Webb was fond of drills. They essentially involved flying their unicorns from one end of the training ground to the other and back again. For Amber and Skandar, who flew with the Peregrine Society, it was very dull—and they usually lapped everyone else.

Sure enough, Scoundrel's Luck and Whirlwind Thief finished within seconds of each other. There'd been a time when Skandar's worst nightmare would have been spending even a minute in Amber Fairfax's company, but since the Well Dance things had changed. Amber had even eaten with him and Flo a couple of times at breakfast.

"What was the point in that?" Amber seethed, as they waited by the pavilion for the others to finish. "There aren't that many air sessions left before the trial; we should be training properly. Where's Instructor Manning?"

"Who knows." Skandar shrugged. Things had been very awkward with Rex since he'd essentially accused Skandar of stealing solstice stones.

"I heard you're missing a water stone," Amber said, but she didn't sound gleeful about it like she might have done before.

"Yep," Skandar said. "And you?"

"Earth," Amber confirmed. "Webb said there'd be four prizes, so I'm really hoping . . ."

"Same."

"I don't think my mother will ever speak to me again if I'm declared a nomad," Amber murmured. "I'm not even sure what I'd do."

"We'll be all right." Skandar tried to sound more confident than he felt. "We're in the Peregrine Society. A race will be easy."

"Nothing about these trials has been easy," Amber said sadly, looking over at Kobi, Alastair, and Meiyi as they landed together nearby.

Skandar was about to agree when he suddenly felt like he was burning up. Instinctively he checked his palm. No red glow. He leaned forward in his saddle, checking to see if Scoundrel had set off a fire blast. Nothing. And then—

"Everyone, into the air! Now!" Instructor Webb yelled, his voice quavering.

Scoundrel bellowed, and Skandar realized that the grass beneath his hooves was turning to molten lava.

"Skandar, take off!" Amber urged him, Whirlwind Thief snapping out her wings. "Forking thunderstorms, it's the whole plateau!"

She was right. The green slice of the Eyrie's hill had turned to fiery rock. Some Fledgling unicorns were going berserk as their hooves burned, and Scoundrel wasn't taking any chances, taking off in three strides.

Once airborne, it quickly became clear who was responsible for the carnage.

Silver Blade was rearing up in the center of the training ground, eyes blazing, while all around him the molten rock began to burn brighter, liquid magma taking its place.

"GET REX!" Flo was yelling. "Get Instructor Manning!"

"FLO!" Skandar shouted, Falcon and Red joining Scoundrel in the air.

"Just get Rex! He's a silver! He can help!"

But almost as soon as she'd said it, Blade's hooves hit the lava-strewn ground, and the grass began to smoke instead of burn.

"What happened?" Skandar asked Flo, as the rest of the quartet landed alongside Blade.

Flo looked like she was trying very hard not to cry. "Don't you see? Your unicorns are almost over their rebellions, but I don't know whether I'll ever be able to control Blade. To trust him."

"You will! Of course you will!" Bobby tried to reassure her.

"You don't understand," Flo choked out. "You're not a silver."

* * *

Later that afternoon, the quartet changed their blue jackets to the yellow of the air season. Skandar hadn't been to the Air Festival before, and there was such a fizz of excitement in the warm evening air that he promised himself that—just for tonight—he'd try to forget about missing eggs, forged bonds, and solstice stones. Flo seemed to have decided something similar and didn't mention the lava incident as they rode through Fourpoint's winding streets.

Air wielders tended to be daring extroverts, and Skandar had never seen a better representation of that than when they turned into Element Square. People walked on tightropes high above the square; others queued for giant trampolines, where they were strapped into harnesses that allowed them to bounce impossibly high. In every corner there was a fierce competition going on—a jousting tournament, archery with lightning bows, and something involving a wind tunnel that Skandar couldn't work out the rules for.

Some Islanders had their heads tipped upward, watching an aerial acrobatics display. Flo had to shut her eyes as one rider threw himself off his unicorn's back in midair and then somersaulted four times, blindfolded. The unicorn zoomed down underneath him, and he landed neatly back in his saddle. The crowd cheered very loudly, and Flo squeaked. "Is it over?"

Next, the quartet headed toward the food stalls lining one side of the square—all painted a bright sunshine yellow.

Each of the quartet's unicorns seemed intent on grabbing something, *anything* for a snack. Falcon managed to snatch an entire loaf of air zone bread—"Thanks, Falcon!" Bobby said, delighted—before a stern-faced Flo made her give it back to the baker. Scoundrel pinched a giant lollipop shaped like a sunflower, Red stole a life-size chocolate bird and then melted it immediately, and Blade—well, Blade got his teeth round an umbrella.

"Blasted Fledgling unicorns!" the owner of Umbrellas for Every Occasion shouted after them.

Skandar got the giggles as he helped Flo dislodge the yellow sparkly object from the silver unicorn's jaw. "Did he think it was edible?" he managed to wheeze out.

"Blade likes sparkly things," Flo said a little defensively. "And he's had a tough day. Maybe he didn't want to eat it; maybe he just wanted to keep it."

Then Bobby insisted they queue up at a stall with a sign that read:

SIMON'S SUPERB SPIRALS! DANGER—
THESE SWEETS WILL BLOW YOUR MIND.

"All his sweets are shaped like the air element symbol," said Bobby, "but depending on the filling, they're either really sour, really sweet, really salty, or really spicy. They're supposed to mimic the tastes of the elements."

"Salty? Urgh!" Mitchell said. "I will *not* be trying one of those."

"That's the water spiral. But don't worry, we'll be trying

all of them," Bobby insisted, a wicked grin on her face.

"Are any of them just ordinary sweets?" Flo asked hopefully.

"Obviously not, Florence. That would be boring. *I've* heard if you put the whole thing into your mouth, it blows your mind." Bobby sighed happily.

"You haven't *heard* that—you read it off the sign!" Mitchell protested.

Bobby shrugged. "I heard it in my head."

Skandar was trying to make out the spirals in their glass jars when the atmosphere at the Air Festival shifted. The acrobats landed their unicorns. The explosions from the jousting competition stopped. The fizzing of the lightning arrows quieted. And the Council of Seven rode right through the middle of the festivities, flanked by two lines of sentinels.

Curious, the quartet drifted toward the center of the square with their unicorns. Nina's air councillors were not dressed in their ceremonial yellow cloaks. They wore rider black from head to toe. They gathered in front of the four elemental statues. Two sentinels quickly constructed a small raised platform, draping it in black. The rest of the silver-masked riders stood to attention in two long lines, creating a narrow path between them.

"What's going on?" Bobby whispered.

Mitchell and Flo looked at each other, something unspoken passing between them.

"Where's Nina?" Skandar asked, looking around for the Commodore.

Whispering erupted from the crowd, as more sentinels draped black fabric over the bright yellow stalls. Sara, Olu, and Ebb Shekoni suddenly melted out of the crowd and came to stand with the quartet. Ebb gripped his sister's hand tightly. Olu had clearly been crying, his dark brown skin wet with tears.

Then Rex Manning rode Silver Sorceress along the path cleared by the sentinels. The head of the Silver Circle was dressed in rider black too, a single circlet of silver visible on his jacket lapel. His cheeks were palest white, and his usually bright green eyes were shadowed. When he reached the Council of Seven, he dismounted from his silver unicorn and stepped onto the platform. The entire festival took a collective breath.

Rex Manning's voice rang out loud and clear across Element Square.

"Nina Kazama is dead."

CHAPTER EIGHTEEN

Agatha's Gift

"THE COMMODORE IS DEAD," REX REPEATED.

At first there was shocked silence, and then the crowd seemed to rouse as one—anguished wails and shouts of disbelief filled the square. Skandar's brain repeated the words over and over. But there was no understanding, no acceptance. Nina couldn't be dead. She was the Commodore. He'd seen her qualify for the Chaos Cup only weeks ago. He'd sat with her on the Sunset Platform. It couldn't possibly be true.

Rex Manning held up a hand for quiet. "It is with deep sorrow that I bring you this news. I was informed at the Eyrie in the early hours of this morning. Our Commodore is not only dead; she was killed." The last word rang out louder than the rest.

Some in the crowd cried out in horror.

"The details are not clear, but we know that Commodore Kazama was out late last night exercising Lightning's Mistake. When she didn't return, her blacksmith, Clara Matthews, raised the alarm. A search party was sent out after midnight, and Lightning's Mistake and Nina Kazama were found in the air zone together. There was, and I say this with sorrow in my heart, nothing anyone could do to save them."

Tears were rolling down cheeks all around Skandar; sobbing echoed across the square. Riders were removing their yellow jackets and holding them limply in their arms. Flo had hidden her face in her brother's shoulder.

"Given the evidence available to us at this time," Rex continued, "we believe that Commodore Kazama was killed by the greatest enemy of this Island—the Weaver—as part of her plan to establish a new order."

The atmosphere became charged with energy; people started shouting out that Nina's death must be avenged. The crowd was very ready to blame the Weaver.

"If the Weaver can kill the Commodore, then we are all in great danger," Rex said, his voice ringing out strong and sure. "We must be ready for when the Weaver tries to seize power with her army of unnatural riders."

Unnatural? Skandar shivered, knowing that Rex was talking about Kenna, too. He felt his throat closing up with distress. Nina had believed Kenna wasn't evil. Nina had helped him identify Goshawk's destined rider. Nina had been a friend to him, to spirit wielders. And now she was gone forever.

"As head of the Silver Circle, it is only right that I take on the heavy burden of leading the Air Council—and with it the Island—at this crucial time," Rex announced. "I will be implementing some emergency measures. Their objective is to ensure the safety of those who are most in danger from the Weaver. As many of you know, my own mother suffered at the hands of Erika Everhart; her unicorn was one of the Fallen Twenty-Four. I am—and will always be— truly committed to protecting others from a similar fate."

"What does that mean?" Mitchell choked out, but Skandar was too full of fear and sadness to process Rex's words.

"Please be assured that I am not seizing power," Rex continued. "I will merely act as caretaker Commodore during this short period before the Chaos Cup, following which the winner will form their own Council in accordance with the usual protocols. Until then we will remain in mourning for our sky-fallen friends, Nina Kazama and Lightning's Mistake. A partnership who made history."

Then Rex bowed his head, before mounting Silver Sorceress to lead the Council and their unicorns from Element Square in a slow, solemn walk.

"I don't like it," Olu muttered. "Did you see the Council's faces? They didn't even *know* Manning was going to announce himself as caretaker Commodore. He's barely managed to keep the Stronghold under control this year. What gives him the right to lead us?"

Sara put a finger to her husband's lips. "Not now. Later. They're here."

Then, as though they'd been waiting for the Council's departure, hundreds of voices joined in one haunting melody. The bards had come down from the Song School to sing the Island's grief. There were no words to the song— for at that moment words would have been too much yet nowhere near enough. The mourning song simply let Skandar remember Nina Kazama as *he* wanted to—as a Commodore who knew doing the right thing was a risk but did it anyway.

Skandar's tear-filled eyes rested on Ebb and Flo, who were still holding hands; then moved to Mitchell, whose eyes were red behind his glasses; then Bobby, who was still staring at the empty black platform. Skandar had so many emotions rushing through him. Sorrow and disbelief, but also a growing sense of unease that Rex—a member of the Silver Circle—would be Commodore, albeit a temporary one. Even if he appeared to be more accepting of spirit wielders than his father, Skandar didn't know whether that would stretch to Kenna. Would it even matter now if Skandar released her from Goshawk's bond? He felt as if everything he'd been trying to do was crashing down around him.

Things got worse when at last the quartet reached the Eyrie's entrance tree. Arctic Swansong was waiting outside,

Agatha rubbing her skeletal cheeks in the lantern light.

She didn't bother greeting them. "Rex is locking up the old spirit wielders in the Silver Stronghold. For their *safety*."

Skandar was confused. "What do you mean, their safety?"

"He's justifying it by saying that the Weaver may target them for new forged bonds. Trying to make it sound perfectly reasonable."

"That's what he meant, wasn't it?" Mitchell breathed from Red's back. "In Element Square?"

"Could the Weaver forge a bond for a spirit wielder whose unicorn has died? Is Rex right?" Skandar wasn't ready to believe Rex was just locking spirit wielders up without a reason. One of his first acts as head of the Silver Circle had been to free Swan.

Agatha shrugged. "I don't see why not. They were destined for a unicorn once. I mean, it's horrifying to think about—a forged bond is a *replacement* for your unicorn. But the riders would be able to use elemental magic again, not like with the false bonds the Weaver created before. I'm guessing that's why Fairfax, Worsham, and Hissington have gone to join her."

"But if that's true," Flo said, her voice small, "the old spirit wielders *should* be protected from the Weaver, shouldn't they? Like Rex said."

Agatha grunted with frustration. "I don't like this *at all.* There's an extremely fine line between protection and imprisonment—I should know that better than anyone else. I am supremely *un*confident that a silver will keep on the right side of it."

"But you've never said this about Rex before," Skandar said, frowning. "You've always liked him." Was Agatha jumping to conclusions? Just because Rex was a silver, it didn't mean he was necessarily a bad person. Searching Skandar's treehouse had been out of order, but he *had* seemed sorry about it.

"*Like* is a strong word, Skandar. I don't really *like* anyone."

"But someone had to take over until the Cup," Mitchell said carefully, clearly not wanting to enrage Agatha further.

"And Rex made sure it was him," Agatha countered.

"What do we do, then? Try to help the old spirit wielders?" Skandar asked, unsure what his aunt wanted from him.

"For now? We do nothing. We hope Rex doesn't win the Chaos Cup," Agatha said darkly. "But before that? We train. Skandar, you cannot afford to be declared a nomad. Not now that there's a silver in charge. Without Nina"— Agatha swallowed—"and without the protection of the Eyrie, I can't promise that you and Scoundrel will be safe. I'd bet my favorite dagger Rex will lock you up *for your own protection* before you can say *Rookie*."

"I really don't think Rex would do that," Flo protested.

Agatha ignored her, appealing to Bobby and Mitchell instead. "Do you understand what I'm saying? You must get Skandar that reward stone or face losing him forever."

And as Agatha opened the door to the Eyrie—the rough indentations in the bark of the tree glowing and spreading in a web of blinding white light—Skandar feared for the first time that the Island might never let spirit wielders return.

As May moved into June, the Island's shock at Commodore Kazama's death ebbed to an aching sadness, and memorials of yellow flowers sprang up all over the Eyrie.

Bobby—who had taken the Commodore's death very badly—had a theory that the Weaver had not wanted Nina to break her record and succeed in winning the Chaos Cup three times in a row. Mitchell argued that this seemed "rather unambitious for a mass-murdering, power-hungry lunatic with an entire generation of unhatched unicorns at her disposal." And Skandar couldn't help agreeing.

Rex Manning had continued Nina's extensive search for the eggs, as well as trying to locate and *protect* the rest of the former spirit wielders, though he wasn't having much luck with either. Skandar worried that some might have gone to join the Weaver. But he knew Craig was hiding at least ten of them in his room above the bookshop, so perhaps other sympathetic Islanders were doing the same. Rex's rounding up of the spirit wielders had certainly made Agatha even more relentless about Skandar's schedule. Skandar got up early every morning, and they spent two hours before breakfast training in the spirit element.

With Arctic Swansong, Agatha was able to demonstrate useful spirit weapons for Skandar to use in a race—
sharp ghostly sabers, beautiful shining bows, misty white
lances. And—when she wasn't getting frustrated with
him—Agatha was a really good teacher.

They worked on the psychological parts of spirit magic
too—the magic of illusion, of accessing another rider's psyche through the bond. Or, as Skandar liked to think of it,
messing with their mind. Agatha demonstrated them all
mercilessly. In one session, Skandar summoned a sand
shield on one side to protect himself from an enormous
wave—only to be soaked through because Agatha had
actually sent it from the other direction. She laughed for
about ten minutes.

And then there was the challenge of duplicating himself and Scoundrel, which was still proving difficult. Of
course, it was impossible on days when Scoundrel wasn't in
the mood to help him. But sometimes—when they were in
sync—Skandar was now able to duplicate either himself or
his unicorn, but not both together. It was very creepy when
he duplicated himself alone, because his double hovered on
thin air with no unicorn beneath him.

Just over a week before the Air Trial, Skandar arrived
bleary-eyed for spirit training. He wasn't sleeping much—
when he wasn't having Mender dreams with Scoundrel, he
would lie in the dark with worries rocketing about in his
head. The missing eggs, exchanging Kenna's bond, being

hunted by the Weaver . . . and Dad would be on the Island soon—what was Skandar going to tell him about Kenna?

For a moment, Skandar thought he might still *be* asleep when Agatha rode Arctic Swansong onto the training ground toward Scoundrel. For the first time ever, they were in full armor, and it was unlike any Skandar had seen before. The chain mail had a pearlescent white sheen so it glowed in the early-morning light. Both rider and unicorn breastplates were inlaid with white spirit element symbols.

Agatha saw Skandar's awed face and smirked. "Turns out my old blacksmith hasn't lost her gift for spirit wielder armor. Best not tell our good old caretaker Commodore about this, though—I think he might faint."

Skandar laughed. "I would *love* to see his face." Then he got suspicious. "Instructor Everhart, why are you wearing that armor today?"

She grinned at him, wolf-like. "I thought we might have a little sky battle."

"Me and Scoundrel? Against you and Swan?"

Agatha reached for the helmet attached to her saddle. "I don't see anyone else here, do you?"

Skandar felt nerves swoop into his stomach. "But it's not like I need to know how to battle other spirit wielders for the Air Trial. Is it really necessary for us to—"

"Are you scared?" Agatha interrupted. "The Air Trial will be all about daring, right?"

"Yes, but," Skandar spluttered, "it's *this* week, Aga—"

Instructor Everhart, and I do need to be *alive* to take part."

"Oh, I'm rusty," Agatha said, waving her hand dismissively. "Give me everything you've got."

Skandar's heart was racing almost as fast as when he'd faced the First Rider and the Wild Unicorn Queen down in their tomb. How could he fight Agatha and win? She was a fully trained spirit wielder—and he was, well, *not*.

"Ready?" Agatha called, and Arctic Swansong took off into the sky.

"Umm, no!" Skandar yelled back, but he rapidly pulled down his helmet anyway. Something about the motion focused his mind. He'd gone into battle with Scoundrel so many times now that all at once it didn't seem to matter that it was his instructor, his aunt, the *Executioner* he was facing. It was a sky battle. And that was all.

Scoundrel's Luck seemed willing to take on Arctic Swansong, eager for takeoff. He galloped five strides and soared up into the sky; then he flapped his great feathered wings opposite Swan, and Agatha unleashed her power.

Her palm glowed bright white, a shining spirit sword bursting into her hand, and the full might of Arctic Swansong soared toward Scoundrel like a terrifying aerial version of the joust. Skandar didn't even have time to block the sword with a shield; it was Scoundrel who took charge and swerved them out of the way with a fraction of an inch to spare.

"Fight, Skandar!" Agatha yelled. "If this was a race, you'd have just given up your position!"

Skandar took a deep breath as Agatha turned Swan in the air.

"We've got to fight together if we're going to stand a chance," Skandar murmured to his unicorn. And as Skandar summoned the spirit element to his palm, cinnamon sweetness filling his nostrils, he could tell from the anticipation in the bond that Scoundrel understood.

Quickly Skandar summoned the fire and spirit elements together, and Scoundrel's mane started to turn to flame. Skandar punched out a fireball at the white unicorn flying toward him. Scoundrel roared, and a column of flame burst from his mouth, engulfing his black body.

"Two spirit wielders can play that game," Agatha yelled, and put up a thick ice shield. Skandar melted it with more blasts of fire—but Swan had already turned entirely to water, shimmering in midair. He pumped his liquid wings, extinguishing the fire attacks and forcing Scoundrel's body to return to black. Agatha laughed gleefully, but Skandar had already started his next move.

His palm turned yellow and—concentrating hard on their bond—he willed Scoundrel to turn to pure air element. Sparks started around Scoundrel's feet and then moved up his legs, until he was a buzzing outline of electricity. Skandar saw Agatha's eyes widen in shock as Skandar molded a lightning bow and notched a fizzing arrow.

Then something was wrong. The bow collapsed. The color in his palm disappeared. Scoundrel's black color returned like ink. She'd used spirit magic to kill his attack inside the bond.

"Oi! Not fair!" Skandar called.

Agatha cackled. "Now you know what it's like to face a spirit wielder in battle. Frustrating, isn't it?"

Skandar thought fast, trying not to get distracted by Agatha's taunting. What could he use to outsmart her? On strength alone they couldn't win. And she had plenty of cunning. He needed to do something she wasn't expecting, something she thought he *couldn't* do.

"Are you with me, boy?" Skandar whispered to Scoundrel. He thought about their life together so far. He thought of that moment in the Hatchery when Scoundrel had looked right at him, the white stripe forming down his head. He thought about their first flight to escape the stampeding unicorns, the way Scoundrel's black feathers had caught the breeze. But most of all Skandar thought about their bond—how it felt when it had first formed round his heart, how it had felt last year when he and Scoundrel had been separated, how it deepened with every Chaos Trial as they learned that together they could face anything.

Holding these thoughts in his mind, Skandar summoned the spirit element to his palm. Arctic Swansong came soaring toward them again, Agatha brandishing a swirling spirit javelin this time. He encouraged the white ball in his hand to shine brighter and brighter—Scoundrel's wing tips glowing too—until he knew Agatha and Swan would struggle to see exactly where they ended and the spirit element began.

And then there were two of them. Two Skandars. Two Scoundrels.

It was like being in a Mender dream. Skandar knew that *he* was the real one, but he could also feel himself in the other Skandar, as though he really had been split in two. Both Scoundrels flew at Arctic Swansong, and Skandar willed the other Skandar—the one that was more spirit magic than human—to raise his palm as though about to attack. Scoundrel got the idea, and the duplicate Scoundrel flapped his wings more aggressively. The real Skandar raised his palm a second later, but tried to make his own movements slow and sloppy, as though *he* was the double.

Arctic Swansong reared, hooves pawing the air in confusion. Agatha's eyes showed shock, though they narrowed as she looked between her two opponents. She drew back her arm, the white javelin point swinging between the two Skandars. Skandar tried to keep his breathing steady. *Don't react.*

Agatha threw her javelin.

At Skandar and Scoundrel.

And it passed right through them.

The real Skandar reacted quickly then, going in for the win. Molding his favorite spirit saber, he flew Scoundrel right at Arctic Swansong. Drawing level with Agatha— still scrambling for a shield—he placed the shining sword against her throat.

The spirit wielders were both breathing hard.

Agatha nodded. And Skandar let the spirit sword wink out.

His aunt ripped off her helmet, eyes sparkling. "You're ready," she told him. "I'm really proud of you."

Skandar's throat was suddenly choked up with emotion. Growing up he'd always wanted his mum to be proud of him—he and Kenna had talked about it all the time, making her proud by becoming riders. Agatha was about as close to a real mother as he was ever going to get. And he had made her *proud*.

Once they'd dismounted, Agatha fed Swan a sugar lump and let him chase a rabbit across the plateau.

"Sit down, Skandar. I want to give you something."

Skandar's armor clinked as he settled on the scorched step of the fire pavilion. "You're giving me a present?" Scoundrel stayed close, casting the occasional jealous glance at Swan's furry snack.

"Of sorts." Agatha grunted, then lifted a chain over her head from beneath her pearly armor. There was a white pouch attached to the chain, and she fidgeted with it. "Don't make a big thing of it," she said, before tipping something out onto her palm.

It was a solstice stone, but not a kind Skandar had seen before. He'd imagined one, of course. He'd even asked Agatha about them all those months ago. Tiny intertwined circles adorned the bright white faces of the stone as it glowed in the sunshine.

"It's a spirit stone," Skandar murmured in wonder. "Where did you get it?"

"It was mine. Well, sort of," Agatha said, her eyes fixed on the white stone. "When I was a Fledgling, I won it during my Spirit Trial. And I kept it."

Skandar was fascinated. "Weren't you supposed to give it back to your instructors?"

"Yes, well . . . they weren't always so tight on security. Erika isn't the only rebel in the family, you know."

At the mention of his mother's name, reality came crashing down on Skandar.

He jumped to his feet. "You can't have this! You told me all the spirit stones were destroyed! Or did you lie to me about that?"

"I didn't *exactly* lie about it," Agatha said sheepishly. "I just . . . discounted this one."

Something else terrible occurred to Skandar. "Does the Weaver know you have a spirit stone?"

Agatha finally snapped. "Calm down, will you? Erika doesn't know. I've been hiding this stone for decades—I've become rather good at it."

"Keep your voice down," Skandar hissed, even though they were completely alone.

"I want you to have it," Agatha insisted, holding out the stone.

"Why?" Skandar thought this was a very inconvenient time for his aunt to take a sudden interest in giving him gifts.

"You've done excellently this year"—Agatha sighed deeply—"and if things had gone differently . . . If Erika . . . Well, I've no doubt you'd have passed your Spirit Trial spectacularly. I want you to remember that, when you're battling in the Air Trial. Remember you belong here."

Skandar had so many emotions, it was hard to keep up. He was incredibly touched that Agatha wanted to give him the stone. He wanted to take it. But there was one more thing he needed to know. "Agatha—does it have power inside?"

Instead of answering, Agatha called Swan over, placed one hand on the unicorn's nose, and summoned the spirit element so her Hatchery wound glowed white under the stone. Skandar watched as the interlocked circles of the spirit element shone brighter against the stone's glassy sides. The rest of the stone stayed dark.

"Empty," Skandar breathed.

"I filled it up after I passed my Chaos Trials—and saved it for a special occasion," Agatha murmured. "And then one presented itself."

"What?" Skandar asked, curious as he remembered Agatha refusing to tell Mitchell why she'd powered up a solstice stone.

"A little trip to Margate." Her eyes were shining.

"When I failed the Hatchery exam." Skandar realized.

"Swan and I needed some extra power—how else do you think we broke out of prison?"

Agatha placed the spirit stone in Skandar's hand. "It feels right that you have it now, little spirit wielder. Take it. Keep it in its pouch. And promise me you won't tell another soul."

Skandar closed his fingers round the stone. "And you're *certain* Erika doesn't know about it? Even though it's empty, she could still try to fill it with power. Come after you . . . or me."

Agatha shook her head. "My sister doesn't know, but even if she did, she'd never guess I'd give something so precious to you."

"Why?"

"Because she's never wanted to believe I could love anyone except her."

Skandar stared at Agatha. *Love.* Did he really have an aunt who loved him? Despite everything, warmth swelled in his chest.

"Agatha, I—I don't know what to say."

His aunt wanted to protect him. She was proud. She loved him.

"Right. Aunt and nephew bonding time over. Get back to the Eyrie."

Skandar hesitated on the pavilion step. "Agatha?"

"Mmm?" Her eyes were already fixed lovingly on the snowy white form of Arctic Swansong, her mouth twitching upward at one corner.

"It's only a week until the summer solstice. The eggs are still missing."

"I know."

"What do you think will happen if the Weaver forges fifty bonds?"

"She doesn't have the power, Skandar."

"But what if she finds a way?"

Agatha looked at him with eyes that looked just like Kenna's. Just like Erika's. Just like his own. "I don't know what will happen."

"We could all fight. We could hold her off."

"We could," Agatha said darkly. "But for how long?"

KENNA

Fear

KENNA SMITH WAS RESTLESS WITH FEAR.

Fear was a Commodore dead in the forest. It was the world's most powerful unicorn buried under an air-allied tree, and the Island wanting someone to blame.

Fear was change. The change of getting fewer visitors every week. The change of being moved to a more secure location. The change of the smile missing on Albert's lips.

Fear was the news she was brought. It was spirit wielders locked in the Silver Stronghold and Rex Manning declaring himself temporary leader.

Fear was the future. The future that was now impossible. The future that was an ending. The future that was coming for them all—no matter what happened next.

Kenna preferred her new hiding place to the water-fall. She'd always loved trees—when she was younger, she'd climbed any that appeared sturdy enough to hide her in their branches. But these redwoods were the tallest and most magnificent she'd ever laid eyes on. When she'd followed Albert up the hidden footholds in the great trunk for the first time, it had felt like they were climbing into the stars. For once, Gos had deigned to follow Eagle's lead; they'd flapped haphazardly upward, avoiding the branches, and accompanied their two riders into a yawning hole in the trunk.

Now that she was up here, Kenna could see that the surrounding trunks had deep holes carved into them, too. "Did the Wanderers make these?" she asked Albert, as they perched on the edge of the hole—legs dangling, their two unicorns lying down behind them. Albert broke off a square of chocolate and, after offering it to Kenna, popped it into his mouth.

"No. They're natural," Albert replied. "We've never used the Sky Forest as our air base, but I've been here occasionally to break a journey." His voice sounded odd, as though he wanted to talk about something else.

Kenna sighed. "What is it?"

She watched Albert's white throat quiver as he swallowed. "Your next mutation. I'm worried. Elora's worried."

She tried to make light of it. "I'll be all right. It's just one tiny little spirit mutation."

Albert stared down at the coals of his knuckles. "The only one I've seen is Skandar's—you can actually *see* the bones and tendons in his arm. What is that going to feel like for you? As a wild mutation?"

Kenna was tired of this. She was tired of everything. "Why do you care so much anyway, Albert?" She knew it was an unkind thing to say. But Goshawk had been pummelling viciousness into the bond all day.

"Kenna, look, I think I—"

"Don't say it." Kenna spoke over him. She knew what he was going to say, and she couldn't bear to hear those words. They had danced round this *thing* between them for so long that she had hoped he'd never get up the courage to put a name to it.

"I don't even know why you want to be friends with me," she said, trying to derail the conversation; trying to keep a lid on his feelings—and hers.

"I wish you wouldn't say that," he said eventually.

In another life she might have said sorry. Might have told him that of course they were friends—best friends. If things were different, she might even have let herself be loved by someone so kind and thoughtful and *good*. But this was the life she had. One where her heart was ensnared by another. By a wild unicorn that gave everything she'd ever wanted and took everything she'd ever wanted at exactly the same time.

"Albert," Kenna said, as gently as she could, "you

shouldn't waste your time with me. Find somebody else. *Anybody* else."

Albert laughed then, and it surprised her. "I don't think that's how this works, Kenn."

"You don't really know me," she insisted. "You have an *idea* of me, but you don't know who I really am. Who you're really dealing with."

"Then tell me."

Kenna closed her eyes and breathed in the air of the forest. Being this high among the fresh smell of the leaves and the bark, she could almost pretend she was back in the Eyrie—that when she opened her eyes, she would see a round treehouse window lit by a lantern and the shadow of her brother climbing the trunk to bed. She wanted to run along the swinging bridges, to hammer on the door. *Help me, Skar. I'm so afraid. I don't know who I am. I don't know what I want. I don't know what to do.*

"I want to know everything about you," Albert insisted.

Kenna shook her head slowly. "Trust me. You don't."

CHAPTER NINETEEN

Something Secret

THE EYRIE WAS A HIVE OF ANXIETY FOR THE week leading up to the summer solstice. The eggs were still missing, and time was running out. Skandar joined his fellow Peregrine Society members in twice-daily sweeps of the Island. Meanwhile, Flo and Mitchell flew with Bobby, searching anywhere the other search parties weren't. But it all felt hopeless. The *Hatchery Herald* reported that the Mainland hadn't found a thing either, and started stoking further panic by publishing a series of articles about how Rex Manning—who, with Nina dead, was the front runner to win the Chaos Cup—was preparing for a battle on the summer solstice. A battle for the Island's future.

"That's all very well," Mitchell spat, folding the

newspaper in disgust. "But there won't *be* a battle for the eggs if nobody finds them, will there?"

"Rex is doing his best," Flo said quietly. "He didn't ask to be in charge."

Skandar knew Agatha would disagree with that.

Bobby fluttered her eyelashes. "If you ask me, I think Rex the dreamboat likes the drama. *And* the Chaos Cup is still going ahead tomorrow. He wants to be captain of the ship when it goes down. I mean, I get it. I'm an air wielder, too."

"We can't not have a Chaos Cup," Flo said, defending Rex again. "The whole Mainland will know something's wrong!"

"They'll know something's *wrong* when every single one of their thirteen-year-old Hatchery candidates gets sent back because there aren't any eggs for them," Mitchell retorted.

Bobby fiddled anxiously with the bracelet Flo had made, clearly thinking of her sister. If Isabel Bruna passed the Hatchery exam, she would be one of those sent back to the Mainland.

Skandar had at least been able to hold on to Chaos Cup day as a shining beacon of hope. While the rest of the Island was busy watching the aerial race, Skandar was going to see Kenna for the first time since the attack on the oasis. He was going to try to talk to her again about the dapple-gray unicorn, about the possibility of freeing her from her wild unicorn—though Goshawk's true rider wouldn't be found until the eggs were. *If* the eggs were. Skandar had promised himself he'd talk about the exchange as a possibility, not a certainty. He would listen to what Kenna wanted this time.

The next morning, Skandar headed down the Eyrie's hill with the rest of his quartet so they could wave him off.

"Say hi from us!" Flo said, to immediate shushing from Mitchell *and* Bobby.

"Just tell everyone, why don't you?" Bobby snapped. "Did you remember the emergency sandwich I made for *you know who?*" she whispered to Skandar.

Skandar nodded, thinking his sister might appreciate it if he "lost" the sandwich on the way, and pointed Scoundrel toward the air zone.

Skandar landed at the edge of a forest of impossibly tall redwood trees. After what had happened in the oasis last time he'd visited Kenna, he was on high alert. Every one of Scoundrel's hoofbeats on the forest floor felt far too loud. Then, as Agatha had instructed him, Skandar pulled the wooden whistle out of his jacket pocket—the one carved in the shape of a swallow—and blew.

The effect was immediate. Elora—who'd obviously been waiting for him—melted out of the trees on her silver unicorn in answer to the swallow's high-pitched chittering call. As Scoundrel and Soldier fell into step alongside each other, Skandar noticed that the Pathfinder of the Wanderers had a nasty new scar on her hand. He wondered guiltily whether it had happened at the oasis.

"It's good to see you, Skandar." Elora's straight white bob shone in the soft light.

"Hi, Elora. How's Kenna?" he asked immediately. "Is she here?"

"She couldn't come out to meet you—a few Islanders have treehouses on the Fourpoint side of the Sky Forest, so it's not safe. But she's fine. She . . ." Elora hesitated, her amethyst eyes guarded. "She's powerful. She's more in control of her magic now—she understands it better, I think. You know about her fire mutation?"

He nodded. "She hasn't mutated again?"

The Pathfinder shook her head. "Not yet."

There was a brief silence between them; the only sound was the rustling of leaves high above them and the swish of the unicorns' wings against low-hanging branches.

"Kenna misses you a great deal," Elora said sadly.

"I miss her, too."

"I fear the months since the oasis attack have been very hard on your sister. She has been alone most of that time."

Skandar frowned. "Hasn't she been with you? Didn't that sentinel return her to the Wanderers?"

Elora shook her head. "The Wanderers are scattered across the zones, though of course we're still welcoming those who need us. Some of the old spirit wielders have chosen to join us rather than take up Rex's offer of *protec-*

tion. Kenna has a visitor most days, but it's too dangerous to have her with the larger groups. It has been hard on . . . everyone. But especially Kenna." Elora's voice caught in her throat.

"I'm sorry that I led the sentinels to the oasis." The apology burst out without warning. "I didn't mean to. I just wanted—"

"To see your sister," Elora said warmly. "You are not to blame for that attack. Ignorance and suspicion and prejudice. *They* are to blame."

"I'm still sorry," Skandar muttered. "Was anyone seriously hurt?"

"Here we are," Elora said, without answering his question.

Silver Soldier had stopped at the roots of one of the tallest redwoods. Skandar couldn't see Kenna—or anything else to indicate they'd arrived.

"Kenna is up there with Albert," Elora said, pointing upward. "He's been her most frequent visitor. They're planning on listening to the Chaos Cup on the radio. She wasn't sure you'd come."

Skandar tipped his head back to look at the high branches; he still couldn't see a thing.

Elora's mouth twitched into a smile. "Trust me. They're up there. Goshawk and Eagle, too. Scoundrel can fly up to join them. Don't ride; it'll be easier for him to get through the branches without you. Use the footholds to climb the redwood trunk. I'll keep guard. If you hear the swallow's call, please do *not* come down." Then Silver Soldier turned back the way they'd come, and Skandar realized he'd been dismissed.

Skandar dismounted and started to climb. Scoundrel launched himself into the air.

As he climbed, muscles screaming, Skandar heard the distant sound of Chaos Cup coverage from above him. The commentators were just audible over the flapping of Scoundrel's wings, as he flew awkwardly to avoid hitting the branches.

". . . and a silver unicorn—that color has *never* been seen in the Chaos Cup, Harry. The name? Silver Sorceress. And she's being ridden by an as-yet-unknown Rex Manning."

"I'm going to cut in here, Mona, and just say what we're all thinking. What. A. Face."

"Well, he's a hit here in the studio, clearly—but being handsome won't help you out on the course."

"Rex has already gathered a lot of fans here on the Mainland. . . ."

It was *Mainland* Chaos Cup coverage. It reminded Skandar so strongly of being back in the living room of Flat 207 that he could almost see their battered old sofa, almost smell the fry-up Dad had just cooked in the kitchen, almost feel the excitement building in his chest.

Scoundrel shrieked as he spotted two unicorn horns— one pure white, one ghostly—poking out from two gigantic holes in opposite redwood trunks. Clumsily Scoundrel managed to land in another hole, the bond a mixture of confusion and excitement.

"Skar!" A hand reached for Skandar and pulled him through an opening in the trunk he was climbing. As his eyes adjusted to the lower light inside the tree, he saw his sister's face for a split second before she pulled him into a tight hug. And suddenly it didn't matter how terrible everything was. It didn't matter that there would be no unicorn eggs for the solstice. It didn't matter that the Weaver was planning to create a whole generation of wild unicorn riders. With Kenna's arms round him, Skandar always felt like everything would be okay.

The feeling quickly disappeared when she pulled back and he took in her four mutations. The thorned vines twisted down her right arm, the feathers studded round both her ears, the ice-spike necklace round her throat—and finally the mutation Skandar had not yet seen. Kenna's left arm was alive with liquid fire. It looked like she'd been tattooed with threads of lava from her elbow to her wrist. It was in constant motion—the molten rock breaking through her skin creases as she moved.

"Kenn," he choked out.

Her gaze dropped to where he was looking. A shadow passed over her face. "Oh, that? It happened ages ago. I'd almost forgotten all about it. I mean, at the time I had to stand in a waterfall for half a day until it stopped burning, but you missed all that excitement. You've missed a lot of things, actually."

Kenna's voice was strange. She didn't sound *angry* with him, but there was something underneath her words that unsettled him.

"I'm so sorry I haven't been able to visit. I didn't want to lead the sentinels to you again. Elora only just told me you haven't been with the Wanderers—that you've been on your own since the oasis. I wish I'd known that!"

"It doesn't matter now," Kenna said stiffly. "I've been fine without you. Without anyone." But her eyes had a bruised look about them.

"Well, *I* haven't been fine without you," Skandar whispered, reaching out. He felt unsure of his sister suddenly. Everything about the way she was behaving felt off—like she was holding something in. Was it anger? Hurt?

"Please, Skar, I don't want to talk about any of that today," Kenna said, her face brighter. "It's the Chaos Cup! I want it to be like the old days!"

She pointed to the back of the oval hole, and he turned to look. The hollow was so tall that he was able to stand upright with no danger of hitting his head, and it was deep enough that he could only just make out Albert. He was sitting on a blanket fiddling with a radio, the Chaos Cup coverage fizzing in and out.

Kenna went to sit on the very edge of the hollow, dangling her legs over the side. She patted the space next to her, and Skandar was grateful that they weren't joining Albert straightaway. He wanted some time with her—just them. But as they sat side by side, looking out at the vast green canopy of leaves ahead, Skandar clammed up. It felt too soon to start talking about the Eyrie and the possibility of releasing her from the forged bond.

"So how's Goshawk?" he ended up asking lamely.

Kenna's brown eyes seemed distant. "A bit of a handful. She's in my head a lot. Elora is trying to help me work out how to block some of the less . . . helpful emotions I'm getting from her, but it's like fighting a war in my mind sometimes. Tiring."

"I'm sorry."

"Don't be. I'd much rather be here with Gos than back on the Mainland."

There was a moment of silence between them.

Skandar cast around for something else to say. He still didn't think it felt right to bring up her future, not when she seemed so . . . He wasn't sure what she seemed. Finally he asked, "Have you seen anything in this forest, Kenn? Did you know that Nina and Lightning's Mistake were found dead here? Has there been any sign of the Weaver?"

"What makes you think Mum killed Nina Kazama?"

Skandar felt a jolt. Kenna seemed to have no problem thinking of their mother that way, but for him she was fractured. *Erika. Commodore. Killer. Mum. Weaver.*

Skandar shrugged. "Who else would it be?"

"How about the person who had the most to gain from her death? The person who was never going to have a chance of winning this Chaos Cup if Nina was racing."

"You think *Rex Manning* killed Nina?"

Kenna shrugged this time. "It's possible."

"I know you don't like him because he ordered the sentinels to find you," Skandar said, "but he can't be a murderer."

"Why?" Kenna raised an eyebrow. "Because he doesn't look like one?"

"The Weaver has stolen the entire contents of the Hatchery, Kenn. She's clearly trying to take over the Island with a new generation of riders. She would definitely want the Commodore out of the way. Nina is—*was*—so powerful."

"If you say so. It's just a theory."

"Come on, Kenn, you're missing it!" Albert called from behind them.

Kenna sprang to her feet.

"You and Albert seem close," Skandar said, bristling slightly at Albert's use of his sister's nickname.

"He's kept me company."

"Nice to see you, Skandar!" Albert said cheerfully. "I'm glad Elora got you here okay."

"Yeah, hi, Albert. How are you—"

"Listen!" Kenna said, and Skandar felt like he was five again and being scolded, but somehow he didn't mind.

". . . and at the halfway point we've got Alodie Birch

in the lead on River-Reed Prince. She's a veteran of this race now. Five years in a row and still chasing that elusive win. But with Nina Kazama no longer with us, she might have a chance. Here comes Ryan Hernandez and Kernow's Kraken, then Ema Templeton and Mountain's Fear— another veteran pairing—coming up on the inside."

"Just like old times, isn't it?" Kenna grinned at Skandar. "Do you remember Ema was my favorite?"

He nodded vigorously, wanting to match Kenna's enthusiasm, but he couldn't help thinking that this wasn't like old times at all. Kenna was on the run. They were hiding in a hole at the top of a tree. Dad wasn't here. *Dad*. Dad was coming to the Island tomorrow, expecting to see Kenna too. What was Skandar going to say to him?

Another commentator cut in. "Mainlander Khadija Malik is currently in second, but Rose's Devil seems to be tiring— Oh!"

The yelling of the crowd was audible from the speakers out on the course.

"What?!" Kenna shouted at the radio.

"I've never seen anything like that, Tim. The sky was alive with lightning—Rex Manning and Silver Sorceress have taken out three riders in the front group. That's Ryan Hernandez, Tom Nazari, and Ema Templeton *out* of the Chaos Cup. I can't believe I'm saying this. Three of the top riders have fallen. And newcomer Rex Manning on Silver Sorceress is now in third place behind water wielder Alodie

Birch and earth-allied Khadija Malik as they head into the final quarter of the course."

Was Rex really going to do it?

"Just to reassure you, I've been informed that Ema, Tom, and Ryan are all fine. Their unicorns managed to catch them long before they hit the ground."

"Back out on the course, Rose's Devil has been taken out by a furious ice shard attack from Alodie. That has *got* to hurt!"

"And they're into the final straight. It's Alodie Birch in the lead, then Rex Manning in second, with Federico Jones on Sunset's Blood gaining on them. In fourth we have Tristan Macfarlane on Acidic Archangel, and in fifth it's Peter Whitaker on Hallowed Hussar. But look at Sorceress fly!"

Skandar could imagine mighty, majestic Sorceress soaring like a silver bullet through the air. No wonder Rex had so many fans on the Mainland already. Young Skandar would have idolized a rider like Rex. Handsome, athletic, successful—and with a rare silver unicorn of extraordinary power. He would have cherished his Chaos Cards of Sorceress or Rex; he wouldn't have traded them for anything. Because they looked like winners. They looked like heroes. They looked like glory.

"Come on, Alodie," Kenna pleaded, grabbing Skandar's hand like she used to back in Margate.

"And Rex Manning and Sorceress have taken the lead,

Alodie and River-Reed Prince still right on their silver tail."

"Rex has summoned the air element as they soar over the stands. This crowd is going *wild* for Manning."

"Rex has molded a lightning bow—bigger than I've ever seen—he's turning in his saddle as Sorceress descends toward the arena. He's pulling back the sparking string; he's loosed it. Ah! It's hit true. A direct hit on Alodie Birch, and she's been slowed by that electric shock."

"Rex Manning and Silver Sorceress have landed. They're down on the sand and they're galloping!"

"No," Albert and Kenna said together.

The cheering of the crowd was deafening now, almost drowning out the commentators.

"He's done it! He's under the finishing arch. Rex Manning and Silver Sorceress have won the Chaos Cup! Rex Manning is the new Commodore of Chaos. It'll be another air council this year. And from the noise of the crowd, he is going to be very popular. That's Rex Manning—"

"Turn it off," Kenna said darkly.

Albert immediately obeyed, and the redwood hole went quiet.

Skandar stared at the radio. It felt like the world had shifted sideways. A silver Commodore. No longer just a caretaker. What would that mean for a spirit wielder like him? He tried to reassure himself. Rex had *freed* Arctic Swansong for Agatha. Maybe he'd challenge the Silver Circle's hatred of spirit wielders. Maybe he'd change it.

Kenna's face told a different story. "Rex is never going to be happy until I'm behind bars."

Albert put a hand on her molten arm, but she withdrew it quickly.

"Kenn, he's not as bad as you think. Maybe it'll be okay. Maybe . . ." Skandar trailed off. Was now the right time to talk about Kenna's future?

But Kenna was inconsolable for the rest of the afternoon and throughout their campfire dinner with Elora and Albert. At one point, Skandar suggested she ride Goshawk so she could show him some of her magic—half hoping they could be alone to talk—but Kenna said she was too tired.

Agatha had decided it would be best for Skandar to stay the night. That way, he could leave in the early morning and avoid any stragglers coming back to the air zone from Chaos Cup celebrations. Skandar was relieved he wasn't leaving yet—he needed more time with Kenna.

The unicorns had already found holes to sleep in, higher up the redwood trunks. The deep hollows were very cozy—stuffed with moss and blankets. Scoundrel was already snoring when Skandar joined him, the occasional spark rippling over his feathery wings.

Goshawk had chosen a hole just above Scoundrel's. Skandar rested his head right on the bottom scoop of the hole—a pillow underneath it—and looked upward. Kenna lay on her stomach, peering down at him from above—so they could just about see each other as it got dark. It was almost like being in bunk beds.

"Kenn," Skandar said, wanting to ask a question that'd been haunting him for months. "Who was that sentinel at the oasis?"

Kenna stared at him for a moment as if she hadn't heard.

"You said he helped you when you were trapped in the Stronghold," Skandar prompted.

"He did. He brought me extra food and things. I think he's just a nice sentinel." She laughed harshly. "Not many of them around."

"But you spent ages with him after the oasis attack. Didn't he tell you who he was? Why he helped you?"

Kenna shrugged. "We didn't talk much. We were too busy running." She changed the subject. "What are you going to say to Dad tomorrow? About me?"

Skandar sighed, dreading it. "I'll tell him you have training, but you'll see him next June."

"You should say we got into an argument, so he thinks that's why I haven't come to your Air Trial."

The words hung in the air as an owl hooted loudly nearby, and they lay in silence for a while. *Are we in an argument?* Skandar wondered, listening to his sister's breathing—like he used to when he couldn't fall asleep back on the Mainland. Those moments between waking and sleeping were when he'd always felt the safest. No Dad to look after, no money to magic out of thin air, and

Kenna right there to protect him from the world.

"Do you want to know something secret, Skar?" Kenna asked quietly, just as Skandar's eyelids were getting heavy. It was a game they'd played when they were younger. They'd admit something silly or scary or secret just before they fell asleep. When it was safe. When nobody else could hear them.

"Yes," Skandar whispered. "Tell me." His stomach turned over with anticipation just like it always used to.

Kenna took a deep breath. "There's a part of me that's hoping you don't pass the Chaos Trials. I can't help thinking that if you're declared a nomad, you can live with me. We can go on the run and be outlaws together! Do you think that's awful?"

Skandar's heart beat wildly. He'd been afraid she might say this. Deep down he'd known tonight wasn't just about her future—it was also about his. "Is that what you want? For me to leave the Eyrie?"

Kenna propped herself up on her elbow, staring down at him.

Skandar crashed on. "I do think it's important what I'm doing, Kenn. If I finish my training at the Eyrie, they'll bring the spirit element back! That's only two more years. And that means you could be a proper rider, too! We could be Chaos riders like we always wanted. We could be together."

"We'd be together if we went on the run too," Kenna pointed out. "And they won't bring the spirit element back,

Skar. I know you want to believe the best in people, but they're never going to. They're too scared of it—of us. And I'm *not* a spirit wielder anyway. I have a forged bond, a wild unicorn. I'm allied to all five elements. Even if they accept the spirit element, they're never going to accept *me*."

Skandar hesitated then, being more careful than he'd been at the oasis. "But I'm worried about your spirit mutation. We've talked about if you weren't bonded to Goshawk, if I—"

"Don't," Kenna said sharply. "It's me and Gos. That's the way it is, whether you like it or not. Don't ruin this time we've got together. Please."

"Okay," he said quietly. The plan he'd made for his sister felt like it was disintegrating into the night. He supposed he'd made it before he really knew how Kenna felt. Before she'd survived four wild mutations. Before he'd seen her magic. Kenna had always been stronger than him. He had underestimated her. "Okay," he said again, and this time the word felt heavier.

"Skandar, I can't tell you to leave the Eyrie," she continued. "I don't want to be the one responsible for you giving that up. You have to do that for yourself; you have to *decide* what you want, what's important to you. It isn't fair to put that on me."

A silence fell between them again that Skandar was desperate to lift.

"Do *you* want to know something secret?" he murmured

into the dark, the stars bright through the redwood leaves. Skandar had promised Agatha he wouldn't tell another soul, but this was his sister, and he felt so distant from her. He wanted another secret to tie them together.

"Always," Kenna whispered.

Skandar unzipped the inside pocket of his yellow jacket and took out a white pouch.

"Reach down your hand," he said, and he placed the spirit stone in Kenna's hanging palm.

Skandar heard her intake of breath. "Is it . . . is it real?" she asked finally, wonder in her voice.

"It's a solstice stone. It's what we collect during the trials. They don't have a Spirit Trial anymore, but Agatha gave me this. She's had it since she was a Fledgling."

"She gave it to you?" Kenna whispered, turning the white stone over in her hand.

"As a sort of *well done* for my spirit training," Skandar said, feeling a bit proud. "I know I'm biased, but I think it's the nicest type of stone."

"It *is* really pretty," Kenna agreed, holding it up in the starlight.

"I'd better hide it away again," Skandar said. "This might be the only one left."

Kenna handed the stone back, and Skandar zipped it into his jacket pocket.

They lay listening to each other's breathing for a while. "You know, I used to forget you weren't there?" Kenna whispered. "Back at Flat 207. I'd speak to you, just like this, and completely forget that you'd gone to the Island."

"I'm so sorry, Kenn," Skandar whispered. When she said things like that, he realized he didn't know the half of what Kenna had been through in the last two years.

"No harm done," Kenna breathed.

But—as Skandar pictured the thorned vines round her arm, the feathers in her ears, the magma under her skin, and the ice spikes at her throat—his last thought before he closed his eyes was that he wasn't sure that was true at all.

CHAPTER TWENTY

The Air Trial

THE FOLLOWING MORNING, WHEN SKAN-dar left for the Air Trial, Kenna was all forced smiles and sharp hugs. Skandar promised he'd be back in a matter of days, but there was a distance in her voice that suggested she didn't believe him.

If you're declared a nomad, you can live with me. Skandar couldn't stop thinking about Kenna's words, as he met Jamie at the Eyrie's entrance for last-minute checks on Scoundrel's armor. Couldn't put them out of his mind, as he forced down breakfast with his quartet, knowing he had to keep his strength up. Every mouthful felt difficult—even with a healthy serving of mayonnaise—as both guilt and the nerves for the trial ahead jangled in his stomach.

Unlike the rest of the Chaos Trials, the Air Trial did not begin at dusk or dawn. It was taking place in the afternoon, which Bobby boasted was proof that air was the best and most civilized element. Mitchell argued it was more to do with the logistics of flying in the Mainlander families to watch. On top of the riders' families, all five instructors—including the new Commodore—were joining the Fledglings in the air zone for the final trial.

At midday, the Fledglings paraded out through the Eyrie's entrance. Mitchell glanced at Skandar, and Flo at Bobby, as they rode under the colorful leaves of the Wild Unicorn Queen's tree. Each of them knew the significance of this—even Bobby didn't make a joke. The quartet had tried not to think about what would happen if they didn't all make it through the Chaos Trials—but there was no stopping those thoughts now as they left the Eyrie behind. If any of them failed to complete their set of solstice stones, they'd never be allowed to enter again.

Skandar felt sheer panic as soon as he was on the other side of the Eyrie's wall. More of Kenna's words echoed in his mind: *We can go on the run and be outlaws together!* Scoundrel shrieked in confusion as Skandar's hand twitched on his rein, as though his body was rebelling against leaving this place he called home. No. He couldn't leave the Eyrie, could he?

Skandar patted the pocket of his air jacket nervously, feeling the lump of the spirit stone in its pouch. Agatha had given it to him for luck and courage. *Remember that you belong here*, she'd said. It calmed him to keep it close, where he could protect it.

The line of Fledgling unicorns stretched out ahead of Scoundrel's Luck, their feathered wings beating like a flock of migrating birds. They'd passed over the redwoods of the Sky Forest already and were now flying over the tall grasses of the prairie—punctuated by blankets of yellow dandelions and sunflowers bending their shining heads in the constant breeze. They flew on over dozens of windmills, then high above valleys with terraced fields rising in steps on either side, which were designed to channel the zone's unpredictable winds into the sails of the mills. Finally the glinting form of Silver Sorceress landed at the very edge of the last valley before the Wilderness.

As Scoundrel touched down, the first person Skandar saw was his dad. He looked slightly older than when he'd last visited the Island—his short dark hair peppered with gray, shoulders a little more stooped. Dressed in a smart striped shirt Skandar had never seen before, he was queuing to enter the makeshift stand built especially for the trial, his head tracking the Fledgling unicorns as they came in to land.

Father and son locked eyes, and then Skandar was dismounting and running toward his dad. Running toward home.

"Ooof!" Dad grunted, as Skandar collided with him in

full armor. But his arms tightened round his son, pulling him close.

"I missed you," Skandar said into his dad's shoulder. *Shoulder.* Skandar was taller now.

"I missed you, too." Dad laughed, finally releasing Skandar so he could see his face. "Are you ready for the race, then? I've heard the new Commodore's watching!"

"As ready as I'll ever be," Skandar said, trying not to think about the possibility that the Weaver might be out on the course hunting stones . . . and him.

"I haven't seen Kenna yet." Dad looked over his shoulder at the other families in the stand.

This was the moment Skandar had been dreading. He took a shaky breath. "Kenna isn't coming today, Dad."

Dad frowned, the lines on his forehead crinkling. "Why not?"

"She, er, we had a bit of a falling-out. And she'd have to get special permission to miss training, anyway, so she decided it wasn't worth coming. We haven't really, um, made up properly yet." It was a half-truth, he supposed.

Dad was a mixture of cross and hurt. "First, I don't get an invitation to her Training Trial because of some kind of administrative error, and now she hasn't come to see me? This place is an organizational nightmare—it's about time I spoke to someone official." He peered at the instructors, as though sizing up which one he could approach. "I've got a right to see her, you know. Maybe after her training this afternoon?"

Facing him now, Skandar couldn't bear to tell Dad that he wouldn't see Kenna after training. That he might not see his daughter for a long time.

Dad gave Skandar a piercing look. "Must have been a bad argument if she isn't supporting you today. That's not like you two. You were always so close."

Skandar swallowed. "I'm sure we'll sort things out."

Dad nodded, satisfied. "Make sure you do. You and your sister have something so special. You'd do anything for each other, wouldn't you? Don't let life come between you. There's only one Kenna in the world, eh? And how lucky are we that she's ours? Come on now, don't cry." Dad reached out and wiped a tear that had escaped down Skandar's cheek. "I'm sure she'll be all smiles when you and Scoundrel come back the winners today!"

Skandar hiccup-laughed at his dad's endless confidence in him. "Dad, I don't think I'm going to actually win the—"

"Skandar, come on!" Mitchell called over bossily. "They're lining everyone up."

Dad gave Skandar one last hug. "Good luck, Son."

Skandar and Scoundrel joined the line on Flo and Blade's right, and realized that the instructors were already giving out the yellow air stones. As he watched Agatha walking purposefully toward his quartet with her canary-colored drawstring bag, Skandar felt queasy—until he remembered that every rider was getting a stone this time.

Agatha dropped the multifaceted gem into Skandar's hand, and he was half tempted to summon the air element to check that it was empty.

The Eyrie's air instructor, head of the Silver Circle, and newly triumphant Commodore of Chaos cleared his throat. The nervous Fledglings quieted immediately—the only sound was the clack of the magnetic solstice stones as they were attached to their armor. Agatha mouthed "Good luck" to Skandar, swung herself back up onto Arctic Swansong, and rode over to join the other four instructors facing the Fledgling unicorns.

"Welcome to the Air Trial," Rex Manning called. Although his voice was upbeat, there were definitely signs of stress in his usually serene face. With the summer solstice so close and no sign of the eggs, he couldn't be getting much rest. "This trial is by far the shortest you have faced so far, but don't let that make you complacent. The primary challenge is perhaps a familiar one: you will be racing cross-country through the air zone. Think of it as an even more unpredictable version of the Chaos Cup. The course—" Rex broke off, his palm glowing yellow, and blasted electricity up into the air on his right, looking every inch the most powerful rider on the Island.

The Mainlanders in the crowd let out an "Oooooh!" of delight, watching sparks explode and then fizz along in midair—as though following an invisible thread—crackling low over the windmills, out of sight, and then back over the terraced valleys and finishing above where they were seated.

The electric loop of the course shimmered in the sunshine, and Rex continued.

"As I was saying, the course is marked out by the electrical field I have just created. You will start and end here, by the stands. Stray outside the course, and you will lose your air stone. All five of us instructors, and two dozen sentinels, will be patrolling to make sure everything goes . . . smoothly." Skandar wondered if Rex would explain *why* the sentinels were here, maybe give a warning about the Weaver and the stones, but of course he left it there. Rex still seemed to be pretending like nothing odd at all had happened during the previous trials.

"The course will take you through the air zone's own obstacles—a dash past rapid windmill blades, a flight over prairie exposed to the worst of the Island's weather, a slalom through giant redwood trunks, and a fight through gale-force winds generated by the sylphs of the terraced valleys—until you return here for the finish."

"What's a sylph?" Skandar whispered to Flo, but she was turned toward Mitchell.

"This seems too easy," Mitchell muttered. "It can't just be a race."

"And what about the reward stones?" Bobby hissed.

Other Fledglings were whispering too, and Rex held his hand up for silence. He chuckled softly, the electricity in his cheeks sparking. "You are quite right, Bobby. I haven't yet given you the full picture, have I? If my fellow instructors wouldn't mind assisting me— Oh, apologies, not you, Instructor Everhart." Skandar thought he glimpsed Instructor O'Sullivan rolling her whirlpool eyes at Agatha, though Celestial Seabird still took off after Moonlight Dust and Desert Firebird.

Commodore Manning summoned the air element again and made a wide circular motion with his palm. The other instructors followed suit, each summoning their own allied element. Though the smell of elemental magic filled the air, the Fledglings could not see what their instructors were doing until the fully grown unicorns landed.

Four elemental hoops were suspended horizontally in the air above them: one of flickering flame, another of crackling electricity, a third of crashing water, and the last of twisting vines. And in the center of each—suspended in a cage of electrical current—was a solstice stone. One of each element. Skandar couldn't help but fixate on the blue stone, encircled by its watery ring a hundred meters above his head. He wanted it—he *needed* it—if he was going to make it to Rookie year.

"To pass the Air Trial, it is not enough simply to finish the race. To keep your air stone—to add it to your collection for re-entry into the Eyrie—you must leap from your unicorn's back in midair and free-fall through one of these four elemental hoops. Once you have passed through the hoop, your unicorn will catch you and you will finish the race as soon as their hooves hit the ground. It is the ultimate test of daring, and of the trust between unicorn and rider. We call it the leap of faith. The final challenge of the Chaos Trials is designed to showcase the relationship you have built with your unicorn this year." He smiled round at them. "Don't look so worried! You're all very capable of this, I know you are. I believe in you."

Skandar saw Flo mouthing "leap of faith" to herself in horror. But Mitchell looked even more afraid. That was when Skandar remembered his fear of heights.

"What if our unicorn decides not to catch us? What if we miss their back? What if—" Romily's panicked voice rose above some of the other murmured conversations between quartets. Skandar knew that—like him—she was missing a stone. She needed fire.

Instructor O'Sullivan answered this time, jumping in before Rex had a chance to speak again. "You do not have to do the leap of faith, but you will lose your air stone if you fail to jump through one of the hoops."

Bobby didn't look fazed. "Who gets the stones in the hoops?" she called. "Is it the fastest finishers?"

"That's exactly right, Bobby," Rex said, his voice warm. "Those who reach the hoops first will get the spare stones. But once you have jumped through one hoop, you cannot go back for another. Choose wisely."

There were some cries of disappointment from down the—now wiggly—line of Fledglings, and Skandar knew why. Some riders needed more than one stone to complete their elemental set. Even if they managed to get to the hoop first and win one of the spare stones they needed, they wouldn't be allowed back into the Eyrie unless they were saved by someone else at its entrance.

"The Air Trial will begin in thirty minutes," Rex said, and he went to greet the healers, who'd just begun erecting their tent. Some blacksmiths—Jamie among them—were also setting up for last-minute armor adjustments. Skandar looked over to the stands for a final glimpse of his dad; he was seated by the Shekonis, and Skandar saw the flashing blue braid belonging to Ira Henderson just behind him.

"They've left us time to discuss tactics!" Mitchell hissed, pointedly *not* looking toward his father as the quartet moved away from the other Fledglings. They bunched their unicorns together so they couldn't be overheard.

"Do we even need to?" Bobby shrugged, her chain mail clinking. "Seems easy to me. Though, you'd better catch me, Falcon," she added to her unicorn. "Else you're a goner too, remember?"

"How can you say that it seems easy?" Flo croaked. "We have to throw ourselves off in midair!"

"So help me, Florence, if you don't leap through that

hoop, I will throw you through myself," Bobby warned. "We haven't come all this way for you to be declared a nomad."

"Oh, I'll do it," Flo mumbled, casting a worried glance at Blade. "But I don't promise to enjoy it."

"Everyone, be quiet a minute," Mitchell said. "We need to plan. Skandar needs that water stone. And what if the Weaver tries to attack him mid-race?"

Flo spoke up. "Wouldn't it make sense if the rest of us protect you, Skar, so Scoundrel can fly as quickly as possible to the finish to get the water stone? Surely if we fight your sky battles for you, you'll get there first?"

"I like it," Mitchell said. "Skandar is the fastest flier of all of us. Being a Grin, I can't imagine he'll have an issue with the leap of faith either. Right, Skandar?"

Skandar didn't like this. He didn't want his friends putting themselves in danger for him . . . again. And was it even worth it? Maybe Kenna was right? Maybe he should leave the Eyrie and not even attempt to reach the spare water stone. Maybe he'd been going about this all wrong.

Bobby looked slightly disappointed with the plan, but she didn't argue. Instead she said, "Amber and Whirlwind Thief are probably Skandar's biggest competition on speed, but Amber needs an earth stone, so it shouldn't matter if she gets to the hoops first."

"But I've worked out that at least ten Fledglings need

a water stone," Mitchell added. "So it's not like we can relax."

"What does it matter?" Bobby said. "Skandar's going to be faster than all of them—like I said, it's just Amber—"

"It's not only about that," Mitchell insisted. "Didn't you hear what Commodore Manning said? This is a cross-country version of the Chaos Cup. Riders are going to try to take each other out during the race too. And Skandar's practically got a target on his back—he's a Grin, so they know he's fast, and they won't necessarily feel bad about taking him out because he's a *scary spirit wielder*."

"You sound like Aunty Agatha," Bobby groaned.

"Please," Skandar begged. His friends were completely unaware of his inner turmoil—he hadn't said a word to them about his time with Kenna. "You don't have to protect me. What if you lose one of your air stones? What if the Weaver's out there? You don't have to—"

"We *want* to," Flo reassured him. "You'd do it for us."

"Also," Bobby added, "Agatha pretty much said she'd murder us if we didn't help you get that water stone, so there really isn't any choice."

"We're a quartet," Mitchell said firmly. "That's the end of it."

Skandar swallowed. They were his quartet. He belonged in the Eyrie with them, didn't he?

Bobby pointed dramatically at Mitchell. "Tell us everything you know about sylphs." She turned to Flo.

"See, Florence. I'm learning not to rush into things. Remember the stalignomes? Well, I've matured, see? I'm *asking*."

Flo cracked a smile, as Mitchell explained that the air elementals were particularly aggressive gusts of wind that had minds of their own and ghostly shifting faces. They occupied the terraced valleys, playing havoc with the air currents. The Fledglings would have to get past them on the last section of the aerial course.

Before they knew it, the thirty minutes were up. The Fledglings gathered along a charred black line that Instructor Anderson had burned into the grass under the four elemental hoops. It would act as the start and the finish. Elemental blasts exploded along the line of unicorns as riders made final adjustments to their armor, tightened girth straps, and pulled down the visors on their helmets.

Scoundrel's eyes were rolling between red and black, the feathers on his wings igniting and then freezing over in anticipation. Skandar could hardly see Blade—clouds of smoke obscured his whole body—and Red was on her fifth fart in a row, igniting them easily with a flick of her flaming hoof. Falcon, on the other hand, was calm—only snorting the occasional spark and pawing the ground. Skandar tried to steady his nerves. *It's just a race*, he told himself. *You don't have to think about Kenna right now. You don't have to think about the Weaver being here. And you could outfly her anyway, right?*

Rex Manning rode to the edge of the starting line. His palm glowed yellow, and Skandar sensed every single Fledgling gathering their reins and crouching low in their saddles. Then the Commodore sent a lightning bolt into the sky—and the Air Trial began.

"Go, Scoundrel!" Skandar called, but he needn't have bothered. He could feel in the bond Scoundrel's desire to race, his love of flying. They had made it through every other Chaos Trial to get here. They were together in this. In everything.

Scoundrel took off in three strides, and Skandar sensed Blade, Red, and Falcon doing the same just behind him. There was a blast of fire magic to his left, the smell of burnt toast, and a wave of heat. Skandar forced himself not to slow. He had one job. He had to be the fastest. He had to reach the water hoop first.

As they weaved their way toward the windmills, Scoundrel's Luck was having the time of his life. He much preferred flying to battling, and right now they were at the front of the fastest group of Fledglings.

"Skandar, above you!" Bobby's voice rang out from a few meters behind. He glanced up through his helmet. Demonic Nymph was descending through the air toward them—Marissa's palm glowing blue—preparing to engage them in a sky battle. There was desperation in her eyes—just like him, she needed that water stone.

But Skandar didn't want to fight her. He wanted to

keep his position at the front, and he knew that if he wasted precious time and energy battling Marissa, then he'd lose his early advantage. So instead he flew Scoundrel down toward the turning sails of the windmills.

The whooshing of wings behind him told Skandar that Marissa had chased after him. Sure enough, shards of ice flew past his shoulder and a few clattered against his chain mail. She wanted a battle.

"All right," Skandar murmured. "If they want a chase, we'll give them one. Do you trust me, boy?"

Skandar flew Scoundrel even lower so they were dangerously close to the sharp sails of the windmills. Then, praying he'd judged the timing correctly, he sent Scoundrel into one of his favorite Peregrine Society moves. An arrow roll. Scoundrel gave an almighty beat of his wings and shot forward like a bullet. The next second, the black unicorn folded his wings tightly to his sides, and Skandar—legs wrapped tightly round Scoundrel to ensure he didn't slip from his saddle—used the reins to roll them to the left, then right, then left again. And it was working. At every windmill, they missed the sails by centimeters until—finally—they were at the last one, and Scoundrel unfolded his wings and flew up to rejoin the race.

Skandar glanced over his shoulder. Marissa was still stuck at the other end of the line of windmills. As Scoundrel soared out over the prairie—the wind battering them from all directions—Skandar heard his quartet whooping behind him. It made his heart sing. They were with him, and he was winning.

Once they'd crossed the prairie, Skandar and Scoundrel were the first pair to reach the halfway point: the Sky Forest. The sparking course line only reached a short way inside—but it was still tricky. The trunks rose up in front of Scoundrel, and he shrieked with frustration as he was forced to slow, slaloming in and out of them. Skandar kept hearing other unicorns enter the trees—the snapping of a branch by a flying hoof, the crackle as wing tips brushed past the leaves. He didn't want a battle in here. And part of him couldn't stop imagining a black shrouded figure, a wild unicorn, and Nina's scream as Lightning's Mistake was attacked for the very last time.

Then finally Skandar saw daylight again, and Scoundrel burst out of the trees. Taking a quick look behind him, Skandar was delighted to see Falcon emerge from the forest, then Red, then Blade—

No.

Flo screamed. Blade let out a terrible shriek of pain. He kicked out and writhed in midair, fighting off some kind of invisible force.

Skandar turned Scoundrel round and flew back toward the forest. Bobby was shouting something at Flo as she clung on for dear life, Falcon hovering just out of reach of Blade's thrashing legs. Mitchell and Red were desperately swooping over the ground near the trees, searching for the source of the attack, as more unicorns emerged from the shadows and continued with their race—oblivious.

"What's happening?" Skandar yelled.

"I can't get to Flo!" Bobby shouted back. "Blade's in some kind of elemental cage. I'm worried he's going to throw her off!"

As Scoundrel flew nearer, Skandar saw coils of flame forming a fire cage round Blade and Flo, watching as it flashed into lightning, then knitted into ice crystals. Then he realized why Blade kept bellowing in pain—the edges of the elemental force field were hurting him as he tried to escape.

Joining Mitchell and Red, Skandar and Scoundrel swooped and dived around the area, looking wildly for the source of the magic. Other Fledglings soared by, focused on the way ahead—Anoushka and Sky Pirate were battling Art and Furious Inferno in the air just beyond the redwoods.

"Help! He's forgotten I'm even here!" Flo screamed, as Blade started to kick elemental blasts at the force field, getting more and more wound up and bellowing every time he hit the cage's edge. Out of desperation, Bobby started to hurl attacks at the cage—alternating the elements to try to outsmart it.

"What *is* this magic?" Bobby yelled. Nothing was working.

"The Weaver must be in the forest!" Mitchell called to Skandar as they circled.

Dread flooded Skandar's whole body. Was the Weaver trying to kill Flo? Just like she'd killed Nina among the redwoods? Wasn't *he* the target?

BANG!

Suddenly the elemental magic around Flo and Blade exploded in a burst of orange light. Blade was blasted sideways and began to spiral down to the ground. Flo screamed as she left the saddle and started to free-fall through the air. Blade was too hurt to catch her, one of his silver wings drooping uselessly as he plummeted toward the ground.

Skandar was too panicked to think, to breathe. *Flo. Not Flo.* But Scoundrel was already diving through the air. Scoundrel's Luck understood how much Flo meant to Skandar. He understood friendship better than anything else. After all, Skandar was his best friend in the whole world.

Falcon and Red were soaring down toward Flo's falling form too. But Scoundrel was already there—right underneath her—waiting to break her fall and—

OOOF! Flo's armored body collided with Skandar's. She grabbed on to his arm with one hand and Scoundrel's mane with the other. She was half crying—winded from the crash and trying to get her breath back. Silver Blade was already on the ground, looking mournfully up at Scoundrel as he circled, one silver wing hanging by his armored side.

"It's okay, it's okay," Skandar said over and over into Flo's hair.

"It's not okay, Skar," Flo choked out.

"What do you—" She turned to face him, and he saw exactly what was wrong.

Flo no longer had an air stone.

CHAPTER TWENTY-ONE

Another Shore

SKANDAR STARED IN HORROR AT THE PLACE where Flo's air stone should have been.

"It must have fallen!" she said desperately.

But Skandar knew better. The Weaver had stolen it. And now she had four solstice stones to fill with elemental power. He tried to stave off the panic by closing his fingers round Agatha's spirit stone in his jacket pocket. *She doesn't have five*, Skandar thought frantically. *This is the only spirit stone, and I'll never let her take it.*

Bobby and Mitchell soared toward Skandar and Flo, who were squashed together on Scoundrel's back. Three more Fledglings raced above them.

"Skandar, Mitchell, you have to go." Bobby hissed.

"What are you talking about?" Mitchell asked. Skandar was still looking down into the shadows of the trees for the attacker. Could he find the Weaver? Could he get Flo's stone back?

"Florence," Bobby said seriously, "climb onto Falcon instead."

Bobby encouraged Falcon to hover in the sky next to Scoundrel. Flo looked skeptical—they were still fifty meters above the ground.

Bobby clapped three times very loudly, trying to shake her quartet into action. "The race! The Air Trial! You're losing time—if you go now, you might still be able to get to the spare stones. We need water *and* air now."

Mitchell was shaking his head. "Roberta, you're faster than me. You go."

"No, I'll wait with Flo until help comes." Bobby glanced at Blade rearing up at them from the ground, unable to take off.

"Instructor Manning," Flo breathed. "He can help with Blade."

"What if the Weaver comes back?" Skandar insisted, as Flo maneuvered herself onto Falcon's back.

"Flo already signaled for help," Bobby said. "The instructors will be here any minute—we don't have time to argue. I'm not going into Rookie year with half a quartet— Mitchell and I will kill each other if we have to live in that treehouse by ourselves."

"She has a point," Mitchell mumbled. "We need those stones."

"I'll follow as soon as Flo and Blade are safe. Go! NOW!" And with that, Bobby flew Flo and Falcon down to Blade.

Skandar and Mitchell rejoined the race. The daunting challenge in front of them hit home as they saw the sheer number of Fledglings soaring along the sparking loop of the course ahead. Scoundrel and Red weren't in last place, but they were definitely toward the back of the competitors.

"Fly as fast as you can!" Mitchell yelled as the shadows of their black and red unicorns passed over the prairie below. "Don't wait for me!"

"Are you sure?" Skandar shouted.

"GO!"

Scoundrel's wingbeats practically doubled in speed, his front legs pumping through the air. The bond was filled with his determination to catch up with the unicorns soaring over more windmills ahead.

Scoundrel swerved around a ferocious sky battle being fought above the final windmill. Through the smoke and elemental debris, Skandar glimpsed Amber and Whirlwind Thief battling against Meiyi and Rose-Briar's Darling and Alastair and Dusk Seeker—members of her own quartet. Skandar forced himself onward. He couldn't slow down now.

Scoundrel's Peregrine Society training was certainly helping. Skandar rocketed past Elias, Ivan, and Aisha as their unicorns tired in the last third of the course.

"C'mon, boy," Skandar whispered, crouching even lower in his Shekoni saddle. "We've got this."

They entered the terraced valleys. The fields on either side were like steps, each higher than the last. The corn swayed violently in the strong gusts. But Skandar had learned with Scoundrel how to listen to the wind and react before it was too late. He leaned left, then right, shifting his weight as Scoundrel tipped his wings to ride through the gales tearing through the valley. And then—

WHOOSH!

The sylphs arrived. The air all around Scoundrel seemed to take the shape of dozens of screaming faces, their shrieks filling Skandar's ears. Scoundrel turned his head from side to side, confused by the elementals as they rushed closer. The direction of the wind changed from one moment to the next; it felt like trying to fly through molasses. Scoundrel bellowed as the sylphs screamed louder, gusts tearing at his wings. Skandar clung to the saddle as the creatures rushed him in dangerous swirls.

They battled on, every muscle they'd built with the Peregrine Society straining for every desperately slow wingbeat, until the sylphs began to drop back to their next target.

Scoundrel was free of them. He increased his speed—passing Romily and Midnight Star, then Anoushka and Sky Pirate, then Farooq and Toxic Thyme—and then they were soaring out of the valley and toward the four elemental hoops glittering in the sky over the finish line.

But there were still Fledglings ahead of them.

Air-allied Zac and Yesterday's Ghost were already approaching the hoops, followed by fire wielder Walker on Savage Salamander. And Walker was missing a water stone.

Skandar started to panic, urging Scoundrel on faster, trying to catch up with Salamander's light brown tail. Skandar would have to battle Walker to stop him from reaching the flowing water hoop first.

Walker—intent on the finish—hadn't noticed Scoundrel behind him. And Skandar decided to use this to his advantage. He summoned the spirit element to his palm and focused on the bond between himself and Scoundrel, imagining their hearts beating as one. And then there was another Skandar and another Scoundrel flying in the air right beside them, mirroring their every wingbeat.

"Walker!" Skandar shouted, and the fire wielder looked over his shoulder.

The terror on the boy's face was absolute. He forgot about flying toward the hoops altogether, half turning Salamander in the air. His head swung from one Skandar to the other.

In that moment, Skandar wished that his duplicate could engage Walker and Salamander in a sky battle—that way *he'd* be free to jump through the water hoop. If only his double could throw a spirit javelin and start the fight, then—

"Argh!" Walker threw up a shield of sand to block a spirit javelin soaring right toward his heart. Skandar snapped his head sideways and saw that the thing he'd wished for—the thing he'd most needed—had happened. Having blocked the spirit javelin thrown by Skandar's double, Walker was now dropping his shield. His palm glowed red as he molded a flaming sword to retaliate with.

Skandar didn't hesitate. With Walker distracted, he pushed Scoundrel on. Zac had taken his leap of faith—the fire stone had already gone from its flaming hoop—but the water stone was still suspended in its watery prison, ready for the taking.

Then Skandar saw the air stone—the one Flo needed—surrounded by its sparking electrical hoop. Down beyond the hoop—cheering and whooping—he could see his dad. A dad he loved so much, even though sometimes loving him had been hard. And Skandar felt as though he'd been zapped by the air element itself. *There's only one Kenna in the world, eh? And how lucky are we that she's ours?* Dad's words made Skandar think more clearly about everything than he had in months, as Scoundrel hovered above the hoops.

Kenna needed him. She had needed him all year—and he'd been so determined to fight for her place in the Eyrie, to find out how to release her bond, that he hadn't been by her side. But Nina Kazama was dead. And with a silver in charge, Kenna's fate, Skandar's fate, and the fate of all spirit wielders was more uncertain than it had been since he'd made his deal with Aspen McGrath. He wasn't sure he could trust Rex to bring back the spirit element. He wasn't even sure he could trust the Eyrie. But he *did* trust his sister. And he'd forgotten how important that was. He would try to convince Kenna to let him release her from Goshawk's Fury, but he would give her all the time she needed. He would listen to her if she said no. They would work it out *together*, like they always had.

And Flo needed the air stone shimmering in front of him. The thought of Flo being unable to re-enter the Eyrie, of being made to live in the Stronghold away from her friends, was impossible—incomprehensible. He thought about her laugh when they'd played in the snow on the night of the Well Dance; he thought about the way the silver in her hair caught the light; the way her mouth curved upward in a half smile when she asked him to breakfast. Then he thought about how she always knew what to say to Mitchell when he was feeling worried about his dad. How she brought out a protective side in Bobby that had been buried long ago. Yes. The three of them would be okay without him—but they would not be okay without Flo.

All his confusion evaporated. Skandar could make two choices with one stone. Two choices that weren't in line with how the Eyrie wanted to train him—to win at any cost, to be a warrior without emotion. He could save Flo, and he could be the kind of brother Kenna deserved. He could be a person he was proud of—even if that meant he was no longer the kind of rider who would win Chaos Cups.

Knowing he had only seconds before other Fledglings started to reach the finish, Skandar hovered Scoundrel above the air hoop.

"You'd better catch me, all right?" Skandar murmured toward his unicorn's black ear, stroking him on the neck.

And then—before the nerves could hit him and before he could change his mind—Skandar lifted his left leg over the saddle, so he was sitting sideways, and threw himself off.

Skandar was falling. The sky rushed by impossibly quickly—everything a blur of blue. He felt Scoundrel's panic in the bond, mixing with his own. He prayed Scoundrel was soaring beneath him—because it was a very, very long way down. He made the mistake of looking and thought he might faint. But he did glimpse his feet entering the sparking air hoop.

The solstice stone. He had to get Flo's stone.

Skandar stuck out his hand just in time and snatched the yellow stone from its elemental prison. He risked looking down again and regretted it immediately. The ground was getting far too close. He could see the instructors on their unicorns—he even spotted Agatha's white cloak. He wondered desperately if he had any chance of survival if he hit the ground at this speed. Would the healers be able to do anything to help? Or would he be—

WHOOSH!

Black wings stretched beneath Skandar, and he landed

on his stomach across his Shekoni saddle. Scoundrel roared in triumph and hovered—beating the air—while he waited for Skandar to sit upright again.

"You took your time!" he said, but his unicorn wasn't listening. Scoundrel was shrieking happily at the sky above him. Skandar looked up. There was a bottleneck forming above the hoops. Riders were clearly nervous to throw themselves off their unicorns. Walker and Salamander were *still* circling.

Then Skandar realized who Scoundrel had seen.

Mitchell Henderson and Red Night's Delight were careering toward the hoops, Red's flaming tail sweeping past the hesitating riders in a streak of smoke. Skandar could almost *see* Mitchell's brain working as he reached the elemental rings and saw that the only two remaining were water and earth. His friend's shoulders dropped as if he'd let out an exasperated sigh—but then he removed his glasses, zipped them into his jacket pocket, swung his leg over Red's back, and . . .

Froze.

Mitchell stared over Red's wing toward the ground, and the terror on his face was clear, even from Skandar's position in the air below him.

"Roaring riptides, Mitchell! Just jump!" Ira's voice pierced the air.

Mitchell stared in his father's direction—wide-eyed and fearful. Then, for some reason, Jamie started climbing past knees and elbows all the way to the very top of the temporary stand, heading right for Mitchell's dad. Skandar saw the flash of Ira Henderson's braid as he turned toward Jamie.

"Please, Mr. Henderson. He needs to know you believe in him either way," Jamie said, putting a hand tentatively on Ira's shoulder. "He needs to know you'll still be proud of him if he doesn't jump."

Skandar held his breath.

"You're doing—er—great, Mitchell!" Ira's voice rang out into the sky, authoritative but a little awkward.

"You can do better than that, Mr. Henderson," Jamie said, winking. "Tell him you'll still love him, even if he doesn't jump."

Ira Henderson looked so shocked, Skandar could see it from Scoundrel's hovering position just above the stand. "Mitchell thinks I won't . . . He thinks I won't *love* him if he fails?"

Jamie shrugged, then—

"YOU DON'T HAVE TO JUMP, MITCHELL!" Ira yelled. "You don't have to jump—for me or for anyone else. Either way, I love you, my boy. I love you so much!"

"Yeah!" Jamie cheered, delighted. "We believe in you, Mitchell. No matter what!"

"We believe in you!" Ira joined in with Jamie's shouts.

And Mitchell started to lower himself very carefully over Red's side—so that his feet were practically dangling within the water hoop. Predictably, Mitchell's technique was a lot more sensible than Skandar's had been. Then, once his arms were fully extended, he let go.

Skandar felt pride swell in his chest. Mitchell was terrified of heights—and yet there were still riders above trying to pluck up their courage to do the leap of faith at all. Red Night's Delight was a blur of scarlet and smoke as she rushed below the water hoop to catch her beloved rider. With a shout of triumph and pain, Mitchell crashed onto his saddle.

"Flaming fireballs, Skandar!" Mitchell shouted, as Red and Scoundrel landed on the finish line, to applause from the crowd. "Do you have any idea how foolish it was for you to take the air stone? We said you were getting the water one! Walker was right there! What if he'd jumped before me and I hadn't managed to get this?" Mitchell shook his fist, fingers pressed round a blue solstice stone.

"Well, I couldn't see you! And I didn't want Flo to be declared a nomad. I had to choose, and I chose—"

"You chose her—over yourself." Mitchell sounded half-irritated, half-impressed. A big smile spread across his face.

It wasn't the whole truth. He *had* chosen Flo, but he'd chosen his sister, too.

It was hard to think about that choice, seeing Mitchell beaming at him now. Mitchell was his friend—and he'd been terrified to jump, but he'd done it for . . . Skandar. It felt so much harder suddenly to leave his quartet. The only friends he'd ever had. But he'd made his choice in the sky. There was no going back now.

Mitchell was laughing, clearly misreading Skandar's expression. "Don't be embarrassed. *We've* all known for ages. It's been pretty obvious, you know."

"What has?"

"That you like Flo, romantically, of course," Mitchell clarified.

Skandar felt his cheeks reddening. Why did Mitchell have to use words like *romantically*? But he was beginning to think perhaps—

"Oh, he's realized, has he?" came a voice from behind them. "Imagine making it snow for someone and still not realizing you were into them." Bobby spoke from Falcon's back, grinning from ear to ear. "Completely clueless."

Skandar's brain had suddenly caught up with *whom* he was talking to. "Bobby, how are you—how are you *here*?" Skandar stuttered. They'd left her and Flo miles back.

In answer, she opened her palm. On it sat a glinting green stone. The last spare.

"But how did you catch up?" Mitchell looked both delighted and confused.

At the same time, Skandar asked, "Is Flo okay?"

"She's fine, spirit boy. Do you think I would have left her otherwise? Rex took Blade back to the Stronghold for his injured wing."

Skandar felt relief wash over him.

"But how, Roberta?" Mitchell asked again. "You were so far behind."

"We went *very* fast, didn't we, girl?" Bobby stroked her unicorn's neck. "I expect they'll be renaming the Peregrine Society the *Falcon* Society now. Maybe I'll insist on that when I'm Commodore?" Bobby mused. Skandar couldn't tell if she was joking.

Mitchell laughed as the three of them dismounted and led their unicorns toward the waiting crowd. Ira Henderson rushed to his son—his usual formality forgotten as he crushed Mitchell against his chest in the most enormous hug.

Skandar feigned excitement when his dad bounded up to him, overjoyed, but he couldn't quite *feel* it. He had survived the Air Trial without the Weaver taking him out, but she'd still stolen an air stone. All Skandar's worries came crashing back. The Weaver. Nina's death. The missing eggs. *Fifty* forged bonds. The quartet had made it through the Chaos Trials, but what did the future of the Island look like? No Hatching ceremony. No new riders to walk the fault lines. Even if the Weaver couldn't fill the stones she had, or if four elements weren't enough, the Island would be waiting. Waiting for the Weaver to forge a new generation of ultra-powerful riders. And meanwhile Kenna's future would hang in the balance. A future that was now *his* future too. Because he had made his decision. The terrible one. The vital one. The one that was going to change everything.

"Skandar!" Agatha interrupted his waterfall of thoughts. Her firm hands were gripping his shoulders and practically shaking him. "You did it! You're going to be a Rookie!" And then, more quietly, "You're going to be safe inside the Eyrie."

"*We* did it," Mitchell corrected Agatha—though he was smiling, Jamie's arm firmly hooked round his waist.

"Why did you jump through the air hoop, Skandar?" Jamie asked curiously. "I thought it was a water stone you needed?"

Bobby rolled her eyes. "Skandar is reckless *and* selfless. Honestly, it's an awful combination for—you know—general survival."

Agatha sighed. "I've been telling him that for years."

"Oi!" Skandar protested. "It all worked out, didn't it?"

"But who did you get the air stone for?" Jamie asked, confused.

"Me." And Flo was suddenly there too, her brown eyes bright and shining. She threw her arms round Skandar, their armor clanking noisily, and he breathed her in. He felt shaky, and different, and he didn't want to let go of her.

"Ah. For Flo?" Skandar heard Jamie say. "That makes sense."

But as Skandar's friends continued to celebrate around him, he couldn't help thinking that right now everything and nothing made sense—all at the same time.

* * *

After saying goodbye to their families, the Fledglings were required to sleep in tents out in the air zone that night. Those who'd been successful in the Chaos Trials would present their stones for re-entry into the Eyrie the following day—the summer solstice—and become Rookies. Some quartet tents went to sleep very early, their fates as nomads sealed; others stayed up late discussing the possibility of their survival, trying to negotiate with those who had spare stones. And some took the opportunity to party the night away, their futures secure. Bobby was so overjoyed that they'd be staying a quartet that she insisted on teaching them a group victory dance while singing a Mainland song about heroes and dragons and crowds going wild. Mitchell and Flo were still happily humming the tune long after lights out. But not Skandar.

As darkness fell, the lone spirit wielder led his black unicorn away from the Fledgling camp unseen. He hadn't spoken to his quartet—he would in time, but he hadn't wanted to ruin tonight for them. His heart was already breaking, and seeing their faces might just make him change his mind. Scoundrel took off into the sky, and Skandar glanced back at the campfires burning behind him, his friends' laughter following him on the wind.

Scoundrel didn't have to fly far. The redwood trees rose up, and Skandar immediately thought of the Weaver. But all was quiet. If the Weaver had any sense, she would be long gone, back to wherever she was hiding the eggs and the lost spirit wielders—Goshawk's destined rider among them. Skandar pushed Scoundrel onward. He wasn't giving up on that. On stopping the Weaver, on finding Goshawk's rider and getting Kenna her dapple-gray. He was just doing it with Kenna, rather than without her.

Skandar didn't have the Wanderers' swallow whistle—he'd been hoping he'd recognize the tree he'd climbed to reach Kenna and Albert. But every tree that loomed above him in the dark looked exactly the same, and he could feel the exhaustion of the Air Trial seeping into his bones and into Scoundrel's emotions in the bond.

"All right, boy," Skandar whispered, dismounting. "We'll just rest for a minute."

They lay down in a mossy hollow between two large trees. Skandar tried not to think about the warm fires or comfy cushioned tents back with his friends. He tucked himself under Scoundrel's wing for what he told himself would be a quick nap—and began to dream.

Skandar saw in snatches through eyes that were not his own. Blink—his vision changed. Blink—a little better through these eyes. Blink—a little worse. Blink—behind a pair of glasses. The emotions came at him in punches: fear, excitement, anticipation, doubt. He was never in one body long enough to get out and see who it belonged to. All he had were snapshots of what they were looking at. A rolling wave. A gray rock.

Where are you? *Skandar thought desperately.* Where am I?

And then, quite unexpectedly, one body held him. In that

moment he felt a kaleidoscope of emotions. *But one thought held them all together.* She is coming.

He saw through the person's eyes for a full five seconds—and their vision was clear. The pieces of the puzzle started to fall into place.

He was looking over a body of water.

Skandar felt a tug on his heart and saw his own bond.

Scoundrel? You're here? *he tried to ask, but he was already traveling along the shining white cord, switching places.*

The wild unicorn he had become was standing on the outer coast of the Island. Beyond Fourpoint, beyond the zones, beyond civilization. Turning his great scarred neck, he could see the barren gray of the Wilderness behind him. His rotting hooves were perched on the very edge of a crumbling cliff, the sea thrashing itself against the rocks below. And Skandar felt an emotion that he had never experienced from a wild unicorn before.

Hope.

And then he screamed as he was torn from the wild unicorn's body and into the next and the next, and there was so much joy that he didn't know how to feel—he didn't know how to be this happy after all this time, all these years of waiting.

Their destined riders were close now.

And as Skandar started to lose himself in the wildness of the unicorns—his vision blurring as he moved between their bloodshot eyes—understanding hit him.

He was looking at an island. An island across a body of water.

And in that moment before oblivion, he knew exactly where the Weaver was.

He knew exactly why they hadn't been able to find her, or the eggs, or the lost spirit wielders.

She wasn't on this Island or the Mainland.

She was on another island altogether.

KENNA

Nostalgia

KENNA SMITH WAS BLINDSIDED BY NOSTALGIA.

Nostalgia was a day on the beach with her family. It was teaching Skandar how to build a sandcastle, and Dad buying them an ice cream and a Chaos Card each.

Nostalgia was escaping. Escaping to a time before bonds. Escaping to a seaside town that still felt like home. Escaping to the place she'd believed she would never want to see again.

Nostalgia was Skandar telling her she was his hero. It was felling his bullies rather than famous trees, and being his best friend in the whole world.

Nostalgia was remembering. Remembering when her biggest fear was failing the Hatchery exam. Remembering how hope for a different future had once guided her. Remembering a time when she still understood the difference between right and wrong.

Kenna watched Skandar sleeping, his body half concealed by his unicorn's feathery wing. He looked younger with his eyes closed. He looked how Kenna remembered him. It was strange how your sibling grew up in front of you, and yet you couldn't really see them doing it. When she thought about Skandar, he was always frozen at eight years old.

That was the age he'd been when he'd first told her he was being bullied at school. That was the age when he'd been old enough to become her best friend as well as her brother. It was the age when he'd started to understand about Dad, and his bad days, and how much Kenna really did around the flat. It was the age when they'd truly become a team.

It was funny, because both Kenna and Skandar had wanted to grow up so badly. They'd wanted to get to thirteen—more precisely, the summer solstice *after* they turned thirteen. But Kenna wondered now whether they had truly believed that the cloudy futures they'd imagined for themselves as Chaos riders would ever come true. Sometimes she wondered whether they had become so obsessed with the Island because it was another part of themselves they had been able to share. Their secret. Their dream. Their escape.

As she watched Skandar sleeping, Kenna wished for the first time in her life that neither of them had got what they'd wished for. She wished that the day of both their

Hatchery exams had gone by and that they'd never found out their mum was alive, and that—like all the other spirit wielders—they had been cheated out of the futures they had longed for.

She wished, with all her heart, that they had never grown up.

CHAPTER TWENTY-TWO

Sister Sorrow

"SKANDAR! CAN YOU HEAR ME?" A VOICE CUT through the fog of pain.

"He's breathing," the same voice called to someone else.

"The unicorn's fine too," someone else replied.

A familiar shriek. *Scoundrel.*

"Has anyone told Kenna he's here?" The first voice resolved itself into Elora's. Skandar blinked, and shards of sunlight pierced his vision. How long had he been asleep?

"She's probably still out on Goshawk." The second voice: Albert.

Skandar tried to sit up, but Elora put a hand on his chest. "Better stay down for now."

But Skandar couldn't just lie here, because it was the

morning of the summer solstice—and he knew. He *knew* where the Weaver had hidden the eggs. He remembered the wild unicorns waiting on the edge of the Wilderness—the destined unicorns of the spirit wielders getting ready to join the Weaver's new generation. Kenna's dapple-gray flashed into his mind, and he sat upright. He wouldn't let that happen again. He wouldn't let the Weaver forge another bond.

The Pathfinder's amethyst eyes tracked Skandar wobbling to his feet, steadying himself against Scoundrel's side. "Skandar, you're in no fit state to go anywhere. You—"

Skandar cut her off, straightening his battered yellow jacket. "I know where the eggs are. The Weaver's on another island, just off the coast of the Wilderness that borders the air zone. Please, can you tell Kenna—" Skandar broke off and swallowed. "Tell Kenna that I'm going to fix everything. That I'm coming back."

"Skandar, you can't!" Albert's voice cracked.

"I'll come with you," Elora said earnestly.

"Please," Skandar said again. He didn't want her to get hurt. Elora wouldn't use magic in combat, but the Weaver would never hesitate to attack. "Go to Agatha. She trusts you. She'll know what to do." There was something else, too, about doing this alone. He wanted to look his mum in the face. After what she'd done to Kenna, he wanted this battle to be his.

Skandar scrambled onto Scoundrel's back without giving Elora or Albert the chance to stop him. Scoundrel weaved through the trees, and—once they were clear of the Sky Forest—took off for the terraced fields.

Skandar glanced—only once—at the Fledgling tents below. Flo, Bobby, and Mitchell would still be fast asleep. The temptation to fly down and wake them was so strong it hurt. But he didn't know how much time he had. He couldn't risk them asking questions or trying to stop him. This time he had to go alone.

Once they'd soared over the last of the tents, Skandar had to rely on Scoundrel to find the way. The Wilderness beyond the air zone was vast, and the sun was already up— he didn't know whether he'd have time to search the entire coast before the Weaver started trying to forge bonds with the unhatched eggs. Perhaps she'd already begun.

"Can you find them, boy?" Skandar stroked Scoundrel's neck as they cut through the cool morning air. In response, Scoundrel's Luck bellowed so loudly across the Wilderness that Skandar thought he must have understood.

Then, distantly but unmistakably, Skandar heard dozens of wild unicorns calling back.

Scoundrel shrieked and dived low, the beating of his wings swirling the dust of the Wilderness around them. Wait, dust?

Beneath them, a dapple-gray unicorn bellowed in welcome. Scoundrel shrieked back, and she raced beneath them, leading them onward through the Wilderness. Scoundrel dived to her right and left, as though playing. As though they were friends who'd done this many times. And Skandar felt tears running down his cheeks because he finally knew where Scoundrel had been going all year, why he'd always come back covered in a thick layer of dust. He hadn't been rebelling at all. Whenever Skandar hadn't been able to check on Kenna's destined unicorn in his Mender dreams, Scoundrel had visited her in real life instead.

They flew above Kenna's dapple-gray until she stopped to join a herd of wild unicorns standing together on the cliff edge. Scoundrel passed over them, and Skandar wondered if they'd follow—even though wild unicorns weren't good fliers. Perhaps the other island was too far out. Or they were afraid that the cliff sentinels would try to stop them. Or perhaps they didn't truly believe their destined riders were so close after all this time. Perhaps the disappointment would be even more unbearable than a life lived in death.

Whatever the wild unicorns were thinking, Skandar knew the image of them bellowing out to sea would stay with him forever. It was a damning illustration of what the Island had done. The consequence of the choice they'd made to outlaw the spirit element. These wild unicorns should have been allied to spirit. They should each have had a rider to take them on adventures. They should have had someone to love them.

But it wasn't too late. Not yet.

Skandar and Scoundrel flew on, the ghostly horns of the unicorns disappearing beneath them. Skandar had never flown Scoundrel over the sea before. He could taste the salt in the air almost immediately, and the wind grew less predictable. Worst of all, he couldn't see the island from his dream at all. He looked desperately out at the vast sea, trying to remember exactly what he'd seen through the wild unicorn's eyes.

"It was there!" Skandar shouted in frustration. And then, out of the corner of his eye, he saw a white glow on the sea below. For a second, something flashed green, and he felt his eyes forced to slide away from it. It reminded him of . . . spirit magic. Illusion, concealment, messing with minds.

She's hidden the other island, Skandar realized with a jolt. *That's why Nina couldn't find the eggs. Why nobody could.* But he'd seen it in a Mender dream, through the eyes of a wild unicorn. He forced his mind to focus on the empty sea ahead. He *knew* it was there, and so did Scoundrel.

And finally a small green island burst into his vision. The *other* island.

Skandar had been hoping that the lost spirit wielders would be standing right where he'd left them in his Mender dream, but as Scoundrel soared toward the cliff edge, it was clear that they were no longer there. Fear gripped him. Had the Weaver already started?

Skandar flew Scoundrel in wide sweeping circles, like he'd done with the Grins. The island was almost entirely covered by trees, making it hard to see anything down below. But on Scoundrel's third sweep, Skandar spotted a clearing. The circular patch of grass shone out like a beacon in the morning light. And there was someone standing in its center.

It was a tricky landing in the forest—Scoundrel's wings caught on branches as he descended—but Skandar didn't want to fly right into the path of the stranger. It hadn't been the Weaver—not tall enough, no black shroud, no wild unicorn—but they might still be dangerous.

Skandar dismounted, keeping his left palm on Scoundrel in case he needed to defend himself. They fought their way through the dense thicket—Scoundrel got so frustrated at one point that he turned an entire branch to ash—until they were hidden in the trees on the edge of the clearing.

The person wore a hooded blue cloak and stood in the center of a circle burned into the grass. Equally spaced round the circle, like compass points, were four wooden poles. And Skandar could see clearly that a solstice stone was strapped to the top of each pole—earth, fire, water, air—their glassy sides reflecting the light of the morning.

A fifth pole was positioned right at the circle's center. The hooded figure was strapping another stone to its top, and this one was pure white.

No. How was there a spirit stone here? Agatha had been *sure* there was only one left.

Skandar's hand went to his jacket pocket. He shook the

white pouch feverishly, and a jagged black rock fell into his palm.

As the hooded figure turned to face him, Skandar realized two things.

His spirit stone had been stolen.

And he was looking at Kenna.

"Kenn?" He took a step out of his hiding place and toward the burned circle. Scoundrel hissed in warning, but Skandar's blood was roaring in his ears. Kenna was the last person he'd been expecting to see.

"Kenn?" he said again, voice shaking. "What are you doing here?"

"What are *you* doing here?" Kenna countered. "You shouldn't have come, Skar."

"Look, listen—the Weaver's here. We need to find the eggs! It's not too late to get them back to the Hatchery for their destined riders today. You can help me! Then everyone will realize . . ."

Kenna cocked her head. "Realize I'm not the bad guy?"

The words hung in the air between them.

Kenna whistled. Goshawk's Fury burst out of the trees and trotted to her side. Scoundrel rumbled a warning. Skandar sent reassurance back. This was Kenna. She'd never hurt him.

"How did you get that spirit stone?" Skandar asked, trying to understand.

"Isn't it obvious?" Kenna said simply. She shrugged, the

blue hood falling back. There was a harshness to her voice, almost like she was daring him to call her a thief. She and Goshawk took a step toward Skandar and away from the fifth pole.

"You jumped for the air stone." It sounded like Kenna was accusing him of something. "You needed the water stone; why did you get the air one instead?"

It seemed so unrelated to anything that was happening— Kenna with his spirit stone, Kenna on an island shrouded by the spirit element, Kenna in the middle of this burned circle—that Skandar almost laughed in confusion.

"What does it matter, Kenn? Why are you—"

"It matters to me!" And suddenly she was yelling. "You risked being declared a nomad! WHY?"

Kenna looked so furiously upset that Skandar reached out for her. She flinched back toward Goshawk, waiting for his answer. Skandar realized that this rage was what she'd been holding back the other night. What he hadn't been able to understand.

"I did it for you," Skandar said quietly. "And for Flo. I did it because I thought I could save her from being declared a nomad *and* come to be with you. Wait, how do you know I jumped through the air hoop?"

"So let me get this straight," Kenna said slowly. "Becoming an outcast with me only occurred to you because you wanted to save someone *else*? My misery on its own wasn't enough to make you give up on your precious Eyrie, but if

Florence Shekoni was also going to lose out, that tipped the balance. Is that it? I've been lonely. I've been in pain. I've been so, so scared—and I haven't known what to do." Kenna's glance flicked to the solstice stones. "But you left me again and again, didn't you? The Island was literally *hunting* me, and you chose them."

"I didn't choose them! I thought I was doing the right thing. I was trying to bring the spirit element back, so you could—"

"Don't kid yourself, Skandar. You haven't stayed at the Eyrie all year for me, or for some big selfless aim of bringing spirit wielders back to the Island, or whatever you tell yourself. You stayed for you. You stayed because you have friends there, like you never did at school. Because you were picked for a fancy flying team. Because you want to become a Chaos rider, just like you always dreamed. And as soon as I arrived on the Island, I got in the way of all of that."

"That's not true!" Skandar's mind was a whirl of panic. "I left the Eyrie, Kenna! I decided!" But then he remembered what he'd admitted to Flo on the day of the Qualifiers: *It's harder with Kenna here.*

"Then the other night you came to me," she continued, "all conflicted, asking whether I wanted you to leave the Eyrie. I could tell you wanted me to be the brave big sister and agree that, of course, you should stay with your friends." The last word was almost a howl.

Skandar took a big gulp of air and tried to argue. "You're

not listening to me! I decided. I've left my friends. I'm not going back to the Eyrie. You asked me to leave, so I—"

"I shouldn't have needed to ask!" Kenna thundered.

But there was more terror crawling to the front of Skandar's mind now, as he looked at Kenna in the circle, at the solstice stones glinting behind her. She hadn't answered his other question. He made himself ask her again.

"How did you know I jumped through the air hoop?"

"You still haven't worked it out, have you?"

But Skandar had. He'd just hoped he was wrong. And, for the first time in Skandar's entire life, he was afraid of his sister. The horror of it was so suffocating that he struggled to breathe deeply enough to get his next words out.

"You were in the air zone," he rasped. "You attacked Flo. That was your elemental cage. *You* stole her air stone."

"Not just the air stone." Kenna sounded proud—like when she used to tell him about a test she'd aced or a funny joke she'd invented. "The fire stone was trickier with you all hemmed in together, but the dark worked in my favor. I targeted one of the Fledglings who was attacking the most people—Alastair, was it? Nobody seemed to care if he lost his stone."

"He blamed me!" Skandar cried. "He mistook you for me."

"Well, everyone *has* always said we look alike," Kenna said, shrugging. "And the water stone—"

"Was mine," Skandar interrupted, suddenly absolutely

furious. Goshawk growled as he jabbed a finger at his sister. "I *knew* there was someone following us in the water zone."

"It's rude to point, Skar," Kenna said, raising an eyebrow. "I told you, I wanted you to fail the Chaos Trials. Taking your stone made complete sense, and it was easy—your quartet didn't really bother to keep their voices down at the floating market."

"But I *saw* the Weaver at the Earth Trial," Skandar remembered. "It was definitely her."

"I . . ." It was the first time Kenna looked unsure. "I wasn't ready to help Mum then. I didn't understand what she was trying to do. She wanted me inside the Eyrie because she thought it'd be an easy way to get information and get access to the trials, but I only agreed because I wanted to be with you. I thought that maybe I'd be accepted as a rider—that maybe Nina would agree to my training." She took a shaky breath. "But then everyone started to turn against me, just like Mum had warned me they would. They were sure I had something to do with the eggs—which I didn't back then, by the way. The sentinels attacked the Wanderers, my friends. Everyone was terrified of my power. Then Nina was murdered and a silver Commodore took her place. And my own brother told me he wanted to break my bond with the unicorn I loved, and then left me all alone. . . . And I realized the Weaver had been right all along, that it was all a hopeless dream. The moment my bond was forged, I was never going to be able to call the Island my home."

"But it *can* still be your home!" Skandar took another step toward her. "Don't you see? You *have* a destined unicorn—you don't have to be an outcast. *We* don't have to be outcasts. Goshawk's rider is probably right here with the Weaver. I can fix everything right now. And if I get spirit wielders back to the Island—"

Kenna mounted Goshawk, her blue cloak draping over the bones poking through the wild unicorn's rotting sides. Skandar took a step back, suddenly realizing how far he was from Scoundrel.

"They are never going to allow spirit wielders back to the Island, Skar. Haven't you realized that yet? There's a silver Commodore now who will do anything for power. A Commodore whose mother died because of something *our* mother did with the spirit element. There is no way Rex Manning is going to allow you to finish your training. There is no way spirit wielders are ever going to be allowed to try the Hatchery door. You're spending all this time trying to get the Island on our side, when they're never going to accept you. They're playing you—all of them. And you're obsessed with the dream you had back on the Mainland: of being a unicorn rider, of belonging somewhere. I don't blame you—it's how I felt at the beginning—but it isn't real. Not for us. Not unless we make a future for ourselves."

"But how would we make a future . . ." Realization hit him. "The eggs."

"Everyone will always see me as a villain, Skar. They've

already made up their minds, so what do I really have to gain by trying to prove them wrong? In time, I think you'll understand that too. You're never going to change how they see you either."

"So we just give up?" Skandar said. "We let the darkness pull us in?"

"We start again," Kenna said from Goshawk's back. "But for now, you need to stay out of my way."

Scoundrel roared, sensing what was about to happen. Skandar was thrown backward by a gust of wind so strong it took his breath away. Bruised and shocked, he realized he was at the edge of the clearing. He was dimly aware of Kenna's palm glowing green—of vines wrapping themselves round him, securing him to a trunk.

Scoundrel sent furious elemental blasts toward Goshawk. The bond reverberated with his rage, the anger filling Skandar's heart too as he struggled against his ties. Then there was a flash of shadow-edged light from Kenna's palm, and a pained shriek.

Scoundrel's body was thrown across the clearing, his roaring silenced.

The black unicorn lay on the ground. He was on his side, wings limp. Skandar's whole body went numb with terror until he realized he could still feel Scoundrel's emotions in the bond, still see his ribs rising and falling. He was alive.

"What did you do to him? Let me go!" Skandar yelled, but Kenna didn't seem to be listening. She'd ridden back inside the burned circle, and halted Goshawk beside the pole holding the spirit stone.

"Kenn! Please! You can't let the Weaver do this!" Skandar shouted again.

She put a finger to her lips. *Quiet now. She's not going to do anything.*

Kenna's voice whispered into Skandar's left ear, and he realized that she'd already learned what it had taken him two years of spirit training to master. What did she mean, the Weaver wasn't doing this? A tiny spark of hope ignited in his heart. His gaze flicked to the solstice stones behind Kenna. Had the Weaver failed to fill them? Had Agatha been right after all?

Here they come.

Leaves rustled, sticks crunched, and dozens of people began to emerge from the dense forest in a long line. Each carried a unicorn egg, slightly hunched over—half weighed down, half protective. Skandar recognized some of them— Simon Fairfax, Joby Worsham—and remembered aspects of others, edges of glasses, pink fingernails, beaded braids, freckled hands. He'd *been* them in his Mender dreams. These were the spirit wielders who'd never had the chance to try the Hatchery door, or whose unicorns had been killed by the Silver Circle's Executioner. Last in line was Tyler Thomson—the boy who'd been destined for Goshawk's Fury.

"Tyler!" Skandar yelled. "Tyler, I need to talk to you!"

But there was no response as the people fanned out round the edge of the burned circle, faced inward, and dropped to one knee. In unison, each placed their right hand on top of the egg in front of them.

They did not turn their heads when Skandar called out to them. They did not even turn when a black-shrouded figure rode out of the forest on a wild unicorn whose skeleton shone in the sun. She was flanked by sentinels—sentinels who'd betrayed the Stronghold.

The Weaver was here.

The white stripe down the middle of Erika's face was just as unsettling as it had been that day on the Restless Mountain, distorting her features so she didn't look quite human. The black shroud whipped around her as she rode toward the circle, her body so thin that the fabric swirled like battle smoke. Her unicorn had a gaping wound on its shoulder, slime dripping from its half-open jaw.

The Weaver rode right for Kenna, and Skandar struggled against his bonds. Though, he needn't have worried for his sister's safety. When mother and daughter greeted each other, they gripped hands over the tattered wings of their wild unicorns like friends, like family. Skandar's whole body shuddered.

The Weaver reached out a skeletal hand to touch the spirit stone strapped to the central pole.

"I knew Agatha would come around once she understood our plan." There was wild joy in her voice. "Was she surprised I knew about her stone? Astonishing that she ever thought she could keep a secret from me."

Kenna shook her head. "I never had to go to Agatha."

Confusion flickered in the Weaver's eyes.

"I took it from Skandar." She inclined her head toward him.

Skandar felt sure the Weaver had known he was there the whole time, but this was the first time she acknowledged the presence of her son. "I see." The joy in her voice was replaced by disappointment, then turned to a hiss, like steam rising off hot coals. "How fitting that you are here to witness this, Skandar. You will see your sister gain a whole new family, with bonds just like hers."

Now Skandar was truly panicking, flinging out anything he could think of to delay her. "There's no way you're strong enough to forge this many bonds in one go. This will kill you! You're—"

The Weaver laughed, high and cold, then looked at Kenna. "He doesn't understand what the stones are for."

Kenna shook her head. The Weaver laughed again, and Skandar struggled harder against his ties, desperate to escape.

"I sense you do not agree with our plan," the Weaver called.

All Skandar could do was stare back at her. With Scoundrel on the ground, out of physical contact, he was powerless to stop what was about to happen.

The Weaver continued. "You do not agree because you do not yet understand. These forged bonds will end the tyranny of elemental allegiance; they will change the path of destiny; they will begin a new age of unbridled power. My generation of riders will master all five elements and share in the might of the immortal wild unicorns. My daughter will grow up in a new age, where she is not shunned but celebrated."

"But those eggs are meant for other people!" Skandar shouted. His gaze rested on the circle of spirit wielders. There had to be fifty of them, enough perhaps to overpower the Weaver. And although it turned out Erika hadn't been trying to kill Skandar during the trials, that didn't mean he wasn't a threat to this plan. His being a Mender might change their minds, maybe even save them all.

"I'm so sorry you never got to open the Hatchery door"—Skandar glanced at Kenna—"but this isn't the right way to fix all this. I'm a Mender. Your destined unicorns have been calling to me. They're waiting on the coast of the Island for you. They *know* you're here." A few heads turned to look at him as he spoke. "I can make you true bonds with your own unicorns—it's not too late. You don't have to do this! It isn't right!"

"Why do you care so much about doing things the *right* way?" Kenna called over. "All the Island has done is reject you, when all *you've* done is save it every year since you arrived. There's never going to be another way. You're always going to be an outcast. But we wouldn't do that to you." She gestured between her and the Weaver. "You could be with Mum and me—maybe even Dad. *We'd* make the rules. We'd let you be a spirit wielder. You could be free, like us."

Skandar was reminded of the time two years ago when he'd been tempted to join the Weaver for the very same reasons. But he wasn't the Hatchling Skandar any longer. He had seen good and he had seen evil—and he understood that the line between them was sometimes blurry.

But all he could think about—as he looked at the eggs held by the lost spirit wielders—was the anguished calling of their wild unicorns in the Wilderness; the searing beauty of the bond in his own heart; the ghostly horns endlessly waiting on the other shore. And there was a dapple-gray unicorn out there—and it was going to die alone forever because of what the Weaver had done to Kenna. What, he realized now, Kenna had done to herself.

As if to cement Skandar's decision, Goshawk's Fury moved closer to the circle of spirit wielders—to one spirit wielder in particular. Tyler stared at his hands in wonder as his bones began to glow through his skin—the bright white of the spirit element—and then his arms, then the bones in his neck and up into his face. Goshawk's bone-splintered knees began to mirror the glow, and then her skeleton lit up so brightly it was almost blinding.

"Please, Kenn!" Skandar begged. "That's Goshawk's

rider—he's right there. Look what's happening between them. It means they belong together!"

As Tyler attempted to move toward Goshawk, a sentinel melted out of the woods and held him firmly in place. Tyler *knew*. He could feel the bond that should have been.

"It means nothing," Kenna said, pulling her wild unicorn back sharply so the glow dimmed. "Goshawk is mine. She will always be mine."

"No, she isn't, Kenna," Skandar choked out. "I never realized that bonding with Goshawk was your choice. You always told me you were the victim, but I don't think that's true, is it?"

Kenna laughed, and it didn't sound like her at all. "Skandar, you have known me my whole life. When have I *ever* been the victim of anything?"

And Skandar realized that it had all been an act a year ago. That when she'd turned up at the Eyrie with her newly hatched wild unicorn—and he had believed he'd lost Kenna forever—that had been the moment. A moment he had chosen to ignore. Perhaps if the Eyrie had let her train? Perhaps if she hadn't been shunned by the other riders? Perhaps if the Wanderers had never been attacked? Perhaps if he had left the Eyrie earlier to join her in the zones? Perhaps then he could have diverted her from this path; perhaps then she wouldn't have handed over her solstice stones to the Weaver. But Kenna was choosing the Weaver over her own brother, and his heart was breaking. Scoundrel stirred on the ground nearby, as though he felt Skandar's pain too.

"Let us begin," the Weaver rasped. And she rode out of the burned circle, leaving Kenna and Goshawk within the stones.

Skandar didn't understand. Why was the Weaver leaving the circle? Why was Kenna still in there?

Kenna summoned the spirit element to her palm, then looked at each of the spirit wielders surrounding her. She smiled at some of them, waved to a few about her own age. Skandar remembered Dad's words in their Christmas card: *Kenna—some of your friends came round asking for you, wanting to make sure you got their messages.* He remembered the people she'd found online after Skandar had left, others who'd missed out on being riders and couldn't accept it. Had some of them been lost spirit wielders like Kenna? Had the Weaver helped Kenna bring them here?

"Kenna!" Skandar cried. "What are you doing?"

Silence. The Weaver's spirit speech crept into his ear like a spider in the night.

Your sister is busy. You were right, I was always too weak to forge these bonds.

Kenna's words from earlier made horrible sense. *She's not going to do anything.*

Skandar's sister was going to create the new generation.

True successor of spirit's dark friend. The truesong had been right after all.

Kenna placed her white palm over the spirit stone. The stone began to glow brighter, until a beam of pure white burst into the air above the clearing and cascaded downward, creating a dome of light over the scorched circle. Kenna and Goshawk's Fury were enclosed within the prism, along with the eggs and the hands of the lost spirit wielders—right palms now outstretched.

At the edge of the dome, the other four stones began to glow more brightly as the spirit magic touched them—a deep green, a flaming red, a brilliant blue, a sparkling yellow. If Skandar hadn't been so afraid of what his sister was about to do, he would have marveled at the elemental firework display. Pulses of color shot up from the stones and arched across the dome, crisscrossing like threads in a magical tapestry. Once complete, it resembled the roof of an elemental cathedral—alive and ancient and beautiful.

Kenna removed her hand from the spirit stone and placed it on her own chest, just where her forged bond surely gripped her heart. As she pulled her palm back, Skandar saw that a torrent of spirit magic was pouring out from her chest and into the spirit stone. And then there was a flood of water magic, a surge of air magic, a column of fire magic, and a steady flow of earth magic—each pouring into their own stones. It reminded him of being able to see the bonds of his fellow riders, though the colors were far brighter. But he didn't understand—why was the elemental power flowing *out* of Kenna?

Skandar winced at the Weaver's voice in his ear again, as though she could sense his confusion.

You were wrong, Skandar. We did not need the stones as a power source. Kenna has power enough to forge these bonds a hundred times over. Your sister needed them for balance. She needed to channel her power into the stones—for stability, for control—so as not to be overcome by the force of her magic completely.

So it hadn't mattered that the stones were empty—that had been exactly what Kenna needed.

Skandar caught sight of his mother through the elemental dome, as power flowed out of Kenna in a waterfall of color. Erika Everhart's face was transformed with fierce joy as she watched her daughter, her successor. More powerful than she'd ever been.

The flow of magic from Kenna ceased, yet the strands still fizzed up and around her to keep the elemental dome in place. Kenna rode Goshawk toward the edge and stopped in front of the first spirit wielder.

Simon Fairfax.

Kenna stretched out her palm, now flashing red, then yellow, then green, then blue, then white. The magic spun down toward Simon and his egg, the color never settling.

There was a sudden bone-chilling shriek to Skandar's right. He recognized it as a unicorn's cry of anguish. He tried to look through the trees, but there was nothing there. The noise had sounded so close—like it was just over his shoulder, just out of sight.

Simon Fairfax's face was determined as Kenna's magic continued to encircle him and the stolen egg. The terrible grief-stricken screeching continued in Skandar's ears, but all Skandar could think about was the young rider—possibly waiting at the Hatchery door right at this very moment— whose chance to bond with their destined unicorn would be gone forever.

Skandar tried to reach out for Scoundrel through the bond, but his unicorn remained on the ground—alive but motionless. Panic engulfing him, all Skandar could think to do was shout for help. He shouted as Kenna's magic intensified, glowing brighter in the morning light. He shouted until his voice was hoarse, hoping someone—anyone— would answer him.

Then somebody did.

CHAPTER TWENTY-THREE

The Everharts

AGATHA EVERHART AND ARCTIC SWAN-
song swooped into the colorful dome—ignoring the spirit
wielders, ignoring the Weaver, ignoring Skandar lashed to
the tree. Agatha only had eyes for the forger of the bonds—
and she slammed right into her.

Kenna was knocked from Goshawk's back, and the
magic she had been spinning to forge the first bond
fizzled out. There were shouts of anger from the older
spirit wielders as some of them recognized Agatha as the
Executioner—the one who had killed their unicorns.

At the exact moment Kenna was thrown from Goshawk, Scoundrel's Luck struggled to his feet. The black

unicorn rushed to Skandar and used his teeth to slice away the tightly knitted vines.

Skandar was free, and he vaulted onto Scoundrel's back.

Visibly shaken, Kenna scrambled back to Goshawk. Anger blazed in her eyes. "What a surprise to see you here, Aunt."

Behind them, the Weaver rode her wild unicorn closer. She seemed serene, perhaps confident in her daughter's power to protect herself.

"Why are you helping her, Kenna?" Agatha asked, sounding genuinely pained.

"You can't stop me!"

"You're only a child," Agatha said sadly. "And what you are trying to do is an abomination. So I *will* stop you if I have to." Agatha's palm glowed, a bone-white spear flashing into her hand.

"NO!" Skandar rode Scoundrel into the burned circle. Scoundrel reared, pawing the air as his rider threw up a flaming shield between Agatha and Kenna. "Please, don't hurt my sister!"

Kenna looked at him, visibly confused, her palm changing color at random as though she was unsure who to attack.

"Get out of the way, Skandar!" Agatha shouted. "She can't be allowed to do this!"

"How about we keep my children out of this, Sister?" the Weaver hissed, riding her wild unicorn into the circle.

"It's about time we settled things ourselves, don't you think?"

As Erika spoke, her palm glowed yellow. Scoundrel and Goshawk were forced backward by the strongest wind Skandar had ever felt. Then a wall of gusts formed round the edge of the scorched circle, trapping Skandar and Kenna on the outside and sealing the Everhart sisters within.

Agatha barely blinked. "I've forgiven you for many mistakes in the past, Erika, but forging a bond for your own daughter?" Agatha gestured toward Kenna. "And now asking *this* of her? You know better than anyone else the price of a bond forged in greed."

Erika's eyes raked over Agatha's white cloak. "I see you've thrown your lot in with some new friends. First the Silver Circle, now the Eyrie? Interesting how you never choose me over your own selfish interests."

"That's not fair at all," Agatha said, grief in her voice. "I have always protected you—more than I should have done. Given you second chances, third chances. But you have *never* been the same since you forged that bond for yourself. That wild unicorn has consumed you completely. This isn't *you*, E. This isn't the sister I grew up with. This has to end now."

The Weaver cocked her head, the movement dangerous. "You always blame my actions on my bond with a wild unicorn. But what if this is just *me*?"

After the last word, Erika's palm glowed bright white

and she opened her mouth in a silent battle cry.

Agatha threw her hands over her ears, yelling in pain, and Skandar realized Erika was using spirit speech to disorient her sister while she prepared a full-blown attack.

"Watch out!" Skandar shouted, as Erika's palm turned yellow and she molded the most incredible bow he'd ever seen. It shimmered in all five elemental colors, and as she shot arrows toward Agatha's chest—one was ice, the next was fire, the next diamond, the next lightning.

The ice arrow grazed Agatha's shoulder, but she ignored the hit and raised shield after shield as more arrows flew toward her.

"Leave!" the Weaver screeched at her sister through the magic, sweat now pouring down the white stripe of paint marking her face. "This is *necessary*."

"It is not necessary; it's barbaric!" Agatha shouted back as a water arrow fizzled out against her fire shield. "These people already have unicorns out in the Wilderness—and *your son* is a Mender. And these eggs you have stolen are due to be hatched by their destined riders this very moment, Erika—you know that!"

"And where has any of that got us Everharts?" Erika said, breathing heavily. "Keeping to tradition, keeping to the rules. My daughter has been hunted this entire year. She will never be safe. Today we start again."

"And what about your son? He's actually been trying to make things better, not worse."

"He is weak. I have no interest in him."

Skandar hated that he felt the pain of those words even now.

"Skandar is brave and strong and good," Agatha said, as an enormous glowing cloud gathered above her head. "If you'd bothered to get to know him, instead of trying to take over the world the whole damned time, you might have noticed."

The white cloud resolved itself into a great sparkling albatross made entirely of spirit magic. Skandar had never seen anything like it, hadn't realized it was even possible. It swooped down toward Erika—beak wide, as though alive—but she was ready with a creature of her own. A great white wolf launched up at the bird—jaws tearing, claws striking its wings until it splintered into glowing pieces. The wolf pounced toward Swan, but the shards of Agatha's albatross rejoined to form a white-striped tiger—twice the bird's size—and they fought each other between the unicorns until their spirit bodies were extinguished.

"Enough!" Erika panted. "You have wasted *too much* of my time." Her hand glowed white, and suddenly there were two Erikas riding two wild unicorns—and they both had a shining spirit javelin poised to be thrown.

"I'm so sorry, Erika. I just want my sister back," Agatha said sadly. And then bright white light burst from her hand toward one of the Erikas and her wild unicorn. The unicorn whose egg she should have returned to the Hatchery all those years ago. The unicorn destined for somebody else.

As the magic spiraled round the color-changing bond between their hearts, Skandar realized that it had been a terrible mistake for the Weaver to split herself. She'd believed her sister incapable of telling which one was real, but Erika had forgotten how much Agatha had loved her. How much Agatha loved her still. And when you love someone for a long time, you see all the tiny details that make them who they are.

The Weaver's double winked out, and her own spirit javelin went up in dark smoke. The real Erika clutched at her heart as Skandar watched Agatha tear apart the forged bond she believed had stolen her sister's soul, the same way she had killed spirit unicorns as the Executioner.

Kenna cried out, trying to push Goshawk through the wind barrier.

"NO!" Skandar shouted. There was a reason he'd stopped considering breaking Kenna's forged bond outright. A reason he'd become obsessed with the idea of the exchange. Elora's warning about breaking a forged bond from all those months ago came back to him now:

It could hurt Kenna. It might even kill her.

Kill. Skandar was not certain of many things in that moment, but the one thing he knew was that Agatha was not intending to kill her own sister. And he didn't want his mum to die—even after all this, even after everything she'd done.

"Agatha, STOP!" Skandar shouted again—but there was too much crackling magic, and the lost spirit wielders were crying out in fear, and everything was so confused, until suddenly—

The wind dropped.

Kenna let out an unearthly scream. Brother and sister rushed into the circle, spirit wielders scattering as Scoundrel and Goshawk passed them.

Skandar arrived at the center of the circle to see Kenna—now dismounted—pushing Agatha away from a black shape on the grass. The Weaver's wild unicorn stood back, aloof.

Agatha's hands were shaking uncontrollably. When she saw Skandar, her brown eyes were pleading. "I didn't mean to hurt her. I just wanted to break the bond. To get her back. I just wanted—" Agatha sounded like a small child.

"I know," Skandar choked out. "I know you didn't mean it."

Kenna was sobbing, and Skandar kneeled down beside her on the other side of their mother. There was no mistaking it—the Weaver was dying.

Two generations of Everhart siblings gathered between the solstice stones. For a moment, there was something like peace between them.

Erika Everhart reached out both her hands—one for her son and one for her daughter. "I promised you both unicorns," she said, looking over toward Scoundrel and

Goshawk standing side by side. One bonded. One wild. "At least I gave my children that."

Erika's brown eyes unfocused, as though looking at something far ahead—something at such a great distance it could not truly be understood. "Ah," she breathed. "Blood-Moon. There you are."

And then her body was glowing white, like the imperfect pieces of the Eyrie's entrance tree. Glowing so brightly they couldn't see her any longer. And when the light went out, all that was left of the Weaver was her black shroud.

Kenna let out a wail of grief so piercing it went through Skandar's body like a knife. Agatha stared at the empty shroud on the ground.

It was horribly simple in the end. To break a forged bond, a spirit wielder only had to unravel the thread between two hearts never destined to be joined. But the price? The life of the human, not the immortal unicorn.

Skandar was leaning against Scoundrel, trying to comprehend what had just happened, when the spirit element was suddenly bright in Kenna's palm: her eyes wild, anger boiling over into every single one of her features. The white light had a shadowy edge, and the grass began to wilt beneath Kenna's feet.

Skandar did not understand. Kenna was nowhere *near* Goshawk's Fury. How was she using magic?

Kenna punched her palm outward, the white light a shard of destruction.

Agatha cried out in pain, clutching her own heart. "Don't, Kenna! I'm sorry! Please don't!" Arctic Swansong screeched over and over—trying to get to his rider—but Goshawk's Fury blocked his way, elemental blasts exploding from his rearing hooves.

Skandar realized Kenna was attacking the bond between Swan and Agatha. As Agatha screamed again, he could imagine their connection splintering—starting at both their hearts and moving slowly toward its center, like a crack running through a frozen river.

Skandar sprang to action, swinging himself up onto Scoundrel. "Kenna! No!" He sent a fireball toward her feet, then a fork of lightning. Something, anything, to slow her down.

But, almost unthinkingly, Kenna raised a spirit shield round her body and continued to attack Agatha's bond. "She deserves it. My mum is *dead*. She killed my—"

Then everything seemed to slow as the ground vibrated with the force of Arctic Swansong hitting the earth.

Kenna stopped her attack, and Agatha clung to Swan's side.

Kenna had got the revenge she wanted.

Skandar rushed to Agatha and looked down at Arctic Swansong. The first unicorn he had ever met. The first unicorn he had ever ridden. The unicorn that had brought him to the Island—to his destiny. Agatha looked completely broken. Words of comfort stuck in Skandar's throat. He couldn't think of anything to say because he knew, just like every other rider, that there were no words that could take away this pain.

"AARGH!" Kenna's cry of agony made Skandar look up from Swan. She'd climbed onto Goshawk's Fury, who was rearing up on her back legs, wings out. Kenna was clutching the right side of her face. She screamed and screamed—and despite everything, Skandar rushed toward her pain. Then she screamed one more time and Goshawk's hooves landed back on the ground.

"Kenn, what—" But as Kenna lowered her hand, Skandar saw what'd happened. She had survived it—the fifth mutation. One side of Kenna's face had become a skull. Like on Skandar's arm, the spirit mutation showed every bone, tendon, and muscle under her skin. The mutation made Kenna look like a monster. And perhaps—after what she had done today—she had become one.

Skandar and Kenna locked eyes, and he understood that she was going. Where? He did not know or care in that moment. He guessed neither did she.

The words the First Rider had spoken down in the tomb came to him then: *The one you love the most will betray you, Skandar Smith.*

Without a word, Kenna galloped Goshawk across the clearing and took off into the sky. And for once, there was no part of Skandar that wished he could follow.

As he stumbled back toward Arctic Swansong's body, Skandar became aware of shouting coming from the spirit wielders in the clearing. They were confused, angry, disappointed; but they seemed afraid to enter the scorched circle.

"What are we supposed to do now that the Weaver's gone?"

"She's not just gone—she'd dead! That one killed her!"

"The Executioner will pay for this. . . ."

"We were promised forged bonds!"

"We've been waiting months. Years."

"Waiting our whole lives, you mean."

And there was Tyler, staring at the gap in the sky where Goshawk's Fury had been only moments before.

Agatha paid no attention, still bent over Swan in grief.

Skandar tried to make himself heard over the angry crowd. "I'm a Mender. Many of your unicorns are still out there in the Wilderness. I've seen them. Once we get you to the Island, I can try to mend your bonds."

A firm hand landed on Skandar's shoulder. There was a ring on one of its fingers that was changing color from orange to red. "I don't think that will be happening, do you?"

Skandar turned sharply and found himself face-to-face with Rex Manning.

Silver-masked sentinels were swarming the clearing. Instructor O'Sullivan, Instructor Webb, and Instructor Anderson swooped in to land. The cliff sentinels must have seen Skandar fly over the sea and let Rex know. And when the Weaver had died, the spirit magic concealing her island must have lifted.

Orders were being shouted; eggs were being pried out of the hands of the spirit wielders. Any who tried to fight were immediately struck down with elemental magic—Joby was already out cold on the ground. Other sentinels were crashing through the forest, clearly looking for the younger eggs—the ones that hadn't been ready this solstice.

"I have potential Hatchlings waiting on the Mirror Cliffs. Do whatever you can to get the eggs back to the Hatchery as safely and quickly as possible," Rex called, his voice commanding. "And somebody capture the Weaver's wild unicorn—I don't know what it's doing just standing there."

"Yes, Commodore," a passing group of sentinels barked.

Rex flashed his perfect smile at Skandar, then addressed another masked guard. "Once the eggs are secured, arrest all the spirit wielders. Including Agatha Everhart."

"Rex, you don't need to do that!" Skandar pleaded. "Agatha saved me. Saved all of us!"

"I'm afraid Agatha used the spirit element outside of your training sessions. She's brought this on herself; *she* is the one who went against our agreement."

"Yes!" Skandar cried. "To stop the Weaver—surely that has to be an exception?"

Rex shrugged. "I've seen no evidence that *she* was the one to defeat the Weaver. And there *were* no exceptions to our agreement. Ah. Talking of exceptions—sentinels!" Rex raised his voice and pointed at Skandar, his ring flashing. "Arrest this spirit wielder too. It seems he was in on the plan all along." Scoundrel hissed, and horror filled Skandar because he suddenly recognized the ring. It had belonged to Nina Kazama.

"Oh, you can't be shocked," Rex hissed, seeing Skandar's face. "Did you really think I was going to let this opportunity go? The opportunity to get rid of you *and* Agatha? You're spirit wielders. The spirit element killed my mother's unicorn—killed *her*. What would you do in my position?" There was a dreadful glint in Rex's eyes that Skandar had never seen before. Something deep-rooted and terribly dangerous.

Agatha had been right. Rex hated spirit wielders. He wanted them all locked up, including Skandar. Had Kenna been right too? Had Rex killed Nina? But why else . . . why else would he have her ring?

Five sentinels crashed toward Skandar, masks gleaming. It was too late to run. He braced himself for impact, but suddenly Instructors O'Sullivan, Anderson, and Webb pushed their unicorns forward and shielded him and Scoundrel.

"Don't. You. Dare. Rex." Instructor O'Sullivan's every word was a warning. "Skandar Smith remains under the Eyrie's protection. Or did you forget he just passed the Chaos Trials?"

Anger flashed over Rex's handsome features before he smoothed his face back into a pleasant smile. "My mistake, Persephone. You're quite right: he's an Eyrie rider. For now, at least."

Rex mounted Silver Sorceress and began shouting more orders, looking every bit the conquering Commodore—the hero who'd saved the fate of an entire generation of unicorn riders. Kenna's words from less than an hour ago floated through his mind: *There is no way Rex Manning is going to allow you to finish your training.*

Skandar swayed on the spot. It was all too much. His mum dead. Agatha broken. Arctic Swansong dead. Kenna gone. Scoundrel was suddenly right beside him, propping him on one side with a wing.

Instructor O'Sullivan hurried to the other. "We need to get you out of here before Rex tries anything else." She turned to Instructors Anderson and Webb. "Fetch Agatha. Don't let the sentinels take her."

Skandar only realized he was crying when he tasted salt on his lips.

"What happened?" Instructor O'Sullivan asked him in the gentlest voice he'd ever heard her use. "Is the Weaver here?"

Skandar felt exactly as he had back at school on the Mainland when children had asked him where his mum was. "She's de— She's de— She's not—" His voice had failed him then, just as it did now. Except then she had been alive after all, and now she truly was . . .

"Dead. The Weaver's dead," Instructor Webb announced. Then more quietly: "So is Arctic Swansong."

Instructor Anderson approached with Agatha, her arm

draped round his broad shoulder. Skandar looked at his aunt through his tears, and he knew they were thinking the same thing: *None of them are going to understand. None of them could possibly understand.*

You aren't supposed to feel sad when a villain dies. It doesn't matter if they're your best friend, or your sister, or your mum. Nobody is supposed to be sad they're gone. But all Skandar wanted to do was sink into the ground and disappear, because he hadn't just lost his mum tonight—he'd lost far, far more than that. And Skandar wasn't sure anymore who the villain was supposed to be. Whether there was one, or two, or dozens.

Agatha reached out for Skandar and pulled him into a hug.

"I want my quartet," he managed to say through shuddering sobs. "I want Flo and Bobby and Mitchell. I need them."

Agatha nodded against the side of his head, and straightened up.

Skandar climbed onto Scoundrel, the effort making his arms shake. Agatha sat behind Instructor O'Sullivan on Celestial Seabird, and—together with Moonlight Dust and Desert Firebird—they left the island behind.

As soon as the unicorns were over the water, Skandar saw Agatha reach into her pocket and bring out five solstice stones. The ones that had almost cost the Island an entire generation. The ones now filled with Kenna's overwhelming elemental power. Agatha held each stone in her fist for a few moments, as though deliberating; then she opened her hand, splaying her fingers over Seabird's wing. The solstice stones plummeted and were swallowed up by the waves of the hungry sea.

Skandar took one last look over his shoulder at the other island and saw a wild unicorn take off over its forests, flying in the direction of the Wilderness. A wild unicorn that had once been tethered to the Weaver. The sight made Skandar so hopelessly sad he had to turn away. The wild unicorn was free of its bond now—the bond the Weaver had forged out of greed all those years ago. It owed her nothing—and it would live on, endlessly, perhaps without ever thinking again about the shrouded rider who had now left this world behind forever.

Who had left Skandar behind forever too.

CHAPTER TWENTY-FOUR

Home Again

A FEW HOURS LATER, THE FLEDGLINGS gathered in front of the Eyrie's colorful entrance tree. Hanging from its lower branches were thirty-six circlets of gold, resembling thin crowns. The circlets had tags displaying the name of each Fledgling, and four sockets around the edge displaying the stones that rider had collected. If a rider had an earth stone, it was nestled in a twist of emerald vines, the water stone rode atop a wave of icy sapphire, the fire stone slotted into a bracket of ruby flames, and the air stone slid within a spiral of yellow diamonds. Each circlet was to be presented to the four main instructors, who would guard the trunk of the entrance tree. Any fewer than four stones in their circlet, and a Fledgling would be unable to re-enter the Eyrie—and immediately be declared a nomad.

Many Fledglings were having frenzied conversations. Those who'd won extra stones during the trials had been given them in pouches only moments before and had the option of saving a fellow rider before re-entering the Eyrie themselves. Niamh's quartet had four spare stones between them, and were being accosted by riders desperate to complete their own collections. Other Fledglings were begging for forgiveness from friends they'd betrayed for a stone during the trials. Some quartets were scattered, no longer speaking after the trust between them had been fractured.

But Skandar Smith, Bobby Bruna, Flo Shekoni, and Mitchell Henderson were very quiet, their arms linked round each other in a tight united line.

Skandar had spent the hours since he'd returned to their air zone tent telling his quartet what had happened on the other island—or the *evil* island, as Bobby had taken to calling it. At points he'd had to stop and cry before he could continue with the story. How he wished it was just a story—or perhaps a nightmare he'd dreamed up to torment himself. But it was real—and somehow he had to carry on.

When he'd finished, it was one of the few times all three of his best friends had been completely speechless. For a moment, they'd stared at him sitting with his knees pulled up to his chest. And then they'd rushed forward—cocooning him in a hug so tight that he was relieved to feel a piece of his heart repair. When Kenna had flown away, he'd thought he might never be able to feel again. That his heart was so shattered by her betrayal that it would be broken forever.

There had been no "I told you so" from Bobby—she wasn't like that—but Skandar had said he was sorry for not listening to her. Sorry for not seeing Kenna's betrayal right in front of him. But all Bobby had said was, "You should have taken us with you, spirit boy," just like he'd known she would.

"We could have come up with a plan," Mitchell had added.

"We could have been there for you when it all happened," Flo had finished.

Skandar had hung his head. "I know. I wish you'd been there. I'm so sorry."

"Don't say *sorry*." Bobby had wagged a finger at him. "Just don't do it again."

Skandar's mouth had curled into a small smile—and he'd started crying all over again.

"You okay?" Flo asked him now, as the instructors moved to block the Eyrie's entrance.

He nodded shakily, though his eyes tracked Rex Manning. The air wielder radiated with triumph. He now occupied three of the highest positions on the Island—Commodore, head of the Silver Circle, and Eyrie instructor. He had averted disaster and returned all the stolen eggs to the Hatchery. There were even rumors that he'd defeated the Weaver himself.

Oh yes, the new silver Commodore was all smiles this afternoon, but Skandar wouldn't make the mistake of falling for his charm again. He'd seen the terrible glint in those sparkling green eyes. He'd seen Nina's ring on the new Commodore's finger—even if Flo insisted he could be wearing it as a mark of respect. But Rex had not hesitated to call for Skandar's arrest. There was a warrant out for Agatha's arrest too, though she'd been whisked off and hidden by the Wanderers. And with all the other spirit wielders locked up *for their own safety*, it seemed Rex was far more dangerous than any of them had ever imagined. Kenna had been right about that.

Kenna. He tried to stop himself from wondering, once again, whether she was okay. It was going to be a hard habit to break.

"Who are you going to give your spare earth stone to?" Skandar whispered to Bobby, trying to distract himself.

Bobby shrugged.

"I know the stones have to go back to the Stronghold for next year, but do you think we'll get to keep the gold circlets?" Flo asked hopefully.

"Absolutely not," Mitchell answered. "Instructor Anderson told me they've been used in the Chaos Trials for centuries."

Instructor O'Sullivan blew a whistle. "The moment is upon us. You have all fought bravely, but for some your journey at the Eyrie will now come to an end. We will call you forward one by one, in the order we consider to be the fairest. Let us begin."

Gabriel was the first to lift down his circlet from the entrance tree's branches. Skandar—along with many of the other Fledglings—craned his neck to see the stones set into the crown. Gabriel led Queen's Price up to the instructors, his stone curls eerily still as he bowed his head and held out the crown for the instructors' inspection.

"He doesn't have a fire stone!" Flo whispered worriedly.

"Relax," Mitchell said. "Zac will save him."

Instructor Anderson's voice boomed out, the fire around his ears flickering. "Without a fire stone, Gabriel is currently unable to re-enter the Eyrie. As his fellow riders, will any of you step forward to ensure he can continue with his training?"

"Me! I will!" Zac—another member of Gabriel's quartet—practically tripped over himself trying to get to Gabriel and Instructor Anderson. He withdrew his extra fire stone from its pouch, and Gabriel grinned at his friend, slotting it into the flaming ruby bracket. Then he handed the complete circlet to Instructor Webb—head of his element—and the instructors cleared a path to the Eyrie's entrance tree.

Gabriel hurried toward the trunk, leading Queen's Price. He placed his palm on the bark, and the entrance opened in a swirl of sand. Cheers went up from the gathered Fledglings, as well as a crowd of other riders who'd gathered on the other side of the entrance to welcome the Fledglings back.

With full circlets—and no more spare stones to offer other Fledglings—Zac and Yesterday's Ghost, Sarika and Equator's Conundrum, and Mabel and Seaborne Lament were called forward to enter the Eyrie after Gabriel. Then Elias gave Aisha his water stone, meaning she could re-enter the Eyrie along with Ajay and Ivan.

But with three stones missing from her circlet, there was no real chance of enough riders being willing to offer their spares to Marissa and Demonic Nymph. It was perhaps even more brutal than the usual way nomads were declared. The eternally poisoned Nomad Tree had been re-erected by a team of expert earth wielders, but Marissa wasn't allowed to see her pin studded into its bark. Instead, Instructor O'Sullivan took Marissa's water pin and smashed it against a rock outside the Eyrie's entrance. Ajay, Aisha, and Ivan didn't even get to say a proper goodbye as Marissa rode Demonic Nymph down the Eyrie's hill alone.

Skandar hoped Marissa would find her way to friends or family, or perhaps even to the Wanderers. He didn't even know her well, but was filled with anger for her. She and Nymph had fought hard. They'd protected their friends, been brave. And now she had to leave the Eyrie. The place that had become her home.

"I know the Chaos Trials are supposed to help us strengthen our connection with our unicorns, but surely there's a better way than this?" Mitchell voiced Skandar's thoughts.

"A kinder way," Flo said.

"This Island has to change," Skandar agreed.

Next was the Threat Quartet. Kobi and Ice Prince had all four elemental stones in their circlet and no spares, so the Eyrie entrance opened for them in a whirl of water.

Then Amber. She emerged from the back of the gathered Fledglings, nowhere near Alastair and Meiyi. Her shoulders were slumped, chestnut hair half covering her face. Skandar had never seen Amber look so defeated. Her hands were shaking so much as she walked toward the instructors that she dropped her circlet. She kneeled quickly to pick it up, but not before Skandar noticed that the emerald vines were empty.

Amber bowed her head, offering up her incomplete circlet. Instructor Webb cleared his gravelly throat, the moss on his head very green in the late-June light. "Without an earth stone, Amber is currently unable to re-enter the Eyrie. As her fellow riders, will any of you step forward to ensure she can continue with her training?"

"I will."

For a moment Skandar couldn't tell who'd spoken, until he saw Bobby move forward.

"You're joking," Mitchell croaked. "Bobby is going to save *Amber*? Amber is her nemesis. Amber—"

"Doesn't deserve this," Bobby said over her shoulder.

The shock on Amber's face was almost funny as Bobby dropped the spare green stone into her palm.

"Don't say I never do anything for you," Bobby joked.

Then something happened that Skandar would have thought impossible only moments before. Amber threw her arms round Bobby and hugged her.

"Gerroff," Bobby said, batting away Amber's hair. "You push me to be my best, all right? Without you to beat, it'd be dead boring around here."

"You won't regret this," Amber choked out through tears.

"Oh, I'm sure I will once you're back to your usual irritating self," Bobby said, and she made her way back toward Flo, Skandar, and Mitchell.

Amber hiccupped and then hurriedly slotted the stone into her circlet.

"That was a really nice thing to do, Bobby," Flo said, squeezing her arm.

"I knew *you'd* approve, earth wielder." Bobby winked, and they all turned back to see Amber and Whirlwind Thief disappear through the Eyrie's entrance in a flash of lightning.

Alastair was next.

"This should be interesting," Mitchell muttered to Skandar. "He's missing earth *and* fire."

Meiyi was the only one of the Threat Quartet with a spare, and luckily for Alastair it *was* an earth stone. To no one's surprise, she immediately handed it over to him, not even waiting to be asked. After slotting it in, Alastair swaggered casually up to the instructors, barely bobbed his head, and presented his incomplete circlet.

"He must know someone is going to save him," Flo murmured.

". . . will any of you step forward to ensure he can continue with his training?" Instructor Webb sounded slightly bored by now.

Nobody moved.

Alastair smirked. "Come on now, Niamh. Don't make me wait. I know you've got a spare fire stone from the Water Trial."

Niamh shook her head, the light catching the ice spike through her right ear. "Not for you I don't."

Alastair laughed, but there was a note of worry in it. "I've done the math, Niamh. There isn't another Fledgling you can save with that fire stone. I'm your only choice."

"Then I choose *not* to choose you," Niamh said venomously.

Skandar knew Alastair had attacked Niamh's quartet multiple times during the trials, but he didn't think it was just that. Water wielder Niamh was unlikely to put up with unkindness or selfishness—and that was exactly who Alastair was.

"You can't be serious," Alastair spluttered; then he appealed to the instructors. "This can't be allowed; she has to—"

"She doesn't *have* to do anything," Instructor O'Sullivan cut in. "Niamh is perfectly entitled not to use her stone to save another Fledgling. That is part of the Chaos Trials."

Niamh strode forward and handed her spare fire stone to Instructor Anderson. And, just like that, the Threat Quartet were a quartet no longer. As Meiyi re-entered the Eyrie, Alastair's pin was smashed and he was sent on his way. It gave Skandar a tiny spark of hope. *Never let anyone tell you who you need to be*, Nina had said up on the Sunset Platform. Perhaps the Island had space for different kinds of Chaos riders after all? Perhaps the most ruthless wouldn't always win.

Finally it was time for Skandar's quartet to take down their circlets. Flo and Silver Blade went first, and even in his state of grief Skandar felt a stab of pride as he handed her the yellow stone he'd won from the Air Trial.

"Well done, Skandar," Rex Manning said stiffly, without any warmth.

Skandar froze, wanting to run a thousand miles in the opposite direction, the note Agatha had sent that afternoon burning in his pocket.

The sentences were short, factual. She was safe. The Wanderers had recovered Arctic Swansong's body from the other island. They would bury him tomorrow so a spirit tree could grow. Skandar was not to come. One day they could visit Swan together, but not yet. Not until it was all over. And at the very end, the note read:

DON'T YOU DARE LET HIM WIN,
SKANDAR SMITH.

Skandar turned his back on Rex.

I won't, Skandar promised his aunt—and himself.

As Flo entered the Eyrie, an almighty cheer went up from the waiting crowd. The silver had made it through the Chaos Trials.

Now Skandar reached up to take his own circlet, Scoundrel sniffing it curiously. He noticed there was another slot for a stone right in the center. It looked like the Divide—with four gold cords connecting to the central circle. Skandar would have bet a lot of mayonnaise it had been designed for a spirit stone.

Instructor O'Sullivan's eyes swirled as Skandar presented his circlet, the sapphire slot empty. "Will any of you step forward to ensure Skandar can continue with his training?"

"Yes! I will! Me!" Mitchell was there in three seconds flat, dropping the blue stone into Skandar's hand.

"Excellent," Instructor O'Sullivan said warmly. "You really have done *your* element proud, Skandar. You and Scoundrel's Luck may return to the Eyrie." She winked at him.

Skandar suddenly felt self-conscious. He'd never opened the Eyrie's entrance in front of anyone except Agatha and his quartet. None of the other riders had seen a spirit wielder do it in decades.

A hush fell over the crowd as Skandar placed a palm on the gnarled bark of the ancient trunk. Under his hand the indentations in the bark shone, joining to form a round web of blinding white light. People gasped as hundreds of tiny cracks glowed brighter and brighter and then winked out like Eyrie lanterns in a storm.

Skandar pulled Scoundrel through the dark hole that remained, and tears sprang to his eyes as he heard his fellow riders cheering. Maybe he could trust the Eyrie to bring back the spirit element after all? Maybe things *could* change. Maybe *he* could change them. And as he—a spirit wielder—was welcomed back through the Eyrie's entrance with joy and celebration, he thought that perhaps he already had.

Scoundrel shrieked with delight as members of the Peregrine Society rushed up to Skandar—Rickesh, Prim, and Marcus crushing him into a hug; Fen whacking him on the back far too hard with an icy fist; Adela, Liam, and Patrick shouting their congratulations. Then Mitchell appeared behind Skandar, with Red farting exuberantly in celebration. Flo beamed at them all as Falcon came through the entrance, too, and Bobby ruffled Skandar's hair, saying something about watching her sister walk the fault lines tonight.

Sister.

If Kenna had seen this, if she'd heard them cheering on a spirit wielder, maybe she'd have understood why he'd fought so hard for her to be allowed back to the Eyrie one day. Why he'd believed he could change things from inside its walls rather than outside them. But it was too late for that.

Sister. Thief. Betrayer. Enemy. Was that who Kenna was to him now?

The noise of the crowd was suddenly too much for Skandar as successful Fledglings continued to pass through the entrance tree. Noticing, his quartet guided him into the quiet of the Eyrie's forest.

When they were hidden among the pines, the worry Skandar had been holding back burst out of him. "Kenna's so powerful. I don't know what she's going to do next."

"Whatever it is, we'll face it together," Mitchell said, his voice confident.

"Don't you worry, spirit boy," Bobby agreed.

In the shadow of an armored tree, Flo slipped her hand into Skandar's.

And for a moment, he let himself believe they could win whatever fight was coming for them.

Epilogue

FAR AWAY FROM THE LANTERN LIGHTS OF THE
Eyrie and the warmth of a treehouse stove, Kenna Everhart
was grieving.

But she was going to make herself feel better.

Kenna Everhart dipped her hand into a bucket of white
paint and slowly drew it down the middle of her face.

This was going to make her feel better.

Kenna Everhart looked out over the barren Wilderness, and
the landscape reflected the desolation of her soul.

Being here was going to make her feel better.

Kenna Everhart kneeled down on the dusty ground and stacked up the broken pieces of the First Rider's bone staff.

She was going to feel so much better once she started.

Kenna Everhart knocked over the stack of bones and then began to build them up again in a different order.

She was already feeling better.

Because although the Weaver was dead . . .

Kenna Everhart wasn't going anywhere.

Acknowledgments

FIRST, I WANT TO THANK YOU, READER—
for outwitting the Restless Mountain, stepping over
noxious salamanders, solving scallop-shell riddles and
battling through sylph-led winds to reach the end of
the Chaos Trials. If I could, I would hand over all my
solstice stones to you, because I am so grateful that
you're still soaring along with the quartet at the end of
their third adventure.

Writing this third book in the Skandar series was
about as challenging as Fledgling year itself. As was keeping these acknowledgments short—having squeezed so
much into this book already—when I owe such immense
gratitude to everyone who has supported me.

Just as family and friends help Skandar through
the Chaos Trials, mine have been a constant source of
comfort and support. Particular thanks to those who
read early drafts of the *Chaos Trials* and gave me such a
vital confidence boost. A special mention to two fellow

writers—Ruth and Aisling—who read this third story first: I don't know if you were telling the truth when you said this was my best one yet, but it didn't half make me cry!

Just as the Eyrie instructors cheer on the Fledgling riders, I feel so lucky to have an agent like Sam Copeland in my corner. Thank you for all your advice and guidance—and that perfect, sweary reaction the first time you finished this book. And thank you to my film agent, Michelle Kroes; screenwriter, Jon Croker; and the whole team at Sony for bringing these unicorns to the big screen.

And just as passing the Chaos Trials relies on having the best team around you, I am overflowing with gratitude that I have the pleasure of continuing to work with the dream-makers at Simon & Schuster. I owe so much to every single one of you.

To Rachel Denwood, Ian Chapman, Jonathan Karp, and Justin Chanda for your passionate support of these ferocious unicorns. To my UK editor, Ali Dougal, for caring so deeply about this world but never at the expense of my well-being. To my US editors, Deeba Zargarpur and Kendra Levin, who also love these characters with all their hearts and help me write them as the best versions of themselves. You all bring a magic to every book that takes my breath away. And huge thanks also to Katie Lawrence, Arub Ahmed, Olive Childs, and Dainese Santos for your eagle-eyed editorial expertise.

To Laura Hough, Dani Wilson, Rich Hawton, Leanne

Nulty, and the whole sales team at S&S across the world, who ensure these unicorns reach as many readers as possible—thank you for your ambition, your competitive spirit, and your bonkers yet brilliant ideas (those T-shirts!). A special thank-you to Eve Wersocki Morris of EWM PR and to Sarah Macmillan, Jess Dean, Dan Fricker, Sam McVeigh, Emily Wilson, Breanna Djamil, and the rest of the S&S marketing and publicity teams both in the UK and abroad. Thank you for putting together incredible book tours that allow me to meet as many Skandar fans as possible, and for spreading awareness and love for this series all over the globe.

To the design team at Simon & Schuster, as well as Two Dots Illustration Studio and Sorrel Packham for creating the most stunning books imaginable—don't the three of them look so wonderful together? A particularly big thank-you for bringing Goshawk's Fury to life on the *Chaos Trials* cover so magnificently. She is bloodthirsty perfection.

To the whole rights team and Skandar's international publishers—thank you for helping the Chaos Trials take place across the world. And to all my editors, translators, copyeditors, proofreaders, and sensitivity readers—I'm so grateful to you for making my words shine as beautifully as solstice stones.

Just as Skandar could never get to Rookie year alone, I owe so much to those who continue to support this series beyond my wildest unicorn dreams. To the incredible booksellers, librarians, and festival organizers who get these books into readers' hands. To all the teachers who are introducing Skandar to whole classes and igniting that reading spark, and to the book bloggers, authors, and cheerleaders who have recommended Skandar to those in their communities—I appreciate everything you do for this series and for children's literacy in general.

And last of all, to my husband, Joseph—my first reader and my best friend. Thank you for creative walks, for talking me up and talking me down, and for giving me every kind of support—from emotional to practical. Because let's be honest: without you, I'd probably be living on emergency sandwiches.